BAD HAIR DAY

Svetz pulled the filter sac over his head and hurriedly smoothed the edges around his neck to form a seal. Blind luck that he hadn't fainted yet. He waited for it to puff up around his head. A selectively permeable membrane, it would pass the right gasses in and out until the composition was . . . was . . .

Svetz was choking, tearing at the sac.

He wadded it up and threw it, sobbing. First the air plant, now the filter sac! Had someone wrecked them both? The inertial calendar too; he was at least a hundred years previous to 50 PostAtomic.

Someone had tried to kill him.

Svetz looked wildly about him. Uphill across a wide green carpet, he saw an angular vertical-sided formation painted in shades of faded green. It had to be artificial. There might be people there. He could—

No, he couldn't ask for help either. Who would believe him? How could they help him anyway? His only hope was the extension cage. And his time must be very short.

The extension cage rested a few yards away, the door a black circle on one curved side. The other side seemed to fade away into nothing. It was still attached to the rest of the time machine, in 1103 PA, along a direction eyes could not follo[illegible]

Svetz hesitated near the door. His only [illegible] disable the air plant. Hold his breath, then . . .

The smell of contaminants wa[illegible]

Svetz sniffed at the air. Ye[illegible]usted itself, drained its contami[illegible] wreck it now. Svetz was si[illegible]

He climbed in.

He remembered th[illegible] filter sac, torn and empty. Then he saw th[illegible]g over him, the coarse thick hair, the yellow eyes[illegible]e taloned hands spread wide to kill.

ALSO IN THIS SERIES

Tomorrow Sucks

Edited by
Greg Cox &
T.K.F.
Weisskopf

With editorial assistance by Hank Davis

TOMORROW BITES

This is a work of fiction. All the characters and events portrayed in this book are fictional, and any resemblance to real people or incidents is purely coincidental.

A Baen Books Original

Baen Publishing Enterprises
P.O. Box 1403
Riverdale, N.Y. 10471

ISBN: 0-671-87691-0

Cover art by Barclay Shaw

First printing, October 1995

Distributed by
SIMON & SCHUSTER
1230 Avenue of the Americas
New York, N.Y. 10020

Printed in the United States of America

DEDICATIONS

T.K.F. Weisskopf
To Jim and Jessica,
in the hope that their tomorrows won't bite.

Greg Cox
To the Science Fiction and Fantasy Club
of Western Washington University

CONTENTS

ACKNOWLEDGMENTS

"Werehouse" is copyright © 1990 by Michael Flynn; first appeared in *New Destinies*; reprinted by permission of the author.

"Operation Afreet" is copyright © 1956 by Fantasy House, Inc.; first appeared in *The Magazine of Fantasy & Science Fiction*; reprinted by permission of the author.

"There Shall Be No Darkness" is copyright © 1950 by Standard Magazines, Inc.; first published in *Thrilling Wonder Stories*; reprinted by permission of Judith Blish and the author's estate.

"There's a Wolf in My Time Machine" is copyright © 1971 by Mercury Press, Inc.; first appeared *The Magazine of Fantasy & Science Fiction*; reprinted by permission of the author.

"Wolf Enough" is copyright © 1995 by Jane Mailander; first published in *Tomorrow*; reprinted by permission of the author.

"A Prophecy of Monsters" is copyright © 1954 by Fantasy House, Inc.; first appeared in *The Magazine of Fantasy & Science Fiction*; reprinted by permission of Arkham House Publishers, Inc. and JABberwocky Literary Agency as agents for the author's estate.

"A Midwinter's Tale" is copyright © 1988 by Michael Swanwick; first appeared in *Asimov's*; reprinted by permission of the author.

"The Hero As Werwolf" is copyright © 1975 by Gene Wolfe; first appeared in *The New Improved Sun*; reprinted by permission of the author and the author's agent, Virginia Kidd.

"flowereW" is copyright © 1995 by John Ordover and is original to this volume.

"Frontier of the Dark" is copyright © 1952 by Street & Smith Publications, Inc.; first appeared in *Astounding Science Fiction*; reprinted by permission of JABberwocky Literary Agency as agents for the author's estate.

"Werewolves of Luna" is copyright © 1994 by Rod Garcia; first appeared in *Asimov's*; reprinted by permission of the author.

A Scientific History of Lycanthropy

GREG COX

It's tempting to call Charles Darwin the father of scientific werewolfry.

Granted, myths and legends about humans transforming into beasts (and vice versa) are probably as old as mankind. The ancient Greco-Roman deities were forever changing themselves and others into swans, rams, stags, and even wolves; one recalls the doomed king Lycaon, transformed into a four-legged wolf by the anger of Zeus. Furthermore, real-life werewolf trials are an ugly part of European history. But these were all creatures born of magic and superstition. Supernatural forces, often a deal with the devil, were required to turn a man into an animal . . . or so it was once believed.

Darwin's *The Origin of Species* (1859) blurred forever the line dividing humanity from the rest of the animal kingdom. Suddenly all manner of hybrids, throwbacks, atavisms, mutants, and manimals became not only possible but plausible. Lycanthropy, defined here as the physical metamorphosis of man into wolf, was no longer a matter of transformation but *evolution* . . . in one direction or another. And modern storytellers were quick to respond to this redefinition of humanity. As Stephen King has pointed out elsewhere, what is Robert Louis Stevenson's *The Strange Case of Dr. Jekyll and Mr. Hyde* (1886) except a classic werewolf story? Significantly, Jekyll does not devolve into the bestial Hyde through the intervention of gods or demons; a scientific experiment involving exotic chemicals is all that is needed to dissolve Jekyll's tenuous veneer of humanity. A few years later, *The Island of Doctor Moreau* (1896) by H. G. Wells offered a temporary form of reverse lycanthropy via experimental surgery and behavior modification. The titular scientist forcibly transforms an entire menagerie of animals (including quite a few wolves) into pathetic imitations of men and women. Alas, despite Moreau's best efforts, that "stubborn beast-flesh" kept creeping back and, like Henry Jekyll and many a werewolf before him, the newly-created people of the island kept devolving back into more primitive forms.

If you doubt that *Jekyll* and *Moreau* really count as early werewolf novels, consider: the first genuine movie werewolf, 1935's *Werewolf of London*, was portrayed as a Victorian scientist complete with chemical laboratory. And the first film adaptation of Wells's novel, *The Island of Lost Souls* (1933), prominently featured a shaggy wolfman played by Bela Lugosi, who, eight years later, played a gypsy werewolf in what is probably the most important and influential of all werewolf movies: *The Wolf Man* (1941). So there!

Seriously, it is almost impossible to discuss the werewolf in fiction without taking Hollywood into account. More so than with vampires, our modern conception of a werewolf has been largely generated by the movies. *The Wolf Man*, written by Curt Siodmak, can be said to occupy the same position in werewolf fiction that *Dracula* holds in the vampiric canon. It is *the* definitive text, and one that owes quite a lot to Darwin. Even today, the standard movie werewolf looks more like a furry, humanoid Missing Link than the four-legged werewolves of myth and folklore.

If Darwin is the father of today's wolfman, then Sigmund Freud must have presided at his christening. Ultimately, most werewolf fiction, scientific or otherwise, is about the eruption of the primal, feral impulses that can sometimes overpower a person's more rational, civilized inclinations and inhibitions. In other words, the triumph of the id over the superego. In the past, we spoke of curses and demonic possession; today we invoke the unconscious mind. The basics remain the same: Even a man who is pure at heart has a raging beast lurking somewhere inside him. The traditional werewolf of legend usually used sorcery to transform himself at will into the actual form of a wolf, but the werewolves of our era are more likely to be man-like creatures driven by uncontrollable and animalistic compulsions. Ultimately, modern lycanthropy turns out to be a very scientific phenomenon.

Over the years, many science fiction writers have carried on the work of Wells and Stevenson, making the scientific roots of the werewolf explicit by providing convincing, non-magical explanations for even the most outrageous of transformations. In his classic *Darker Than You Think* (1940), Grand Master Jack Williamson postulates an entire species of shapeshifters, "*homo lycanthropus,*" who can reorganize their bodies on a molecular level by controlling the laws of probability. (For you vampire fans who enjoyed our first book, *Tomorrow Sucks*, Williamson eventually provides a scientific justification for the Undead as well.) Clifford Simak examines both physical and psychological metamorphoses in *The Werewolf Principle* (1967), about an infinitely malleable android with multiple personalities, one of which happens to be that of a wolflike alien. More recently, Whitley Strieber speculates about another evolutionary offshoot in his 1978 bestseller *The Wolfen*, about a breed of super-intelligent predators who have managed to co-exist with humanity without ever revealing their presence among us. And continuing in the Darwinian tradition, Charles Sheffield's *Erasmus Magister* (1982) has Erasmus Darwin (grandfather of Charles) proving that an apparent case of lycanthropy is actually the result of a rare form of moonlight-induced epilepsy.

No doubt more variations on the werewolf theme await us in the future. Indeed, only a few pages away stalk a pack of the strangest werewolves that ever prowled the cutting edge of science and technology: alien werewolves, virtual reality werewolves, nanotech werewolves, and even time-traveling werewolves. There may even be a vampire or two lurking around in the shadows. Only one thing can be predicted for certain:

Tomorrow bites!

Nanotechnology promises the most intriguing Pandora's box of temptations for the human race since printing was invented. Michael Flynn's series of future history stories (published in one volume as The Nanotech Chronicles*) reveal the bright and wondrous possibilities that the ability to change one's personal reality by means of very very small machines can bring to humanity. He also explores the dark side. That's where the werewolves come in.*

Werehouse

MICHAEL FLYNN

Me and Pinky and the Wag was sitting around bored one day when we decided to pay a visit to the carter. We was just hanging out on the corner and there was nothing going down, so Pinky ups and says he'd like to get himself informed.

Well, it sounded okay. We never went in for that stuff before; but you know how it is. You keep your ears open and you hear things, and it was supposed to be a real kick. Besides, it was a slow day and we was itching for something new, and we wasn't too particular what. You know how it is: Different day; same shit.

It was Pinky brought it up. Pinky was an albino. His hair was as white as a Connecticut suburb and his eyes was red, which was spooky. He was skinny and liked to dress in black. He wore vinyl bomber jackets and pants tucked into his boots. The Wag always told him how it made him look like a prock.

We was flush and we figured to blow it on something; because what the hell good was a wad if it just sits in your pants? So we knowed we was gonna buy some kicks, the only questions being what kind and how many. Gambling? That was for suckers. Besides, the crap games had floated downtown and the numbers was run by The State and was crooked as a snake. Drugs? Most drugs didn't kick no more. Not since that guy Singer doped the water supply with Anydote; and that was a long time ago.

Sex? Like I said, what good is it if it just sits in your pants? There was plenty of janes in the neighborhood, and they didn't charge much; but then they wasn't worth much, neither. We figured with what we had on us we could get parked about two million times each; which, no matter how you look at it, is a tough row; and, whatever enthusiasm we might start with would wilt a whole lot sooner than our wad. And there was always the chance of Catching Something—State Cleanliness Certificates not being worth the paper they was forged on.

Besides, we had all them janes so many times already there wasn't no more kick to it. I mean, how many different ways can you do it? It was a long time since we seen anything new along those lines.

And what was there worth doing, besides gambling, drugs and sex?

So Pinky, who was maybe thinking about parking Red Martha for the millionth time and not thinking too highly of it, gives a shudder and says, "I don't want to dribble this wad away. How bout we try something really new?"

The Wag looks at me and shrugs. "What?"

"How bout we go look up a carter? I hear there's one up by 72nd Street."

"A carter?" The Wag touches his lips with his tongue and rubs his face with his hand to show how he's thinking it over. "That's a stiff tick." He says that to show how cost conscious he is. As if it was our money to start with.

"Hey," I said. "You only live once." (And yeah, I know it shows religious prejudice, but the Dots live mostly over in Jersey, so who gives a shit?)

Pinky looks at me. "You wanna do it?"

What I heard is that informing hurts like hell. They dope you up with Thal, which helps; but which also makes you a dick, which is how they get a lot of repeat business. "I dunno. You gonna?"

We kick it around and what it come down to is that each of us would do it if the other two would; so it ain't like nobody made a decision or nothing. Shit happens. You know. So we started walking north. We wasn't exactly going to the carter, but if we found ourselves near there, we might look in just to see what it was like.

Werehouses was never easy to find. Seeing as how they was illegal, they tried to stay quiet. Make too much noise and a prock was sure to come nosing around. Carters didn't exactly hang out no signs, so if you wanted to get informed you had to listen to The Street. The Street knew, like it always did.

We was passing 69th when a crop of janes come a-cruisin the other way. They was dressed in twin glitterbelts. One on top and one below and neither one much wider than a promise. The Wag, he smiles at them and unzips so richard can wave at them. That's how he got his name. "Hi, jane," he says. "Show me your smile."

The janes, they look at him and one kinda raises her eyebrow the way a proctor might, but they don't stop walking and one glance is all they make. So the Wag, he points and says, "Hey, don't you know who this is?"

And the chocolate one, with the eyebrow, she answers and says, "It looks like richard, only smaller."

The janes laugh. And Pinky and me, we kinda

laugh, too; cause it was funny, you know. But the Wag, he gets red in the face.

"Oh, he be blushing. Ain't it cute?"

The Wag growls deep in his throat and makes a snatch at them but Pinky and me grab him instead and hang on. He stretched his arms out like claws and tugged and twisted himself, trying to break our grip. He called them janes some pretty bad names, but they didn't pay him no mind. Hell, they was called those things near every day of the year and some of it was no more than the truth anyway, so who cared? That made him madder and he screamed some more. I admired his vocabulary and studied some of it for future use.

The Wag is like that. Most times he's as sweet as your mama's milk. Other times, he's as sour as the smile. There was no telling what would yank him off.

"Hey, Wag," I says. "Calm down. Get hold of yourself."

He looks at me and cusses. There's spit at the corners of his mouth. He tells me what he's gonna do to them janes—and I had to admit it was real creative—but they're gone around the corner and out of sight out of mind. The Wag laughs high and funny like he does sometimes. Then he does get hold of himself, and after a while he smiles.

"Let's go find the carter," he says when he's done.

I kinda scuff my sneaks a little. "You sure you wanna?"

He looks where the janes went. "Yeah. I'm sure."

The werehouse was in an old Chink restaurant uptown on Serpent turf. When we passed 70th and saw the local colors policing, we knowed we was close. Carters bring a lot of cash onto a turf; so the colors, they don't let nobody bother 'em. An op gets ripped off too much, he shifts the scene and the colors lose the Tax. And werehouses was about the biggest op around, legal or illegal. Some of the colors even put the Word around through the Street sayin' they would cut breaks to any op what staked out on their turf.

Pinky asked a jimmy on 71st if he knowed where we could get informed and the Serpent, he looked us up and down like we was procks. He spit a gob into the street and allowed as how he might know something or he might not. So the Wag goes how much was the Tax and the Serpent goes how much you got and they haggled a little. No big thing and we all knew it. The little shit wanted some grease on top of the Tax. Pinky and me kinda waited around, pretending to be scenery. The Serps were a chink gang and were supposed to be straight as any colors north of 48th, but who ever knew for sure? I hadn't hearda no wars on the East Side lately; but we seen plenty of old burned out buildings when we crossed the line.

I studied the jimmy's jacket a while, trying to read his badges and pins. Some of the colors go in for a lot of deco, showing how long the jimmy been stooled or how much weight he threw. But the gangs all used different systems and some didn't use any at all so who cared?

Besides, the lookout who was lounging in the fifth floor window across the street got my attention. Not that I ever thought the Serps would leave their man uncovered, but that jimmy with the smear gun made me a little nervous, you know what I mean? If he was a dick he might not care if we was legit or not and blow us away just for fun. He didn't have no expression on his face and he wore flatshades so I couldn't make out his eyes. He was dressed all in black, and nothing reflected any sunlight. Not his shades; not his leather; not his gun barrel. Nothing to make him stand out against his background; except that he was so damn flat that he did stand out.

Pinky sees him, too, and leans over and whispers. "To keep their man here from getting too much grease on his fingers. He's probably got a mike so's he can hear what goes down."

"So shut up, stupid. We ain't supposed to notice him."

Pinky shrugs. "Why pretend?" And the sunuvabitch *waves* at the lookout.

I don't want to see the lookout's reaction, but I can't help myself; so I kinda glance sideways. And the jimmy hasn't moved so much as a muscle since I first seen him. His flatshades look like two more gun barrels, and he stared at us like we was meat.

The Wag punched us on the shoulder. "C'mon," he said. "I got the skinny."

I don't know how long the restaurant was abandoned. I could still smell the chop suey and mustard sauce and the Wag makes a joke about sweet and sour park which we didn't think was too funny. The tables and counters was layered in dust and grease. There was newspapers and broken glass all over, and the heavy smell of yourn.

There was a zombie crouched by the kitchen doors, watching us, and I kinda stop for a second or two, you know. Not that I'm scared or nothing. I know that they don't have no more brains than a dog; but he gimme the creeps. You look in a zombie's eyes and there ain't nobody home, you know what I mean? Even when they juice a stiff with his own DNA, there's always something missing. What they call free will and innerlect. So all a zombie's good for is fetchin' and guardin' and stuff like that.

The Churches wasn't too happy about zombies when they first come out, but even the legit ops all said they was good, cheap labor that couldn't be organized. So everyone looked in the Book and found out that, sure enuf, old Jesus H. had pulled the same stunt with Lazarus and a little dead girl, and maybe even with Himself. It was a great thing, that Book. You could find whatever you were looking for, if you only looked hard enough.

(Golems was tougher to find. That's where they

juice the stiff with someone else's DNA. And sometimes the stiff wasn't really a body, but just buy-o-mass or whatever. They hadda go all the way back to Genesis to make golems legit. You know. The part where God breathes on a lump of clay. Golems had to be registered with a synagogue and have a special mark on their forehead; but zombies could be marked and registered by anyone, even a mosque.)

The Wag walked up to the zombie and said something which I suppose was the password, because it pushed the swinging door open and let us go in with no more than a hungry look in our direction.

The carter was a skinny man who looked like a ferret. He must have been fat once, but went on a diet and forgot to tell his skin, cause it hung on him kind of loose. His green doctor gown was all stained and tore and his chin was a mess of stubble, like his whiskers couldn't decide whether to grow or not. He paid us no mind at first, but sat behind a battered old metal desk marking a tablet with a stylus. Every time he made a mark the computer screen beside him would wink at us.

After he made us wait long enough to show us he was important and we wasn't, he looked up and blinked his red, watery eyes. "Well?" he said. "What do you want?" His voice said he didn't particularly approve of us or what we wanted, which was funny because what we wanted was him.

Pinky looks at us, then at the carter. "We wanta be informed." Me, I wasn't so sure, but I didn't want to make Pinky look stupid.

The carter scans us, like he was checking the janes at a smile auction. "Have you ever patronized a were-house before? No?" He steepled his fingers. "I thought as much. Go home to your mamas, boys. This is not for you." He bends over his stylus and pad.

Have you ever seen how a little kid acts when you try to take a toy away, even if he wasn't too sure he wanted to play with it in the first place? The carter talked like an educated man, maybe even high school—there was ragged and stained papers thumbtacked to the wall that looked official—so he ought of knowed that. And maybe he did. Maybe he was playing games, teasing us. Maybe he liked to see people beg for it.

The Wag pulls our wad from his purse and waves it at the carter. "We got the cash. You selling or what?"

The carter looks at the stash and wets his lips. "Is that government money?" he asks and the Wag nods. "It might be enough for one treatment," he allows.

"Nuts. It's all three of us or none of us."

The carter nods his head at the wad. "That is insufficient to cover three fees."

"You ain't counted it."

"That isn't necessary. I can gauge its thickness."

The Wag looks uncertain and I'm keeping my mouth shut; but Pinky, he ups and says, "So, what's better: three cheapies, or nothing?"

Well, I can see how that makes him think some. "You're too young," he says again, but his heart ain't really in it. Nobody makes money turning customers away.

"We're old enough to park janes," says the Wag, which makes me wonder if he's still thinking about them smilers that shot him down on 69th street. "I probably got a dozen kids around the City."

"An accomplishment requiring great skill and study, I'm sure." The carter makes a steeple of his fingers again. "Very well," he says through the fingertips. "You understand that the treatment will be quite painful. I will give you drugs to deaden the pain; but nevertheless, the nanomachines restructuring your cells will twist your bones and organs into new shapes. That there will be some pain involved is regrettable, but unavoidable."

Me, I could feel my organs twisting already, but the Wag says, "Yeah. We can take it."

The carter looks doubtful, but shrugs. "Very well. The original procedure was developed by Henry Carter over a generation ago when he adapted some of the earliest cell repair nanomachines to change the body's shape. Of course, it was far more painful and took much longer than it does now. Great strides have been made since then. I have an extensive library of DNA samples"—And he points to a refrigerator humming in the corner—"that I can use to program the cell machines for the original alteration; and I will, of course, retain your own DNA samples in my cell library, and culture nanomachines from them, so that I may restore your bodies to their original configuration when you return."

He pulls open a drawer and lays some papers on his desk. "These are the usual release forms stating that I have explained the procedure and the risks to you. Read them and sign where I've indicated."

Read? He's gotta be kidding. I couldn't understand none of his explanation, and I didn't care. What difference did it make how old informing was, or who done it first? I see Pinky and the Wag look at each other. Then they take pens from the desk and scratch their X's. They show the carter their City passes so he can copy their vitals onto the form.

I try to read my form like he says. I wasn't from the City original, so I can read some. I can recognize some of the words on the form, which makes me happy; but too many are long or unfamiliar, so I give up. I stick my tongue out the corner of my mouth and draw my name. I'm proud I can do that, but the carter, when he sees what I done, looks kinda sad and says, "Are you sure you want to go through with this, son?"

No, I'm not. For just a second the carter sounded like my old man and I wanted to tell him everything and let him tell me what was right. But what can I say with my friends sitting right next to me? The next second I remember the carter is a smelly old man who doesn't shave and that reminds me what my old man was really like so it doesn't bother me any more.

"Yeah, I'm sure."

He sighs. "Very well, then." He gives all three of us a look. "My cell library includes several of the more famous pornstars and athletes. You understand, by the way, that the transformation will not be total. Your brain cells, in particular, will be affected only to the extent necessary to, ah, 'run' your new bodies. That was the law when this procedure was legal, and I still abide by it."

That explained why he made us sign release forms. I didn't think he would file them with the proctors, though.

"After you have been informed by the nanomachine, your bodies will become a reasonable compromise between your present form and that of your chosen model. You will not look precisely like Big Pete Hardy does on his videos, if he should be your choice; but you will have his craggy good looks and his, shall we say, virility?" He waved us to a row of cracked plastic chairs salvaged from the restaurant and asked us what form we wanted.

Pinky looks at us and says, "I'll tell you when we go in there." And he nods toward the curtained off area that I been trying not to look at.

The carter doesn't say anything to that. "And you gentlemen?"

"I ain't decided yet," says the Wag. "Me, too," I agree.

The carter looks disgusted but it ain't his problem. So he takes Pinky behind the curtains. I hear all kinds of sounds, like metal and glass and stuff. As soon as they're gone the Wag was out of his chair and at the refrigerator. He opened it and began pawing through the vials racked inside.

"Hey, Wag. What you doing?"

"Shut up. I wanna see if he got what I want."

"What's that?"

"Wolf."

Before I can say anything, the curtain parts and the carter comes out. He sees what the Wag is doing and shouts. "Get your ass away from there!" And aims a kick at him. The Wag rolls away from it and bares his teeth in a snarl. For a second I thought he would flip out again like he did with those janes; but he calmed down right away and grinned. "Just wanta see what you got."

"Don't mess with things you don't understand." The carter reaches into the fridge and pulls out a vial. When he closes the door, he puts a deadlock through the handle. Before he retreats behind the curtains again he turns and looks at us.

"Your friend is under anesthetic now. Do you wish to watch the transformation? It is quite remarkable to see the bones and muscles changing shape before your very eyes. There are some who find the sight enjoyable."

"Nah," says the Wag, who's thinking about more important things. I just shake my head.

After that it was quiet and I wondered what form Pinky picked for himself. It was his idea to get informed, so he musta had something in mind before we ever come uptown.

I look at the Wag. "Wolf?"

When he grins back, I see all his teeth.

Screams I think I could have took, but what we heard was moans. Long, low, and drawn out, like someone having a bad dream. The Wag and me look at the curtain, then at each other; and the Wag's tongue darts out and wets his lips. A jimmy moans, you know the pain goes on and on and he can't do nothing about it, like he give up the struggle. I began to wish for one, pure, defiant scream.

After a while, it began to get to me, so I stood up and walked around. The carter had some old yellowed newspaper clippings tacked to the wall and I spent the time trying to sound out the headlines. Some had pictures and, if the words weren't too long, I could mostly figure them out, which made me feel good. *Clones Not Legit, Sez Council. Sawyer Rules on Zombie Law. Kops Katch Killer Klone.* Before my time, all of it. Some of the clippings was so old they was falling apart; but I did figure out from one old photo that the carter's name was Benny.

Then the carter pulls the curtain aside and Pinky walked out dressed in a tattered, white robe. He was wet and shiny, like he just took a bath. The carter stood to one side, watching us. Pinky was walking unsteady and looked a little dopey from the drug. I looked and the Wag looked and neither of us said anything for a while.

Cause Pinky was a jane.

I knowed it was still Pinky. If anything, his skin and his hair was whiter than ever, so his eyes looked like spots of blood. He looked about the same mass, but it was all set up different, you know what I mean? His face looked like a Chink ivory carving I seen once in a picture book. I remembered a phrase I heard one time: alabaster body. Pinky sure enough had that.

"Well?" he says after a minute of us gawking.

"Shit, Pink. You're parking beautiful." And he was, too. Richard tried to sit up and look for himself. It embarrassed me and I hoped nobody noticed.

Pinky looks kinda pleased—and, who knows, maybe he did notice—and turns to get his clothes. But the Wag jumps up and grabs his wrist.

"Hey, hold on there," he says. "We ain't seen everything." And he pulls Pinky's robe open. "Show us your smile."

I was kinda curious myself to see how complete the informing was. Pinky lets us look for a moment, then he pulls shut again. "It's your turn now," he says. "I'm gonna get dressed."

"Wait up a sec," the Wag says to the carter. "Me and my friends got some talking to do."

The carter shrugs and points. "Use that room over there."

It was a small room, that used to be a storeroom or office or something, and there wasn't no furniture. The Wag kicked the door shut and it got dark, with just a little light coming in a small, dirty window high on the wall.

"Hey, Wag," says Pinky. "Leggo my arm."

"What's up?" I ask. Then I hear the Wag unzip and I know what's up.

"C'mon, jane," he says. "Smile for richard."

"Hey!—" And Pinky sounds scared. "Quit foolin."

"No foolin." And the Wag pulls the robe so hard it tears at the sleeve. Pinky is whiter than the robe and he glows in the light from the window. He always was built light and he makes a fine looking jane; so I can't help it if richard wants to look, too.

The Wag hooks a foot behind Pinky's ankle and trips him down. I can hear Wag's boots scraping on the dirt. Then he kneels hard on Pinky's belly to make him smile. "Quit yer bitchin," he says, and his voice was hard and angry. "We was looking for something different, weren't we?"

"Yeah, but—"

"C'mon. Don't you even wanna know what it's like from the other side? Whydja change if you didn't want to do it?"

Pinky yells a couple times and says it hurt, but the Wag goes shut up and enjoy it; and it wasn't like Pinky never said the same thing to janes himself. The Wag says over and over how good it feels, but I look close at his face and he ain't smiling no more than Pinky is.

After a while I can't look no more. I ain't squeemish or nothing. We'd all watched each other plenty of times. But this was different, somehow.

Wag doesn't take long. He never does. When he's done, he tells me it's my turn. "I gotta see the Man about a dog." And he laughs that laugh of his again and leaves us in that little dark room.

Pinky watched him go. "Bastard," he said, hugging himself.

"Hey, Pink. You come dancing out with nothing but a robe on, what do you expect? It ain't his fault. Shit happens."

"Yeah." He didn't sound like he believed me.

"And it ain't like you never done it to janes yourself."

He looked at me and his eyes were twin pools of blood. "It's different being done to."

I didn't say anything. I didn't want to be in the room with Pinky. I didn't want to be in the werehouse at all. I don't know where I wanted to be.

I looked at Pinky out of the corner of my eye. He was sitting there, naked, picking little pieces of wood or plastic off the floor and tossing them into the dark. I had to admit he made a good looking jane. Better looking than he ever was as a jimmy.

He sees me staring. "Well?" he says, and his voice has a defiance to it. "You gonna take your turn or what?"

I look away. "I dunno. I'm not real interested."

He pointed. "I got eyes. You wanna do it. So why don't you?"

"Christ, Pinky. You're a jimmy."

"Hey! Look at me. Look at me," he demanded. I looked and he showed me the smile. "Does this look jimmy to you?" I had to admit that it didn't and he leaned back on his elbows. "So go do it. It ain't like I'm a virgin or nothin."

I put my hand out and touched him/her. He looked like a jane; and he felt like a jane; and he smelt like a jane. And the eyes and the skin and the nose are a lot smarter than the brain any day. Besides, it was getting hot in that little room. So, what the hell? Shit happens. You know what I mean?

▼▼▼

Afterward me and Pinky was back in the waiting room and the Pink was all dressed up and ready to go. He was wearing the same clothes he come in with, but they fit different. Snug in some places, you know. His hair hadn't grown any longer, but s/he had combed it different. S/he didn't look butch or nothing. Pinky was a real cruising jane. If I seen him on the street, not knowing who s/he was, I don't know what I'da thought.

Pink shouldered his bag and paused kinda awkward. "Well," he said. "So long."

"See you later," I said.

Pinky shook her head. "I ain't coming back."

I wasn't surprised. Somehow I knowed that already. "Cause of the Wag?"

His face hardened. "I'll fix that bastard good," she said, looking toward the ratty curtains. "And that carter. He knowed what the Wag wanted. I'll fix him, too. But they ain't the real reason. I always wanted to be a jane. I don't know why, but I always did. Now I am, and I ain't changing back. It was too boring, doing the same stuff every day."

"Yeah, I know." Life's a bore. Different day, same shit. But I wondered how long it would take Pinky to get bored of smiling, too.

That was a scary thought. Anything new is a thrill the first time you try it; but the thrill wears off. So what do you do when there ain't no more new thrills to try? The Ultimate Thrill? The one that no one ever does twice, because you only can do it once? The one you could never get bored of? A lotta jimmies and janes I knew tried it. No one ever came back to say how it felt.

A long moan came from behind the curtain and me and Pinky look that way. Pinky spits on the floor. "I hope that sunuvabitch hurts for a week. What did he pick? Pornstar?"

"Wolf," I say, and Pink looks at me funny.

"Wolf?"

"Yeah. He's gonna be a 'laskan grey wolf."

Pinky shook her head. "Wolf ain't possible. The size. . . ."

"Nah. He tol' me how a wolf is 150 pounds or less, which is about all any of us mass. So there shouldn't be too much stretching or squashing."

"Too bad," says Pink. "He should hurt more. But then, he always was part animal." She looks at me. "What about you? You gonna do it?"

I shook my head. "It ain't sounded like too much fun so far."

She grins and claps me on the shoulder. "And why change what's perfect, right?"

"Yeah. Something like that." I grin back at her, knowing I prob'ly won't never see him again. "I'll miss you, Pink."

She looks at the curtain once more. "Yeah. Look me up. I better be going. Good luck."

"Yeah. Good luck." And I waited a while longer in that dank, empty room, listening to the moans from behind the curtain, smelling the medicines and the zombie outside the door, and Pinky, even tho she was gone. Well, we wanted something different, didn't we?

The Wag looked like a wolf, but you could tell he really wasn't. His head was bigger than a real wolf's and was shaped different. The muzzle was shorter and blunter. The carter goes how that's because the human and lupine (that's what he said, human and lupine) DNA juices had to blend together. The brain stayed mostly human; which meant the skull had to be bigger; which took away from the jaws. The carter told me all about it. He called it Morfo Jenny, or something like that. I almost understood what he was saying.

"Can he talk?" I asked the carter.

"Somewhat. He has vocal cords, but the lips and palate and teeth are shaped differently. That was part of the humano-lupine compromise. So—"

"Of course I can talk," says the Wag/Wolf. Except I have to ask him to repeat a couple times before I get it, which pisses him off.

"What's it like, being a wolf?" I ask. I see his tail whisking back and forth and thought: *He's still the Wag.* I thought it was kinda funny but I didn't say nothing to him. The Wag had a bad temper and a lot of teeth.

"I'll tell you later. Better yet, why don't you join me? It'll be more fun the two of us together." He barked. "Tonite's my night to howl."

Yeah. A load of laughs. "Well . . . I tole Pinky I wasn't gonna do it."

His hairs stood up and he growled at me. "You wimping out on me, shithead? You hop in the vat like I did, or I'll tell the janes tomorrow how you couldn't do it."

"Well. . . ." I didn't want to do it; not really. But I didn't want to back down, either. I mean, you don't let your friends down, right? And I didn't want Wag to think I was scared or nothing.

"Come on," he goes. "Ain't you never wondered what it was like to park a dog? This way you can do it without being no prevert or nothing." He made a whuffing sound, which I thought might have been laughter. "Everything looks different. Everything smells different. I can tell how many people been in here just by the number of smells. Shit. You wanted something different? This is as different as you can get."

Just before I climb into the vat, the carter leans over and whispers in my ear. "Last chance to back out, boy."

I don't look at him. "I ain't scared. Why should I back out?"

"Because you don't really want to do this. Because you aren't like your two friends. Because—" He hesitates and rattles a couple of needle valves in his hand. "Because you can read," he says.

I tell him I can't read nohow; and he better not let on. People find out you can read, even a little, and they call you a nerd. A 'worm. "Besides," I tell him, "reading ruins your eyes. They proved it."

"Who's 'They'?" The carter looks angry for a moment. Then he sags and shrugs. "To hell with it, then. Climb into the vat." And he turns on a faucet and a thick, greenish liquid oozes into the tank. I climb in and it's like swimming into gelatin.

I won't bother telling you what it was like. If you been through it, you already know; and if you ain't, nothing I can say will mean shit. I hoped I would die and was afraid I wouldn't. I felt like I was made of tiny twisted threads and every thread was on fire. It was a nightmare even with the dope.

Afterwards, I scampered out of the vat and stood on the floor. I shook the excess water off and it come to me that I was standing on all fours and I was covered with fur. My eyes was three foot off the floor, about level with the Wag. I felt like I was on hands and knees, with my legs cut off at the knees. I twisted my head to try to get a good look at me and saw long, hairy, grey flanks. Things looked a little blurred. Out of focus like.

Shit. I was a wolf.

"Hey," I said. "I can't see so well." Were wolves nearsighted? Or just my wolf?

"Take a deep breath," says the Wag. He's grinning with his teeth.

I do and all of a sudden I can "see" real well. Not colors and shapes, but smells. The far corner of the room smells pungent, like stale yourn, but it fades off toward the ceiling into something more like mildew. There are fireflies dancing in the air. Molly Cools, the carter tells me. Chemicals and medicines he's used. I know it's my nose, not my eyes, but my brain is telling me it's my eyes. So, I "see" sparks. The floor has a million smells from a million feet; and each footprint glows with its own individual color. I snuffed one or two like I was tracking and it was like blowing on a hot coal. The smells seemed to brighten.

Wag and me stagger around the waiting room a while until we get our coordination back. The carter tell us our physio-jimmy has all the wolf's nerves. What he called the auto-something nervous system. That way it didn't take long to learn our new bodies.

"Hey," I says, "this is all right."

The Wag shook himself. "Then let's howl." He looks back at the carter. "We'll be back in the morning. You have our juice ready by then."

The carter was already planting himself behind his desk. He looked at us with those empty eyes of his and shrugs. "Certainly. Mind the zombie as you leave."

We bounded out from the old restaurant and onto the streets. The zombie howled and shook its chains as we passed, which made me feel good; a zombie being afraid of me and all.

It was night when we come out and I was surprised 'cause I didn't think we'd been in there so long. *Evening Mists* was shining bright high overhead in its orbit and me and the Wag howled at the gooks up there.

I always thought the City smelled; but shit, I never smelled it like I did that night. The smokey grey of old, burnt out buildings; and the fresher yellow of a new fire somewhere off downtown. The garbage along the curb and in the alleyways. The greasy trails of cars, their exhaust plumes twisting like brown streamers in the air long after the cars was gone. The black smell of rubber on the road.

And the people! I didn't know they could stink so many different ways. They stank in stripes. The carter smelled one way; the footprints on the sidewalk smelled another. I could smell Serpents: chinks smelled different from regular people. I knowed some of the smells were me and Pinky and the Wag, but I couldn't tell which was which.

And there were dogs and pigeons and rats. Each one unique. Each one different.

Somehow, that rat smell made me hungry.

I could smell the Wag-wolf, too; and that made me nervous. I don't know why; but every time we got a little too close, he would growl or I would growl, and we'd back away from each other. In-stink, the Wag called it.

"Hey," he said. "Let's go find those janes we saw before and give 'em a scare."

I knew he was wanting to get back at them for what they done to him earlier; but hell, it sounded okay to me, so we bounded off downtown. It was a wonderful feeling, the way I could run and leap. I was strong. I was fast. The air was a wind on my face, sparkling with odors.

A jimmy and jane was walking toward us, up Fourth. She was leaning on him and rubbing her hand over his chest. He had his hand on her ass, squeezing. I could hear them whispering to each other from half a block away. They wasn't saying nothing too original.

We streak past them like an express train, leaping into the air and snapping our teeth in their faces. She shrieks and he cries out and tries to pull her in front of him and the Wag and I disappear around the corner on 71st. I find out what fear smells like. It is a heavy, pale smell. It rolls off them in waves and makes me want to chase them.

I can hear the slap she lays on his face as clear as a bell. The Wag and me look at each other and we both rear back our heads and howl at the moon.

We zig-zagged our way down the avenue, snapping and growling at pedestrians. Mostly, they yelled and ran. Some of them yelled and froze stiff. One man pulled out a cross and aimed it at us, but it didn't hurt none. The fear smell made me jumpy. I don't remember ever feeling so high before. I wanted to jitterbug.

I remembered the Serp lookout at 70th just in time. The Wag was all set to have a go at the turf guard, but I gave him a bump and he went ass over teakettle.

Man, he whipped up and was on me in a flash. He bit me on the left hind leg but I shook loose. "The lookout!" I shouted. Except it was more like "The woof-au!" and he was so excited that I had to say it over and over before he got the idea. When he did, he quieted down.

"Don't screw with the Serps," I said. "Or any of the other colors when we're on their turf. They don't mind a little hell-raising; but you can't touch one of their own."

He growled at me a little, but he had to admit that I was right. "Don't never bump me again," he said. "I couldn't help myself. Biting you. It was those in-stinks again."

He wasn't gonna get no closer to an apology. I didn't know if it was wolf in-stinks or Wag in-stinks, though, that made him do it. I twisted my neck backward and sniffed at the wound. There was a metallic smell I recognized as blood. I sniffed again and licked at it. It was stopped already, clotting up.

We cut down an alleyway, bumping over all the trash cans. One of them fell and a couple of big, grey rats cut out in front of us.

I struck like lightning!

That rat was in my jaws before I even thought about it. I bit down hard and felt the bones crack. Bright, hot copper-smelling blood gushed around my teeth, down my throat. The rat squealed once and tried to bite back, but he never had no chance. I dropped the body to the ground and snuffed it. It sure did smell good.

Then I realized I was thinking about eating a dead rat, raw, and I wanted to puke. Except that it didn't really make me feel sick. Just in my head I wanted to feel sick. I backed away a step or two.

The Wag had lunged at one of the other rats but had missed. He come over and looked at mine. "Lucky bite," he says.

Lucky, hell. I think I was just quicker to learn the body, is all. He sniffs at the rat and I feel the hairs on my back go up. So I growl at him and he backs away.

"You gonna eat it or what?" he asks.

I didn't want to, but the thought of the Wag eating what I killed don't feel right. "Just leave it," I say. "You wanna eat, we can get steak from the market."

"Yeah? With what?"

"Our smile." I show him my teeth and he catches on.

When we reached 69th, the Wag snuffed around some looking for the trail the janes had left. But the trail was cold. We'd met them early in the afternoon and now it was late night—about one ayem. About a million feet had walked around that block and the smells was all the color of mud.

We tried around the corner on Sixth, where we seen them go, and all of a sudden Wag pulled up sharp. He took in a sharp sniff and let it out. "Park," he says.

I sniff, too; and suddenly I know what got him. A scarlet smell mixed with pink shimmering in the air. A bitch in heat.

My wolf's body responded. I sat on my haunches and yipped at the moon. Wag did, too. Then we set off following the scent. We could tell we was going the right direction cause the smell got brighter as we loped along.

She was inside an alleyway taking a leak by a trash dumpster. She was a regular dog; a collie mix, I think. She looks up and sees us, and her head darts left, then right, but we got her cornered. Between the brick wall of the building and the dumpster there wasn't no way out except past the Wag or me.

Understand. She wasn't pretty or nothing. Hell, she was a dog. But I guess the 'lupo' part of my "lupo-human" body didn't go by looks. It was the smell that hooked us, and it was automatic. Pure in-stink. I could no more *not* want to do it than I could play the saxaphone with my paws.

We was sliding up real slow and easy. The Wag, he was sweet-talking her as if she could understand a word he was saying. I was starting to realize that I didn't know *how* to do it and figured to rely on those in-stinks again, when she howled and the decision was taken away from us.

He came bounding toward us from the dark end of the alley, snarling and snapping. The Wag and me, we cut out of there real fast without even looking. He sounded a whole lot meaner and tougher than we was. We didn't turn around till we passed a lamppost that had his marker scent on it. Then we looked back to see what it was that had chased us.

I don't suppose we was the first jimmies ever to get ourselves informed with wolf juice. Still, it was kind of a surprise to meet another one. He was standing by the entrance to the alleyway, pacing back and forth and growling at us. Three, four other dogs, all bitches, crowded up behind him; and one other wolf-man guarded the—harem?—and kept a watch in the other direction.

We tucked our tails. I could tell the Wag wanted to fight; but he wasn't any dumber than I was. Two against two and both of them was bigger than us. We slunk off. I wondered if them wolf-men we seen made the change-over regular-like; or even if they'd given up being men at all. A short-timer can always tell a lifer, and them two had acted like they knowed what they was doing.

Wouldn't you know it. The bitch had took our

minds off them janes we was trying to track; and, as soon as we stopped looking for them, there they was.

We saw 'em when we turned crosstown on 67th. There was only three of them by now. The others had probably found customers to stay with; or maybe these three was working overtime. Anyhow, I recognized the tall chocolate one that put the Wag down earlier and figured the other two orbited with her.

The Wag sees them, too. He pushes me back around the corner before they can spot us and takes a strong whiff of the air so he'll know their scent. He put his muzzle next to my ear and whispered. "Let's run at 'em barking and knock 'em down. Snarl right in their faces; show 'em some teeth. Maybe tear their glitterbelts off. Make 'em pee their pants, if they was wearing any." He looked once at the corner. "The nigger bitch is mine. I'll teach her a thing or two." I think he was wondering if a wolf could do it to a human.

"We're just gonna like scare 'em, right?"

He sniffed the air again. "Get ready. They're almost here . . . Now!"

We cut around the corner and spring into the air. The janes see us and scream. I hit the skinny white one and knock her down. She tries to squirm away and she hits me with her fists, but it's like being hit with feathers. I put my face close to hers and growl and she freezes with her mouth wide open and not a sound coming out. "Don't move," I say. I don't think she understands me; but she understands I spoke.

"Werewolf!" She tries to scream it, but it only comes out a whisper.

I smile with my wolf-mouth to show she's right. She's afraid of me, all right. I can feel her shivering underneath me. It makes me feel funny. Nobody was ever afraid of me before. The fear smell is starting to get to me, so I take a snap at her torso-belt, to pull it loose. It's vinyl or something like that, so it doesn't tear, but I stretch it enough so that she pops out of it like twin seeds from a melon. I start licking and she squeezes her eyes shut and gets real stiff.

"Son of a bitch!"

That was the Wag.

I turn and look and see that his jane is loose. Maybe he missed his jump and didn't hit her square on. I don't know. All I know is I see she's loose, but she ain't running. She's backed up against a lamppost and has a gravity knife in her hand. Her lips are pulled back from her teeth and she looks for the moment every bit as dangerous as we do.

A swipe with the knife and a line of red opens up along the Wag's side. He howls with rage and leaps at her. She tries to put her arm in front of her throat. And that's all I see, because the jane underneath me decides to fight back, too. She swings and connects to my nose.

None of her other punches so much as bothered me, but that left to the nose was another story. It was like I was poked in the eyes. All the smells around me shattered into a kaleidoscope. I howl and snap and my teeth sink into something tender.

There is a scream in my ear and the fear smell is overpowering. I snap again and the scream turns into a gurgle. My mouth is full of warm, salty water. I pull and tear and swallow. It tastes good. Almost like pork. I hadn't realized how hungry I am.

There are more screams, too, from somewheres else; and that warm liquid squirts at me like from a hose. I keep biting and tearing until the pain in my nose goes away. I bite and I chew and . . .

And I realize what I done.

I jerk away from the body like I was burned. I see it twitch two, three times as the last of the blood spurts out. Then it gets real still. Part of the rib cage is sticking out. The smell—a blend of fear and blood and yourn—starts to cool, and I commence to shaking, but I can't tear my nose away from it.

"Wag?" I call, and I can hear the strain in my own voice. He doesn't answer and I turn and look. "Wag!"

And he's still at it.

The chocolate jane is lying stiff and her eyes is like glass. One arm still has a tight hold on the knife, which stands there sharp and upright; but the rest of her is limp. She flops all loose every time he takes a bite. Her throat is all tore up and there's blood sprayed all over everything. The jane is covered with it and the street is covered with it and the Wag is covered with it.

"Wag!" I call again.

This time he hears me because I can see him come into focus. He looks at me and at the janes and he snuffs the body. Then we both cut out for the alleyway.

When we was back in the alleyway, we turned and looked. It was all blurred at that distance, but I could smell what it looked like. The two janes laid there not moving. Not that I expected them to. If they had, I might have lost my mind. But there was a tiny shred of thought that maybe it was just a bad dream.

"Wag," I said again and reared back my head and howled. "What did we do?"

"We didn't do nothing," the Wag said. "It was all them in-stinks. When the bitch cut me I couldn't think. I went crazy. Like you. It ain't our fault. Shit happens. They shouldn't have fought."

I sniffed a little at the Wag's idea. It sounded right and I wanted to believe it. That wolf juice gave us wolf in-stinks along with our bodies. It was like we was just along for the ride. You know what I mean? It all happened without me wanting it; and it was over before I knowed it.

I remembered how good it felt, though. Like catching prey was what I was built to do. I don't remember ever feeling that good about something; and I didn't ever want to feel that good again. I began shaking again.

"Where'd the third jane go?"

"What?" I look at him.

"The third jane," he snarled. "She'll nark to the proctors. We've got to find her!" And he was off like lightning. I didn't know what else to do, so I followed him.

We picked up the scent real easy. It was so heavy with fear that it glowed like neon. We trailed it down the street and across into the alley opposite. We ran like the wind, knocking over trashcans and newspaper stands. There wasn't no one around at that hour.

Then we seen her, about a crosstown block ahead of us. Wag howls as he runs and the jane turns and sees us coming and shrieks. She's running, too; but she's tired and clumsy and she stumbles and the Wag is on top of her.

"Wag, wait! What are you doing?" I jump around a little, feeling skittish from the scents around me.

He was getting better at it. Practice, I suppose. He knew to go for the neck right off and I suppose that was the fastest and kindest way to do it. But the jane kept right on trying to scream, even with no throat to make the sound; with the blood spraying the walls instead of going up into her head. Then her brain finally got the message and shut down for good. It couldn't have taken more than a minute, but it seemed to last forever.

When he was done, the Wag was breathing heavy. He took a bite from the thigh muscle. "You want any?" he asked me.

I just shook my head. "No! Wag, what's got into you?"

"It ain't me, chickenshit. It's the wolf. I ain't the one doing it. I'm just inside watching. This is great, man. When we go back to the carter and get reinformed, it'll be like we never done it ourselves."

And he took off again, howling. Somewhere off downtown I heard an answering howl and I thought about those other wolves we seen.

I chased after the Wag. I didn't know what I'd do if I caught him. I wanted to be back at the werehouse. I wanted to be myself again. I hated Pinky for ever suggesting we try it; and I hated the Wag for making me climb in the vat.

Something had gone terribly wrong with the Wag. He never was any too right to start with, but he was never a stone killer. I didn't know too much about wolves; but I didn't think they acted this way, either. Even wolves have rules.

I caught up with him in another dark alley. He was crouched at one end, watching and sniffing. There was two figures at the far end of it. I sniffed a jimmy and a jane parking it and I could hear them telling each other lies. They was doing it standing up, with him pushing her up against the wall. But it was too far to smell any more than that through the garbage.

"Watch this," says the Wag. "Two at once." And he runs and leaps.

The two screw-balls hear him. The jimmy turns and starts to shout an obscenity, but then he sees what's coming, and he pulls out and she falls on her ass. He tries to run, but his pants are down around his ankles and he trips and sprawls into the trash along the building wall.

Then the Wag is on him; but he just makes a snap in passing. The jimmy, he shrieks and grabs himself with both hands between the legs. He twists and curls along the pavement, splashing in the rancid puddles that dripped down from the gutters overhead. He was dressed downtown slick, and I wondered what he would tell his wife when he went home to the suburbs.

The Wag bounced over him and snapped the jane. I thought he would make short work of her like he did the other one. But he bites and tears; then he freezes, and backs off.

By that time I catch up with him. The jimmy is

moaning and cursing. His legs and hands is all bloody, but I got no eyes for him. I sniff the jane and know who she is.

It's Pinky.

She ain't dead; but that's just a formality. She's all messed up, blood everywhere; the red sharp against her milky skin. Her jaws is clenched tight so no scream'll come out. She don't look decent. I want to pull her glitterbelts back in place—sometime during the night she musta got herself regular cruising clothes—but I don't got the hands for it. Folks should look decent when they die. I look into those blood red eyes and she's looking right back.

"You, too?" The words trickled from her ruined throat. "You did it anyway?"

I sat on my haunches. "Yeah. I was bored. Didn't know what else to do."

"Pinky," says the Wag. "I didn't mean it. I was just—"

"Doing what . . . always . . . wanted." The words came fast, in bunches. Short gasps of sound. "Fuck . . . both. Fixed . . . good, Wag . . . Narked . . . carter." She sucked in her breath and held it. "No screams. Finish job . . . bastard."

The Wag looks at me and I look at him.

"Finish it!" she screamed.

The Wag howled and lunged and it was over.

Then he laid down and put his head on his forelegs and whimpered. "It ain't my fault," he kept saying. "It was the in-stinks."

I just kept looking at Pinky, not thinking anything. Until I thought: *Narked on the carter?*

I stood bolt upright. We had to get back there fast! That carter had our juice.

We ran back uptown as fast as we could. The Wag was winded already from what he done, but he found his second breath when I told him what was coming down. While we ran he kept trying to tell me that it wasn't his fault about Pinky. I wanted to tell him to shut up but I wanted to save my breath.

The Wag was tired from all his running and leaping, and maybe he had too full a belly, you know what I mean? So I pulled ahead and it wasn't in me to wait up for him. I wished I'd never see him again.

Then I turned the corner on 72nd and seen I was too late.

I stop short by a brownstone on the corner and scramble behind some ashcans under the stairway. The grating is hard and cold on my flanks. I listen and sniff.

The proctors is all over the chink restaurant like a fungus. They got the zombie on a leash and it's just sitting there snuffling in confusion. The carter is standing nearby with his hands clasped over his head. They got dart guns aimed at him from all over but I don't smell no fear. I'm not sure what his smell was. It was dull colored with sparks. He's just watching everything and not saying nothing. I think maybe he's relieved.

I smell some Serpents nearby watching. I know they don't like losing the Tax on the werehouse, but they ain't about to mess with no proctors. And for that matter the procks ain't gonna mess with the Serpents. Officially, this was City turf and the Serps didn't have no legal standing. I see one proctor, though, in his flat black leathers, watching the window at the far corner. He's standing easy with a smear gun over his shoulder. I think he's admiring the view the chink lookout has. Hell, maybe they was saluting each other. One colors to another.

It gradually came through to me that I wasn't going to get reinformed. The carter had my juice, and the procks had the carter. I began to shake, but I didn't dare move. I couldn't let the proctors see me. By their code I committed not just a crime, but a sin. Just being a wolf was a sin; and since changing me back would be a sin, too, there was only one thing they could do.

The Wag comes panting around the corner just as the procks start smashing the vials with the juices in them. They got the fridge hauled out; and they got the rack of glass jars; and they're picking them up one by one and throwing them against the wall of the building. I flinch with each smash. They crash and splash and stain the bricks. The broken glass sparkles in the light from the streetlamps. They sparkle with the odors of men and beasts.

The Wag sees what they's doing and he lets out a howl. It sends a shiver down my spine. It is a howl filled with such anger and hopelessness that I hope never to hear it again.

The proctors spot him right away and a squad takes off in his direction. That brings them close to where I'm hiding, so I hunker down close in the shadows. My heart is doing a rock beat.

The Wag knows he done a stupid thing. I could hear him in my mind blaming his in-stinks. He turns and runs, but he's all run out. The procks get him in range and one of them brings him down with a dart. He flops down in the middle of the street right where I can see him. He's stunned and looks around with glazed eyes. The fear stench is so strong it makes me want to run myself, but I keep ahold of myself, fighting the in-stink, and don't so much as twitch.

The procks reach where the Wag is lying and one of them pulls a shiny spike and a mallet from his kit. The Wag sees what they're doing and starts to whimper and tries to lick the hand of the nearest prock; but the prock yanks his hand away as if there was acid on the tongue.

Four of them get down and grab the Wag's legs and a fifth, his head, and they pull and the Wag is all spread out. The fur on his underbelly is pale and bright in the streetlight. Then the prock with the mallet positions his silver spike and drives it home with two well-aimed blows.

There is a pause like a freeze frame in an old movie. The Wag staring at the spike in his chest. The procks crouching around him on one knee, almost like they was genuflecting. The carter still under guard of the other procks, watching with no expression on his face.

Then the blood spurts out around the spike, and the proctors let go, and the Wag starts to twist and jerk in the street, and the carter closes his eyes and his head sags down on his chest.

And I cross my forelegs over my muzzle so I can't see or smell anything.

It was a long time before the procks cleaned out the werehouse. They were coming and going all night and I began to get worried that it would get light enough that they would see me where I was hiding. But there was still only a hope of grey in the east, when the last of the black cars with the star-cross-and-crescent pulled away and roared down the street and I was alone.

I lay there shaking for a long time, not daring to move. Not even knowing where to go. I couldn't go back. I was a wolf now, for good. I didn't even know where another carter might be. And no one else had my juice, anyway; and he couldn't get it from me anymore because I was a "lupo-human compromise." Funny how I remember that phrase of the carter's. I was alone. No family; no friends. There'd be no more janes; no more numbers or dice. No more pizza and hoagies and soda. No more. . . .

It come to me that I wasn't losing a lot. That there never was much to lose. Yet, I felt sad, like I had lost everything in the world.

I looked at myself and I couldn't see what to do. Sure, when the three of us went hunting kicks yesterday, this was never what we intended.

I remembered the other wolves we seen on 69th and thought maybe they could use a new jimmy. Maybe there was a whole gang of us hiding in the alleys and sewers of the City. It wasn't much, maybe; but it looked to be all the future I had.

I left my hiding place and darted from stairwell to stairwell until I reached the corner. When I looked back, I saw *Morning Star* rising. It shined bright and steady and I snarled at it. There was men up there, and women, too; looking down on us from orbit. But hardly any of them spoke English and they never paid a mind to what happened in the City. And then it came to me that I had lost a lot, but that I had lost it a long, long time ago, and there wasn't no going back.

I sat on my haunches and bayed at *Morning Star*. A mournful cry that echoed between the old decaying buildings. Then I tucked my tail between my legs and slunk off to find the wolf-pack.

Witches have always been associated with animals and shapechanging. Indeed, more primitive versions of the werewolf legend confuse the two phenomena (we, enjoying in the twentieth century a firm, enlightened idea of the werewolf's nature, are no longer so confused). In Poul Anderson's alternate history World War II espionage tale, the witch and the werewolf are reunited in their separate modern guises, the better to battle the enemy.

Operation Afreet

POUL ANDERSON

I

It was sheer bad luck, or maybe their Intelligence was better than we knew, but the last raid, breaking past our air defenses, had spattered the Weather Corps tent from here to hell. Supply problems being what they were, we couldn't get replacements for weeks, and meanwhile the enemy had control of the weather. Our only surviving Corpsman, Major Jackson, had to save what was left of his elementals to protect us against thunderbolts; so otherwise we took whatever they chose to throw at us. At the moment, it was rain.

There's nothing so discouraging as a steady week of cold rain. The ground turns liquid and runs up into your boots, which get so heavy you can barely lift them. Your uniform is a drenched rag around your shivering skin, the rations are soggy, the rifles have to have extra care, and always the rain drums down on your helmet till you hear it in dreams. You'll never forget that endless gray washing and beating; ten years later a rainstorm will make you feel depressed.

The one consolation, I thought, was that they couldn't very well attack us from the air while it went on. Doubtless they'd yank the cloud cover away when they were ready to strafe us, but our broomsticks could scramble as fast as their carpets could arrive. Meanwhile, we slogged ahead, a whole division of us with auxiliaries—the 45th, the Lightning Busters, pride of the United States Army, turned into a wet misery of men and dragons hunting through the Oregon hills for the invader.

I made a slow way through the camp. Water ran off tents and gurgled in slit trenches. Our sentries were, of course, wearing Tarnkappen, but I could see their footprints form in the mud and hear the boots squelch and the tired monotonous cursing.

I passed by the Air Force strip; they were bivouacked with us, to give support as needed. A couple of men stood on guard outside the knockdown hangar, not bothering with invisibility. Their blue uniforms were as mucked and bedraggled as my OD's, but they had shaved and their insignia—the winged broomstick and the anti-Evil Eye beads—were polished. They saluted me, and I returned the gesture idly. *Esprit de corps*, wild blue yonder, nuts.

Beyond was the armor. The boys had erected portable shelters for their beasts, so I only saw steam rising out of the cracks and caught the rank reptile smell. Dragons hate rain, and their drivers were having a hell of a time controlling them.

Nearby lay Petrological Warfare, with a pen full of hooded basilisks writhing and hissing and striking out with their crowned heads at the men feeding them. Personally, I doubted the practicality of that whole corps. You have to get a basilisk quite close to a man, and looking straight at him, for petrifaction; and the aluminum-foil suit and helmet you must wear to deflect the influence of your pets is an invitation to snipers. Then, too, when human carbon is turned to silicon, you have a radioactive isotope, and maybe get such a dose of radiation yourself that the medics have to give you St. John's Wort plucked from a graveyard in the dark of the moon.

So, in case you didn't know, cremation hasn't simply died out as a custom; it's become illegal under the National Defense Act. We have to have plenty of old-fashioned cemeteries. Thus does the age of science pare down our liberties.

I went on past the engineers, who were directing a gang of zombies carving another drainage ditch, and on to General Vanbrugh's big tent. When the guard saw my Tetragrammaton insigne, for the Intelligence Corps, and the bars on my shoulders, he saluted and let me in. I came to a halt before the desk and brought my own hand up.

"Captain Matuchek reporting, sir," I said.

Vanbrugh looked at me from beneath shaggy gray brows. He was a large man with a face like weathered rock, 103 percent Regular Army, but we liked him as well as you can like a buck general. "At ease," he said. "Sit down. This'll take a while."

I found a folding chair and lowered myself into it. Two others were already seated whom I didn't know. One was a plump man with a round red face and a fluffy white beard, a major bearing the crystal-ball emblem of the Signal Corps. The other was a young woman. In spite of my weariness, I blinked and looked twice at her. She was worth it—a tall green-eyed redhead with straight high-cheeked features and a figure too good for the WAC clothes or any other. Captain's bars, Cavalry spider . . . or Sleipnir, if you want to be official about it.

"Major Harrigan," grumfed the general. "Captain

Graylock. Captain Matuchek. Let's get down to business."

He spread a map out before us. I leaned over and looked at it. Positions were indicated, ours and the enemy's. They still held the Pacific seaboard from Alaska halfway down through Oregon, though that was considerable improvement from a year ago, when the Battle of the Mississippi had turned the tide.

"Now then," said Vanbrugh, "I'll tell you the overall situation. This is a dangerous mission, you don't have to volunteer, but I want you to know how important it is."

What I knew, just then, was that I'd been told to volunteer or else. That was the Army, at least in a major war like this, and in principle I couldn't object. I'd been a reasonably contented Hollywood actor when the Saracen Caliphate attacked us. I wanted to go back to more of the same, but that meant finishing the war.

"You can see we're driving them back," said the general, "and the occupied countries are primed and cocked to revolt as soon as they get a fighting chance. The British have been organizing the underground and arming them while readying for a cross-Channel jump. The Russians are set to advance from the north. But we have to give the enemy a decisive blow, break this whole front and roll 'em up. That'll be the signal: If we succeed, the war will be over this year. Otherwise, it might drag on for another three."

I knew it. The whole Army knew it. Official word hadn't been passed yet, but somehow you feel when a big push is impending.

His stumpy finger traced along the map. "The 9th Armored Division is here, the 12th Broomborne here, the 14th Cavalry here, the Salamanders here where we know they've concentrated their fire-breathers. The Marines are ready to establish a beachhead and retake Seattle, now that the Navy's bred enough Krakens. One good goose, and we'll have 'em running."

Major Harrigan snuffled into his beard and stared gloomily at a crystal ball. It was clouded and vague; the enemy had been jamming our crystals till they were no use whatsoever, though naturally we'd retaliated. Captain Graylock tapped impatiently on the desk with a perfectly manicured nail. She was so clean and crisp and efficient, I decided I didn't like her looks after all. Not while I had three days' beard bristling from my chin.

"But apparently something's gone wrong, sir," I ventured.

"Correct, damn it," said Vanbrugh. "In Trollburg."

I nodded. The Saracens held that town: a key position, sitting as it did on U.S. Highway 20 and guarding the approach to Salem and Portland.

"I take it we're supposed to seize Trollburg, sir," I murmured.

Vanbrugh scowled. "That's the job for the 45th," he grunted. "If we muff it, the enemy can sally out against the 9th, cut them off, and throw the whole operation akilter. But now Major Harrigan and Captain Graylock come from the 14th to tell me the Trollburg garrison has an afreet."

I whistled, and a chill crawled along my spine. The Caliphate had exploited the Powers recklessly—that was one reason why the rest of the Moslem world regarded them as heretics and hated them as much as we did—but I never thought they'd go as far as breaking Solomon's seal. An afreet getting out of hand could destroy more than anybody cared to estimate.

"I hope they haven't but one," I whispered.

"No, they don't," said the Graylock woman. Her voice was low and could have been pleasant if it weren't so brisk. "They've been dredging the Red Sea in hopes of finding another Solly bottle, but this seems to be the last one left."

"Bad enough," I said. The effort to keep my tone steady helped calm me down. "How'd you find out?"

"We're with the 14th," said Graylock unnecessarily.

Her Cavalry badge had surprised me, however. Normally, the only recruits the Army can dig up to ride unicorns are pickle-faced schoolteachers and the like.

"I'm simply a liaison officer," said Major Harrigan in haste. "I go by broomstick myself." I grinned at that. No American male, unless he's in holy orders, likes to admit he's qualified to control a unicorn. He saw me and flushed angrily.

Graylock went on, as if dictating. She kept her tone flat, though little else. "We had the luck to capture a bimbashi in a commando attack. I questioned him."

"They're pretty close-mouthed, those noble sons of . . . um . . . the desert," I said. I'd bent the Geneva Convention myself, occasionally, but didn't relish the idea of breaking it completely—even if the enemy had no such scruples.

"Oh, we practiced no brutality," said Graylock. "We housed him and fed him very well. But the moment a bite of food was in his throat, I'd turn it into pork. He broke pretty fast, and spilled everything he knew."

I had to laugh aloud, and Vanbrugh himself chuckled; but she sat perfectly deadpan. Organic-organic transformation, which merely shuffles molecules around without changing atoms, has no radiation hazards but naturally requires a good knowledge of chemistry. That's the real reason the average dogface hates the technical corps: pure envy of a man who can turn K rations into steak and French fries. The quartermasters have enough trouble conjuring up the rations themselves, without branching into fancy dishes.

"Okay, you learned they have an afreet in Trollburg," said the general. "What about their strength otherwise?"

"A small division, sir. You can take the place handily, if that demon can be immobilized," said Harrigan.

"Yes, I know." Vanbrugh swiveled his eyes around to me. "Well, Captain, are you game? If you can carry the stunt off, it'll mean a Silver Star at least—pardon me, a Bronze."

"Uh—" I paused, fumbling after words. I was more interested in promotion and ultimate discharge, but that might follow too. Nevertheless . . . quite apart from my own neck, there was a practical objection. "Sir, I don't know a damn thing about the job. I nearly flunked Demonology 1 in college."

"That'll be my part," said Graylock.

"You!" I picked my jaw off the floor again, but couldn't find anything else to say.

"I was head witch of the Arcane Agency in New York before the war," she said coldly. Now I knew where she got that personality: the typical big-city career girl. I can't stand them. "I know as much about handling demons as anyone on this coast. Your task will be to escort me safely to the place and back."

"Yeah," I said weakly. "Yeah, that's all."

Vanbrugh cleared his throat. He didn't like sending a woman on such a mission, but time was too short for him to have any choice. "Captain Matuchek is one of the best werewolves in the business," he complimented me.

Ave, Caesar, morituri te salutant, I thought. No, that isn't what I mean, but never mind. I can figure out a better phrasing at my leisure after I'm dead.

I wasn't afraid, exactly. Besides the spell laid on me to prevent that, I had reason to believe my personal chances were no worse than those of any infantryman headed into a firefight. Nor would Vanbrugh sacrifice personnel on a mission he himself considered hopeless. But I did feel less optimistic about the prospects than he.

"I think two adepts can get past their guards," the general proceeded. "From then on, you'll have to improvise. If you can put that monster out of action, we attack at noon tomorrow." Grimly: "If I haven't got word to that effect by dawn, we'll have to regroup, start retreating, and save what we can. Okay, here's a geodetic survey map of the town and approaches—"

He didn't waste time asking me if I had really volunteered.

II

I guided Captain Graylock back to the tent I shared with two brother officers. Darkness was creeping across the long chill slant of rain. We plodded through the muck in silence until we were under canvas. My tentmates were out on picket duty, so we had the place to ourselves. I lit the saintelmo and sat down on the sodden plank floor.

"Have a chair," I said, pointing to our one camp stool. It was an animated job we'd bought in San Francisco: not especially bright, but it would carry our duffel and come when called. It shifted uneasily at the unfamiliar weight, then went back to sleep.

Graylock took out a pack of Wings and raised her brows. I nodded my thanks, and the cigaret flapped over to my mouth. Personally, I smoke Luckies in the field: self-striking tobacco is convenient when your matches may be wet. When I was a civilian and could afford it, my brand was Philip Morris, because the little red-coated smoke sprite can also mix you a drink.

We puffed for a bit in silence, listening to the rain. "Well," I said at last, "I suppose you have transportation."

"My personal broomstick," she said. "I don't like this GI Willys. Give me a Cadillac anytime. I've souped it up, too."

"And you have your grimoires and powders and whatnot?"

"Just some chalk. No material agency is much use against a powerful demon."

"Yeah? What about the sealing wax on the Solly bottle?"

"It isn't the wax that holds an afreet in, but the seal. The spells are symbolic; in fact, it's believed their effect is purely psychosomatic." She hollowed the flat planes of her cheeks, sucking in smoke, and I saw what a good bony structure she had. "We may have a chance to test that theory tonight."

"Well, then, you'll want a light pistol loaded with silver slugs; they have weres of their own, you know. I'll take a grease gun and a forty-five and a few grenades."

"How about a squirter?"

I frowned. The notion of using holy water as a weapon has always struck me as blasphemous, though the chaplain said it was permissible against Low World critters. "No good to us," I said. "The Moslems don't have that ritual, so of course they don't use any beings that can be controlled by it. Let's see, I'll want my Polaroid flash too. And that's about it."

Ike Abrams stuck his big nose in the tent flap. "Would you and the lady captain like some eats, sir?" he asked.

"Why, sure," I said. Inwardly, I thought: Hate to spend my last night on Midgard standing in a chow line. When he had gone, I explained to the girl: "Ike's only a private, but we were friends in Hollywood—he was a prop man when I played in *Call of the Wild* and *Silver Chief*—and he's kind of appointed himself my orderly. He'll bring us some food here."

"You know," she remarked, "that's one good thing about the technological age. Did you know there used to be widespread anti-Semitism in this country? Not just among a few Johannine cranks; no, among ordinary respectable citizens."

"Fact?"

"Fact. Especially a false belief that Jews were cowards and never found in the front lines. Now, when religion forbids most of them to originate spells, and the Orthodox don't use goetics at all, the proportion of them who serve as dogfaces and Rangers is simply too high to ignore."

I myself had gotten tired of comic-strip supermen and pulp-magazine heroes having such monotonously Yiddish names—don't Anglo-Saxons belong to our culture too?—but she'd made a good point. And it showed she was a trifle more than a money machine. A bare trifle.

"What'd you do in civilian life?" I asked, chiefly to drown out the incessant noise of the rain.

"I told you," she snapped, irritable again. "I was with the Arcane Agency. Advertising, public relations, and so on."

"Oh, well," I said. "Hollywood is at least as phony, so I shouldn't sneer."

I couldn't help it, however. Those Madison Avenue characters gave me a pain in the rear end. Using the good Art to puff some self-important nobody, or to sell a product whose main virtue is its total similarity to other brands of the same. The SPCA has cracked down on training nixies to make fountains spell out words, or cramming young salamanders into glass tubes to light up Broadway, but I can still think of better uses for slick paper than trumpeting Ma Chère perfume. Which is actually a love potion anyway, though you know what postal regulations are.

"You don't understand," she said. "It's part of our economy—part of our whole society. Do you think the average backyard warlock is capable of repairing, oh, say a lawn sprinkler? Hell, no! He'd probably let loose the water elementals and flood half a township if it weren't for the inhibitory spells. And we, Arcane, undertook the campaign to convince the Hydros they had to respect our symbols. I told you it's psychosomatic when you're dealing with these really potent beings. For that job, I had to go down in an aqualung!"

I stared at her with more respect. Ever since mankind found how to degauss the ruinous effects of cold iron, and the goetic age began, the world has needed some pretty bold people. Apparently she was one of them.

Abrams brought in two plates of rations. He looked wistful, and I would have invited him to join us except that our mission was secret and we had to thresh out the details.

Captain Graylock chanted the coffee into martinis—not quite dry enough—and the dog food into steaks—a turn too well done; but you can't expect the finer sensibilities in a woman, and it was the best chow I'd had in a month. She relaxed a bit over the brandy, and I learned that her repellent crispness was simply armor against the slick types she dealt with, and we found out that our first names were Steven and Virginia. But then dusk had become dark outside, and we must be going.

III

You may think it was sheer lunacy, sending two people, one of them a woman, into an enemy division on a task like this. It would seem to call for a Ranger brigade, at least. But present-day science has transformed war as well as industry, medicine, and ordinary life. Our mission was desperate in any event, and we wouldn't have gained enough by numbers to make reinforcements worthwhile.

You see, while practically anyone can learn a few simple cantrips, to operate a presensitized broomstick or vacuum cleaner or turret lathe or whatever, only a small minority of the human race can qualify as adepts. Besides years of study and practice, that takes inborn talent. It's kind of like therianthropy; if you're one of the rare persons with chromosomes for that, you can change into your characteristic animal almost by instinct; otherwise you need a transformation performed on you by powerful outside forces.

My scientific friends tell me that the Art involves regarding the universe as a set of Cantorian infinities. Within any given class, the part is equal to the whole and so on. One good witch could do all the runing we were likely to need; a larger party would simply be more liable to detection, and would risk valuable personnel. So Vanbrugh had very rightly sent us two alone.

The trouble with sound military principles is that sometimes you personally get caught in them.

Virginia and I turned our backs on each other while we changed clothes. She got into an outfit of slacks and combat jacket, I into the elastic knit garment which would fit me as well in wolf-shape. We put on our helmets, hung our equipment around us, and turned about. Even in the baggy green battle garb she looked good.

"Well," I said tonelessly, "shall we go?"

I wasn't afraid, of course. Every recruit is immunized against fear when they put the geas on him. But I didn't like the prospect.

"The sooner the better, I suppose," she answered. Stepping to the entrance, she whistled.

Her stick swooped down and landed just outside. It had been stripped of the fancy chrome, but was still a neat job. The foam-rubber seats had good shock absorbers and well-designed back rests, unlike Army transport. Her familiar was a gigantic tomcat, black as a furry midnight, with two malevolent yellow eyes. He arched his back and spat indignantly. The weatherproofing spell kept rain off him, but he didn't like this damn air.

Virginia chucked him under the chin. "Oh, so, Svartalf," she murmured. "Good cat, rare sprite, prince of darkness, if we outlive this night you shall sleep on cloudy cushions and lap cream from a golden bowl." He cocked his ears and raced his motor.

I climbed into the rear seat, snugged my feet in the stirrups, and leaned back. The woman mounted in front of me and crooned to the stick. It swished upward, the ground fell away and the camp was hidden in gloom. Both of us had been given witch-sight—infrared vision, actually—so we didn't need lights.

When we got above the clouds, we saw a giant vault of stars overhead and a swirling dim whiteness below. I also glimpsed a couple of P-56's circling on patrol, fast jobs with six brooms each to lift their weight of armor and machine guns. We left them behind and streaked northward. I rested the BAR on my lap and sat listening to the air whine past. Underneath us, in the rough-edged murk of the hills, I spied occasional flashes, an artillery duel. So far no one had been able to cast a spell fast enough to turn or implode a shell. I'd heard rumors that General Electric was developing a gadget which could recite the formula in microseconds, but meanwhile the big guns went on talking.

Trollburg was a mere few miles from our position. I saw it as a vague sprawling mass, blacked out against our cannon and bombers. It would have been nice to have an atomic weapon just then, but as long as the Tibetans keep those antinuclear warfare prayer wheels turning, such thoughts must remain merely science-fictional. I felt my belly muscles tighten. The cat bottled out his tail and swore. Virginia sent the broomstick slanting down.

We landed in a clump of trees and she turned to me. "Their outposts must be somewhere near," she whispered. "I didn't dare try landing on a rooftop; we could have been seen too easily. We'll have to go in from here."

I nodded. "Okay. Gimme a minute."

I turned the flash on myself. How hard to believe that transforming had depended on a bright full moon till only ten years ago! Then Wiener showed that the process was simply one of polarized light of the right wavelengths, triggering the pineal gland, and the Polaroid Corporation made another million dollars or so from its WereWish Lens. It's not easy to keep up with this fearful and wonderful age we live in, but I wouldn't trade.

The usual rippling, twisting sensations, the brief drunken dizziness and half-ecstatic pain, went through me. Atoms reshuffled into whole new molecules, nerves grew some endings and lost others, bone was briefly fluid and muscles like stretched rubber. Then I stabilized, shook myself, stuck my tail out the flap of the skin-tight pants, and nuzzled Virginia's hand.

She stroked my neck, behind the helmet. "Good boy," she whispered. "Go get 'em."

I turned and faded into the brush.

A lot of writers have tried to describe how it feels to be were, and every one of them has failed, because human language doesn't have the words. My vision was no longer acute, the stars were blurred above me and the world took on a colorless flatness. But I heard with a clarity that made the night almost a roar, way into the supersonic; and a universe of smells roiled in my nostrils, wet grass and teeming dirt, the hot sweet little odor of a scampering field mouse, the clean tang of oil and guns, a faint harshness of smoke—Poor stupefied humanity, half-dead to such earthy glories!

The psychological part is the hardest to convey. I was a wolf, with a wolf's nerves and glands and instincts, a wolf's sharp but limited intelligence. I had a man's memories and a man's purposes, but they were unreal, dreamlike. I must make an effort of trained will to hold to them and not go hallooing off after the nearest jackrabbit. No wonder weres had a bad name in the old days, before they themselves understood the mental changes involved and got the right habits drilled into them from babyhood.

I weigh a hundred and eighty pounds, and the conservation of mass holds good like any other law of nature, so I was a pretty big wolf. But it was easy to flow through the bushes and meadows and gullies, another drifting shadow. I was almost inside the town when I caught a near smell of man.

I flattened, the gray fur bristling along my spine, and waited. The sentry came by. He was a tall bearded fellow with gold earrings that glimmered wanly under the stars. The turban wrapped around his helmet bulked monstrous against the Milky Way.

I let him go and followed his path until I saw the next one. They were placed around Trollburg, each pacing a hundred-yard arc and meeting his opposite number at either end of it. No simple task to—

Something murmured in my ears. I crouched. One of their aircraft ghosted overhead. I saw two men and a couple of machine guns squatting on top of the carpet. It circled low and lazily, above the ring of sentries. Trollburg was well guarded.

Somehow, Virginia and I had to get through that picket. I wished the transformation had left me with full human reasoning powers. My wolf-impulse was simply to jump on the nearest man, but that would bring the whole garrison down on my hairy ears.

Wait—maybe that was what was needed!

I loped back to the thicket. The Svartalf cat scratched at me and zoomed up a tree. Virginia Graylock started, her pistol sprang into her hand, then she relaxed and laughed a bit nervously. I could work the flash hung about my neck, even as I was, but it went more quickly with her fingers.

"Well?" she asked when I was human again. "What'd you find out?"

I described the situation, and saw her frown and bite her lip. It was really too shapely a lip for such purposes. "Not so good," she reflected. "I was afraid of something like this."

"Look," I said, "can you locate that afreet in a hurry?"

"Oh, yes. I've studied at Congo U. and did quite well at witch-smelling. What of it?"

"If I attack one of those guards and make a racket doing it, their main attention will be turned that way. You should have an even chance to fly across the line unobserved, and once you're in the town your Tarnkappe—"

She shook her red head. "I didn't bring one. Their detection systems are as good as ours. Invisibility is actually obsolete."

"Mmm—yeah, I suppose you're right. Well, anyhow, you can take advantage of the darkness to get to the afreet house. From there on, you'll have to play by ear."

"I suspected we'd have to do something like this," she replied. With a softness that astonished me: "But Steve, that's a long chance for you to take."

"Not unless they hit me with silver, and most of their cartridges are plain lead. They use a tracer principle like us; every tenth round is argent. I've got a ninety percent probability of getting home free."

"You're a liar," she said. "But a brave liar."

I wasn't brave at all. It's inspiring to think of Valley Forge, or the Alamo, or San Juan Hill, or Casablanca where our outnumbered Army stopped three Panther divisions of von Ogerhaus' Afrika Korps—but only when you're safe and comfortable yourself. Down underneath the antipanic geas, a cold knot was in my guts. Still, I couldn't see any other way to do the job, and failure to attempt it would mean court-martial.

"I'll run their legs off once they start chasing me," I told her. "When I've shaken 'em, I'll try to circle back and join you."

"Okay." Suddenly she rose on tiptoe and kissed me. The impact was explosive.

I stood for a moment, looking at her. "What are you doing Saturday night?" I asked, a mite shakily.

She laughed. "Don't get ideas, Steve. I'm in the Cavalry."

"Yeah, but the war won't last forever." I grinned at

her, a reckless fighting grin that made her eyes linger. Acting experience is often useful,

We settled the details as well as we could. She herself had no soft touch: the afreet would be well guarded, and was plenty dangerous in itself. The chances of us both seeing daylight were nothing to feel complacent about.

I turned back to wolf-shape and licked her hand. She rumpled my fur. I slipped off into the darkness.

I had chosen a sentry well off the highway, across which there would surely be barriers. A man could be seen to either side of my victim, tramping slowly back and forth. I glided behind a stump near the middle of his beat and waited for him.

When he came, I sprang. I caught a dark brief vision of eyes and teeth in the bearded face, I heard him yelp and smelled the upward spurt of his fear, then we shocked together. He went down on his back, thrashing, and I snapped for the throat. My jaws closed on his arm, and blood was hot and salty on my tongue.

He screamed again. I sensed the call going down the line. The two nearest Saracens ran to help. I tore out the gullet of the first man and bunched myself for a leap at the next.

He fired. The bullet went through me in a jag of pain and the impact sent me staggering. But he didn't know how to deal with a were. He should have dropped on one knee and fired steadily till he got to the silver bullet; if necessary, he should have fended me off, even pinned me with his bayonet, while he shot. This one kept running toward me, calling on the Allah of his heretical sect.

My tissues knitted as I plunged to meet him. I got past the bayonet and gun muzzle, hitting him hard enough to knock the weapon loose but not to bowl him over. He braced his legs, grabbed my neck, and hung on.

I swung my left hind leg back of his ankle and

shoved. He fell with me on top, the position an infighting werewolf always tries for. My head swiveled; I gashed open his arm and broke his grip.

Before I could settle the business, three others had piled on me. Their trench scimitars went up and down, in between my ribs and out again. Lousy training they'd had. I snapped my way free of the heap—half a dozen by then—and broke loose.

Through sweat and blood I caught the faintest whiff of Chanel No. 5, and something in me laughed. Virginia had sped past the confusion, riding her stick a foot above ground, and was inside Trollburg. My next task was to lead a chase and not stop a silver slug while doing so.

I howled, to taunt the men spilling from outlying houses, and let them have a good look at me before making off across the fields. My pace was easy, not to lose them at once; I relied on zigzags to keep me unpunctured. They followed, stumbling and shouting.

As far as they knew, this had been a mere commando raid. Their pickets would have re-formed and the whole garrison been alerted. But surely none except a few chosen officers knew about the afreet, and none of those knew we'd acquired the information. So they had no way of telling what we really planned. Maybe we *would* pull this operation off—

Something swooped overhead, one of their damned carpets. It rushed down on me like a hawk, guns spitting. I made for the nearest patch of woods.

Into the trees! Given half a break, I could—

They didn't give it. I heard a bounding behind me, caught the acrid smell, and whimpered. A weretiger could go as fast as I.

For a moment I remembered an old guide I'd had in Alaska, and wished to blazes he were here. He was a were-Kodiak bear. Then I whirled and met the tiger before he could pounce.

He was a big one, five hundred pounds at least. His eyes smoldered above the great fangs, and he lifted a paw that could crack my spine like a dry twig. I rushed in, snapping, and danced back before he could strike.

Part of me heard the enemy, blundering around in the underbrush trying to find us. The tiger leaped. I evaded him and bolted for the nearest thicket. Maybe I could go where he couldn't. He ramped through the woods behind me, roaring.

I saw a narrow space between a pair of giant oaks, too small for him, and hurried that way. But it was too small for me also. In the half second that I was stuck, he caught up. The lights exploded and went out.

IV

I opened my eyes. For a while I was aware entirely of the horror. Physical misery rescued me, driving those memories back to where half-forgotten nightmares dwell. The thought flitted by me that shock must have made me briefly delirious.

A natural therianthrope in his beast shape isn't quite as invulnerable as most people believe. Aside from things like silver—biochemical poisons to a metabolism in that semifluid state—damage which stops a vital organ will stop life; amputations are permanent unless a surgeon is near to sew the part back on before its cells die; and so on and so on, no pun intended. We are a hardy sort, however. I'd taken a blow that probably broke my neck. The spinal cord not being totally severed, the damage had healed at standard therio speed.

The trouble was, they'd arrived and used my flash to make me human before the incidental hurts had quite gone away. My head drummed and I retched.

"Get up." Someone stuck a boot in my ribs.

I lurched erect. They'd removed my gear, including

the flash. A score of them trained their guns on me. Tiger Boy stood close. In man-shape he was almost seven feet tall and monstrously fat. Squinting through the headache, I saw he wore the insignia of an emir—which was a military rank these days rather than a title, but pretty important nevertheless.

"Come," he said. He led the way, and I was hustled along behind.

I saw their carpets in the sky and heard the howling of their own weres looking for spoor of other Americans. I was still too groggy to care very much.

We entered the town, its pavement sounding hollow under the boots, and went toward the center. Trollburg wasn't big, maybe five thousand population once. Most of the streets were empty. I saw a few Saracen troops, anti-aircraft guns poking into the sky, a dragon lumbering past with flames flickering around its jaws and cannon projecting from the armored howdah. No trace of the civilians, but I knew what had happened to them. The attractive young women were in the officers' harems, the rest dead or locked away pending shipment to the slave markets.

By the time we got to the hotel where the enemy headquartered, my aches had subsided and my brain was clear. That was a mixed blessing under the circumstances. I was taken upstairs to a suite and told to stand before a table. The emir sat down behind it, half a dozen guards lined the walls, and a young pasha of Intelligence seated himself nearby.

The emir's big face turned to that one, and he spoke a few words—I suppose to the effect of "I'll handle this, you take notes." He looked back at me. His eyes were the pale tiger-green.

"Now then," he said in good English, "we shall have some questions. Identify yourself, please."

I told him mechanically that I was called Sherrinford Mycroft, Captain, AUS, and gave him my serial number.

"That is not your real name, is it?" he asked.

"Of course not!" I replied. "I know the Geneva Convention, and you're not going to cast name-spells on me. Sherrinford Mycroft is my official johnsmith."

"The Caliphate has not subscribed to the Geneva Convention," said the emir quietly, "and stringent measures are sometimes necessary in a jehad. What was the purpose of this raid?"

"I am not required to answer that," I said. Silence would have served the same end, delay to gain time for Virginia, but not as well.

"You may be persuaded to do so," he said.

If this had been a movie, I'd have told him I was picking daises, and kept on wisecracking while they brought out the thumbscrews. In practice it would have fallen a little flat.

"All right," I said. "I was scouting."

"A single one of you?"

"A few others. I hope they got away." That might keep his boys busy hunting for a while.

"You lie," he said dispassionately.

"I can't help it if you don't believe me," I shrugged.

His eyes narrowed. "I shall soon know if you speak truth," he said. "If not, may Eblis have mercy on you."

I couldn't help it, I jerked where I stood and sweat pearled out on my skin. The emir laughed. He had an unpleasant laugh, a sort of whining growl deep in his fat throat, like a tiger playing with its kill.

"Think over your decision," he advised, and turned to some papers on the table.

It grew most quiet in that room. The guards stood as if cast in bronze. The young shavetail dozed beneath his turban. Behind the emir's back, a window looked out on a blankness of night. The sole sounds were the loud tickings of a clock and the rustle of papers. They seemed to deepen the silence.

I was tired, my head ached, my mouth tasted foul and thirsty. The sheer physical weariness of having to stand was meant to help wear me down. It occurred to me that the emir must be getting scared of us, to take this much trouble with a lone prisoner. That was kudos for the American cause, but small consolation to me.

My eyes flickered, studying the tableau. There wasn't much to see, standard hotel furnishings. The emir had cluttered his desk with a number of objects: a crystal ball useless because of our own jamming, a fine cut-glass bowl looted from somebody's house, a set of nice crystal wineglasses, a cigar humidor of quartz glass, a decanter full of what looked like good Scotch. I guess he just liked crystal.

He helped himself to a cigar, waving his hand to make the humidor open and a Havana fly into his mouth and light itself. As the minutes crawled by, an ashtray soared up from time to time to receive from him. I guessed that everything he had was 'chanted so it would rise and move easily. A man that fat, paying the price of being a really big werebeast, needed such conveniences.

It was very quiet. The light glared down on us. It was somehow hideously wrong to see a good ordinary GE saintelmo shining on those turbaned heads.

I began to get the forlorn glimmerings of an idea. How to put it into effect I didn't yet know, but just to pass the time I began composing some spells.

Maybe half an hour had passed, though it seemed more like half a century, when the door opened and a fennec, the small fox of the African desert, trotted in. The emir looked up as it went into a closet, to find darkness to use its flash. The fellow who came out was, naturally, a dwarf barely one foot high. He prostrated himself and spoke rapidly in a high thready voice.

"So." The emir's chins turned slowly around to me. "The report is that no trace was found of other tracks than yours. You have lied."

"Didn't I tell you?" I asked. My throat felt stiff and strange. "We used owls and bats. I was the lone wolf."

"Be still," he said tonelessly. "I know as well as you

that the only werebats are vampires, and that vampires are—what you say—4-F in all armies."

That was true. Every so often, some armchair general asks why we don't raise a force of Draculas. The answer is routine: they're too light and flimsy; they can't endure sunshine; if they don't get a steady blood ration they're apt to turn on their comrades; and you can't possibly use them around Italian troops. I swore at myself, but my mind had been too numb to think straight.

"I believe you are concealing something," went on the emir. He gestured at his glasses and decanter, which supplied him with a shot of Scotch, and sipped judiciously. The Caliphate sect was also heretical with respect to strong drink; they maintained that while the Prophet forbade wine, he said nothing about beer, gin, whisky, brandy, rum, or akvavit.

"We shall have to use stronger measures," the emir said at last. "I was hoping to avoid them." He nodded at his guards.

Two held my arms. The pasha worked me over. He was good at that. The werefennec watched avidly, the emir puffed his cigar and went on with his paperwork. After a long few minutes, he gave an order. They let me go, and even set forth a chair for me, which I needed badly.

I sat breathing hard. The emir regarded me with a certain gentleness. "I regret this," he said. "It is not enjoyable." Oddly, I believed him. "Let us hope you will be reasonable before we have to inflict permanent injuries. Meanwhile, would you like a cigar?"

The old third degree procedure. Knock a man around for a while, then show him kindness. You'd be surprised how often that makes him blubber and break.

"We desire information about your troops and their plans," said the emir. "If you will cooperate and accept the true faith, you can have an honored position with us. We like good men in the Caliphate." He smiled. "After the war, you could select your harem out of Hollywood if you desired."

"And if I don't squeal—" I murmured.

He spread his hands. "You will have no further wish for a harem. The choice is yours."

"Let me think," I begged. "This isn't easy."

"Please do," he answered urbanely, and returned to his papers.

I sat as relaxed as possible, drawing the smoke into my throat and letting strength flow back. The Army geas could be broken by their technicians only if I gave my free consent, and I didn't want to. I considered the window behind the emir. It was a two-story drop to the street.

Most likely, I'd just get myself killed. But that was preferable to any other offer I'd had.

I went over the spells I'd haywired. A real technician has to know at least one arcane language—Latin, Greek, classical Arabic, Sanskrit, Old Norse, or the like—for the standard reasons of sympathetic science. Paranatural phenomena are not strongly influenced by ordinary speech. But except for the usual tag-eads of incantations, the minimum to operate the gadgets of daily life, I was no scholar.

However, I knew one slightly esoteric dialect quite well. I didn't know if it would work, but I could try.

My muscles tautened as I moved. It was a shuddersome effort to be casual. I knocked the end of ash off my cigar. As I lifted the thing again, it collected some ash from the emir's.

I got the rhyme straight in my mind, put the cigar to my lips, and subvocalized the spell.

"Ashes-way of the urningbay,
upward-way ownay eturningray,
as-way the arksspay do yflay,
ikestray imhay in the eye-way!"

I closed my right eye and brought the glowing cigar end almost against the lid.

The emir's El Fumo leaped up and ground itself into *his* right eye.

He screamed and fell backward. I soared to my feet. I'd marked the werefennec, and one stride brought me over to him. I broke his vile little neck with a backhanded cuff and yanked off the flash that hung from it.

The guards howled and plunged for me. I went over the table and down on top of the emir, snatching his decanter en route. He clawed at me, wild with pain, I saw the ghastliness in his eye socket, and meanwhile I was hanging on to the vessel and shouting:

"Ingthay of ystalcray,
ebay a istralmay!
As-way I-way owthray,
yflay ouyay osay!"

As I finished, I broke free and hurled the decanter at the guards. It was lousy poetics, and might not have worked if the fat man hadn't already sensitized his stuff. As if was, the ball, the ashtray, the bowl, the glasses, the humidor, and the windowpanes all took off after the decanter. The air was full of flying glass.

I didn't stay to watch the results, but went out that window like an exorcised devil. I landed in a ball on the sidewalk, bounced up, and began running.

V

Soldiers were around. Bullets sleeted after me. I set a record reaching the nearest alley. My witch-sight showed me a broken window, and I wriggled through that. Crouching beneath the sill, I heard the pursuit go by.

This was the back room of a looted grocery store, plenty dark for my purposes. I hung the flash around my neck, turned it on myself, and made the change-over. They'd return in a minute, and I didn't want to be vulnerable to lead.

Wolf, I snuffled around after another exit. A rear door stood half open. I slipped through into a court-yard full of ancient packing cases. They made a good hideout. I lay there, striving to control my lupine nature, which wanted to pant, while they swarmed through the area.

When they were gone again, I tried to consider my situation. The temptation was to hightail out of this poor, damned place. I could probably make it, and had technically fulfilled my share of the mission. But the job wasn't really complete, and Virginia was alone with the afreet—if she still lived—and—

When I tried to recall her, the image came as a she-wolf and a furry aroma. I shook my head angrily. Weariness and desperation were submerging my rea-son and letting the animal instincts take over. I'd bet-ter do whatever had to be done fast.

I cast about. The town smells were confusing, but I caught the faintest sulfurous whiff and trotted cau-tiously in that direction. I kept to the shadows, and was seen twice but not challenged. They must have supposed I was one of theirs. The brimstone reek grew stronger.

They kept the afreet in the courthouse, a good solid building. I went through the small park in front of it, snuffed the wind carefully, and dashed over street and steps. Four enemy soldiers sprawled on top, throats cut open, and the broomstick was parked by the door. It had a twelve-inch switchblade in the handle, and Virginia had used it like a flying lance.

The man side of me, which had been entertaining stray romantic thoughts, backed up in a cold sweat;

but the wolf grinned. I poked at the door. She'd 'chanted the lock open and left it that way. I stuck my nose in, and almost had it clawed off before Svartalf recognized me. He jerked his tail curtly, and I passed by and across the lobby. The stinging smell was coming from upstairs. I followed it through a thick darkness.

Light glowed in a second-floor office. I thrust the door ajar and peered in. Virginia was there. She had drawn the curtains and lit the elmos to see by. She was still busy with her precautions, started a little on spying me but went on with the chant. I parked my shaggy behind near the door and watched.

She'd chalked the usual figure, same as the Pentagon in Washington, and a Star of David inside that. The Solly bottle was at the center. It didn't look impressive, an old flask of hard-baked clay with its hollow handle bent over and returning inside—merely a Klein bottle, with Solomon's seal in red wax at the mouth. She'd loosened her hair, and it floated in a ruddy cloud about the pale beautiful face.

The wolf of me wondered why we didn't just make off with this crock of It. The man reminded him that undoubtedly the emir had taken precautions and would have sympathetic means to uncork it from afar. We had to put the demon out of action . . . somehow . . . but nobody on our side knew a great deal about his race.

Virginia finished her spell, drew the bung, and sprang outside the pentacle as smoke boiled from the flask. She almost didn't make it, the afreet came out in such a hurry. I stuck my tail between my legs and snarled. She was scared, too, trying hard not to show that but I caught the adrenaline odor.

The afreet must bend almost double under the ceiling. He was a monstrous gray thing, nude, more or less anthropoid but with wings and horns and long ears, a mouthful of fangs and eyes like hot embers. His assets were strength, speed, and physical near-invulnerability. Turned loose, he could break any attack of Vanbrugh's, and inflict frightful casualties on the most well-dug-in defense. Controlling him afterward, before he laid the countryside waste, would be a problem. But why should the Saracens care? They'd have exacted a geas from him, that he remain their ally, as the price of his freedom.

He roared something in Arabic. Smoke swirled from his mouth. Virginia looked tiny under those half-unfurled bat membranes. Her voice was less cool than she would have preferred: "Speak English, Marid. Or are you too ignorant?"

The demon huffed indignantly. "O spawn of a thousand baboons!" My eardrums flinched from the volume. "O thou white and gutless infidel thing, which I could break with my least finger, come in to me if thou darest!"

I was frightened, less by the chance of his breaking loose than by the racket he was making. It could be heard for a quarter mile.

"Be still, accursed of God!" Virginia answered. That shook him a smidgen. Like most of the hell-breed, he was allergic to holy names, though only seriously so under conditions that we couldn't reproduce here. She stood hands on hips, head tilted, to meet the gaze that smoldered down upon her. "Suleiman bin Daoud, on whom be peace, didn't jug you for nothing, I see. Back to your prison and never come forth again, lest the anger of Heaven smite you!"

The afreet fleered. "Know that Suleiman the Wise is dead these three thousand years," he retorted. "Long and long have I brooded in my narrow cell, I who once raged free through earth and sky and will now at last be released to work my vengeance on the puny sons of Adam." He shoved at the invisible barrier, but one of that type has a rated strength of several million p.s.i. It would hold firm—till some adept dissolved it. "O thou shameless unveiled harlot with hair of hell, know that I am Rashid the Mighty, the glorious in power, the smiter of rocs! Come in here and fight like a man!"

I moved close to the girl, my hackles raised. The hand that touched my head was cold. "Paranoid type," she whispered. "A lot of these harmful Low Worlders are psycho. Stupid, though. Trickery's our single chance. I don't have any spells to compel him directly. But—" Aloud, to him, she said: "Shut up, Rashid, and listen to me. I also am of your race, and to be respected as such."

"Thou?" He hooted with fake laughter. "Thou of the Marid race? Why, thou fish-faced antling, if thou'dst come in here I'd show thee thou'rt not even fit to—" The rest was graphic but not for any gentle-were to repeat.

"No, hear me," said the girl. "Look and hearken well." She made signs and uttered a formula. I recognized the self-geas against telling a falsehood in the particular conversation. Our courts still haven't adopted it—Fifth Amendment—but I'd seen it used in trials abroad.

The demon recognized it, too. I imagine the Saracen adept who pumped a knowledge of English into him, to make him effective in this war, had added other bits of information about the modern world. He grew more quiet and attentive.

Virginia intoned impressively: "I can speak nothing to you except the truth. Do you agree that the name is the thing?"

"Y-y-yes," the afreet rumbled. "That is common knowledge."

I scented her relief. First hurdle passed! He had *not* been educated in scientific geotics. Though the name is, of course, in sympathy with the object, which is the principle of nymic spells and the like—nevertheless, only in this century has Korzybski demonstrated that the word and its referent are not identical.

"Very well," she said. "My name is Ginny."

He started in astonishment. "Art thou indeed?"

"Yes. Now will you listen to me? I came to offer you advice, as one jinni to another. I have powers of my own, you know, albeit I employ them in the service of Allah, the Omnipotent, the Omniscient, the Compassionate."

He glowered, but supposing her to be one of his species, he was ready to put on a crude show of courtesy. She couldn't be lying about her advice. It did not occur to him that she hadn't said the counsel would be good.

"Go on, then, if thou wilst," he growled. "Knowest thou that tomorrow I fare forth to destroy the infidel host?" He got caught up in his dreams of glory. "Aye, well will I rip them, and trample them, and break and gut and flay them. Well will they learn the power of Rashid the bright-winged, the fiery, the merciless, the wise, the . . ."

Virginia waited out his adjectives, then said gently: "But Rashid, why must you wreak harm? You earn nothing thereby except hate."

A whine crept into his bass. "Aye, thou speakest sooth. The whole world hates me. Everybody conspires against me. Had he not had the aid of traitors, Suleiman had never locked me away. All which I have sought to do has been thwarted by envious ill-wishers— Aye, but tomorrow comes the day of reckoning!"

Virginia lit a cigaret with a steady hand and blew smoke at him. "How can you trust the emir and his cohorts?" she asked. "He too is your enemy. He only wants to make a cat's-paw of you. Afterward, back in the bottle!"

"Why . . . why . . ." The afreet swelled till the space-warp barrier creaked. Lightning crackled from his nostrils. It hadn't occurred to him before; his race isn't bright; but of course a trained psychologist would understand how to follow out paranoid logic.

"Have you not known enmity throughout your long days?" continued Virginia quickly. "Think back, Rashid.

Was not the very first thing you remember the cruel act of a spitefully envious world?"

"Aye—it was." The maned head nodded, and the voice dropped very low. "On the day I was hatched . . . aye, my mother's wingtip smote me so I reeled."

"Perhaps that was accidental," said Virginia.

"Nay. Ever she favored my older brother—the lout!"

Virginia sat down cross-legged. "Tell me about it," she urged. Her tone dripped sympathy.

I felt a lessening of the great forces that surged within the barrier. The afreet squatted on his hams, eyes half-shut, going back down a memory trail of millennia. Virginia guided him, a hint here and there. I didn't know what she was driving at, surely you couldn't psychoanalyze the monster in half a night, but—

"—Aye, and I was scarce turned three centuries when I fell into a pit my foes must have dug for me."

"Surely you could fly out of it," she murmured.

The afreet's eyes rolled. His face twisted into still more gruesome furrows. "It was a pit, I say!"

"Not by any chance a lake?" she inquired.

"Nay!" His wings thundered. "No such damnable thing . . . 'twas dark, and wet, but—nay, not wet either, a cold which burned . . ."

I saw dimly that the girl had a lead. She dropped long lashes to hide the sudden gleam in her gaze. Even as a wolf, I could realize what a shock it must have been to an aerial demon, nearly drowning, his fires hissing into steam, and how he must ever after deny to himself that it had happened. But what use could she make of—

Svartalf the cat streaked in and skidded to a halt. Every hair on him stood straight, and his eyes blistered me. He spat something and went out again with me in his van.

Down in the lobby I heard voices. Looking through the door, I saw a few soldiers milling about. They'd come by, perhaps to investigate the noise, seen the dead guards, and now they must have sent for reinforcements.

Whatever Ginny was trying to do, she needed time for it. I went out that door in one gray leap and tangled with the Saracens. We boiled into a clamorous pile. I was almost pinned flat by their numbers, but kept my jaws free and used them. Then Svartalf rode that broomstick above the fight, stabbing.

We carried a few of their weapons back into the lobby in our jaws, and sat down to wait. I figured I'd do better to remain wolf and be immune to most things than have the convenience of hands. Svartalf regarded a tommy gun thoughtfully, propped it along a wall, and crouched over it.

I was in no hurry. Every minute we were left alone, or held off the coming attack, was a minute gained for Ginny. I laid my head on my forepaws and dozed off. Much too soon I heard hobnails rattle on pavement.

The detachment must have been a good hundred. I saw their dark mass, and the gleam of starlight off their weapons. They hovered for a while around the squad we'd liquidated. Abruptly they whooped and charged up the steps.

Svartalf braced himself and worked the tommy gun. The recoil sent him skating back across the lobby, swearing, but he got a couple. I met the rest in the doorway.

Slash, snap, leap in, leap out, rip them and gash them and howl in their faces! After a brief whirl of teeth they retreated. They left half a dozen dead and wounded.

I peered through the glass in the door and saw my friend the emir. He had a bandage over his eye, but lumbered around exhorting his men with more energy than I'd expected. Groups of them broke from the main bunch and ran to either side. They'd be coming in the windows and the other doors.

I whined as I realized we'd left the broomstick outside. There could be no escape now, not even for Ginny. The protest became a snarl when I heard glass breaking and rifles blowing off locks.

That Svartalf was a smart cat. He found the tommy gun again and somehow, clumsy though paws are, managed to shoot out the lights. He and I retreated to the stairway.

They came at us in the dark, blind as most men are. I let them fumble around, and the first one who groped to the stairs was killed quietly. The second had time to yell. The whole gang of them crowded after him.

They couldn't shoot in the gloom and press without potting their own people. Excited to mindlessness, they attacked me with scimitars, which I didn't object to. Svartalf raked their legs and I tore them apart—whick, snap, clash. Allah Akbar and teeth in the night!

The stair was narrow enough for me to hold, and their own casualties hampered them, but the sheer weight of a hundred brave men forced me back a tread at a time. Otherwise one could have tackled me and a dozen more have piled on top. As things were, we gave the houris a few fresh customers for every foot we lost.

I have no clear memory of the fight. You seldom do. But it must have been about twenty minutes before they fell back at an angry growl. The emir himself stood at the foot of the stairs, lashing his tail and rippling his gorgeously striped hide.

I shook myself wearily and braced my feet for the last round. The one-eyed tiger climbed slowly toward us. Svartalf spat. Suddenly he zipped down the banister past the larger cat and disappeared in the gloom. Well, he had his own neck to think about—

We were almost nose to nose when the emir lifted a paw full of swords and brought it down. I dodged somehow and flew for his throat. All I got was a mouthful of baggy skin, but I hung on and tried to work my way inward.

He roared and shook his head till I swung like a bell clapper. I shut my eyes and clamped on tight. He raked my ribs with those long claws. I skipped away but kept my teeth where they were. Lunging, he fell on me. His jaws clashed shut. Pain jagged through my tail. I let go to howl.

He pinned me down with one paw, raising the other to break my spine. Somehow, crazed with the hurt, I writhed free and struck upward. His remaining eye was glaring at me, and I bit it out of his head.

He screamed! A sweep of one paw sent me kiting up to slam against the banister. I lay with the wind knocked from me while the blind tiger rolled over in his agony. The beast drowned the man, and he went down the stairs and wrought havoc among his own soldiers.

A broomstick whizzed above the melee. Good old Svartalf! He'd only gone to fetch our transportation. I saw him ride toward the door of the afreet, and rose groggily to meet the next wave of Saracens.

They were still trying to control their boss. I gulped for breath and stood watching and smelling and listening. My tail seemed ablaze. Half of it was gone.

A tommy gun began stuttering. I heard blood rattle in the emir's lungs. He was hard to kill. *That's the end of you, Steve Matuchek*, thought the man of me. *They'll do what they should have done in the first place, stand beneath you and sweep you with their fire, every tenth round argent.*

The emir fell and lay gasping out his life. I waited for his men to collect their wits and remember me.

Ginny appeared on the landing, astride the broomstick. Her voice seemed to come from very far away. "Steve! Quick! Here!"

I shook my head dazedly, trying to understand. I was too tired, too canine. She stuck her fingers in her mouth and whistled. That fetched me.

She slung me across her lap and hung on tight as Svartalf piloted the stick. A gun fired blindly from below. We went out a second-story window and into the sky.

A carpet swooped near. Svartalf arched his back and poured on the Power. That Cadillac had legs! We left the enemy sitting there, and I passed out.

VI

When I came to, I was prone on a cot in a hospital tent. Daylight was bright outside; the earth lay wet and steaming. A medic looked around as I groaned. "Hello, hero," he said. "Better stay in that position for a while. How're you feeling?"

I waited till full consciousness returned before I accepted a cup of bouillon. "How am I?" I whispered; they'd humanized me, of course.

"Not too bad, considering. You had some infection of your wounds—a staphylococcus that can switch species for a human or canine host—but we cleaned the bugs out with a new antibiotic technique. Otherwise, loss of blood, shock, and plain old exhaustion. You should be fine in a week or two."

I lay thinking, my mind draggy, most of my attention on how delicious the bouillon tasted. A field hospital can't lug around the equipment to stick pins in model bacteria. Often it doesn't even have the enlarged anatomical dummies on which the surgeon can do a sympathetic operation. "What technique do you mean?" I asked.

"One of our boys has the Evil Eye. He looks at the germs through a microscope."

I didn't inquire further, knowing that *Reader's Digest* would be waxing lyrical about it in a few months. Something else nagged at me. "The attack . . . have they begun?"

"The— Oh. That! That was two days ago, Rin-Tin-Tin. You've been kept under asphodel. We mopped 'em up along the entire line. Last I heard, they were across the Washington border and still running."

I sighed and went back to sleep. Even the noise as the medic dictated a report to his typewriter couldn't hold me awake.

Ginny came in the next day, with Svartalf riding her shoulder. Sunlight striking through the tent flap turned her hair to hot copper. "Hello, Captain Matuchek," she said. "I came to see how you were, soon as I could get leave."

I raised myself on my elbows, and whistled at the cigaret she offered. When it was between my lips, I said slowly: "Come off it, Ginny. We didn't exactly go on a date that night, but I think we're properly introduced."

"Yes." She sat down on the cot and stroked my hair. That felt good. Svartalf purred at me, and I wished I could respond.

"How about the afreet?" I asked after a while.

"Still in his bottle." She grinned. "I doubt if anybody'll ever be able to get him out again, assuming anybody would want to."

"But what did you *do*?"

"A simple application of Papa Freud's principles. If it's ever written up, I'll have every Jungian in the country on my neck, but it worked. I got him to spinning out his memories and illusions, and soon found he had a hydrophobic complex—which is fear of water, Rover, not rabies—"

"You can call me Rover," I growled, "but if you call me Fido, gives a paddling."

She didn't ask why I assumed I'd be sufficiently close in future for such laying on of hands. That encouraged me. Indeed, she blushed, but went on: "Having gotten the key to his personality, I found it simple to play on his phobia. I pointed out how common a substance water is and how difficult total dehydration is. He got more and more scared. When I showed him that all animal tissue, including his own, is about eighty percent water, that was that. He crept back into his bottle and went catatonic."

After a moment, she added thoughtfully: "I'd like to have him for my mantelpiece, but I suppose he'll wind up in the Smithsonian. So I'll simply write a little treatise on the military uses of psychiatry."

"Aren't bombs and dragons and elfshot gruesome enough?" I demanded with a shudder.

Poor simple elementals! They think they're fiendish, but ought to take lessons from the human race.

As for me, I could imagine certain drawbacks to getting hitched with a witch, but—"C'mere, youse."

She did.

I don't have many souvenirs of the war. It was an ugly time and best forgotten. But one keepsake will always be with me, in spite of the plastic surgeons' best efforts. As a wolf, I've got a stumpy tail, and as a man I don't like to sit down in wet weather.

That's a hell of a thing to receive a Purple Heart for.

The late James Blish was an astonishingly versatile author whose works include both A Case of Conscience, *which won the Hugo Award for Best Novel in 1956, and the first original* Star Trek *novel (*Spock Must Die, *1970). This classic werewolf story was filmed in 1974 as* The Beast Must Die, *one of my favorite "guilty pleasure" horror movies. Rumor has it that two versions of this story exist, one with a scientific explanation for lycanthropy and one without. Guess which version we used. . . .*

There Shall Be No Darkness

JAMES BLISH

1

It was about 10:00 P.M. when Paul Foote decided that there was a monster at Newcliffe's house party.

Foote was tight at the time—tighter than he liked to be ever. He sprawled in a too-easy chair in the front room, slanted on the end of his spine, his forearms resting on the high arms of the chair. A half-empty glass depended laxly from his right hand. A darker spot on one gray trouser leg showed where some of the drink had gone. Through half-shut eyes he watched Jarmoskowski at the piano.

The pianist was playing, finally, his transcription of the Wolf's-Glen scene from von Weber's *Der Freischuetz.* Though it was a tremendous technical showpiece, Jarmoskowski never used it in concert, but only at social gatherings. He played it with an odd, detached amusement which only made more astounding the way the notes came swarming out of Newcliffe's big Baldwin; the rest of the gathering had been waiting for it all evening.

For Foote, who was a painter with a tin ear, it wasn't music at all. It was an enormous, ominous noise, muted occasionally to allow the repetition of a cantrap whose implications were secret.

The room was stuffy and was only half as large as it had been during the afternoon, and Foote was afraid that he was the only living man in it except for Jan Jarmoskowski. The rest of the party were wax figures, pretending to be humans in an aesthetic trance.

Of Jarmoskowski's vitality there could be no question. He was not handsome, but there was in him a pure brute force that had its own beauty—that and the beauty of precision with which the force was controlled. When his big hairy hands came down it seemed that the piano should fall into flinders. But the impact of fingers upon keys was calculated to the single dyne.

It was odd to see such delicacy behind such a face. Jarmoskowski's hair grew too long on his rounded head, despite the fact that he had avoided carefully any suggestion of Musician's Haircut. His brows were straight, rectangular, so shaggy that they seemed to meet over his high-bridged nose.

From where Foote sat he noticed for the first time the odd way the Pole's ears were placed—tilted forward as if in animal attention, so that the vestigial "point" really was in the uppermost position. They were cocked directly toward the keyboard, reminding Foote irresistibly of the dog on the His Master's Voice trademark.

Where had he seen that head before? In Matthias Gruenewald, perhaps—in that panel on the Isenheim Altar that showed the Temptation of St. Anthony. Or had it been in one of the illustrations in the *Red Grimoire*, those dingy, primitive woodcuts which Chris Lundgren called "Rorschach tests of the medieval mind"?

On a side-table next to the chair the painter's cigarette burned in an onyx ash tray which bore also a tiny dancer frozen in twisted metal. From the unlit end of the cigarette a small tendril of white smoke flowed downward and oozed out into a clinging pool, an ameboid blur against the dark mahogany. The river of sound subsided suddenly and the cantrap was spoken, the three even, stony syllables and the answering wail. The pool of smoke leapt up in the middle exactly as if something had been dropped into it. Then the piano was howling again under Jarmoskowski's fingers, and the tiny smoke-spout twisted in the corner of Foote's vision, becoming more and more something like the metal dancer. His mouth dry, Foote shifted to the outer edge of the chair.

The transcription ended with three sharp chords, a "concert ending" contrived to suggest the three plucked notes of the cantrap. The smoke-figurine toppled and slumped as if stabbed; it poured over the edge of the table and disintegrated swiftly on the air. Jarmoskowski paused, touched his fingertips together reflectively, and then began a work more purely his own: the *Galliard Fantasque*.

The wax figures did not stir, but a soft eerie sigh of recognition came from their frozen lips. Through the window behind the pianist a newly risen moon showed another petrified vista, the snowy expanse of Newcliffe's Scottish estate.

There was another person in the room, but Foote could not tell who it was. When he turned his unfocused eyes to count, his mind went back on him and he never managed to reach a total; but somehow there was the impression of another presence that had not been of the party before. Someone Tom and Caroline hadn't invited was sitting in. Not Doris, nor the

Laborite Palmer, either; they were too simple. By the same token, Bennington, the American critic, was much too tubbily comfortable to have standing as a menace. The visiting psychiatrist, Lundgren, Foote had known well in Sweden, and Hermann Ehrenberg was only another refugee novelist and didn't count; for that matter, no novelist was worth a snap in a painter's universe, so that crossed out Alec James, too.

His glance moved of itself back to the composer. Jarmoskowski was not the presence. He had been there before. But he had something to do with it. There was an eleventh presence now, and it had something to do with Jarmoskowski.

What was it?

For it was there—there was no doubt about that. The energy which the rest of Foote's senses ordinarily would have consumed was flowing into his instincts now, because his senses were numbed. Acutely, poignantly, his instincts told him of the monster. It hovered around the piano, sat next to Jarmoskowski as he caressed the musical beast's teeth, blended with the long body and the serpentine fingers.

Foote had never had the horrors from drinking before, and he knew he did not have them now. A part of his mind which was not drunk and could never be drunk had recognized real horror somewhere in the room; and the whole of his mind, its barriers of skepticism tumbled, believed and trembled within itself.

The batlike circling of the frantic notes was stilled abruptly. Foote blinked, startled.

"Already?" he said stupidly.

"Already?" Jarmoskowski echoed. "But that's a long piece, Paul. Your fascination speaks well for my writing."

His eyes turned directly upon the painter; they were almost completely suffused, though Jarmoskowski never drank. Foote tried frantically to remember whether or not his eyes had been red during the afternoon, and whether it was possible for any man's eyes to be as red at any time as this man's were now.

"The writing?" he said, condensing the far-flung diffusion of his brain. Newcliffe's highballs were damn strong. "Hardly the writing, Jan. Such fingers as those could put fascination into 'Three Blind Mice.' "

He snickered inside at the parade of emotions which marched across Jarmoskowski's face: startlement at a compliment from Foote—for the painter had a reputation for a savage tongue, and the inexplicable antagonism which had arisen between the two since the pianist had first arrived had given Foote plenty of opportunity to justify it—then puzzled reflection—and then at last veiled anger as the hidden slur bared its fangs in his mind. Nevertheless the man could laugh at it.

"They are long, aren't they?" he said to the rest of the group, unrolling the fingers like the party noisemakers which turn from snail to snake when blown through. "But it's a mistake to suppose that they assist my playing, I assure you. Mostly they stumble over each other. Especially over this one."

He held up his hands for inspection. On both, the index fingers and the middle fingers were exactly the same length.

"I suppose Lundgren would call me a mutation," Jarmoskowski said. "It's a nuisance at the piano. I have to work out my own fingerings for everything, even the simplest pieces."

Doris Gilmore, once a student of Jarmoskowski's in Prague, and still obviously, painfully in love with him, shook coppery hair back from her shoulders and held up her own hands.

"My fingers are so stubby," she said ruefully. "Hardly pianist's hands at all."

"On the contrary—the hands of a master pianist," Jarmoskowski said. He smiled, scratching his palms abstractedly, and Foote found himself in a universe of brilliant, perfectly even teeth. No, not perfectly even. The polished rows were bounded almost mathematically by slightly longer canines. They reminded him of that idiotic Poe story—was it *Berenice*? Obviously Jarmoskowski would not die a natural death. He would be killed by a dentist for possession of those teeth.

"Three fourths of the greatest pianists I know have hands like truck drivers," Jarmoskowski was saying. "Surgeons too, as Lundgren will tell you. Long fingers tend to be clumsy."

"You seem to manage to make tremendous music, all the same," Newcliffe said, getting up.

"Thank you, Tom." Jarmoskowski seemed to take his host's rising as a signal that he was not going to be required to play any more. He lifted his feet from the pedals and swung them around to the end of the bench. Several of the others rose also. Foote struggled up onto numb feet from the infernal depths of the armchair. Setting his glass on the side-table a good distance away from the onyx ash tray, he picked his way cautiously over to Christian Lundgren.

"Chris, I'm a fan of yours," he said, controlling his tongue with difficulty. "Now I'm sorry. I read your paper, the one you read to the Stockholm Endocrinological Congress. Aren't Jarmoskowski's hands—"

"Yes, they are," the psychiatrist said, looking at Foote with sharp, troubled eyes. Suddenly Foote was aware of Lundgren's chain of thought; he knew the scientist very well. The gray, craggy man was assessing Foote's drunkenness, and wondering whether or not he would have forgotten the whole affair in the morning.

Lundgren made a gesture of dismissal. "I saw them too," he said, his tone flat. "A mutation, probably, as he himself suggested. Not every woman with a white streak through her hair is a witch; I give Jan the same reservation."

"That's not all, Chris."

"It is all I need to consider, since I live in the twentieth century. I am going to bed and forget all about it. Which you may take for advice as well as for information, Paul, if you will."

He stalked out of the room, leaving Foote standing alone, wondering whether to be reassured or more alarmed than before. Lundgren should know, and certainly the platinum path which parted Doris Gilmore's absurdly red hair indicated nothing about Doris but that her coiffure was too chic for her young, placid face. But Jarmoskowski was not so simple; if he was despite Lundgren just what he seemed—

The party appeared to be surviving quite nicely without Foote, or Lundgren either. Conversations were starting up about the big room. Jarmoskowski and Doris shared the piano bench and were talking in low tones, punctuated now and then by brilliant bits of passage work; evidently the Pole was showing her better ways of handling the Hindemith sonata she had played before dinner. James and Ehrenberg were dissecting each other's most recent books with civilized savagery before a fascinated Newcliffe. Blandly innocent Caroline Newcliffe was talking animatedly to Bennington and Palmer about nothing at all. Nobody missed Lundgren, and it seemed even less likely that Foote would be missed.

He walked with wobbly nonchalance into the dining room, where the butler was still clearing the table.

" 'Scuse me," he said. "Little experiment, if y'don't mind. Return it in the morning." He snatched a knife from the table, looked for the door which led directly from the dining room into the foyer, propelled himself through it. The hallway was dim, but intelligible; so was the talk in the next room.

As he passed the French door, he saw Bennington's figure through the ninon marquisette, now standing by the piano watching the progress of the lesson. The critic's voice stopped him dead as he was sliding the knife into his jacket. Foote was an incurable eavesdropper.

"Hoofy's taken his head to bed," Bennington was

remarking. "I'm rather relieved. I thought he was going to be more unpleasant than he was."

"What was the point of that fuss about the silverware, at dinner?" the girl said. "Is he noted for that sort of thing?"

"Somewhat. He's really quite a brilliant artist, but being years ahead of one's time is frequently hard on the temper."

"He had me worried," Jarmoskowski confessed. "He kept looking at me as if I had forgotten to play the repeats."

Bennington chuckled. "In the presence of another inarguable artist he seems to become very malignant. You were being flattered, Jan."

Foote's attention was attracted by a prodigious yawn from Palmer. The Laborite was showing his preliminary signals of boredom, and at any moment now would break unceremoniously for his bed. Reluctantly Foote resumed his arrested departure; still the conversations babbled on indifferently behind him. The corners of his mouth pulled down, he passed the stairway and on down the hall.

As he swung closed the door of his bedroom, he paused a moment to listen to Jarmoskowski's technical exhibition on the keys, the only sound from the living room which was still audible at this distance. Then he shut the door all the way with a convulsive shrug. Let them say about Foote what they liked, even if it sometimes had to be the truth; but nevertheless it might be that at midnight Jarmoskowski would give another sort of exhibition.

If he did, Foote would be glad to have the knife.

2

At 11:30, Jarmoskowski stood alone on the terrace of Newcliffe's country house. Although there was no wind, the night was frozen with a piercing cold—but he did not seem to notice it. He stood motionless, like a black statue, with only the long streamers of his breathing, like twin jets of steam from the nostrils of a dragon, to show that he was alive.

Through the haze of watered silk which curtained Foote's window, Jarmoskowski was an heroic pillar of black stone—a pillar above a fumarole.

The front of the house was evidently entirely dark: there was no light on the pianist's back or shoulders. He was silhouetted against the snow, which gleamed dully in the moonlight. The shadow of the heavy tower which was the house's axis looked like a donjon-keep. Thin slits of embrasures, Foote remembered, watched the landscape with a dark vacuity, and each of the crowning merlons wore a helmet of snow.

He could feel the house huddling against the malice of the white Scottish night. A sense of age invested it. The curtains smelled of dust and spices. It seemed impossible that anyone but Foote and Jarmoskowski could be alive in it.

After a long moment, Foote moved the curtain very slightly and drew it back. His face was drenched in reflected moonlight and he stepped back into the dark again, leaving the curtains parted.

If Jarmoskowski saw the furtive movement he gave no sign. He remained engrossed in the acerb beauty of the night. Almost the whole of Newcliffe's estate was visible from where he stood. Even the black border of the forest, beyond the golf course to the right, could be seen through the dry frigid air. A few isolated trees stood nearer the house, casting sharply etched shadows on the snow, shadows that flowed and changed shape with the slow movement of the moon.

Jarmoskowski sighed and scratched his left palm. His lips moved soundlessly.

A cloud floated across the moon, its shadow preceding it, gliding in a rush of ink athwart the house. The gentle ripples of the snow field reared ahead of the wave, like breakers, falling back, engulfed, then surging again much closer. A thin singing of wind rose briefly, whirling crystalline showers of snow from the terrace flagstones.

The wind died as the umbra engulfed the house. For a long instant, the darkness and silence persisted. Then, from somewhere near the stables and greenhouses behind the house, a dog raised his voice in a faint sustained throbbing howl. Others joined in.

Jarmoskowski's teeth gleamed in the occluded moonlight. He stood a moment longer; then his head turned with a quick jerk and his eyes flashed a feral scarlet at the dark window where Foote hovered. Foote released the curtains hastily. Even through them he could see the pianist's phosphorescent smile.

The dog keened again. Jarmoskowski went back into the house. Foote scurried to his door and cocked one eye around the jamb.

Some men, as has somewhere been remarked, cannot pass a bar; some cannot pass a woman; some cannot pass a rare stamp or a good fire. Foote could not help spying, but in this one case he knew that one thing could be said for him: *this* time he wanted to be in the wrong.

There was a single small light burning in the corridor. Jarmoskowski's room was at the end of the hall, next to Foote's. As the pianist walked reflectively toward it, the door of the room directly across from Foote's swung open and Doris Gilmore came out, clad in a quilted sapphire housecoat with a high Russian collar. The effect was marred a little by the towel over her arm and the toothbrush in her hand, but nevertheless she looked startlingly pretty.

"Oh!" she said. Jarmoskowski turned toward her, and then neither of them said anything for a while.

Foote ground his teeth. Was the girl, too, to be a witness to the thing he expected from Jarmoskowski? That would be beyond all decency. And it must be nearly midnight now.

The two still had not moved. Trembling, Foote edged out into the hall and slid behind Jarmoskowski's back along the wall to Jarmoskowski's room. By the grace of God, the door was open.

In a quieter voice, Doris said, "Oh, it's you, Jan. You startled me."

"So I see. I'm most sorry," Jarmoskowski's voice said. Foote again canted his head until he could see them both. "It appears that we are the night owls of the party."

"I think the rest are tight. Especially that horrible painter. I've been reading the magazines Tom left by my bed, and I finally decided I'd better try to sleep, too. What have you been up to?"

"I was out on the terrace, getting a breath. I like the winter night—it bites."

"The dogs are restless, too," she said. "Did you hear them? I suppose Brucey started them off."

Jarmoskowski smiled. "Very likely. Why does a full moon make a dog feel so sorry for himself?"

"Maybe there's a banshee about."

"I doubt it," Jarmoskowski said. "This house isn't old enough to have any family psychopomps; it's massive, but largely imitation. And as far as I know, none of Tom's or Caroline's relatives have had the privilege of dying in it."

"Don't. You talk as if you believed it." She wrapped the housecoat tighter about her waist; Foote guessed that she was repressing a shiver.

"I came from a country where belief in such things is common. In Poland most skeptics are imported."

"I wish you'd pretend to be an exception," she said. "You're giving me the creeps, Jan."

He nodded seriously. "That's—fair enough," he said gently.

There was another silence, while they looked at each other anew in the same dim light. Then Jarmoskowski stepped forward and took her hands in his.

Foote felt a long-belated flicker of embarrassment.

Nothing could be more normal than this, and nothing interested him less. He was an eavesdropper, not a voyeur. If he were wrong after all, he'd speedily find himself in a position for which no apology would be possible.

The girl was looking up at Jarmoskowski, smiling uncertainly. Her smile was so touching as to make Foote writhe inside his skin. "Jan," she said.

"No . . . Doris, wait," Jarmoskowski said indistinctly. "Wait just a moment. It has been a long time since Prague."

"I see," she said. She tried to release her hands.

Jarmoskowski said sharply: "You don't see. I was eighteen then. You were—what was it?—eleven, I think. In those days I was proud of your school-girl crush, but of course infinitely too old for you. I am not so old any more, and when I saw this afternoon how lovely you have become the years went away like dandelion fluff—no, no, hear me out, please! There is much more. I love you now, Doris, as I can see you love me; but—"

In the brief pause Foote could hear the sharp indrawn breaths that Doris was trying to control. He felt like crawling. He had no business—

"But we must wait a little, Doris. I know something that concerns you that you do not know yourself. And I must warn you of something in Jan Jarmoskowski that neither of us could even have dreamed in the old days."

"Warn—me?"

"Yes." Jarmoskowski paused again. Then he said: "You will find it hard to believe. But if you can, we may be happy. Doris, I cannot be a skeptic. I am—"

He stopped. He had looked down abstractedly at her hands, as if searching for precisely the right English words. Then, slowly, he turned her hands over until they rested palms up on his. An expression of absolute shock transformed his face, and Foote saw his grip tighten spasmodically.

In that tetanic silence Foote heard his judgment of Jarmoskowski confirmed. It gave him no pleasure. He was frightened.

For an instant Jarmoskowski shut his eyes. The muscles along his jaw stood out with the violence with which he was clenching his teeth. Then, deliberately, he folded Doris' hands together, and his curious fingers made a fist about them. When his eyes opened again they were as red as flame in the weak light.

Doris jerked her hands free and crossed them over her breasts. "Jan—Jan, what is it? What's the matter?"

His face, that should have been flying into flinders under the force of the knowledge behind it, came under control muscle by muscle.

"Nothing," he said. "There's really no point in what I was going to say. I have been foolish; please pardon me. Nice to have seen you again, Doris. Good night."

He brushed past her and stalked on down the corridor. Doris turned to look after him, her cheeks beginning to glisten, one freed hand clutching her toothbrush.

Jarmoskowski wrenched the unresisting doorknob of his room and threw the door shut behind him. Foote only barely managed to dodge out of his way.

Behind the house, a dog howled and went silent again.

3

In Jarmoskowski's room the moonlight played in through the open window upon a carefully turned-down bed. The cold air had penetrated every cranny. He ran both hands through his hair and went directly across the carpet to the table beside his bed. As he crossed the path of colorless light his shadow was oddly foreshortened, so that it looked as if he were walking on all fours. There was a lamp on the side-table and he reached for it.

Then he stopped dead still, his hand halfway to the switch. He seemed to be listening. Finally, he turned and looked back across the room, directly at the spot behind the door where Foote was standing.

It was the blackest spot of all, for it had its back to the moon; but Jarmoskowski said immediately, "Hello, Paul. Aren't you up rather late?"

Foote did not reply for a while. His senses were still alcohol-numbed, and he was further poisoned by the sheer outrageous impossibility of the thing he knew to be true. He stood silently in the darkness, watching the Pole's barely visible figure beside the fresh bed, and the sound of his own breathing was loud in his ears. The broad flat streamer of moonlight lay between them like a metallic river.

"I'm going to bed shortly," he said at last. His voice sounded flat and dead and faraway, as if it belonged to someone else entirely. "I just came to issue a little warning."

"Well, well," said Jarmoskowski pleasantly. "Warnings seem to be all the vogue this evening. Do you customarily pay your social calls with a knife in your hand?"

"That's the warning, Jarmoskowski. The knife. I'm sleeping with it. It's made of silver."

"You must be drunker than usual," said the composer. "Why don't you just go to bed—with the knife, if you fancy it? We can talk again in the morning."

"Don't give me that," Foote snapped savagely. "You can't fool me. I know you for what you are."

"All right, you know me. Is it a riddle? I'll bite, as Bennington would say."

"Yes, you'd bite," Foote said, and his voice shook a little despite himself. "Should I really give it a name, Jarmoskowski? Where you were born it was *vrolok*, wasn't it? And in France it was *loup-garou*. In the

Carpathians it was *stregoica* or *strega*, or sometimes *vlkolak*. In—"

"Your command of languages is greater than your common sense," Jarmoskowski said. "And *stregoica* and *strega* are different in sex, and neither of them is equivalent to *loup-garou*. But all the same you interest me. Isn't it a little out of season for all such things? Wolfsbane does not bloom in the dead of winter. And perhaps the things you give so many fluent names are also out of season in 1952."

"The dogs hate you," Foote said softly. "That was a fine display Brucey put on this afternoon, when Tom brought him in from his run and he found you here. I doubt that you've forgotten it. I think you've seen a dog behave like that before, walking sidewise through a room where you were, growling, watching you with every step until Tom or some other owner dragged him out. He's howling now.

"And that shock you got from the table silverware at dinner—and your excuse about rubber-soled shoes. I looked under the table, if you recall, and your shoes turned out to be leather-soled. But it was a pretty feeble excuse anyhow, for anybody knows that you can't get an electric shock from an ungrounded piece of tableware, no matter how long you've been scuffing rubber. Silver's deadly, isn't it, Jarmoskowski?

"And those fingers—the index fingers as long as the middle ones—you were clever about those. You were careful to call everybody's attention to them. It's supposed to be the obvious that everybody misses. But Jarmoskowski, that 'Purloined Letter' mechanism has been ground through too often already in detective stories. It didn't fool Lundgren, it didn't fool me."

"Ah, so," Jarmoskowski said. "Quite a catalogue."

"There's more. How does it happen that your eyes were gray all afternoon, and turned red as soon as the moon rose? And the palms of your hands—there was some hair growing there, but you shaved it off, didn't you, Jarmoskowski? I've been watching you scratch them. Everything about you, the way you look, the way you talk, every move you make—it all screams out your nature in a dozen languages to anyone who knows the signs."

After a long silence, Jarmoskowski said, "I see. You've been most attentive, Paul—I see you are what people call the suspicious drunk. But I appreciate your warning, Paul. Let us suppose that what you say of me is true. What then? Are you prepared to broadcast it to the rest of the house? Would you like to be known until the day you die as 'The Boy Who Cried—' "

"I don't intend to say anything unless you make it necessary. I want you to know that I know, in case you've seen a pentagram on anyone's palm tonight."

Jarmoskowski smiled. "Have you thought that, knowing that you know, I could have no further choice? That the first word you said to me about it all might brand *your* palm with the pentagram?"

Foote had not thought about it. He had spent far too much time convincing himself that it had all come out of the bottle. He heard the silver knife clatter against the floor before he was aware that he had dropped it; his eyes throbbed with the effort to see through the dimness the hands he was holding before them.

From the other side of his moonlit room, Jarmoskowski's voice drifted, dry, distant, and amused. "So—you hadn't thought. That's too bad. *Better never* than late, Paul."

The dim figure of Jarmoskowski began to sink down, rippling a little in the reflected moonlight. At first it seemed only as if he were sitting down upon the bed; but the foreshortening proceeded without any real movement, and the pianist's body was twisting, too, and his clothing with it, his shirt-bosom dimming to an indistinct blaze upon his broadening chest, his shoulders hunching, his pointed jaw already squared into a blunt muzzle, his curled pads ticking as they struck the bare floor and moved deliberately toward Foote. His tail was thrust straight out behind him, and the ruff of coarse hair along his back stirred gently. He sniffed.

Somehow Foote got his legs to move. He found the doorknob and threw himself out of Jarmoskowski's room into the corridor.

A bare second after he had slammed the door, something struck it a massive blow from inside. The paneling split sharply. He held it shut by the knob with all the strength in his body. He could see almost nothing; his eyes seemed to have rolled all the way back into his head.

A dim white shape drifted down upon him through the dark corridor, and a fresh spasm of fear sent rivers of sweat down his back, his sides, his cheeks. But it was only the girl.

"Paul! What on Earth! What's the *matter?*"

"Quick!" he said, choking. "Get something silver—something heavy made out of silver—quick, *quick!*"

Despite her astonishment, the frantic urgency in his voice drove her away. She darted back into her room. Kalpas of eternity went by after that while he listened for sounds inside Jarmoskowski's room. Once he thought he heard a low rumble, but he was not sure. The sealike hissing and sighing of his blood, rushing through the channels of the middle ear, seemed very loud to him. He couldn't imagine why it was not arousing the whole countryside. He clung to the doorknob and panted.

Then the girl was back, bearing a silver candlestick nearly three feet in length—a weapon that was almost too good, for his fright-weakened muscles had some difficulty in lifting it. He shifted his grip on the knob to the left hand alone, and hefted the candlestick awkwardly with his right.

"All right," he said, in what he hoped was a grim voice. "Now let him come."

"What in heaven's name is this all about?" Doris

said. "You're waking everybody in the house with this racket. Look—even the dog's come in to see—"

"The dog!"

He swung around, releasing the doorknob. Not ten paces from them, an enormous coal-black animal, nearly five feet in length, grinned at them with polished fangs. As soon as it saw Foote move it snarled. Its eyes gleamed red under the single bulb.

It sprang.

Foote heaved the candlestick high and brought it down—but the animal was not there. Somehow the leap was never completed. There was a brief flash of movement at the open end of the corridor, then darkness and silence.

"He saw the candlestick," Foote panted. "Must have jumped out the window and come around through the front door. Then he saw the silver and beat it."

"Paul!" Doris cried. "What—how did you know that thing would jump? It was so big! And what has silver—"

He chuckled, surprising even himself. He had a mental picture of what the truth was going to sound like to Doris. "That," he said, "was a wolf and a whopping one. Even the usual kind isn't very friendly and—"

Footsteps sounded on the floor above, and the voice of Newcliffe, grumbling loudly, came down the stairs. Newcliffe liked his evenings noisy and his nights quiet. The whole house now seemed to have heard the commotion, for in a moment a number of half-clad figures were elbowing out into the corridor, wanting to know what was up or plaintively requesting less noise.

Abruptly the lights went on, revealing blinking faces and pajama-clad forms struggling into robes. Newcliffe came down the stairs. Caroline was with him, impeccable even in disarray, her face openly and honestly ignorant and unashamedly beautiful. She was no lion-hunter but she loved parties. Evidently she was pleased that the party was starting again.

"What's all this?" Newcliffe demanded in a gravelly voice. "Foote, are you the center of this whirlpool? Why all the noise?"

"Werewolf," Foote said, as painfully conscious as he had expected to be of how meaningless the word would sound. "We've got a werewolf here. And somebody's marked out for him."

How else could you put it? Let it stand.

There was a chorus of "What's" as the group jostled about him. "Eh? What was it? . . . Werewolf, I thought he said . . . What's this all about? . . . Somebody's seen a wolf . . . Is that new? . . . What an uproar!"

"Paul," Lundgren's voice cut through. "Details, please."

"Jarmoskowski's a werewolf," Foote said grimly, making his tone as emotionless and factual as he could. "I suspected it earlier tonight and went into his room and accused him of it. He changed shape, right on the spot while I was watching."

The sweat started out afresh at the recollection of that half-seen mutation. "He came around into the hall and went for us. I scared him off with a silver candlestick for a club." He realized that he still held the candlestick and brandished it as proof. "Doris saw the wolf—she'll vouch for that."

"I saw a big doglike thing, all right," Doris admitted. "And it did jump at us. It was black and had a lot of teeth. But—Paul, was that supposed to be Jan? Why, that's ridiculous."

"It certainly is," Newcliffe said feelingly. "Getting us all up for a practical joke. Probably one of the dogs is loose."

"Do you have any all-black dogs five feet long?" Foote demanded desperately. "And where's Jarmoskowski now? Why isn't he here? Answer me that!"

Bennington gave a skeptical grunt from the background

and opened Jarmoskowski's door. The party tried to jam itself as a unit into the room. Foote forced his way through the clot.

"See? He isn't here, either. And the bed's not been slept in. Doris—" He paused for an instant, realizing what he was about to admit, then plunged ahead. The stakes were now too big to hesitate over social conventions. "Doris, you saw him go in here. Did you see him come out again?"

The girl looked startled. "No, but I was in my room—"

"All right. Here. Look at this." Foote led the way over to the window and pointed out. "See? The prints on the snow?"

One by one the others leaned out. There was no arguing it. A set of animal prints, like large dog-tracks, led away from a spot just beneath Jarmoskowski's window—a spot where the disturbed snow indicated the landing of some heavy body.

"Follow them around," Foote said. "They lead around to the front door, and away again—I hope."

"Have you traced them?" James asked.

"I didn't have to. I saw the thing, James."

"The tracks could be coincidence," Caroline suggested. "Maybe Jan just went for a walk."

"Barefoot? There are his shoes."

Bennington vaulted over the windowsill with an agility astonishing in so round a man, and plowed away with slippered feet along the line of tracks. A little while later he entered the room behind their backs.

"Paul's right," he said, above the hubbub of excited conversation. "The tracks go around to the terrace to the front door, then away again and around the side of the house toward the golf course." He rolled up his wet pajama cuffs awkwardly. A little of the weight came off Foote's heart; at least the beast was not still in the house, then—

"This is crazy," Newcliffe declared angrily. "We're

like a lot of little children, panicked by darkness. There's no such thing as a werewolf."

"I wouldn't place any wagers on that," Ehrenberg said. "Millions of people have believed in the werewolf for hundreds of years. One multiplies the years by the people and the answer is a big figure, *nicht wahr*?"

Newcliffe turned sharply to Lundgren. "Chris, I can depend upon you at least to have your wits about you."

The psychiatrist smiled wanly. "You didn't read my Stockholm paper, did you, Tom? I mean my paper on psychoses of Middle Ages populations. Much of it dealt with lycanthropy—werewolfism."

"You mean—you believe this idiot story?"

"I spotted Jarmoskowski early in the evening," Lundgren said. "He must have shaved the hair on his palms, but he has all the other signs—eyes bloodshot with moonrise, first and second fingers of equal length, pointed ears, merged eyebrows, domed prefrontal bones, elongated upper cuspids. In short, the typical hyperpineal type—a lycanthrope."

"Why didn't you say something?"

"I have a natural horror of being laughed at," Lundgren said dryly. "And *I didn't want to draw Jarmoskowski's attention to me.* These endocrine-imbalance cases have a way of making enemies very easily."

Foote grinned ruefully. If he had thought of that part of it before he had confronted Jarmoskowski, he would have kept his big mouth shut. It was deflating to know how ignoble one's motives could be in the face of the most demanding situations.

"Lycanthropy is no longer common," Lundgren droned, "and so seldom mentioned except in out-of-the-way journals. It is the little-known aberration of a little-known ductless gland; beyond that we know only what we knew in 1400, and that is that it appears to enable the victim to control his shape."

"I'm still leery of this whole business," Bennington

growled, from somewhere deep in his teddy-bear chest. "I've known Jan for years. Nice fella—helped me out of a bad hole once, without owing me any favors at all. And I think there's enough discord in this house so that I won't add to it much if I say I wouldn't trust Paul Foote as far as I could throw him. By God, Paul, if this does turn out to be some practical joke of yours—"

"Ask Lundgren," Foote said.

There was dead silence, disturbed only by heavy breathing. Lundgren was known to almost all of them as the world's ultimate authority on hormone-created insanity. Nobody seemed to want to ask him.

"Paul's right," Lundgren said at last. "You must take it or leave it. Jarmoskowski is a lycanthrope. A hyperpineal. No other gland could affect the blood vessels of the eyes like that or make such a reorganization of the soma possible. Jarmoskowski is inarguably a werewolf."

Bennington sagged, the light of righteous incredulity dying from his eyes. "I'll be damned!" he muttered. "It can't be. It can't be."

"We've got to get him tonight," Foote said. "He's seen the pentagram on somebody's palm—somebody in the party."

"What's that?" asked James.

"It's a five-pointed star inscribed in a circle, a very old magical symbol. You find it in all the old mystical books, right back to the so-called fourth and fifth Books of Moses. The werewolf sees it on the palm of his next victim."

There was a gasping little scream from Doris. "So that's it!" she cried. "Dear God, I'm the one! He saw something on my hand tonight while we were talking in the hall. He was awfully startled and went away with hardly another word. He said he was going to warn me about something and then he—"

"Steady," Bennington said, in a soft voice that had all the penetrating power of a thunderclap. "There's safety in numbers. We're all here." Nevertheless, he could not keep himself from glancing surreptitiously over his shoulder.

"It's a common illusion in lycanthropic seizures," Lundgren agreed. "Or hallucination, I should say. But Paul, you're wrong about its significance to the lycanthrope; I believe you must have gotten that idea from some movie. The pentagram means something quite different. Doris, let me ask you a question."

"Why—certainly, Dr. Lundgren. What is it?"

"What were you doing with that piece of modelling clay this evening?"

To Foote, and evidently to the rest of the party, the question was meaningless. Doris, however, looked down at the floor and scuffed one slippered toe back and forth over the carpet.

"Answer me, please," Lundgren said patiently. "I watched you manipulating it while Jan was playing, and it seemed to me to be an odd thing for a woman to have in her handbag. What were you doing with it?"

"I—was trying to scare Paul Foote," she said, in so low a voice that she could scarcely be heard at all.

"How? Believe me, Doris, this is most important. How?"

"There was a little cloud of smoke coming out of his cigarette. I was—trying to make it take—"

"Yes. Go on."

"—take the shape of a statuette near it," Foote said flatly. He could feel droplets of ice on his forehead. The girl looked at him sideways; then she nodded and looked back at the floor. "The music helped," she murmured.

"Very good," Lundgren said. "Doris, I'm not trying to put you on the spot. Have you had much success at this sort of game?"

"Lately," she said, not quite so reluctantly. "It doesn't always work. But sometimes it does."

"Chris, what does this mean?" Foote demanded.

"It means that we have an important ally here, if only we can find out how to make use of her," Lundgren said. "This girl is what the Middle Ages would have called a witch. Nowadays we'd probably say she's been given a liberal helping of extrasensory powers, but I must confess that never seems to me to explain much that the old term didn't explain.

"That is the significance of the pentagram, and Jarmoskowski knows it very well. The werewolf hunts best and ranges most widely when he has a witch for an accomplice, as a mate when they are both in human form, as a marker or stalker when the werewolf is in the animal form. The appearance of the pentagram identifies to the lycanthrope the witch he believes appointed for him."

"That's hardly good news," Doris said faintly.

"But it is. In all these ancient psychopathic relationships there is a natural—or, if you like, a supernatural—balance. The werewolf adopts such a partner with the belief—for him of course it is a certain foreknowledge—that the witch inevitably will betray him. That is what so shocked Jarmoskowski; but his changing to the wolf form shows that he has taken the gambit. He knows as well as we do, probably better, that as a witch Doris is only a beginner, unaware of most of her own powers. He is gambling very coolly on our being unable to use her against him. It is my belief that he is most wrong."

"So we still don't know who Jan's chosen as a victim," James said in earnest, squeaky tones. "That settles it. We've got to trail the—the beast and kill him. We must kill him before he kills one of us—if not Doris, then somebody else. Even if he misses us, it would be just as bad to have him roaming the countryside."

"What are you going to kill him with?" Lundgren asked matter-of-factly.

"Eh?"

"I said, what are you going to kill him with? With

that pineal hormone in his blood he can laugh at any ordinary bullet. And since there are no chapels dedicated to St. Hubert around here, you won't be able to scare him to death with a church-blessed bullet."

"Silver will do," Foote said.

"Yes, silver will do. It poisons the pinearin-catalysis. But are you going to hunt a full-grown wolf armed with table silver and candlesticks? Or is somebody here metallurgist enough to cast a decent silver bullet?"

Foote sighed. With the burden of proof lifted from him, and completely sobered up by shock, he felt a little more like his old self, despite the pall which hung over him and the others.

"Like I always tell my friends," he said, "there's never a dull moment at a Newcliffe house party."

4

The clock struck 1:30. Foote picked up one of Newcliffe's rifles and hefted it. It felt—useless. He said, "How are you coming?"

The group by the kitchen range shook their heads in comical unison. One of the gas burners had been jury-rigged as a giant Bunsen burner, and they were trying to melt down over it some soft unalloyed silver articles, mostly of Mexican manufacture.

They were using a small earthenware bowl, also Mexican, for a crucible. It was lidded with the bottom of a flower pot, the hole in which had been plugged with shredded asbestos yanked forcibly out of the insulation of the garret; garden clay gave the stuff a dubious cohesiveness. The awkward flame leapt uncertainly and sent fantastic shadows flickering over their intent faces.

"We've got it melted, all right," Bennington said,

lifting the lid cautiously with a pair of kitchen tongs and peering under it. "But what do we do with it now? Drop it from the top of the tower?"

"You can't kill a wolf with buckshot unless you're damned lucky," Newcliffe pointed out. Now that the problem had been reduced temporarily from a hypernatural one to a matter of ordinary hunting, he was in his element. "And I haven't got a decent shotgun here anyhow. But we ought to be able to whack together a mold. The bullet should be soft enough so that it won't stick in the rifling of my guns."

He opened the door to the cellar stairs and disappeared down them, carrying in one hand several ordinary rifle cartridges. Faintly, the dogs renewed their howling. Doris began to tremble. Foote put his arm around her.

"It's all right," he said. "We'll get him. You're safe enough."

She swallowed. "I know," she agreed in a small voice. "But every time I think of the way he looked at my hands, and how red his eyes were— You don't suppose he's prowling around the house? That that's what the dogs are howling about?"

"I don't know," Foote said carefully. "But dogs are funny that way. They can sense things at great distances. I suppose a man with pinearin in his blood would have a strong odor to them. But he probably knows that we're after his scalp, so he won't be hanging around if he's smart."

She managed a tremulous smile. "All right," she said. "I'll try not to be hysterical." He gave her an awkward reassuring pat, feeling a little absurd.

"Do you suppose we can use the dogs?" Ehrenberg wanted to know.

"Certainly," said Lundgren. "Dogs have always been our greatest allies against the abnormal. You saw what a rage Jarmoskowski's very presence put Brucey in this afternoon. He must have smelled the incipient seizure. Ah, Tom—what did you manage?"

Newcliffe set a wooden transplanting box on the kitchen table. "I pried the slug out of one shell for each gun," he said, "and used one of them to make impressions in the clay here. The cold has made the stuff pretty hard, so the impressions should be passable molds. Bring the silver over here."

Bennington lifted his improvised crucible from the burner, which immediately shot up a tall, ragged blue flame. James carefully turned it off.

"All right, pour," Newcliffe said. "Chris, you don't suppose it might help to chant a blessing or something?"

"Not unless Jarmoskowski overheard it—probably not even then, since we have no priest among us."

"Very well. Pour, Bennington, before the goo hardens."

Bennington decanted sluggishly molten silver into each depression in the clay, and Newcliffe cleaned away the oozy residue from the casts before it had time to thicken. At any other time the whole scene would have been funny—now it was grotesque, as if it had been composed by a Holbein. Newcliffe picked up the box and carried it back down to the cellar, where the emasculated cartridges awaited their new slugs.

"Who's going to carry these things, now?" Foote asked. "There are six rifles. James, how about you?"

"I couldn't hit an elephant's rump at three paces. Tom's an expert shot. So is Bennington here, with a shotgun anyhow; he holds skeet-shooting medals."

"I can use a rifle," Bennington said diffidently.

"So can I," said Palmer curtly. "Not that I've got much sympathy for this business. This is just the kind of thing you'd expect to happen in this place."

"You had better shelve your politics for a while," James said, turning an unexpectedly hard face to the Laborite. "Lycanthropy as a disease isn't going to limit its activities to the House of Lords. Suppose a werewolf got loose in the Welsh coal fields?"

"I've done some shooting," Foote said. "During the show at Dunkirk I even hit something."

"I," Lundgren said, "am an honorary member of the Swiss Militia."

Nobody laughed. Even Palmer was aware that Lundgren in his own oblique way was bragging, and that he had something to brag about. Newcliffe appeared abruptly from the cellar.

"I pried 'em loose, cooled 'em with snow and rolled 'em smooth with a file. They're probably badly crystallized, but we needn't let that worry us. At worst it'll just make 'em go dum-dum on us—no one here prepared to argue that that would be inhumane, I hope?"

He put one cartridge into the chamber of each rifle in turn and shot the bolts home. "There's no sense in loading these any more thoroughly—ordinary bullets are no good anyhow, Chris says. Just make your first shots count. Who's elected?"

Foote, Palmer, Lundgren and Bennington each took a rifle. Newcliffe took the fifth and handed the last one to his wife.

"I say, wait a minute," James objected. "Do you think that's wise, Tom? I mean, taking Caroline along?"

"Why, certainly," Newcliffe said, looking surprised. "She shoots like a fiend—she's snatched prizes away from me a couple of times. I thought *everybody* was going along."

"That isn't right," Foote said. "Especially not Doris, since the wolf—that is, I don't think she ought to go."

"Are you going to subtract a marksman from the hunting party to protect her? Or are you going to leave her here by herself?"

"Oh no!" Doris cried. "Not here! I've got to go! I don't want to wait all alone in this house. He might come back, and there'd be nobody here. I couldn't stand it."

"There is no telling what Jarmoskowski might learn from such an encounter," Lundgren added, "or, worse, what he might teach Doris without her being aware of it. For the rest of us—forgive me, Doris, I must be brutal—it would go harder with us if he did not kill her than if he did. Let us keep our small store of magic with us, not leave it here for Jan."

"That would seem to settle the matter," Newcliffe said grimly. "Let's get under way. It's after two now."

He put on his heavy coat and went out with the heavy-eyed groom to rouse out the dogs. The rest of the company fetched their own heavy clothes. Doris and Caroline climbed into ski suits. They assembled again, one by one, in the living room.

Lundgren's eyes swung on a vase of irislike flowers on top of the closed piano. "Hello, what are these?" he said.

"Monkshood," Caroline informed him. "We grow it in the greenhouse. It's pretty, isn't it? Though the gardener says it's poisonous."

"Chris," Foote said. "That isn't—wolfsbane, is it?"

The psychiatrist shook his head. "I'm no botanist. I can't tell one aconite from another. But it doesn't matter; hyperpineals are allergic to the whole group. The pollen, you see. As in hay fever, your hyperpineal case breathes the pollen, anaphylaxis sets in, and—"

"The last twist of the knife," James murmured.

A clamoring of dogs outside announced that Newcliffe was ready. With somber faces the party filed out onto the terrace. For some reason all of them avoided stepping on the wolf's prints in the snow. Their mien was that of condemned prisoners on the way to the tumbrels. Lundgren took one of the sprigs of flowers from the vase.

The moon had long ago passed its zenith and was almost halfway down the sky, projecting the Bastille-like shadow of the house a long way out onto the grounds; but there was still plenty of light, and the house itself was glowing from cellar to tower room. Lundgren located Brucey in the milling, yapping pack and abruptly thrust the sprig of flowers under his muzzle. The animal sniffed once, then crouched back and snarled softly.

"Wolfsbane," Lundgren said. "Dogs don't dislike the other aconites—basis of the legend, no doubt. Better fire your gardener, Caroline. In the end he may be the one to blame for all this happening in the dead of winter. Lycanthropy normally is an autumn affliction."

James said:

"Even a man who says his prayers
Before he sleeps each night
May turn to a wolf when the wolfsbane blooms
And the moon is high and bright."

"Stop it, you give me the horrors," Foote snapped angrily.

"Well, the dog knows now," said Newcliffe. "Good. It would have been hard for them to pick up the trail from hard snow, but Brucey can lead them. Let's go."

The tracks of the wolf were clear and sharp in the ridged drifts. The snow had formed a hard crust from which fine, powdery showers of tiny ice crystals were whipped by a fitful wind. The tracks led around the side of the house, as Bennington had reported, and out across the golf course. The little group plodded grimly along beside them. The spoor was cold for the dogs, but every so often they would pick up a faint trace and go bounding ahead, yanking their master after them. For the most part, however, the party had to depend upon its eyes.

A heavy mass of clouds had gathered in the west over the Firth of Lorne. The moon dipped lower. Foote's shadow, knobby and attenuated, marched on before him, and the crusted snow crunched and crackled beneath his feet. The night seemed unnaturally still and watchful, and the party moved in tense silence except for an occasional growl or subdued bark from the dogs.

Once the marks of the werewolf doubled back a short distance, then doubled again, as if the monster had turned for a moment to look back at the house before resuming his prowling. For the most part, however, the trail led directly toward the dark boundary of the woods.

As the brush began to rise around them they stopped by mutual consent and peered warily ahead, rifles lifted halfway, muzzles weaving nervously as the dogs' heads shifted this way and that. Far out across the countryside behind them, the great cloud-shadow continued its sailing. The brilliantly lit house stood out against the gloom as if it were on fire.

"Should have turned those out," Newcliffe muttered, looking back at it. "Outlines us."

The dogs strained at their leashes. In the black west there was a barely audible muttering, as of winter thunder. Brucey pointed a quivering nose at the woods and snarled.

"He's in there, all right."

"We'd better step on it," Bennington said, whispering. "Going to be plenty dark in about five minutes. Looks like a storm."

Still they hesitated, looking at the noncommittal darkness of the forest. Then Newcliffe waved his gun hand and his dog hand in the conventional deploy-as-skirmishers signal and plowed forward. The rest spread out in a loosely spaced line and followed him. Foote's finger trembled over his trigger.

The forest was shrouded and very still. Occasionally a branch groaned as someone pushed against it, or twigs snapped with sharp, tiny musical explosions. Foote could see almost nothing. The underbrush tangled his legs; his feet broke jarringly through the crust of snow, or were supported by it when he least expected support. Each time his shoulder struck an unseen trunk gouts of snow fell on him.

After a while the twisted, leafless trees began to remind him of something; after a brief mental search he found it. It was a Doré engraving of the woods of Hell, from an illustrated Dante which had frightened him green as a child: the woods where each tree was a sinner in which harpies nested, and where the branches bled when they were broken off. The concept still frightened him a little—it made the forest by Newcliffe's golf course seem almost cozy.

The dogs strained and panted, weaving, no longer growling, silent with a vicious intentness. A hand touched Foote's arm and he jumped; but it was only Doris.

"They've picked up something, all right," Bennington's whisper said. "Turn 'em loose, Tom?"

Newcliffe pulled the animals to a taut halt and bent over them, snapping the leashes free. One by one, without a sound, they shot ahead and vanished.

Over the forest the oncoming storm clouds cruised across the moon. Total blackness engulfed them. The beam of a powerful flashlight splashed from Newcliffe's free hand, flooding a path of tracks on the brush-littered snow. The rest of the night drew in closer about the blue-white glare.

"Hate to do this," Newcliffe said. "It gives us away. But he knows we're— Hello, it's snowing."

"Let's go then," Foote said. "The tracks will be blotted out shortly."

A many-voiced, clamorous baying, like tenor bugles, rang suddenly through the woods. It was a wild and beautiful sound! Foote, who had never heard it before, thought for an instant that his heart had stopped. Certainly he would never have associated so pure a choiring with anything as prosaic as dogs.

"That's it!" Newcliffe shouted. "Listen to them! That's the vie-whalloo. Go get him, Brucey!"

They crashed ahead. The belling cry seemed to ring all around them.

"What a racket!" Bennington panted. "They'll raise the whole countryside."

They plowed blindly through the snow-filled woods. Then, without any interval, they broke through into a small clearing. Snowflakes flocculated the air. Something dashed between Foote's legs, snapping savagely, and he tripped and fell into a drift.

A voice shouted something indistinguishable. Foote's mouth was full of snow. He jerked his head up—and looked straight into the red rage-glowing eyes of the wolf.

It was standing on the other side of the clearing, facing him, the dogs leaping about it, snapping furiously at its legs. It made no sound at all, but stood with its forefeet planted, its head lowered below its enormous shoulders, its lips drawn back in a travesty of Jarmoskowski's smile. A white streamer of breath trailed horizontally from its long muzzle, like the tail of a malign comet.

It was more powerful than all of them, and it knew it. For an instant it hardly moved, except to stir lazily the heavy brush of tail across its haunches. Then one of the dogs came too close.

The heavy head lashed sidewise. The dog yelped and danced back. The dogs already had learned caution: one of them already lay writhing on the ground, a black pool spreading from it, staining the snow.

"Shoot, in God's name!" James screamed.

Newcliffe clapped his rifle to his shoulder with one hand, then lowered it indecisively. "I can't," he said. "The dogs are in the way—"

"To hell with the dogs—this is no fox hunt! Shoot, Tom, you're the only one of us that's clear—"

It was Palmer who shot first. He had no reason to be chary of Newcliffe's expensive dogs. Almost at the same time the dogs gave Foote a small hole to shoot through, and he took it.

The double flat crack of the two rifles echoed through the woods and snow puffed up in a little explosion behind the wolf's left hind pad. The other shot—whose had come closest could never be known—struck a frozen tree trunk and went squealing away. The wolf settled deliberately into a crouch.

A concerted groan had gone up from the party;

above it Newcliffe's voice thundered, ordering his dogs back. Bennington aimed with inexorable care.

The werewolf did not wait. With a screaming snarl it launched itself through the ring of dogs and charged.

Foote jumped in front of Doris, throwing one arm across his own throat. The world dissolved into rolling pandemonium, filled with shouts, screams, snarls, and the frantic hatred of dogs. The snow flew thick. Newcliffe's flashlight fell and tumbled away, coming to rest at last on the snow on its base, regarding the treetops with an idiot stare.

Then there was the sound of a heavy body moving swiftly away. The noise died gradually.

"Anybody hurt?" James' voice asked. There was a general chorus of "no's."

"That's not good enough," Bennington puffed. "How does a dead man answer No? Let's have a nose-count."

Newcliffe retrieved his flashlight and played it about, but the snowstorm had reached blizzard proportions, and the light showed nothing but shadows and cold confetti. "Caroline?" he said anxiously.

"Yes, dear. Soaked, but here."

"Doris? Good. Paul, where are you—oh, I see you, I think. Ehrenberg? And Palmer? So; there you have it, Bennington. We didn't invite anybody else to this party—except—"

"He got away," Bennington said ironically. "Didn't like the entertainment. And the snow will cover his tracks this time. Better call your dogs back, Tom."

"They're back," Newcliffe said. He sounded a little tired, for the first time since the beginning of the trouble. "When I call them off, they come off."

He walked heavily forward to the body of the injured animal, which was still twitching feebly, as if trying to answer his summons. He squatted down on his hams and bent his shoulders, stroking the restlessly rolling head.

"So—so," he said softly. "So, Brucey. Easy—easy. So, Brucey—so."

Still murmuring, he brought his rifle into position with one arm. The dog's tail beat once against the snow.

The rifle leapt noisily against Newcliffe's shoulder.

Newcliffe arose slowly, and looked away.

"It looks like we lose round one," he said tonelessly.

5

It seemed to become daylight very quickly. The butler went phlegmatically around the house, snapping off the lights. If he knew what was going on he gave no sign of it.

Newcliffe was on the phone to London. "Cappy? Tom here—listen and get this straight, it's damned important. Get Consolidated Warfare—no, no, not the Zurich office, they've offices in the city—and place an order for a case of .30 caliber rifle cartridges—listen to me, dammit, I'm not through yet—with *silver slugs*. Yes, that's right—silver—and it had better be the pure stuff, too. No, not sterling, that's too hard for my purposes. Tell them I want them flown up, and that they've got to arrive here tomorrow . . . I don't care if it is impossible. Make it worth their while; I'll cover it. And I want it direct to the house here. On Loch Rannoch 20 kilometers due west of Blair Atholl . . . Of course you know the house but how will CWS's pilot unless you tell them? Now read it back to me."

"Garlic," Lundgren was saying to Caroline. She wrote it dutifully on her marketing list. "How many windows does this house have? All right, buy one clove for each, and get a half-dozen tins of ground rosemary, also."

He turned to Foote. "We must cover every possibility," he said somberly. "As soon as Tom gets off the line I will try to raise the local priest and get him out here with a drayload of silver crucifixes. Understand, Paul, there is a strong physiological basis beneath all that medieval mumbo-jumbo.

"The herbs, for example, are anti-spasmodics—they act rather as ephedrine does, in hay fever, to reduce the violence of the seizure. It's possible that Jan may not be able to maintain the wolf shape if he gets a heavy enough sniff.

"As for the religious trappings, their effects are perhaps solely psychological—and perhaps not, I have no opinion in the matter. It's possible that they won't bother Jan if he happens to be a skeptic in such matters, but I suspect that he's—" Lundgren's usually excellent English abruptly gave out on him. The word he wanted obviously was not in his vocabulary. "*Aberglaeubig,*" he said. "*Criandre.*"

"Superstitious?" Foote suggested, smiling grimly.

"Is that it? Yes. Yes, certainly. Who has better reason, may I ask?"

"But how does he maintain the wolf shape at all, Chris?"

"Oh, that's the easiest part. You know how water takes the shape of the vessel it sits in? Well, protoplasm is a liquid. This pineal hormone lowers the surface tension of the cells; and at the same time it short-circuits the sympathetic nervous system directly through to the cerebral cortex by increasing the efficiency of the cerebrospinal fluid as an electrolyte beyond the limits in which it's supposed to function—"

"Whoa there, I'm lost already."

"I'll go over it with you later, I have several books in my luggage which have bearing on the problem which I think you should see. In any event, the result is a plastic, malleable body, within limits. A wolf is the easiest form because the skeletons are so similar. Not much pinearin can do to bone, you see. An ape would be easier still, but lycanthropes don't assume shapes outside their own ecology. A were-ape would be logical in Africa, but not here. Also, of course, apes don't eat people; there is the really horrible part of this disease."

"And vampires?"

"Vampires," Lundgren said pontifically, "are people we put in padded cells. It's impossible to change the bony structure *that* much. They just think they are bats. But yes, that too is advanced hyperpinealism.

"In the last stages it is quite something to see. As the pinearin blood level increases, the cellular surface tension is lowered so much that the cells literally begin to boil away. At the end there is just a—a mess. The process is arrested when the vascular systems no longer can circulate the hormone, but of course the victim dies long before that stage is reached."

Foote swallowed. "And there's no cure?"

"None yet. Palliatives only. Someday, perhaps, there will be a cure—but until then— Believe me, we will be doing Jan a favor."

"Also," Newcliffe was saying, "drive over and pick me up six automatic rifles. No, not Brownings, they're too hard to handle. Get American T-47's. All right, they're secret—what else are we paying CWS a retainer for? What? Well, you might call it a siege. All right, Cappy. No, I won't be in this week. Pay everybody off and send them home until further notice. No, that doesn't include you. All right. Yes, that sounds all right."

"It's a good thing," Foote said, "that Newcliffe has money."

"It's a good thing," Lundgren said, "that he has me—and you. We'll see how twentieth-century methods can cope with this Middle Ages madness."

Newcliffe hung up, and Lundgren took immediate possession of the phone.

"As soon as my man gets back from the village," Newcliffe said, "I'm going to set out traps. Jan may be able to detect hidden metal—I've known dogs that could do it by smell in wet weather—but it's worth a try."

"What's to prevent his just going away?" Doris asked hopefully. The shadows of exhaustion and fear around her eyes touched Foote obscurely; she looked totally unlike the blank-faced, eager youngster who had bounded into the party in ski clothes so long ago.

"I'm afraid you are," he said gently. "As I understand it, he believes he's bound by the pentagram." At the telephone, where Lundgren evidently was listening to a different speaker with each ear, there was an energetic nod. "In the old books, the figure is supposed to be a sure trap for demons and such, if you can lure or conjure them into it. And once the werewolf has seen his appointed partner marked with it, he feels compelled to remain until he has made the alliance good."

"Doesn't it—make you afraid of me?" Doris said, her voice trembling.

He touched her hand. "Don't be foolish. There's no need for us to swallow all of a myth just because we've found that part of it is so. The pentagram we have to accept; but I for one reserve judgment on the witchcraft."

Lundgren said "Excuse me," and put one hand over the mouthpiece. "Only lasts seven days," he said.

"The compulsion? Then we'll have to get him before then."

"Well, maybe we'll sleep tonight anyhow," Doris said dubiously.

"We're not going to do much sleeping until we get him," Newcliffe announced. "I could boil him in molten lead just for killing Brucey."

"Brucey!" Palmer snorted. "Don't you think of anything but your damned prize dogs, even when all our lives are forfeit?" Newcliffe turned on him, but Bennington grasped his arm.

"That's enough," the American said evenly. "Both

of you. We certainly don't dare quarrel among ourselves with this thing hanging over us. I know your nerves are shot. We're all in the same state. But dissension among us would make things just that much easier for Jan."

"Bravo," Lundgren said. He hung up the phone and rejoined them. "I didn't have much difficulty in selling the good Father the idea," he said. "He was stunned, but not at all incredulous. Unfortunately, he has only crucifixes enough for our ground-floor windows, at least in silver; gold, he says, is much more popular. By the way, he wants a picture of Jan, in case he should turn up in the village."

"There are no existing photographs of Jarmoskowski," Newcliffe said positively. "He never allowed any to be taken. It was a headache to his concert manager."

"That's understandable," Lundgren said. "With his cell radiogens under constant stimulation, any picture of him would turn out overexposed anyhow—probably a total blank. And that in turn would expose Jan."

"Well, that's too bad, but it's not irreparable," Foote said. He was glad to be of some use again. He opened Caroline's secretary and took out a sheet of stationery and a pencil. In ten minutes he had produced a head of Jarmoskowski in three-quarter profile, as he had seen him at the piano that last night so many centuries ago. Lundgren studied it.

"To the life," he said. "Tom can send this over by messenger. You draw well, Paul."

Bennington laughed. "You're not telling him anything he doesn't know," he said. Nevertheless, Foote thought, there was considerably less animosity in the critic's manner.

"What now?" James asked.

"We wait," Newcliffe said. "Palmer's gun was ruined by that one hand-made slug, and Foote's isn't in much better shape. The one thing we can't afford is to have our weapons taken out of action. If I know

Consolidated, they'll have the machine-made bullets here tomorrow, and then we'll have some hope of getting him. Right now we'll just have to lie doggo and hope that our defenses are effective—he's shown that he's more than a match for us in open country."

The rest looked at each other uneasily. Some little understanding of what it would be like to wait through helpless, inactive days and dog-haunted nights already showed on their faces. But before the concurrence of both master hunters—Newcliffe and Lundgren—they were forced to yield.

The conference broke up in silence.

When Foote came into the small study with one of the books Lundgren had given him, he was surprised and somewhat disappointed to find that both Caroline and Doris had preceded him. Doris was sitting on a hassock near the grate, with the fire warming her face, and a great sheaf of red-gold hair pouring down her back. Caroline, seated just behind her, was brushing it out with even strokes.

"I'm sorry," he said. "I didn't know you were in here. I had a little reading to do and this looked like the best place for it—"

"Why, of course, Paul," Caroline said. "Don't let us distract you in the least. We came in here for the fire."

"Well, if you're sure it's all right—"

"Of course it's all right," Doris said. "If our talking won't annoy you—"

"No, no." He found the desk with the gooseneck lamp on it, turned on the lamp, and put down the heavy book in the pool of light. Caroline's arm resumed its monotonous, rhythmic movement over Doris' bent head. Both of them made a wonderful study: Caroline no longer the long-faced hounds-and-horses Englishwoman in jodhpurs, but now the exactly opposite type, tall, clear-skinned, capable of carrying a bare-shouldered evening gown with enchanting naturalness, yet in both avatars clearly the wife of the same man; Doris transformed from the bouncing youngster to the preternaturally still virgin waiting beside the lake, her youth not so much emphasized as epiphanized by the maternal shape stroking her head.

But for once in his life he had something to do that he considered more pressing than making a sketch for an abstraction. He turned his back on them and sat down, paging through the book to the chapter Lundgren had mentioned. He would have preferred studying it with Lundgren at his side, but the psychiatrist, wiry though he was, felt his years as the hour grew late, and was now presumably asleep.

The book was hard going. It was essentially a summary of out-of-the-way psychoses associated with peasant populations, and it had been written by some American who assumed an intolerably patronizing attitude toward the beliefs he was discussing, and who was further handicapped by a lack of basic familiarity with the English language. Foote suspected that sooner or later someone like Lundgren was going to have to do the whole job over again from scratch.

Behind him the murmuring of the two women's voices blended with the sighing of the fire in the grate. It was a warm, musical sound, so soothing that Foote found himself nodding at the end of virtually every one of the book's badly constructed paragraphs, and forced to reread nearly every other sentence.

"I do believe you've conquered Tom completely," Caroline was saying. The brush went crackle . . . crackle . . . through the girl's hair. "He hates women who talk. About anything. That's hard on him, for he loves artists of all sorts, and so many of them are women, aren't they?"

. . . *Within a few years I was able to show to a startled world that between sympathetic magic and the sympatheticomimetic rituals of childhood there are a distinct relationship, directly connectable to the benighted fantasies of Balkan superstition of which I have just given so graphic a series of instances. Shortly thereafter, with the aid of Drs. Egk and Bergenweiser, I was able to demonstrate . . .*

"So many of them are pianists, anyhow," Doris said. "Sometimes I wish I'd taken to the harp, or maybe the bassoon."

"Well, now, I sometimes feel that way about being a woman. There really is a great deal of competition abroad in the world. Your hair is lovely. That white part is so fashionable now that it's a pleasure to see one that's natural."

"Thank you, Caroline. You've been very brave and kind. I feel better already."

"I've never known a woman," Caroline said, "who didn't feel better with the tangles out of her hair. Does this affair really disturb you greatly?"

. . . *in order to make it clear that this total misconception of the real world can have no REAL consequences except in the mind of the ignorant. To explain the accounts of the deceived observers we must first of all assume . . .*

"Shouldn't it? I wouldn't have taken it seriously for a moment a few days ago, but—well, we did go out to hunt for Jan, and there really doesn't seem to be much doubt about it. It is frightening."

"Of course it is," Caroline said. "Still I wouldn't dream of losing my sleep over it. I remember when Brucey had the colic when he was five weeks old; London was being bombed at the same time by those flying things. Tom carried on terribly, and the house was full of refugees, which simply made everything more difficult. And Jan is really very sweet and he's been most effective in the World Federation movement, really one of the best speakers we've ever had; I can't imagine that he would hurt anyone. I know what Tom would do if he discovered he could turn himself into a wolf. He'd turn himself in to the authorities; he's really very serious-minded, and fills every weekend with these artists until one wonders if anybody else in the world is sane. But Jan has a sense of humor. He'll be back tomorrow laughing at us."

Foote turned a page in the book, but he had given up everything but the pretense of reading it.

"Chris takes it very seriously," Doris said.

"Of course, he's a specialist. There now, that should feel better. And there's Paul, studying his eyes out; I'd forgotten you were there. What have you found?"

"Nothing much," Foote said, turning to look at them. "I really need Chris to understand what I'm reading. I haven't the training to extract meaning out of this kind of study. I'll tackle it with him tomorrow."

Caroline sighed. "Men are so single-minded. Isn't it wonderful how essential Chris turned out to be? I'd never have dreamed that he'd be the hero of the party."

Doris got up. "If you're through with me, Caroline, I'm very tired. Good night, and thank you. Good night, Paul."

"Good night," Foote said.

"Quite through," Caroline said. "Good night, dear."

Then it was deep night again. The snowstorm had passed, leaving fresh drifts, and the moon was gradually being uncovered. The clouds blew across the house toward the North Sea on a heavy wind which hummed under the gutters, rattled windows, ground together the limbs of trees.

The sounds stirred the atmosphere of the house, which was hot and stuffy because of the closed windows and reeking with garlic. It was not difficult to hear in them other noises less welcome. In the empty room next to Foote's there was the imagined coming and going of thin ghosts to go with them, and the crouched expectancy of a turned-down bed which awaited a curiously deformed guest—a guest who might depress its sheets regardless of the tiny glint of the crucifix upon the pillow.

The boundary between the real and the unreal had

been let down in Foote's mind, and between the comings and goings of the cloud-shadows and the dark errands of the ghosts there was no longer any way of making a selection. He had entered the cobwebby borderland between the human and the animal, where nothing is ever more than half true, and only as much as half true for the one moment.

After a while he felt afloat on the stagnant air, ready to drift all the way across the threshold at the slightest motion. Above him, other sleepers turned restlessly, or groaned and started up with a creak of springs. Something was seeping through the darkness among them. The wind followed it, keeping a tally of the doors that it passed.

One.

Two.

Three. Closer now.

Four. The fourth sleeper struggled a little; Foote could hear a muffled squeaking of floorboards above his head.

Five.

Six. Who was six? Who's next? When?

Seven—

Oh my God, I'm next . . . I'm next . . .

He curled into a ball, trembling. The wind died away and there was silence, tremendous and unquiet. After a long while he uncurled, swearing at himself; but not aloud, for he was afraid to hear his own voice. Cut that out, now, Foote, you bloody fool. You're like a kid hiding from the trolls. You're perfectly safe. Lundgren says so.

Mamma says so.

How the hell does Lundgren know?

He's an expert. He wrote a paper. Go ahead, be a kid. Remember your childhood faith in the printed word? All right, then. Go to sleep, will you?

There goes that damned counting again.

But after a while his worn-down nerves would be excited no longer. He slept a little, but fitfully, falling in his dreams through such deep pits that he awoke fighting the covers and gasping for the vitiated, garlic-heavy air. There was a foulness in his mouth and his heart pounded. He threw off the blankets and sat up, lighting a cigarette with shaking hands and trying not to sêe the shadows the match-flame threw.

He was no longer waiting for the night to end. He had forgotten that there had ever been such a thing as daylight. He was waiting only to hear the low, inevitable snuffling that would tell him he had a visitor.

But when he looked out the window, he saw dawn brightening over the forest. After staring incredulously at it for a long while, he snubbed out his cigarette in the socket of the candlestick—which he had been carrying about the house as if it had grown to him—and fell straight back. With a sigh he was instantly in profound and dreamless sleep.

When he finally came to consciousness he was being shaken, and Bennington's voice was in his ears. "Get up, man," the critic was saying. "No, you needn't reach for the candlestick—everything's okay thus far."

Foote grinned and reached for his trousers. "It's a pleasure to see a friendly expression on your face, Bennington," he said.

Bennington looked a little abashed. "I misjudged you," he admitted. "I guess it takes a crisis to bring out what's really in a man so that blunt brains like mine can see it. You don't mind if I continue to dislike your latest abstractions, I trust?"

"That's your function: to be a gadfly," Foote said cheerfully. "Now, what's happened?"

"Newcliffe got up early and made the rounds of the traps. We got a good-sized rabbit out of one of them and made Hassenpfeffer—very good—you'll see. The other one was empty, but there was blood on it and on the snow around it. Lundgren's still asleep, but we've saved scrapings for him; still there doesn't seem to be much doubt about it—there's a bit of flesh with coarse black hair on it—"

James poked his head around the doorjamb, then came in. "Hope it cripples him," he said, dexterously snaffling a cigarette from Foote's shirt pocket. "Pardon me. All the servants have deserted us but the butler, and nobody will bring cigarettes up from the village."

"My, my," Foote said. "You're a chipper pair of chaps. Nice sunrise, wasn't it?"

"Wasn't it, though."

In the kitchen they were joined by Ehrenberg, his normally ruddy complexion pale and shrunken from sleeplessness.

"Greetings, Hermann. How you look! And how would you like your egg?"

"*Himmel, Asch und Zwirn,* how can you sound so cheerful? You must be part ghoul."

"You must be part angel—nobody human could be so deadly serious so long, even at the foot of the scaffold."

"Bennington, if you burn my breakfast I'll turn you out of doors without a shilling. Hello, Doris; can you cook?"

"I'll make some coffee for you." Newcliffe entered as she spoke, a pipe between his teeth. "How about you, Tom?"

"Very nice, I'm sure," Newcliffe said: "Look—what do you make of this?" He produced a wad of architect's oiled tracing cloth from his jacket pocket and carefully unwrapped it. In it were a few bloody fragments. Doris choked and backed away.

"I got these off the trap this morning—you saw me do it, Bennington—and they had hair on 'em then. Now look at 'em."

Foote poked at the scraps with the point of his pencil. "Human," he said.

"That's what I thought."

"Well, isn't that to be expected? It was light when

you opened the trap, evidently, but the sun hadn't come up. The werewolf assumes human form in full daylight—these probably changed just a few moments after you wrapped them up. As for the hair—this piece here looks to me like a bloodstained sample of Jarmoskowski's shirt cuff."

"We've nipped him, all right," Bennington agreed.

"By the way," Newcliffe added, "we've just had our first desertion. Palmer left this morning."

"No loss," James said. "But I know how he feels. When this affair is over, I'm going to take a month off at Brighton and let the world go to hell."

"What? In the winter?"

"I don't care. I'll watch the tides come in and out in the W.C."

"Just be sure to live to get there," Ehrenberg said gloomily.

"Hermann, you are a black cloud and a thunderclap of doom."

There was a sound outside. It sounded like the world's biggest teakettle. Something flitted through the sky, wheeled and came back. Foote went to the nearest window.

"Look at that," he said, shading his eyes. "An Avro jet—and he's trying to land here. He must be out of his mind."

The plane circled silently, engines cut. It lost flying speed and glided in over the golf course, struck, and rolled at breakneck speed directly for the forest. At the last minute the pilot ground-looped the ship expertly, and the snow fountained under its wheels.

"By heaven, I'll bet that's Newcliffe's bullets!"

They pounded through the foyer and out onto the terrace. Newcliffe, without bothering to don coat or hat, plowed away toward the plane. A few minutes later, he and the pilot came puffing into the front room, carrying a small wooden case between them. Then they went back and got another, larger but obviously not so heavy.

Newcliffe pried the first crate open. Then he sighed. "Look at 'em," he said. "Shiny brass cartridges, and dull silver heads, machined for perfect accuracy—there's a study in beauty for you artist chaps. Where'd you leave from?"

"Croydon," said the pilot. "If you don't mind, Mr. Newcliffe, the company said I was to collect from you. That's six hundred pounds for the weapons, two-fifty for the ammo and a hundred fifty for me, just a thousand in all."

"Fair enough. Hold on, I'll write you a check."

Foote whistled. It was obvious—not that there had ever been any doubt about it—that Tom Newcliffe did not paint for a living.

The pilot took the check, and shortly thereafter the teakettle began to whistle again. From the larger crate Newcliffe was handing out brand-new rifles, queer ungainly things with muzzle brakes and disproportionately large stocks.

"Now let him come," he said grimly. "Don't worry about wasting shots. There's a full case of clips. As soon as you see him, blaze away like mad. Use it like a hose if you have to. This is a high-velocity weapon: if you hit him square anywhere—even if it's only his hand—you'll kill him from shock. If you get him in the body, there won't be enough of that area left for him to reform, no matter what his powers."

"Somebody go wake Chris," Bennington said. "He should have lessons, too. Doris, go knock on his door like a good girl."

Doris nodded and went upstairs. "Now this stud here," Newcliffe said, "is the fire-control button. You put it in this position and the gun will fire one shot and reload itself, like the Garand. Put it here and it goes into automatic operation, firing every shell in the clip, one after the other and in a hurry."

"Thunder!" James said admiringly. "We could stand off an army."

"Wait a minute—there seem to be two missing."

"Those are all you unpacked," Foote pointed out.

"Yes, but there were two older models of my own. I never used 'em because it didn't seem sporting to hunt with such cannon. But I got 'em out last night on account of this trouble."

"Oh," Bennington said with an air of sudden enlightenment. "I thought that thing I had looked odd. I slept with one last night. I think Lundgren has the other."

"Where is Lundgren? Doris should have had him up by now. Go see, Bennington, and fetch back that rifle while you're at it."

"Isn't there a lot of recoil?" Foote asked.

"Not a great deal; that's what the muzzle brake is for. But it would be best to be careful when you have the stud on fully automatic. Hold the machine at your hip, rather than at your shoulder—what's *that!*"

"Bennington's voice," Foote said, his jaw muscles suddenly almost unmanageable. "Something must be wrong with Doris." The group stampeded for the stairs.

They found Doris at Bennington's feet in front of Lundgren's open door. She was perfectly safe; she had only fainted. The critic was in the process of being very sick. On Lundgren's bed something was lying.

The throat had been ripped out, and the face and all the soft parts of the body were gone. The right leg had been gnawed in one place all the way to the bone, which gleamed white and polished in the reassuring sunlight.

6

Foote stood in the living room by the piano in the full glare of all the electric lights. He hefted the T-47 and surveyed the remainder of the party, which was standing in a puzzled group before him.

"No," he said, "I don't like that. I don't want you all bunched together. String out in a line, please, against the far wall, so that I can see everybody."

He grinned briefly. "Got the drop on you, didn't I? Not a rifle in sight. Of course, there's the big candlestick behind you, Tom—aha, I saw you sneak your hopeful look at it—but I know from experience that it's too heavy to throw. I can shoot quicker than you can club me, too." His voice grew ugly. "*And I will,* if you make it necessary. So I would advise everybody—including the women—not to make any sudden movements.'"

"What's this all about, Paul?" Bennington demanded angrily. "As if things weren't bad enough—"

"You'll see directly. Get into line with the rest, Bennington. *Quick!*" He moved the gun suggestively. "And remember what I said about moving too suddenly. It may be dark outside, but I didn't turn on all the lights for nothing."

Quietly the line formed. The eyes that looked at Foote were narrowed with suspicion of madness, or something worse.

"Good. Now we can talk comfortably. You see, after what happened to Chris I'm not taking any chances. That was partly his fault, and partly mine. But the gods allow no one to err twice in matters of this kind. He paid for his second error—a price I don't intend to pay, or to see anyone else here pay."

"Would you honor us with an explanation of this error?" Newcliffe said icily.

"Yes. I don't blame you for being angry, Tom, since I'm your guest. But you see I'm forced to treat you all alike for the moment. I was fond of Lundgren."

There was silence for a moment, then a thin indrawing of breath from Bennington. "All alike?" he whispered raggedly. "My God, Paul. Tell us what you mean."

"You know already, I see, Bennington. I mean that Lundgren was not killed by Jarmoskowski. He was killed by someone else. Another werewolf—yes, we have two now. One of them is standing in this room at this moment."

A concerted gasp went up.

"Surprised?" Foote said, coldly, and deliberately. "But it's true. The error for which Chris paid so dearly, an error which I made too, was this: we forgot to examine everyone for injuries after the encounter with Jan. We forgot one of the cardinal laws of lycanthropy.

"A man who survives being bitten by a werewolf himself becomes a werewolf. That's how the disease is passed on. The pinearin in the wolf's saliva evidently gets into the bloodstream, stimulates the victim's own pineal gland, and—"

"But nobody was bitten, Paul," Doris said in a suspiciously reasonable voice.

"Somebody was, even if only lightly. None of you but Chris and myself could have known about the bite-infection. Evidently somebody got a few small scratches, didn't think them worth mentioning, put iodine on them and forgot about them—until it was too late."

There were slow movements in the line—heads turning surreptitiously, eyes swinging to neighbors left and right.

"Paul, this is merely a hypothesis," Ehrenberg said. "There is no reason to suppose that it is so, just because it sounds likely."

"But there is. Jarmoskowski can't get in here."

"Unproven," Ehrenberg said.

"I'll prove it. Once the seizure occurred, Chris was the logical first victim. The expert, hence the most dangerous enemy. I wish I had thought of this before lunch. I might have seen which one of you was uninterested in his lunch. In any event, if I'm right, Chris' safeguards against letting Jarmoskowski in also keep you from getting out. If you think you'll ever leave this room again, you're bloody wrong—"

He gritted his teeth and brought himself back into control. "All right," he said. "This is the end of the line. Everybody hold up both hands in plain view."

Almost instantly there was a ravening wolf in the room.

Only Foote, who could see at one glance the order of the people in the staggered line, could know who it was. His drummed-up courage, based solely on terror, went flooding out of him on a tide of sick pity; he dropped the rifle and began to weep convulsively. The beast lunged for his throat like a reddish projectile.

Newcliffe's hand darted back and grasped the candlestick. He leapt forward with swift clumsy grace and brought it down, whistling, against the werewolf's side. Ribs burst with a sharp splintering sound. The wolf spun, its haunches hitting the floor. Newcliffe hit it again. It fell, screaming like a great dog run down by a car, its fangs slashing the air.

Three times, with scientific viciousness, Newcliffe heaved the candlestick back and struck at its head. Then it cried out in an almost-familiar voice, and died.

Slowly the cells of its body groped back toward their natural positions. Even its fur moved, becoming more matted, more regular—more fabriclike.

The crawling metamorphosis was never completed; but the hairy-haunched thing with the crushed skull which sprawled at Newcliffe's feet was recognizable.

It had been Caroline Newcliffe.

Tears coursed along Foote's palms, dropped from under them, fell to the carpet. After a while he dropped his hands. Blurrily he saw a frozen tableau of wax figures in the yellow lamplight. Bennington's face was gray with illness, but rigidly expressionless, like a granite statue. James' back was against the wall;

he watched the anomalous corpse as if waiting for some new movement. Ehrenberg had turned away, his pudgy fists clenched.

As for Newcliffe, he had no expression at all. He merely stood where he was, the bloody candlestick hanging straight down from a limp hand.

His eyes were quite empty.

After a moment Doris walked over to Newcliffe and touched his shoulder compassionately. The contact seemed to let something out of him. He shrank visibly into himself, shoulders slumping, his whole body withering to a dry husk.

The candlestick thumped against the floor, rocked wildly on its base, toppled across the body. As it struck, Foote's cigarette butt, which had somehow remained in its socket all day, tumbled out and rolled crazily along the carpet.

"Tom," Doris said softly. "Come away now. There's nothing you can do."

"It was the blood," his empty voice said. "She had a cut. On her hand. Handled the scrapings from the trap. My trap. I did it to her. Just a breadknife cut from making canapés. I did it."

"No you didn't, Tom. You're not to blame. Let's get some rest."

She took his hand. He followed her obediently, stumbling a little as his spattered shoes scuffed over the thick carpet, his breath expelling from his lungs with a soft whisper. The French doors closed behind them.

Bennington bolted for the kitchen sink.

Foote sat down on the piano bench, his worn face taut with dried tears. Like any nonmusician he was drawn almost by reflex to pick at the dusty keys. Ehrenberg remained standing where he was, so motionless as to absent himself from the room altogether, but the lightly struck notes aroused James. He crossed the room, skirting the body widely, and looked down at Foote.

"You did well," the novelist said shakily. "Don't condemn yourself, Paul. What you did was just and proper—and merciful in the long run."

Foote nodded. He felt—nothing. Nothing at all.

"The body?" James said.

"Yes. I suppose so." He got up from the bench. Together they lifted the ugly shape; it was awkward to handle. Ehrenberg remained dumb, blind and deaf. They maneuvered their way through the house and on out to the greenhouse.

"We should leave her here," Foote said, the inside of his mouth suddenly sharp and sour. "Here's where the wolfsbane bloomed that started the whole business."

"Poetic justice of sorts, I suppose," James said. "But I don't think it's wise. Tom has a tool shed at the other end that isn't steam-heated. It should be cold enough there."

Gently they lowered the body to the cement floor, laid down gunnysacks and rolled it onto them. There seemed to be nothing available to cover it. "In the morning," Foote said, "we can have someone come for her."

"How about legal trouble?" James said, frowning. "Here's a woman whose skull has been crushed with a blunt instrument—"

"I think we can get Lundgren's priest to help us there, and with Lundgren, too," Foote said somberly. "They have authority to make death certificates in Scotland. Besides, Alec—is that a woman? Inarguably it isn't Caroline."

James looked sidewise at the felted, muscular haunches. "No. It's—legally it's nothing. I see your point."

Together they went back into the house. "Jarmoskowski?" James said.

"Not tonight, I imagine. We're all too tired and sick. And we do seem to be safe enough in here. Chris saw to that."

Ehrenberg had gone. James looked around the big empty room.

"Another night. What a damnable business. Well, good night, Paul."

He went out. Foote remained in the empty room a few minutes longer, looking thoughtfully at the splotch of blood on the priceless Persian carpet. Then he felt of his face and throat, looked at his hands, arms and legs, and explored his chest under his shirt.

Not a scratch. Tom had been very fast.

He was exhausted, but he could not bring himself to go to bed. With Lundgren dead, the problem was his; he knew exactly how little he knew about it still, but he knew as well how much less the rest of the party knew. Hegemony of the house was his now—and the next death would be his responsibility.

He went around the room, making sure that all the windows were tightly closed and the crucifixes in place, turning out the lights as he went. The garlic was getting rancid—it smelled like mercaptan—but as far as he knew it was still effective. He clicked out all but the last light, picked up his rifle and went out into the hall.

Doris' room door was open and there was no light coming out of it. Evidently she was still upstairs tending Newcliffe. He stood for a few moments battling with indecision, then toiled up the staircase.

He found her in Caroline's room, her head bowed upon her arm among the scattered, expensive vials and flasks which had been Caroline's armamentarium. The room was surprisingly froufrou; even the telephone had a doll over it. This, evidently, had been the one room in the house which Caroline had felt was completely hers, where her outdoorsy, estate-managing daytime personality had been ousted by her nocturnal femininity.

And what, in turn, had ousted that? Had the womanly Caroline been crowded, trying not to weep, into some remote and impotent corner of her brain as the monster grew in her? What did go on in the mind of a werewolf?

Last night, for instance, when she had brushed Doris' hair, she had seemed completely and only herself, the Caroline Newcliffe with the beautiful face and the empty noggin, toward whom Foote had so long felt a deep affection mixed with no respect whatsoever. But she had already been taken. It made his throat ache to realize that in her matronly hovering over the girl there had already been some of the tenseness of the stalker.

Men are so single-minded. Isn't it wonderful how essential Chris turned out to be?

At that moment she had shifted her target from Doris to Chris, moved by nothing more than Foote's remark about being unable to progress very far without the psychiatrist. Earlier this evening he had said that Chris had been the most logical target because he was the expert—yet that had not really occurred to Caroline except as an afterthought. It was wolf-reasoning; Caroline's own mind had seen danger first in single-mindedness.

And it had been Caroline's mind, not the wolf's, which had dictated the original fix on Doris. The girl, after all, was the only other woman in the party, thanks to Tom's lion-hunting and his dislike of the Modern Girl; and Caroline had mentioned that Tom seemed drawn to Doris. Which was wolf, which human? Or had they become blended, like two innocuous substances combining to form a poison? Caroline had once been incapable of jealousy—but when the evil had begun to seethe in her bloodstream she had been no longer entirely Caroline . . .

He sighed. Doris had seemed to be asleep on the vanity, but she stirred at the small sound, and the first step he took across the threshold brought her bolt upright. Her eyes were reddened and strange.

"I'm sorry," he said. "I was looking for you. I have

to talk to you, Doris; I've been putting it off for quite a while, but I can't do that any longer. May I?"

"Yes, of course, Paul," she said wearily. "I've been very rude to you. It's a little late for an apology, but I am sorry."

He smiled. "Perhaps I had it coming. How is Tom?"

"He's—not well. He doesn't know where he is or what he's doing. He ate a little and went to sleep, but he breathes very strangely." She began to knead her hands in her lap. "What did you want?"

"Doris—what about this witchcraft business? Lundgren seemed to think it might help us. God knows we need help. Have you any idea why Chris thought it was important? Beyond what he told us, that is?"

She shook her head. "Paul, it seemed a little silly to me then, and I still don't understand it. I can do a few small tricks, that's all, like the one I did to you with the smoke. I never thought much about them; they came more or less naturally, and I thought of them just as a sort of sleight-of-hand. I've seen stage conjurers do much more mystifying things."

"But by trickery—not by going right around natural law."

"What do I know about natural law?" she said reasonably. "It seems natural to me that if you want to make something plastic behave, you mold something else that's plastic nearby. To make smoke move, you move clay, or something else that's like smoke. Isn't that natural?"

"Not very," he said wryly. "It's a law of magic, if that's any comfort to either of us. But it's supposed to be a false law."

"I've made it work," she said, shrugging.

He leaned forward. "I know that. That's why I'm here. If you can do that, there should be other things that you can do, things that can help us. What I want to do is to review with you what Chris thought of your talents, and see whether or not anything occurs to you that we can use."

She put her hands to her cheeks, and then put them back in her lap again. "I'll try," she said.

"Good for you. Chris said he thought witches in the old days were persons with extrasensory perception and allied gifts. I think he believed also that the magic rituals that were used in witchcraft were just manipulative in intention—symbolic objects needed by the witch to focus her extrasensory powers. If he was right, the 'laws' of magic really were illusions, and what was in operation was something much deeper."

"I think I follow that," Doris said. "Where does it lead?"

"I don't know. But I can at least try you on a catalogue. Have you ever had a prophetic dream, Doris? Or read palms? Or cast horoscopes? Or even had the notion that you could look into the future?"

She shook her head decidedly.

"All right, we'll rule that out. Ever felt that you knew what someone else was thinking?"

"Well, by guesswork—"

"No, no," Foote said. "Have you ever felt certain that you knew—"

"Never."

"How about sensing the positions of objects in another room or in another city—no. Well, have you ever been in the vicinity of an unexplained fire? A fire that just seemed to happen because you were there?"

"No, Paul, I've never seen a single fire outside of a fireplace."

"Ever moved anything larger and harder to handle than a column of smoke?"

Doris frowned. "Many times," she said. "But just little things. There was a soprano with a rusty voice that I had to accompany once. She was overbearing and a terrible stage hog. I tied her shoe-bows together so that she fell when she took her first bow, but it was awfully hard work; I was all in a sweat."

Foote suppressed an involuntary groan. "How did you do it?"

"I'm not quite sure. I don't think I could have done it at all if we hadn't wound up the concert with *Das Buch der Haengenden Gaerten.*" She smiled wanly. "If you don't know Schoenberg's crazy counterpoint that wouldn't mean anything to you."

"It tells me what I need to know, I'm afraid. There really isn't much left for me to do but ask you whether or not you've ever transformed a woman into a white mouse, or ridden through the air on a broomstick. Doris, doesn't *anything* occur to you? Chris never talked without having something to talk about; when he said that you could help us, he meant it. But he's dead now, and we can't ask him for the particulars. It's up to you."

She burst into tears. Foote got clumsily to his feet, but after that he had no idea what to do.

"Doris—"

"I don't know," she wailed. "I'm not a witch! I don't want to be a witch! I don't know anything, anything at all, and I'm so tired and so frightened and please go away, please—"

He turned helplessly to go, then started to turn back again. At the same instant, the sound of her weeping was extinguished in the roar of an automatic rifle, somewhere over their heads, exhausting its magazine in a passionate rush.

Foote shot out of the room and back down the stairs. The ground floor still seemed to be deserted under the one light. Aloft there was another end-stopped snarl of gunfire; then Bennington came bouncing down the stairs.

"Watch out tonight," he panted as soon as he saw Foote. "He's around. I saw him come out of the woods in wolf form. I emptied the clip, but he's a hard target against those trees. I sprayed another ten rounds around where I saw him go back in, but I'm sure I didn't hit him. The rifle just isn't my weapon."

"Where were you shooting from?"

"The top of the tower." His face was very stern. "Went up for a breath and a last look around, and there he was. I hope he comes back tonight. I want to be the one who kills him."

"You're not alone."

"Thank God for that. Well, good night. Keep your eyes peeled."

Foote stood in the dark for a while after Bennington had left. Bennington had given him something to think about. While he waited, Doris picked her way down the stairs and passed him without seeing him. She was carrying a small, bulky object; since he had already put the light out, he could not see what it was. But she went directly to her room.

I want to be the one who kills him.

Even the mild Bennington could say that now; but Foote, who understood the feeling behind it all too well, was startled to find that he could not share it.

How could one hate these afflicted people? Why was it so hard for equal-minded men like Bennington to remember that lycanthropy was a disease like any other, and that it struck its victims only in accordance with its own etiology, without regard for their merits as persons? Bennington had the reputation of being what the Americans called a liberal, all the way to his bones; presumably he could not find it in his heart to hate an alcoholic or an addict. He knew also—he had been the first to point it out—that Jarmoskowski as a human being had been compassionate and kindly, as well as brilliant; and that Caroline, like the poor devil in Andreyev's *The Red Laugh,* had been noble-hearted and gentle and had wished no one evil. Yet he was full of hatred now.

He was afraid, of course, just as Foote was. Foote wondered if it had occurred to him that God might be on the side of the werewolves.

The blasphemy of an exhausted mind; but he had been unable to put the idea from him. Suppose

Jarmoskowski should conquer his compulsion and lie out of sight until the seven days were over. Then he could disappear; Scotland was large and sparsely populated. It would not be necessary for him to kill all his victims thereafter—only those he actually needed for food. A nip here, a scratch there—

And then from wherever he hunted, the circle of lycanthropy would grow and widen and engulf—

Perhaps God had decided that proper humans had made a muddle of running the world; had decided to give the *nosferatu*, the undead, a chance at it. Perhaps the human race was on the threshold of that darkness into which he had looked throughout last night.

He ground his teeth and made a noise of exasperation. Shock and exhaustion would drive him as crazy as Newcliffe if he kept this up. He put his hands to his forehead, wiped them on his thighs, and went into the little study.

The grate was cold, and he had no materials for firing it up again. All the same, the room was warmer than his bed would be at this hour. He sat down at the small desk and began to go through Lundgren's book again.

Cases of stigmata. Accounts of Sabbats straight out of Krafft-Ebing. The dancing madness. Theory of familiars. Conjuration and exorcism. The besom as hermaphroditic symbol. Fraser's Laws. Goety as an international community. Observations of Lucien Levy-Bruehl. The case of Bertrand. Political commentary in *Dracula*. Necromancy vs. necrophilia. Nordau on magic and modern man. Basic rituals of the Anti-Church. Fetishism and the theory of talismans . . .

Round and round and round, and the mixture as before. Without Chris there was simply no hope of integrating all this material. Nothing would avail them now but the rifles with the silver bullets in them; their reservoir of knowledge of the thing they fought had been destroyed.

Foote looked tiredly at the ship's clock on the

mantel over the cold grate. The fruitless expedition through the book had taken him nearly two hours. He would no longer be able to avoid going to bed. He rose stiffly, took up the automatic rifle, put out the light, and went out into the cold hall.

As he passed Doris' room, he saw that the door was now just barely ajar. Inside, two voices murmured.

Foote was an incurable eavesdropper. He stopped and listened.

7

It was years later before Foote found out exactly what had happened at the beginning. Doris, physically exhausted by her hideous day, emotionally drained by tending the childlike Newcliffe, feeding him from a blunt spoon, parrying his chant about traps and bread-knives, and herding him into bed, had fallen asleep almost immediately. It was a sleep dreamless except for a vague, dull undercurrent of despair. When the light tapping against the windowpanes finally reached through to her, she had no idea how long she had been lying there.

She struggled to a sitting position and forced her eyelids up. Across the room the moonlight, gleaming in patches against the rotting snow outside, glared through the window. Silhouetted against it was a tall human figure. She could not see its face, but there was no mistaking the red glint of its eyes. She clutched for her rifle and brought it awkwardly into line.

Jarmoskowski did not dodge. He moved his forearms out a little way from his body, palms forward in a gesture that looked almost supplicating, and waited. Indecisively she lowered the gun again. What was he asking for?

As she dropped the muzzle she saw that the fire-control stud was at *automatic*. She shifted it carefully to *repeat*. She was afraid of the recoil Newcliffe had mentioned; she could feel surer of her target if she could throw one shot at a time at it.

Jarmoskowski tapped again and motioned with his finger. Reasoning that he would come in of his own accord if he were able, she took time out to get into her housecoat. Then, holding her finger against the trigger, she went to the window. All its sections were closed tightly, and a crucifix, suspended from a silk thread, hung exactly in the center of it. She touched it, then opened one of the small panes directly above Jarmoskowski's head.

"Hello, Doris," he said softly. "You look a little like a clerk behind that window. May I make a small deposit, miss?"

"Hello." She was more uncertain than afraid. Was this really happening, or was it just the recurrent nightmare? "What do you want? I should shoot you. Can you tell me why I shouldn't?"

"Yes, I can. Otherwise I wouldn't have risked exposing myself. That's a nasty-looking weapon."

"There are ten silver bullets in it."

"I know that too. I had some fired at me earlier tonight. And I would be a good target for you, so I have no hope of escape—my nostrils are full of rosemary." He smiled ruefully. "And Lundgren and Caroline are dead, and I am responsible. I deserve to die; that is why I am here."

"You'll get your wish, Jan," she said. "But you have some other reason, I know. I'll back my wits against yours. I want to ask you questions."

"Ask."

"You have your evening clothes on. Paul said they changed with you. How is that possible?"

"But a wolf has clothes," Jarmoskowski said. "He is not naked like a man. And surely Chris must have spoken of the effect of the pineal upon the cell radiogens. These little bodies act upon any organic matter, wool, cotton, linen, it hardly matters. When I change, my clothes change with me. I can hardly say how, for it is in the blood—the chromosomes—like musicianship, Doris. Either you can or you can't. If you can—they change."

"Jan—are there many like you? Chris seemed to think—"

Jarmoskowski's smile became a little mocking. "Go into a great railroad station some day—Waterloo, or a Metro station, or Grand Central in New York; get up above the crowd on a balcony or stairway and look down at it in a mirror. We do not show in a silvered mirror. Or if you are in America, find one of the street photographers they have there who take 'three action pictures of yourself' against your will and try to sell them to you; ask him what percentage of his shots show nothing but background."

His voice darkened gradually to a somber diapason. "Lundgren was right throughout. This werewolfery is now nothing but a disease. It is not prosurvival. Long ago there must have been a number of mutations which brought the pineal gland into use; but none of them survived but the werewolves, and the werewolves are madmen—like me. We are dying out.

"Someday there will be another mutation, the pineal will come into better use, and all men will be able to modify their forms without this terrible cannibalism as a penalty. But for us, the lycanthropes, the failures of evolution, nothing is left.

"It is not good for a man to wander from country to country, knowing that he is a monster to his fellowmen and cursed eternally by his God—if he can claim a God. I went through Europe, playing the piano and giving pleasure, writing music for others to play, meeting people, making friends—and always, sooner or later, there were whisperings and strange looks and dawning horror.

"And whether I was hunted down for the beast I

was, or whether there was only a gradually growing revulsion, they drove me out. Hatred, silver bullets, crucifixes—they are all the same in the end.

"Sometimes, I could spend several months without incident in some one place, and my life would take on a veneer of normality. I could attend to my music, and have people around me that I liked, and be—human. Then the wolfsbane bloomed and the pollen frightened the air, and when the moon shone down on that flower my blood surged with the thing I carry within me—

"And then I made apologies to my friends and went north to Sweden, where Lundgren was and where spring came much later. I loved him, and I think he missed the truth about me until night before last; I was careful.

"Once or twice I did *not* go north, and then the people who had been my friends would be hammering silver behind my back and waiting for me in dark corners. After years of this few places in Europe would have me. With my reputation as a composer and a pianist spread darker rumors, none of them near the truth, but near enough.

"Towns I had never visited closed their gates to me without a word. Concert halls were booked up too many months in advance for me to use them, inns and hotels were filled indefinitely, people were too busy to talk to me, to listen to my playing, to write me any letters.

"I have been in love. That—I will not describe.

"Eventually I went to America. There no one believes in werewolves. I sought scientific help—which I had never sought from Lundgren, because I was afraid I would do him some harm. But overseas I thought someone would know enough to deal with what I had become. I would say, 'I was bitten during a hunt on Graf Hrutkai's estate, and the next fall I had my first seizure—'

"But it was not so. No matter where I go, the

primitive hatred of my kind lies at the heart of the human as it lies at the heart of the dog. There was no help for me.

"I am here to ask for an end to it."

Slow tears rolled over Doris' cheeks. The voice faded away indefinitely. It did not seem to end at all, but rather to retreat into some limbo where men could not hear it. Jarmoskowski stood silently in the moonlight, his eyes burning bloodily, a somber sullen scarlet.

Doris said, "Jan—Jan, I am sorry, I am so sorry. What can I do?"

"Shoot."

"I—can't!"

"Please, Doris."

The girl was crying uncontrollably. "Jan, don't. I can't. You know I can't. Go away, *please* go away."

Jarmoskowski said, "Then come with me, Doris. Open the window and come with me."

"Where?"

"Does it matter? You have denied me the death I ask. Would you deny me this last desperate hope for love, would you deny your own love, your own last and deepest desire? That would be a vile cruelty. It is too late now, too late for you to pretend revulsion. Come with me."

He held out his hands.

"Say goodbye," he said. "Goodbye to these self-righteous humans. I will give you of my blood and we will range the world, wild and uncontrollable, the last of our race. They will remember us, I promise you."

"Jan—"

"I am here. Come now."

Like a somnambulist, she swung the panes out. Jarmoskowski did not move, but looked first at her, then at the crucifix. She lifted one end of the thread and let the little thing tinkle to the floor.

"After us, there shall be no darkness comparable

to our darkness," Jarmoskowski said. "Let them rest—let the world rest."

He sprang into the room with so sudden, so feral a motion that he seemed hardly to have moved at all. From the doorway an automatic rifle yammered with demoniac ferocity. The impact of the silver slugs hurled Jarmoskowski back against the side of the window. Foote lowered the smoking muzzle and took one step into the room.

"Too late, Jan," he said stonily.

Doris wailed like a little girl awakened from a dream. Jarmoskowski's lips moved, but there was not enough left of his lungs. The effort to speak brought a bloody froth to his mouth. He stood for an instant, stretched out a hand toward the girl. Then the long fingers clenched convulsively and the long body folded.

He smiled, put aside that last of all his purposes, and died.

"Why did he come in?" Foote whispered. "I could never have gotten a clear shot at him if he'd stayed outside."

He swung on the sobbing girl. "Doris, you must tell me, if you know. With his hearing, he should have heard me breathing. But he stayed—and he came in, right into my line of fire. *Why?*"

The girl did not answer; but stiffly, as if she had all at once become old, she went to her bedside light and turned it on. Standing beneath it was a grotesque figurine which Foote had difficulty in recognizing as Caroline's telephone doll. All the frills had been stripped off it, and a heavy black line had been penciled across its innocuous forehead in imitation of Jarmoskowski's eyebrows. Fastened to one of its wrists with a rubber band was one of the fragments of skin Newcliffe had scraped out of his trap; and completely around the doll, on the surface of the table, a pentagram had been drawn in lipstick.

The nascent witch had turned from white magic to black. Doris had rediscovered the malign art of poppetry, and had destroyed her demon lover.

Compassionately, Foote turned to her, and very slowly, as if responding to the gravitational tug of a still-distant planet, the muzzle of his rifle swung, too. Together, the man and the machine, they waited for her.

Both would have to be patient.

When most SF readers think Larry Niven, they think hard SF. *And while I'm far from saying that the creator of the "Known Universe" and the author of* Ringworld *should* not *be known as "Mr. Hard SF," I associate Larry with hard* fun. *Here Larry Niven has fun with werewolves, fun with time travel, and fun with his main character Svetz, one of my all-time favorite guys.*

Svetz is just someone trying to do his job as best he can. He works in the Department of Temporal Research, a cushy civil service position. But sometimes he has to run errands for the Secretary-General's family: Svetz is the designated flunky who travels in time to fetch back extinct animals. Simple job description. But somehow things always get complicated for poor old Svetz.

There's a Wolf in My Time Machine

LARRY NIVEN

The old extension cage had no fine controls, but that hardly mattered. It wasn't as if Svetz were chasing some particular extinct animal. Ra Chen had told him to take whatever came to hand.

Svetz guided the cage back to preindustrial America, somewhere in midcontinent, around 1000 AnteAtomic Era. Few humans, many animals. Perhaps he'd find a bison.

And when he pulled himself to the window, he looked out upon a vast white land.

Svetz had not planned to arrive in midwinter.

Briefly he considered moving into the time stream again and using the interrupter circuit. Try another date, try the luck again. But the interrupter circuit was new, untried, and Svetz wasn't about to be the first man to test it.

Besides which, a trip into the past cost over a million commercials. Using the interrupter circuit would nearly double that. Ra Chen would be displeased.

Svetz began freezing to death the moment he opened the door. From the doorway the view was also white, with one white bounding shape far away.

Svetz shot it with a crystal of soluble anesthetic.

He used the flight stick to reach the spot. Now that it was no longer moving, the beast was hard to find. It was just the color of the snow, but for its open red mouth and the black pads on its feet. Svetz tentatively identified it as an arctic wolf.

It would fit the Vivarium well enough. Svetz would have settled for anything that would let him leave this frozen wilderness. He felt uncommonly pleased with himself. A quick, easy mission.

Inside the cage, he rolled the sleeping beast into what might have been a clear plastic bag, and sealed it. He strapped the wolf against one curved wall of the extension cage. He relaxed into the curve of the opposite wall as the cage surged in a direction vertical to all directions.

Gravity shifted oddly.

A transparent sac covered Svetz's own head. Its lip was fixed to the skin of his neck. Now Svetz pulled it loose and dropped it. The air system was on; he would not need the filter sac.

The wolf would. It could not breathe industrial-age air. Without the filter sac to remove the poisons, the wolf would choke to death. Wolves were extinct in Svetz's own time.

Outside, time passed at a furious rate. Inside, time crawled. Nestled in the spherical curve of the extension cage, Svetz stared up at the wolf, who seemed fitted into the curve of the ceiling.

Svetz had never met a wolf in the flesh. He had seen pictures in children's books . . . and even the children's books had been stolen from the deep past. Why should the wolf look so familiar?

It was a big beast, possibly as big as Hanville Svetz, who was a slender, small-boned man. Its sides heaved with its panting. Its tongue was long and red, and its teeth were white and sharp.

Like the dogs, Svetz remembered. The dogs in the Vivarium, in the glass case labeled:

DOG
Contemporary

Alone of the beasts in the Vivarium, the dogs were not sealed in glass for their own protection. The others could not breathe the air outside. The dogs could.

In a very real sense, they were the work of one man. Lawrence Wash Porter had lived near the end of the Industrial Period, between 50 and 100 Post-Atomic Era, when billions of human beings were dying of lung diseases while scant millions adapted. Porter had decided to save the dogs.

Why the dogs? His motives were obscure, but his methods smacked of genius. He had acquired members of each of the breeds of dog in the world and bred them together over many generations of dogs and most of his own lifetime.

There would never be another dog show. Not a purebred dog was left in the world. But hybrid vigor had produced a new breed. These, the ultimate mongrels, could breathe industrial-age air, rich in oxides of carbon and nitrogen, scented with raw gasoline and sulfuric acid.

The dogs were behind glass because people were afraid of them. Too many species had died. The people of 1100 PostAtomic were not used to animals.

Wolves and dogs . . . could one have sired the other?

Svetz looked up at the sleeping wolf and wondered. He was both like and unlike the dogs. The dogs grinned out through the glass and wagged their tails when children waved. Dogs liked people. But the wolf, even in sleep . . .

Svetz shuddered. Of all the things he hated about his profession, this was the worst; the ride home, staring up at a strange and dangerous extinct animal. The first time he'd done it, a captured horse had seriously damaged the control panel. On his last mission an ostrich had kicked him and broken three ribs.

The wolf was stirring restlessly . . . and something about it had changed.

Something was changing now. The beast's snout was shorter, wasn't it? Its forelegs lengthened peculiarly; its paws seemed to grow and spread.

Svetz caught his breath, and instantly forgot the wolf. Svetz was choking, dying. He snatched up his filter sac and threw himself at the control.

Svetz stumbled out of the extension cage, took three steps, and collapsed. Behind him, invisible contaminants poured into the open air.

The sun was setting in banks of orange cloud.

Svetz lay where he had fallen, retching, fighting for air. There was an outdoor carpet beneath him, green and damp, smelling of plants. Svetz did not recognize the smell, did not at once realize that the carpet was alive. He would not have cared at that point. He knew only that the cage's air system had tried to kill him. The way he felt, it had probably succeeded.

It had been a near thing. He had been passing 30 PostAtomic when the air went bad. He remembered clutching the interrupter switch, then waiting, waiting. The foul air stank in his nostrils and caught in his throat and tore at his larynx. He had waited through twenty years, feeling every second of them. At 50

PostAtomic he had pulled the interrupter switch and run choking from the cage.

50 PA. At least he had reached industrial times. He could breathe the air.

It was the horse, he thought without surprise. The horse had pushed its wickedly pointed horn through Svetz's control panel, three years ago. Maintenance was supposed to fix it. They *had* fixed it.

Something must have worn through.

The way he looked at me every time I passed his cage. I always knew the horse would get me, Svetz thought.

He noticed the filter sac still in his hand. Not that he'd be—

Svetz sat up suddenly.

There was green all about him. The damp green carpet beneath him was alive; it grew from the black ground. A rough, twisted pillar thrust from the ground, branched into an explosion of red and yellow papery things. More of the crumpled colored paper lay about the pillar's base. Something that was not an aircraft moved erratically overhead, a tiny thing that fluttered and warbled.

Living, all of it. A preindustrial wilderness.

Svetz pulled the filter sac over his head and hurriedly smoothed the edges around his neck to form a seal. Blind luck that he hadn't fainted yet. He waited for it to puff up around his head. A selectively permeable membrane, it would pass the right gasses in and out until the composition was . . . was . . .

Svetz was choking, tearing at the sac.

He wadded it up and threw it, sobbing. First the air plant, now the filter sac! Had someone wrecked them both? The inertial calendar too; he was at least a hundred years previous to 50 PostAtomic.

Someone had tried to kill him.

Svetz looked wildly about him. Uphill across a wide green carpet, he saw an angular vertical-sided formation painted in shades of faded green. It had to be artificial. There might be people there. He could—

No, he couldn't ask for help either. Who would believe him? How could they help him anyway? His only hope was the extension cage. And his time must be very short.

The extension cage rested a few yards away, the door a black circle on one curved side. The other side seemed to fade away into nothing. It was still attached to the rest of the time machine, in 1103 PA, along a direction eyes could not follow.

Svetz hesitated near the door. His only hope was to disable the air plant. Hold his breath, then . . .

The smell of contaminants was gone.

Svetz sniffed at the air. Yes, gone. The air plant had exhausted itself, drained its contaminants into the open air. No need to wreck it now. Svetz was sick with relief.

He climbed in.

He remembered the wolf when he saw the filter sac, torn and empty. Then he saw the intruder towering over him, the coarse thick hair, the yellow eyes glaring, the taloned hands spread wide to kill.

The land was dark. In the east a few stars showed, though the west was still deep red. Perfumes tinged the air. A full moon was rising.

Svetz staggered uphill, bleeding.

The house on the hill was big and old. Big as a city block, and two floors high. It sprawled out in all directions, as though a mad architect had built to a whim that changed moment by moment. There were wrought-iron railings on the upper-floor windows, and wrought-iron handles on the screens on both floors, all painted the same dusty shade of green. The screens were wood, painted a different green. They were closed across every window. No light leaked through anywhere.

The door was built for someone twelve feet tall.

The knob was huge. Svetz used both hands and put all his weight into it, and still it would not turn. He moaned. He looked for the lens of a peeper camera and could not find it. How would anyone know he was here? He couldn't find a doorbell either.

Perhaps there was nobody inside. No telling what this building was. It was far too big to be a family dwelling, too spread out to be a hotel or apartment house. Might it be a warehouse or a factory? Making or storing what?

Svetz looked back toward the extension cage. Dimly he caught the glow of the interior lights. He also saw something moving on the living green that carpeted the hill.

Pale forms, more than one.

Moving this way?

Svetz pounded on the door with his fists. Nothing. He noticed a golden metal thing, very ornate, high on the door. He touched it, pulled at it, let it go. It clanked.

He took it in both hands and slammed the knob against its base again and again. Rhythmic clanking sounds. Someone should hear it.

Something zipped past his ear and hit the door hard. Svetz spun around, eyes wild, and dodged a rock the size of his fist. The white shapes were nearer now. Bipeds, walking hunched.

They looked too human—or not human enough.

The door opened.

She was young, perhaps sixteen. Her skin was very pale, and her hair and brows were pure white, quite beautiful. Her garment covered her from neck to ankles, but left her arms bare. She seemed sleepy and angry as she pulled the door open—manually, and it was heavy, too. Then she saw Svetz.

"Help me," said Svetz.

Her eyes went wide. Her ears moved too. She said something Svetz had trouble interpreting, for she spoke in Ancient American.

"What *are* you?"

Svetz couldn't blame her. Even in good condition his clothes would not fit the period. But his blouse was ripped to the navel, and so was his skin. Four vertical parallel lines of blood ran down his face and chest.

Zeera had been coaching him in American speech. Now he said carefully, "I am a traveler. An animal, a monster, has taken my vehicle away from me."

Evidently the sense came through. "You poor man! What kind of animal?"

"Like a man, but hairy all over, with a horrible face—and claws—claws—"

"I see the marks they made."

"I don't know how he got in. I—" Svetz shuddered. No, he couldn't tell her that. It was insane, utterly insane, this conviction that Svetz's wolf had become a bloodthirsty humanoid monster. "He only hit me once. On the face. I could get him out with a weapon, I think. Have you a bazooka?"

"What a funny word! I don't think so. Come inside. Did the trolls bother you?" She took his arm and pulled him in and shut the door.

Trolls?

"You're a strange person," the girl said, looking him over. "You look strange, you smell strange, you move strangely. I did not know that there were people like you in the world. You must come from very far away."

"Very," said Svetz. He felt himself close to collapse. He was safe at last, safe inside. But why were the hairs on the back of his neck trying to stand upright?

He said, "My name is Svetz. What's yours?"

"Wrona." She smiled up at him, not afraid despite his strangeness . . . and he must look strange to her, for surely she looked strange to Hanville Svetz. Her skin was sheet white, and her rich white hair would better have fit a centenarian. Her nose, very broad and flat, would have disfigured an ordinary girl. Somehow it fit Wrona's face well enough; but her face was most odd, and her ears were too large, almost pointed, and her eyes were too far apart, and her grin stretched *way* back . . . and Svetz liked it. Her grin was curiosity and enjoyment, and was not a bit too wide. The firm pressure of her hand was friendly, reassuring. Though her fingernails were uncomfortably long and sharp.

"You should rest, Svetz," she said. "My parents will not be up for another hour, at least. Then they can decide how to help you. Come with me. I'll take you to a spare room."

He followed her through a room dominated by a great rectangular table and a double row of high-backed chairs. There was a large microwave oven at one end, and beside it a platter of . . . red things. Roughly conical they were, each about the size of a strong man's upper arm, each with a dot of white in the big end. Svetz had no idea what they were; but he didn't like their color. They seemed to be bleeding.

"Oh," Wrona exclaimed. "I should have asked. Are you hungry?"

Svetz was, suddenly. "Have you any dole yeast?"

"Why, I don't know the word. Are those dole yeast? They are all we have."

"We'd better forget it." Svetz's stomach lurched at the thought of eating something that color. Even if it turned out to be a plant.

Wrona was half supporting him by the time they reached the room. It was rectangular and luxuriously large. The bed was wide enough, but only six inches off the floor, and without coverings. She helped him down to it. "There's a wash basin behind that door, if you find the strength. Best you rest, Svetz. In perhaps two hours I will call you."

Svetz eased himself back. The room seemed to rotate. He heard her go out.

How strange she was. How odd he must look to her. A good thing she hadn't called anyone to tend him. A doctor would notice the differences.

Svetz never dreamed that primitives would be so

different from his own people. During the thousand years between now and the present, there must have been massive adaptation to changes in air and water, to DDT and other compounds in foods, to extinction of food plants and meat animals until only dole yeast was left, to higher noise levels, less room for exercise, greater dependence on medicines. . . . Well, why shouldn't they be different? It was a wonder humanity survived at all.

Wrona had not feared his strangeness, nor cringed from the scratches on his face and chest. She was only amused and interested. She had helped him without asking too many questions. He liked her for that.

He dozed.

Pain from deep scratches, stickiness in his clothes made his sleep restless. There were nightmares. Something big and shadowy, half man and half beast, reached far out to slash his face. Over and over. At some indeterminate time he woke completely, already trying to identify a musky, unfamiliar scent.

No use. He looked about him, at a strange room that seemed even stranger from floor level. High ceiling. One frosted globe, no brighter than a full moon, glowed so faintly that the room was all shadow. Wrought-iron bars across the windows; black night beyond.

A wonder he'd awakened at all. The preindustrial air should have killed him hours ago.

It had been a futz of a day, he thought. And he shied away from the memory of the thing in the extension cage. Snarling face, pointed ears, double row of pointed white teeth. The clawed hand reaching out, swiping down. The nightmare conviction that a wolf had turned into *that*.

It could not be. Animals did not change shape like that. Something must have gotten in while Svetz was fighting for air. Chased the wolf out, or killed it.

But there were legends of such things, weren't there? Two and three thousand years old and more, everywhere in the world, were the tales of men who could become beasts and vice versa.

Svetz sat up. Pain gripped his chest, then relaxed. He stood up carefully and made his way to the bathroom.

The spigots were not hard to solve. Svetz wet a cloth with warm water. He watched himself in the mirror, emerging from under the crusted blood. A pale, slender young man topped with thin blond hair . . . and an odd distortion of chin and forehead. That must be the mirror, he decided. Primitive workmanship. It might have been worse. Hadn't the first mirrors been two-dimensional?

A shrill whistle sounded outside his door. Svetz went to look, and found Wrona. "Good, you're up," she said. "Father and Uncle Wrocky would like to see you."

Svetz stepped into the hall, and again noticed the elusive musky scent. He followed Wrona down the dark hallway. Like his room, it was lit only by a single white frosted globe. Why would Wrona's people keep the house so dark? They had electricity.

And why were they all sleeping at sunset? With breakfast laid out and waiting . . .

Wrona opened a door, gestured him in.

Svetz hesitated a step beyond the threshold. The room was as dark as the hallway. The musky scent was stronger here. He jumped when a hand closed on his upper arm—it felt wrong; there was hair on the palm; the hard nails made a circlet of pressure points—and a gravelly male voice boomed, "Come in, Mister Svetz. My daughter tells me you're a traveler in need of help."

In the dim light Svetz made out a man and woman seated on backless chairs. Both had hair as white as Wrona's, but the woman's hair bore a broad black stripe. A second man urged Svetz toward another backless chair. He too bore black markings: a single black eyebrow, a black crescent around one ear.

And Wrona was just behind him. Svetz looked around at them all, seeing how alike they were, how different from Hanville Svetz.

The fear rose up in him like a strong drug. Svetz was a xenophobe.

They were all alike. Rich white hair and eyebrows, black markings. Narrow black fingernails. The broad flat noses and the wide, wide mouths, the sharp white conical teeth, the high, pointed ears that moved, the yellow eyes, the hairy palms.

Svetz dropped heavily onto the padded footstool.

One of the males noticed: the larger one, who was still standing. "It must be the heavier gravity," he guessed. "It's true, isn't it, Svetz? You're from another world. Obviously you're not quite a man. You told Wrona you were a traveler, but didn't say from how far away."

"Very far," Svetz said weakly. "From the future."

The smaller male was jolted. "The future? You're a time traveler?" His voice became a snarl. "You're saying that we will evolve into something like you!"

Svetz cringed. "No. Really."

"I hope not. What, then?"

"I think I must have gone sidewise in time. You're descended from wolves, aren't you? Not apes? Wolves?"

"Yes, of course."

The seated male was looking him over. "Now that he mentions it, he does look much more like a troll than any man has a right to. No offense intended, Svetz."

Svetz, surrounded by wolf men, tried to relax. And failed. "What is a troll?"

Wrona perched on the edge of his stool. "You must have seen them on the lawn. We keep about thirty."

"Plains apes," the smaller male supplied. "Imported from Africa, sometime in the last century. They make good watchbeasts and meat animals. You have to be careful with them, though. They throw things."

"Introductions," the other said suddenly. "Excuse our manners, Svetz. I'm Flakee Wrocky. This is my brother Flakee Worrel, and Brenda, his wife. My niece you know."

"Pleased to meet you," Svetz said hollowly.

"You say you slipped sideways in time?"

"I think so. A futz of a long way, too," said Svetz. "Marooned. Gods protect me. It must have been the horse—"

Wrocky broke in. "Horse?"

"The horse. Three years ago, a horse damaged my extension cage. It was supposed to be fixed. I suppose the repairs just wore through, and the cage slipped sideways in time instead of forward. Into a world where wolves evolved instead of *Homo habilis.* Gods know where I'm likely to wind up if I try to go back."

Then he remembered. "At least you can help me there. Some kind of monster has taken over my extension cage."

"Extension cage."

"The part of the time machine that does the moving. You'll help me evict the monster?"

"Of course," said Worrel, at the same time that the other was saying, "I don't think so. Bear with me, please, Worrel. Svetz, it would be a disservice to you if we chased the monster out of your extension cage. You would try to reach your own time, would you not?"

"Futz, yes!"

"But you would only get more and more lost. At least in our world you can eat the food and breathe the air. Yes, we grow food plants for the trolls; you can learn to eat them."

"You don't understand. I can't stay here. I'm a xenophobe!"

Wrocky frowned. His ears flicked forward enquiringly. "What?"

"I'm afraid of intelligent human beings who aren't human. I can't help it. It's in my bones."

"Oh, I'm sure you'll get used to us, Svetz."

Svetz looked from one male to the other. It was obvious enough who was in charge. Wrocky's voice was much louder and deeper than Worrel's; he was bigger than the other man, and his white fur fell about his neck in a mane like a lion's. Worrel was making no attempt to assert himself. As for the women, neither had spoken a word since Svetz entered the room.

Wrocky was emphatically the boss. And Wrocky didn't want Svetz to leave.

"You don't understand," Svetz said desperately. "The air—" He stopped.

"What about the air?"

"It should have killed me by now. A dozen times over. In fact, why hasn't it?" Odd enough that he'd ever stopped wondering about that. "I must have adapted," Svetz said half to himself. "That's it. The cage passed too close to this line of history. My heredity changed. My lungs adapted to preindustrial air. Futz it! If I hadn't pulled the interrupter switch, I'd have adapted back."

"Then you can breathe our air," said Wrocky.

"I still don't understand it. Don't you have any industries?"

"Of course," Worrel said in surprise.

"Internal-combustion cars and aircraft? Diesel trucks and ships? Chemical fertilizers, insect repellents—?"

"No, none of that. Chemical fertilizers wash away, ruin the water. The only insect repellents I ever heard of smelled to high heaven. They never got beyond the experimental stage. Most of our vehicles are battery powered."

"There *was* a fad for internal-combustion once," said Wrocky. "It didn't spread very far. They stank. The people inside didn't care, of course, because they were leaving the stink behind. At its peak there were over two hundred cars tootling around the city of Detroit, poisoning the air. Then one night the citizenry rose in a pack and tore all the cars to pieces. The owners too."

Worrel said, "I've always thought that men have more sensitive noses than trolls."

"Wrona noticed my smell long before I noticed hers. Wrocky, this is getting us nowhere. I've *got* to go home. I seemed to have adapted to the air, but there are other things. Foods; I've never eaten anything but dole yeast; everything else died out long ago. Bacteria."

Wrocky shook his head. "Anywhere you go, Svetz, your broken time machine will only take you to more and more exotic environments. There must be a thousand ways the world could end. Suppose you stepped out into one of them? Or just passed near one?"

"But—"

"Here, on the other paw, you will be an honored guest. Think of all the things you can teach us! You, who were born into a culture that builds time-traveling vehicles!"

So that was it. "Oh, no. You couldn't use what I know," said Svetz. "I'm no mechanic. I couldn't show you how to do anything. Besides, you'd hate the side effects. Too much of past civilizations was built on petrochemicals. And plastics. Burning plastics produces some of the strangest—"

"But even the most extensive oil reserves could not last forever. You must have developed other power sources by your own time." Wrocky's yellow eyes seemed to bore right through him. "Controlled hydrogen fusion?"

"But I can't tell you how it's done!" Svetz cried desperately. "I know nothing of plasma physics!"

"Plasma physics? What are plasma physics?"

"Using electromagnetic fields to manipulate ionized gasses. You *must* have plasma physics."

"No, but I'm sure you can give us some valuable hints. Already we have fusion bombs. And so do the Europeans . . . but we can discuss that later." Wrocky stood up. His black nails made pressure points on Svetz's arm. "Think it over, Svetz. Oh, and make yourself free of the house, but don't go outside without an escort. The trolls, you know."

Svetz left the room with his head whirling. The wolves would not let him leave.

"Svetz, I'm glad you're staying," Wrona chattered. "I like you. I'm sure you'll like it here. Please let me show you over the house."

Down the length of the hallway one frosted globe burned dimly in the gloom, like a full moon transported indoors. Noctunal, they were nocturnal.

Wolves.

"I'm a xenophobe," he said. "I can't help it. I was born that way."

"Oh, you'll learn to like us. You like me a little already, don't you, Svetz?" She reached up to scratch him behind the ear. A thrill of pleasure ran through him, unexpectedly sharp, so that he half closed his eyes.

"This way," she said.

"Where are we going?"

"I thought I'd show you some trolls. Svetz, are you really descended from trolls? I can't believe it!"

"I'll tell you when I see them," said Svetz. He remembered the *Homo habilis* in the Vivarium. It had been a man, an Advisor, until the Secretary-General had ordered him regressed.

They went through the dining room, and Svetz saw unmistakable bones on the plates. He shivered. His forebears had eaten meat; the trolls were brute animals here, whatever they might be in Svetz's world—but Svetz shuddered. His thinking seemed turgid, his head felt thick. He had to get out of here.

"If you think Uncle Wrocky's tough, you should meet the European ambassador," said Wrona. "Perhaps you will."

"Does he come here?"

"Sometimes." Wrona growled low in her throat. "I don't like him. He's a different species, Svetz. Here it was the wolves that evolved into men; at least that's what our teacher tells us. In Europe it was something else."

"I don't think Uncle Wrocky will let me meet him. Or even tell him about me." Svetz rubbed at his eyes.

"You're lucky. Herr Dracula smiles a lot and says nasty things in a polite voice. It takes you a minute to—Svetz! What's wrong?"

Svetz groaned like a man in agony. "My eyes!" He felt higher. "My forehead! I don't have a forehead anymore."

"I don't understand."

Svetz felt his face with his fingertips. His eyebrows were a caterpillar of hair on a thick, solid ridge of bone. From the brow ridge his forehead sloped back at forty-five degrees. And his chin, his chin was gone, too. There was only a regular curve of jaw into neck.

"I'm regressing. I'm turning into a troll," said Svetz. "Wrona, if I turn into a troll, will they eat me?"

"I don't know. I'll stop them, Svetz!"

"No. Take me down to the extension cage. If you're not with me, the trolls will kill me."

"All right. But, Svetz, what about the monster?"

"He should be easier to handle by now. It'll be all right. Just take me there. Please."

"All right, Svetz." She took his hand and led him.

The mirror hadn't lied. He'd been changing, even then, adapting to this line of history. First his lungs had lost their adaption to normal air. There had been no industrial age here. But there had been no *Homo sapiens* either. . . .

Wrona opened the door. Svetz sniffed at the night. His sense of smell had become preternaturally acute. He smelled the trolls before he saw them, coming uphill toward him across the living green carpet. Svetz's fingers curled, wishing for a weapon.

Three of them. They formed a ring around Svetz

and Wrona. One of them carried a length of white bone. They all walked upright on two legs, but they walked as if their feet hurt them. They were as hairless as men. Apes' heads mounted on men's bodies.

Homo habilis, the killer plains apes. Man's ancestor.

"Pay them no attention," Wrona said offhandedly. "They won't hurt us." She started down the hill. Svetz followed closely.

"He really shouldn't have that bone," she called back. "We try to keep bones away from them. They use them as weapons. Sometimes they hurt each other. Once one of them got hold of the iron handle for the lawn sprinkler and killed a gardener with it."

"I'm not going to take it away from him."

"That glaring light, is that your extension cage?"

"Yes."

"I'm not sure about this, Svetz." She stopped suddenly. "Uncle Wrocky's right. You'll only get more lost. Here you'll at least be taken care of."

"No. Uncle Wrocky was wrong. See the dark side of the extension cage, how it fades away into nothing. It's still attached to the rest of the time machine. It'll just reel me in."

"Oh."

"No telling how long it's been veering across the time lines. Maybe ever since that futzy horse poked his futzy horn through the controls. Nobody ever noticed before. Why should they? Nobody ever stopped a time machine halfway before."

"Svetz, horses don't have horns."

"Mine does."

There was a noise behind them. Wrona looked back into a darkness Svetz's eyes could not pierce. "Somebody must have noticed us! Come on, Svetz!"

She pulled him toward the lighted cage. They stopped just outside.

"My head feels thick," Svetz mumbled. "My tongue too."

"What are we going to do about the monster? I can't hear anything—"

"No monster. Just a man with amnesia, now. He was only dangerous in the transition stage."

She looked in. "Why, you're right! Sir, would you mind—Svetz, he doesn't seem to understand me."

"Sure not. Why should he? He thinks he's a white arctic wolf." Svetz stepped inside. The white-haired wolf man was backed into a corner, warily watching. He looked a lot like Wrona.

Svetz became aware that he had picked up a tree branch. His hand must have done it without telling his brain. He circled, holding the weapon ready. An unreasoning rage built up and up in him. Invader! The man had no business here in Svetz's territory.

The wolf man backed away, his slant eyes mad and frightened. Suddenly he was out the door and running, the trolls close behind.

"Your father can teach him, maybe," said Svetz.

Wrona was studying the controls. "How do you work it?"

"Let me see. I'm not sure I remember." Svetz rubbed at his drastically sloping forehead. "That one closes the door—"

Wrona pushed it. The door closed.

"Shouldn't you be outside?"

"I want to come with you," said Wrona.

"Oh." It was getting terribly difficult to think. Svetz looked over the control panel. Eeeny, meeny—that one? Svetz pulled it.

Free fall. Wrona yipped. Gravity came, vectored radially outward from the center of the extension cage. It pulled against the walls.

"When my lungs go back to normal, I'll probably go to sleep," said Svetz. "Don't worry about it." Was there something else he ought to tell Wrona? He tried to remember.

Oh, yes. "You can't go home again," said Svetz. "We'd never find this line of history again."

"I want to stay with you," said Wrona.

"All right."

Within a deep recess in the bulk of the time machine, a fog formed. It congealed abruptly—and Svetz's extension cage was back, hours late. The door popped open automatically. But Svetz didn't come out.

They had to pull him out by the shoulders, out of air that smelled of beast and honeysuckle.

"He'll be all right in a minute. Get a filter over that other thing," Ra Chen ordered. He stood over Svetz with his arms folded, waiting.

Svetz began breathing.

He opened his eyes.

"All right," said Ra Chen. "What happened?"

Svetz sat up. "Let me think. I went back to preindustrial America. It was all snowed in. I . . . shot a wolf."

"We've got it in a tent. Then what?"

"No. The wolf left. We chased him out." Svetz's eyes went wide. "Wrona!"

Wrona lay on her side in the filter tent. Her fur was thick and rich, white with black markings. She was built something like a wolf, but more compactly, with a big head and a short muzzle and a tightly curled tail. Her eyes were closed. She did not seem to be breathing.

Svetz knelt. "Help me get her out of there! Can't you tell the difference between a wolf and a dog?" He zipped open the tent. The beast snorted, then began panting. Her eyes opened and found Svetz.

Ra Chen said, "We don't need this. We've got dogs."

"That's all right. She can come with me. I'll take care of you, Wrona."

There must be something in the air. No sooner had we decided to assemble a collection of futuristic werewolf stories, then "Wolf Enough" popped up in the February 1995 issue of Tomorrow *magazine edited by Algis Budrys. A mixture of artificial lycanthropy with high-tech future warfare, this story couldn't have been a better fit if we'd commissioned it ourselves. (See also "Werewolves of Luna" by R. Garcia y Roberston.) It also is a fine example of a new wave of feminist werewolf stories, where the traditional victim becomes predator, taking back the night in a big way.*

Wolf Enough

JANE MAILANDER

Four of them were hiding up ahead; a female and three males, all but one of the males up in the trees. They were all armed, and—Tag raised her nose higher, flared her nostrils for the top scent, for any other important clue—the woman sniper was having her period.

She got rid of the irrelevant odor with a loud snort, and her guys jumped; Lori almost yelled, but turned it into a cough.

Tag did not look behind her; let the four up ahead think the company was walking into a trap. She reached behind with her left arm to scratch her back (felt good to scratch her own back with her hand—one tiny gain from a great loss), and showed four fingers to her company. She pointed to where the four were hiding, indicated which of her company were to act and where they were to go. She showed three fingers.

"Aw, geez, I gotta take a crap again," Wilbur said, and moved off into the brush. Good, Tag thought, he's been bitching about the runs all day anyway.

"Fuck, I wish you hadn't said that, Rocky Raccoon," Mike said. "Coon, get it?" The skin turned and hunkered off in another direction as if he had to go, too. Tag looked at Lori, leaned on a nearby tree and dangled her AK, yawned, scratched under her chin, and sneezed. One, two, three.

Wilbur was good with the AK. Mike was too good—he didn't think of the Nicaraguans as people anyway. They turned the snipers' trees into colanders; bits of red meat came down with the leaves and vines. The man on the ground jumped up and ran, and did a little dance at the end of Mike's gunsight before he fell. Mike yelled something that was probably "Gotta Nicky" or something equally kind. The birds were louder than the guns—they didn't even leave, just sat there and screamed, screamed long after the shooting had stopped.

Tag waved her arm, and the company edged up to the perforated area, watching for boobies. Lori turned aside and threw up. Tag watched her, nodding. She herself looked at the big mess—only because her nose was never wrong did she know that that big mess used to be four people—and her stomach growled at the smell of all that blood and meat. She had been in Lukos for too long: she still had the nose and stomach of a sarker.

Skin Mike bent down with his knife and came up with an ear from one of the undamaged heads; the eight withered ears hanging from the loop of gold chain on his right earring swayed with the movement.

"Drop it, Mike," Tag said. That warm drippy thing—one good swallow. . . . "You wanna get Buddha earlobes?"

"The Nick chicks like it; they think I'm a real

fighter," Mike said. The cross around his neck flashed as he turned toward the corporal. Its stink turned Tag's stomach, and she didn't want the ear any more. "Anyway the Nicks do this to our dicks. They make necklaces out of 'em, like bear's teeth. Five or six dicks."

Tag stared straight into Mike's watery blue Aryan eyes. "You don't cut ears in my company. Drop it, Mike, and if you don't I'll cut one of yours off." She let her hate for skins rise up to warm her spirit, light her yellow eyes, flare her nostrils. Her teeth showed a little, the canines still long and inhumanly sharp.

Mike's white skin turned whiter. He dropped the ear. He had once seen Tag cut someone's ear off. "Goddamn monkeyface cunt. Fucking bitch." His voice was a whisper, rage boiled down to a thin syrup.

Lori's face tightened at the "cunt" reference.

"You're right I'm a bitch, and don't you ever forget it, stag." Now Tag grinned and let him see her full complement of wolf-teeth, the length of which was the reason her jaw was bowled outward like an ape's. Once again she let Mike know who was in charge of her pack. He backed off, with the human body-language equivalent of a lowered nose and tail; but his eyes said that the fight was only delayed.

A dark spotted shape dropped from a nearby tree, small with shining eyes. An ocelot. A cat.

Cat—

Tag's gun whipped up and squeezed off a round. The cat's head turned to pulp just before it did a backflip in the air.

"No!" Lori put her hand out as if to stop the bullets, but the ocelot had been dead for seconds. "Oh, God, it was so pretty, why'd you do that . . . ?" She turned away, her face crumpling and tears leaking out of her squeezed-up eyes. This, on top of the snipers' massacre, was too much for her first billy-walk.

"Jeez, I'm stringier than I thought." Tag put the gun down slow and took a couple of deep breaths, averting her face to let Lori have some privacy and to lessen the woman's embarrassment later. She remembered the tearing pain inside after the first billy-walk she had commanded, when two of her guys had come in on the shoulders of baggie boys because she hadn't trusted her blunted sense of smell on guns. Her eyes had burned with dry heat for a long time—Tag had not shed tears since she had first put on a wolfsark.

Lori gulped for air, dragging a khaki sleeve across her face. Tag made sure Mike and Wilbur read the message in their commander's face: the first one to call Lori a baby for crying gets to go back to base alone with no gun.

Wilbur called the baggie boys and Mike nailed the beacon to the remnants of the tree, pounding the device home as if he were crucifying a sniper.

"Mike, go up ahead."

Without looking at Tag, Mike grabbed his AK and pack and crackled forward into the bush, snapping the branches aside. The undergrowth stopped swaying and the clearing lightened considerably.

"Whew." Wilbur grinned, with a smile that looked as if he'd stolen it from Mickey Mouse. "That's better."

"He sure hates you," Lori said, looking toward the parted bush where Mike could be heard crunching his way through the jungle.

"Oh hell, he's mad at everybody. Pick up your pack, Basarnian." Tag stepped through the mangled bush, AK pointed down and ready. "Poor little skinhead, can you blame him? He's forced to travel with the scum of the Earth."

"Scum . . . ?" It was Lori's first day with Tag's company.

"Yeah," Wilbur said, "a gang-banger with a stunted gene pool like me." Tag knew, from the tone, that Wilbur was grinning the Mickey-mouse grin. "And a shell like you."

"Polk." Tag's voice came down like a stamping machine.

"Sorry, Corporal." Wilbur's face and stricken voice showed that he really was sorry. But in that moment, if only for a moment, the oldest conflict of all divided the allies. *Figures*, Tag thought resentfully. *When all other racial terms are forbidden, it's still okay to call women the worst names. He sure didn't call himself the n-word just now, did he?* Her teeth clacked together in reflex.

"Shell?" Lori was learning lots of new things today.

"Skinhead word. And *only* a skinhead would use 'shell' out loud in a joke," Tag growled, still angry at Wilbur. "It's a hate word, Lori. You are an affront to Mike because you're not home like a housefly churning out little white maggots. The term comes from their book *How to Save the United States:* 'A barren white woman is a traitor to her race. She is as white, empty, and useless as an eggshell.' "

"That—!" Lori choked off her words as quickly as she'd stopped her crying; Tag could hear the private's teeth grating, a dam holding back a flood of angry words. Good soldier.

"One thing I've learned is you can't change someone like that," Wilbur said. "Leave him alone, that's the best way to deal with Mike. He's out there; he'll shoot whatever he finds, scare some snipers, use up his clip. Maybe he'll bring back a nice parrot for dinner."

"Eeww."

Tag grinned at the sound from Lori. "Forget the parrot, Wilbur," she said, louder than was necessary. "Let's hope he finds us one of those big lizards!"

"Or a nice juicy dog. Yum!"

But they couldn't keep up the joke when they heard the noises Lori was making, and they burst out laughing. When Basarnian got it, she looked ready to frag someone.

"Steady, soldier. Welcome to Nicaragua."

"No wonder Mike can't stand to stay with you." But Lori's tone let her in on the joke.

"Yeah, he can't stand unAmerican shit like Negroes and Army women, and saying 'Yes sir' to a werewolf."

Oh dammit, Wilbur.

From the abrupt silence behind her, Tag knew that Wilbur realized too late what he'd done, and Lori understood what Wilbur meant. For a long time there was no sound from the back. *Damn, damn, damn. . . .* But the ripped wolfsark can't be repaired.

Tag slogged ahead through the forest, eyes and ears forward and back, trying to put what had just happened out of her mind and concentrate on *now*. It had once been easier to do that.

Think about something else . . . think about her boots. Her boots were big and heavy, good for slogging. It was still a strange sensation to stalk on two legs, even after nearly two years; her feet hurt a lot at the end of the day, complaining about carrying all her weight.

Nicaragua was hot and sticky, like breathing and walking through a hot wet washcloth. But it was marvelous for carrying scents; to Tag's nose, the air was a smorgasbord to be sifted and appraised. She was sure she was missing all the smells that would reek through a rain forest, things she wouldn't have smelled in a city. But she was getting used to her human nose. Tag had lost the two on her first billywalk because the smell of guns wasn't as strong as she'd remembered from sarking. (It certainly wasn't because she was careless about guns. The stags had learned about silver bullets, and the sarkers had learned that being shot could once again mean death. Before then Tag had loved the rush of adrenaline when she leapt at someone firing point-blank and felt the bullets whip through her head and body without leaving a path or a mark. Not a wound, not till the cat.)

"You—you were a, a Lupus?" Lori's voice was nearly

drowned in the muffled squish of the undergrowth beneath their boots.

Time to face the music after all. "Lukos," Tag said. "I was a member of Lukos. And 'was' is the operative word, Basarnian." Her voice was iron. "I'm retired. That's all you need to know." She heard and smelled Lori's tension; rustling, human sweat. "Basarnian, if you even think of running on me now, Wilbur will stay with me and you'll be on solitary billy-walk with a short clip." From the sudden silence in the back she knew she'd stopped Lori from doing exactly that.

"Why'd you think we kept out of that ambush, Lori?" Wilbur's voice was soft. "I didn't hear or see anything wrong, neither did Mike. Did you?"

"I . . . I just. . . ." More silence. Tag wondered if Lori had enough left in her stomach to throw up, after seeing the snipers cut to bits; she'd no doubt make a valiant effort. Not everyone can handle the news that her CO used to eat human beings for a living—especially someone who can't tolerate the thought of eating a parrot or a dog.

"That's why Mike wears that big ugly silver cross around his neck. He thinks it'll keep him safe from me." Tag laughed once, a short exhalation. "He might as well wear a dildo on a string of dental floss—work just as well."

"Then it's true." Tiny voice. Another long silence. "You've—you've eaten. . . ."

"Those who deserved it." Tag even put the Errol Flynn swagger into her voice. "The cruel and the unjust."

"People like Mike, but worse." Wilbur's voice had its own ring of authority. "You know what skins are like back home. They get worse out here. One of Mike's buddies shot at me back at the base, shot at my feet—said he wanted to see my genetic dancing ability." He said nothing for about 20 yards of slogging. "A couple of years ago, a friend of mine, back in the States, drove into a skins neighborhood by accident. They found his car, but all they ever found of *him* was some blood and brains on the upholstery. The cops didn't exactly bust their butts looking for the murderer, either." Bitterness flattened his voice.

Silence. "But that still doesn't give you—"

"The subject is closed, Private." Tag turned and nailed Lori with the yellow stare less than eight inches from her face and watched Basarnian's pupils enlarge. She switched from Errol Flynn to Captain Kirk. "I did not bring this up for discussion. You will not bring it up for discussion again."

The thin, pale, freckled face moved in a nod; Basarnian's hands tightened on her AK.

Damn. Tag turned and made herself walk through the tall trees as easily and alertly as if she didn't fear Lori's gun behind her now.

The day after the funeral for her brother's family, her phone rang, and the only message left was a woman's voice (a friend's voice, hard to pinpoint) reciting a phone number into the answering machine. Two days later she had unbenumbed herself long enough to call the number she had memorized—for some reason she felt the number should not be written down. Three days after that she was given her clearance and her wolfsark, and was made a member of Lukos.

Tag was astonished to find that the rumors were true—that the specially-raised and treated wolves produced pelts lined with a sensitive underskin that, when the pelt was removed in one piece, was sensitized to human physiology, enough to imprint lupine nature directly into the living tissue it contacted.

Tag was also told the brief history of the organization. Dr. Reva Maklis, the genetic researcher who'd created the wolfsark, had had her paper on her work with wolves treated with human DNA rejected from all the usual publications. She'd expected no less, having dealt with all the hostilities and harassments encountered by female scientists the world over. But the crowning blow that had turned a scientist into an activist came when she was raped in the lab by one of her own assistants. Rather than press charges, she had silently taken all her notes, her wolves, her sarks, and had gone to Greenland with the new name Raksha. The remains of her lab assistant had been found a few days after she disappeared. Not long after that, Raksha began to organize a few of her similarly treated friends; she herself stayed in Greenland with her lab equipment and her wolf litters, creating the wolfsarks; she was the sole source for the pelts to that day.

The next night Tag ate, for the first time since the Aryan Brothers had raided Eric's house to set an example for whites who married Filipino women and bred mongrel children.

She did not walk on two legs for a month; even when she peeled off the wolfsark to air-dry the fragile skin and was back in a human shape, she stayed on hands and knees, and slept curled up on the floor or her couch. She learned how to kill as easily as she had learned how to knit, bunching the muscles in the broad furry shoulders to drive her forepaws through a man's chest and splinter his ribcage; how to reach into the wet opening, bite here, bite there, and pull out the heart—that and the liver were the prize for the killer. She ate nothing while in human shape, and regained her weight that first month. Organ meats are rich.

Basarnian's fear was only natural, of course. Who hadn't heard all about Lukos women? They went berserk, they ate babies (but always *someone else's* babies), they attacked the people they were supposed to protect, they had sold their souls, they could fly. Catholic women who joined Lukos were automatically excommunicated. A lot of non-Lukos women blamed Lukos for the rising viciousness of crimes against women, saying the men were retaliating and that things were better in the old days (few of them credited Lukos with the overall *drop* in crime rate).

Cows, Tag snarled to herself, remembering some of the editorials written by *Eagle Forum* and *Traditional Family Values* members. "Know your place, girls! Relax and enjoy it! It's God's will!" *Don't those stupid little fawns realize it's a war we're fighting for them?* Pain twisted her gut. *A war Lukos is fighting.* The "expanded military presence" Tag was currently stalking her way through was a war she was fighting for herself.

Wilbur kept up his guard in the rear just behind Basarnian, gun pointed down, armed and ready and safe. Wilbur was always last; Lori was brand-new, and Tag would dance in a minefield before she'd let Mike get behind all three of them with his AK.

Tag spared a backwards cant of her eyes to check on Wilbur's progress. He'd been billy-walking with her for two months now. She had suspected from the first that he knew she'd once been a member of that controversial sorority. One drunken night at the base, not long after she'd been demoted for the ear incident, she had whispered it to him; he in turn had told her about his friend in the car. From then on he had treated her with a respect beyond the mere obedience due a superior. It smelled of gratitude for the work Tag had once done; that Lukos, and by extension Tag, had avenged his murdered friend in a way Wilbur could not. *As if I personally killed and ate the guys who did it. . . .* But Tag did not grudge his respect. She never thought about Wilbur when he guarded her back, the way one does not think about the white blood cells that continually stave off infection.

Poor Wilbur. Everybody assumed he was a ganger doing AS; it was as if black people didn't volunteer. A black man wearing a blue sweatshirt when the Alternative Sentencing trucks drove into gang neighborhoods got recruited and sent into C.A. before you could say Bill of Rights. Mike's cronies made life hell for anyone with dark skin, beating them up and worse when they weren't forcibly restricted to taunts. And skins purely hated to see a poor helpless white woman like Tag left alone with someone like Wilbur.

Tag grinned an inhuman grin to herself, remembering Mike's pal who had wanted to see Wilbur tap dance. Wilbur had neglected to tell Lori that Tag had shot the skin in the shoulder and hacked his left ear off (*THAT for Eric, since I can't eat you!*). Another skin had pounced on the gory thing to add to his earring collection; that was how she'd been introduced to Mike. Tag had gotten her ass chewed and lost a stripe, but Deadear Dick had been sent home under arrest—it was still illegal to *act* on one's racist beliefs. Tag was too valuable to be sent home—not with her nose and ears.

Who knew what underground people Raksha had contacted, what things had been used to treat the pelts? After a year or so of shootings or woundings in her wolf-people, she had created a true werewolf-hide, impervious to all but the silver that counteracted all metanatural influences.

Six years with Lukos. Tag ran fast, tail high, teeth snapping for a pants leg or jacket sleeve. How she yelled with mirth when they pointed guns at her and at her comrades! Bullets whizzed through wolfsarks like neutrinos; laughing wolf muzzles were the last things the gunmen ever saw.

Formaya specialized in cars. She would wait on the top of a parked car, looking like someone's big dog taking a nap. When a slow-moving BMW or Volvo came down the street, full of the sweat of blind hate and a glint of gunmetal, she would leap right through the open window to bite off the top of the gunman's head, and leap out the window again just as the panicked driver wrapped the car around a telephone pole. When she had done that seven times, there were no more drive-by shootings in Formaya's neighborhood. It wasn't known if she'd named herself after Maya Angelou, or if she'd had a little girl named Maya who hadn't ducked fast enough during a drive-by.

Rache took her name from her beloved Sherlock Holmes stories. (It was her second choice; she was pissed when she found out that another Lukos member already had the name Baskerville.) She made a big long-legged wolf, like a Russian mastiff, and was the fastest runner in the L.A. chapter. Rache led the beach chase of the Malibu Slasher—she was the one who broke his back and got his heart and liver. (Tag's only contribution to that night's hunting was a joke—she walked over to a lifeguard station and dropped a turd beneath the NO DOGS ADMITTED ON BEACH *sign. Everyone else did the same thing, yowling in glee. It was no joke for the lifeguard who had to pick up the wolf shit the next day, but all agreed it was a small price to pay for bringing the tourists back to the beach.)*

Tag got her name from Tagalog, the Filipino language—the language of her dead sister-in-law Abbie. Tag's best kill had been in her fifth year of sarking. She had pounced on three stags gang-raping a woman in an alley, biting and clawing till they jumped up from the bruised, naked body and ran after her. They had cornered Tag in the dead end, all of them firing the converted semis with which they had also been promising to rape their victim when Tag found them. In the time it took them to realize that their clouds of bullets didn't bother the short burly wolf, all three of them had been hamstrung. Tag had paced around them as the screaming, wounded men emptied their guns at her in vain, occasionally nipping fingers off grabbing hands—shamelessly enjoying her terrorization of the brutes. Finally she neatly bit through the back of each neck; three bites, no more noise. Three hearts and three livers—Tag was stuffed for two days after that. The glow from stopping that crime in the very act never left her.

Mike's gun went off now and then—maybe they *would* have parrot for dinner. Tag could still smell Mike ahead, and hear him scuttling along out of sight (and human earshot) of the company; she could smell the big stinking cross around his neck. Tag shook her head once; as if that dumb ugly thing would keep her away! Non-sarkers still didn't know how the process worked. *Let him think, though. Let him keep thinking that the next full Moon will send me running after his Nazi ass. If ever there was fragger-material, he's it, and anything that'll keep him in line I'm not questioning.*

And for the hundredth time she asked herself why the higher-ups had assigned a skin to her troop. *Someone* should have known there would be a dangerous conflict. . . . The past week of having Mike in her company had felt more like three months—it had been nonstop standoffs and confrontations. Today he'd started off a little easier to live with; he'd been downright cheerful right up to her finding the snipers. She had foolishly thought he might be acclimating himself to her troop, or—wilder thought still—that he had been trying to make a good impression on the newcomer Lori.

The damp earthiness of the jungle filled her nose and she inhaled deeply. It was lovely, just as the smell of horse manure or human sweat was pleasing to many people. Tag dropped the worn and unprofitable questioning, and set her mind to the puzzle she made out of nearly every inhalation, sifting and classifying as many separate odors as she could. Trees, creepers (just the small wiry ones), grass, animal droppings (one strong stab that was probably fox), and the birds everywhere, flavoring every inhalation with their dirty feathers and guano. Wasn't that sour smell coming from that particular bright blue bird, the one that ate fruit?

Tag smiled. She was starting to make up for the loss of her wolf-sense of smell; by osmosis or practice her own human nose was getting sharper and more discriminating.

She thought of how it would feel to be a wolf in this jungle. Lukos members had done their running and hunting through urban jungles; streets, parks, beaches. She would have liked to trot through this undergrowth at an easy lupine lope with no heavy load on her back that made her shoulders ache, spread her weight all along four feet, sniffing out snipers by herself. Here she would be a real wolf, not just a Lukos sarker doing a job. Here she could go far away from other humans, see the little lives of this place, howl at the moon if she felt like it, stalk four-footed prey as well as two-footed, ravage all the damn ocelot cats she wanted—

But if Tag could still be a wolf, she wouldn't hate cats so. Six years. . . .

A vine dangled before Tag; she swung the butt of her gun against the plant and crushed it against a tree trunk, all her teeth bared.

Silver bullets started showing up about four years after Tag joined Lukos. The one thing the sarks couldn't deflect, silver was instantly fatal even if the bullet didn't hit heart or brain—a punctured sark became just a smelly old wolf skin; its wearer a human woman alone, wounded and unarmed, surrounded by angry, frightened armed men. The L.A. chapter had heard about deaths from other cities: then Formaya had gotten her brains blown out by a guy with an Uzi clip full of silver bullets.

It was then that Tag knew she had wolf in her blood. The Lukos group stayed in human form all night at someone's house, and Tag joined the others in screaming and howling for the loss of Formaya, as hot-eyed and tearless with rage as they all were. The next night they met, ready for work, and to Tag it was as if she had grieved for Formaya years ago. No one hesitated about going out again that night; Renfield, the chapter head, merely cautioned everyone to sniff the guns for silver before attacking head-on.

"Shit, no parrot," Wilbur said as Mike came back holding only his AK. Tag resolutely put aside the thought of the slaughtered snipers behind them, which was hard because the contents of their kit made her want to gag. Pre-Vietnam rations were no match for a fresh warm liver.

Mike pulled two small bright-red birds that looked something like orioles from his pockets. "Nothing for you dingoes—these are mine. You can gag down your Zion rations if you want. The government puts hormones in them—"

" '—to make us sterile,' " Wilbur chorused with Mike.

" 'They're trying to wipe out the true white men of America that come here.' " Tag took up the refrain. "Old news, Mike. You need fresh propaganda."

"Yeah. Like, they're making white men sterile so they won't have mixed children when they're forced at gunpoint to screw Nicaraguan women," Wilbur said, the Hi, Mouseketeers! look on his face. Lori burst out laughing. Tag grinned widely—a human grin.

She saw Mike's AK move, and was up gripping his gun barrel in an iron fist before he could aim at anyone, holding it in a downpointed position. The barrel was hot in her hand; she would get blisters later. . . . She stared her yellow eyes into his, and her human grin of humor phased effortlessly into the bared-teeth wolf grin of rage. She heard fast breathing from the others behind her.

"You are a dog-fucking bitch." He was so quiet-voiced, compared to the terror in his watery eyes.

"So I am," she said without moving her teeth; like a phantom severed limb she felt the hair rising all along her back and her tail rising in the air. "Got a lotta cute little puppies waiting for their mama to come home in one piece."

Mike tried to pull his gun free, but Tag's forearms were strong from years of running on them; the AK muzzle stayed pointed at the ground. His cross was bedewed with his sweat; a savory smell tempered the silver reek.

"Watch your step, bitch." Mike's watery blue eyes matched the yellow ones stare for stare. "Or you'll end up like the other one, from 43rd." His hands tightened on the gun stock. "They can give us a shell, but they can't make it stay."

Wilbur started to lift his gun into place. "No," Tag snapped without turning around, and he lowered it again. She could smell sweat from all four of them. Deliberately, she drove all expression out of her face and kept staring into the skin's eyes, her nostrils flared. Again he tried to jerk the gun from her fist, and she tightened her hold on the hot barrel. The standoff stretched on. His blue eyes unfocused in panic. She kept staring into the mad eyes, thinking fast.

Forty-third had been Sergeant Baynes' outfit. Paula Baynes had gotten fragged less than six months ago. She had been a brand-new sergeant in charge of her third billy-walk. The news article about the death in the *Billy-Walk Blues* reported that the man who had shot her was hopped up on Ultra, and was going back to the states under psychiatric observation. In his rush of inhuman strength (Ultra made PCP look like baby powder), the junkie had mutilated Baynes' body after shooting her, digging out chunks of her flesh and swallowing them before he was subdued.

There had been a photo of Sgt. Baynes with the article. Anyone else would have said that the woman had had a frightened look in her pale eyes, and a nervous closed-mouth smile; but Tag knew, from the other facial clues, that Baynes had smiled that way to hide the long canine teeth. The article had mentioned in passing that Baynes had been a competent stalker. Paula Baynes sounded like a corruption of Paulsbane—a woman who joined Lukos after she had been raped often took the name of her rapist and added the suffix that denoted a conqueror.

Tag had considered that the junkie's mutilation of Baynes' body might not be just the Ultra. If he'd known her background, he could have done that to pay an ex-Lukos woman back, by eating the eater.

So Mike thought he could threaten his commander. . . .

At the right moment, just before Mike's terror would have toppled him into berserker violence, Tag's fingers unclenched from his gun barrel. "Deal, skin. Use your hate words. All you want. But no shooting. No aiming. Or I swear to Jesus Christ I'll bite you." This time she gave him only the partly-bared-teeth warning grin of the pack leader. "And you know what happens when a werewolf bites you."

Mike grinned himself, the bared-teeth grin of a frightened chimp—or an enraged baboon. The gun stayed down. "Deal. Cunt."

Tag then flashed her version of Wilbur's smile, purely human and good-natured. "Right. Nuff said." She turned her back on Mike and walked to Wilbur and Lori. "Was that so hard?" She plopped down on a rock and quelled her desire to shit the fear out of her right where she was sitting—six years of doggy carelessness about defecation tried her control severely. But the fear was an acid wine in her blood—still nearly as sweet as in the days of killing. "Eat your dead birds. Let's break out the gruel, children."

Mike opened his bag to get out a can of Sterno, and the billowing stink from his pack made Tag want to vomit. It was exponentially stronger than the smell from his cross. She made sure not to let any expression show her reaction to the smell, and thought again. All Mike should have had in the rucksack were his clothes and food, some flares, and his boxes of ammo.

Silver suddenly made the job interesting. Some newcomers turned in their wolfsarks, but most stayed—they had been wolves too long to be frightened by death. They stopped being pack animals and became snipers, solitary predators springing and lying low in unpredictable patterns.

Tag didn't expect to die of old age. She didn't WANT *to anymore—the Language Arts major who wouldn't get on a roller coaster had disappeared the moment she'd walked into her brother's slippery, swastika-covered kitchen. Tag had grown to love the excitement of feeling lead bullets whip through her—then she became addicted to the rush when she sprang for a throat and didn't know if the gun would kill or not. The hearts got sweeter, the chases wilder. She had no history of that time (apart from her proud disruption of the gang-rape); she lived it day to day to day.*

The other three opened cans and Mike cooked his small birds on sharpened sticks, the plucked feathers like an arterial splash on the ground.

"Ech." Lori gulped down a cold ravioli, making a face. "Isn't there anything that grows around here we could put in this to make it taste better?"

"Well, there just happens to be this local mushroom," Wilbur said blithely, lifting out a forkful of gray chili. "Round and brown, big as your fist. Give you stomach cramps so bad you won't be able to eat anything for a week. After that, this stuff will taste like caviar."

"Hmp. Bad enough getting cramps *once* a month," Lori muttered, twitching a little because she had obviously been raised to feign ignorance about female body functions.

Wilbur chuckled. Mike guffawed, spraying out bird and bones, and the other two looked at him. Tag laughed with them at Lori's comment and kept thinking, her nerves still piano wire after the latest showdown with Mike. *Why* had they assigned her a skin, one teetering on the edge, if they knew what she used to be? If they knew. . . .

Tag held herself very still, repeated the last two words to herself.

They knew. That stink—Mike couldn't afford that kind of ammo, and so much of it, by himself. The article about Baynes mentioned that she'd been mutilated after her death by the Ultra-head who'd shot her. Tag had assumed he'd been paying her back for the people she'd eaten as a Lukos member—but perhaps he had been digging the bullets out of his victim and swallowing them so people wouldn't find out they were silver bullets. Cover-up. Silver. . . .

Then again, they *didn't* know.

Tag choked a laugh into her canned tamales, and kept choking till Wilbur whacked her on the back. Mike's eyes were slits looking at Wilbur; this obviously Wilbur's way of expressing his uncontrollable lust for a white woman. "Eat it, you baby," Wilbur said, grinning. "Corporal, we don't have any raw meat."

But it was so perfectly, typically *government*! At the current price for silver (with crack dealers and wealthy felons in a desperate buying war, the price was beginning to rival gold's), and the amount of silver needed per bullet, the number of bullets per box of ammo. . . . For a moment Tag wanted a calculator, to find out exactly how much money was being wasted for the rub-out when four or five standard-issues. . . .

"Got any ammo left, Mike?"

Mike choked a little on his birds, but it was an ordinary enough question. There was no way Tag could know about the silver bullets he was assigned for his job (as Tag had always been careful never to let on how she reacted to silver smell). He recovered well enough. "Some."

"I can't take this shit any more." Tag handed the rest of her tamales to Lori, who seized them eagerly. For a moment Tag felt a vague pity for the virgin taste buds that had never gloried in jalapeño or chipotle. Hormel Mexican food was as exotic as it got in the little Ohio town Basarnian had left to fight for her country. "You're a good shot. What do you charge for getting a couple of birds like that? That is, if you'd actually take money from a non-Aryan wolf-bitch."

He had his Nazi pride to think about. He was going to be paid well (if they let him live) and he could always hock what silver bullets he didn't use. But she would get suspicious, she knew he couldn't turn down the right cash offer. . . . "Ten bucks each. And I keep the money whether I get anything or not. Take it or leave it, cunt."

Tag yawned and scratched under her chin, pondering. "Mm." She found a twenty wadded in her boot. Of course he knew how much she had with her.

He took his time eating his birds, made a documentary on proper hygiene after meals, quadruple checked his gun, and stuffed an extra box of ammo in his pants.

"Need a sniper buddy?" Lori asked. Mike gave her the finger. "Okay, get your fucking head blown off, see if I care."

Tag smiled a human smile. *She's catching on.*

Five minutes after Mike disappeared, Tag looked up a nearby tree as if to check for ocelots, and flared her nostrils. There was no silver reek. The bastard was downwind. He wasn't hunting for birds this time.

"Aw, geez, I gotta take a crap again," Tag said.

Wilbur started; Tag caught his eye and nodded. He thumbed his chest and mouthed a question; she shook her head, looked at Lori for a second, who was still angrily absorbed in the tamales, and back to him. One jerk of his head: yes. Tag was in the undergrowth before Lori could react to the shadow play.

Stalking a stag. These ears were always forward; no tail to help shift her body weight. Weight. . . . Tag dropped forward onto her hands and strong forearms. But that pushed her nose downward, nearly into the snake-infested undergrowth. She cursed soundlessly and leapt upright again.

He went in the wind's path. She would have to cut a 90-degree path—but from which direction?

Silver bullets. Old superstitions made real, so the people behind the scenes would brief their tools on other superstitions. What side does evil come from—what is the sinister side?

Tag went to the right, and kept going. There were patches of bare unsheltered ground to cross that were scarier than the squishy undergrowth, but the soldiers weren't wearing camouflage for nothing. She rustled and creaked abominably through the growth—at least she did to her own ears. She flared nostrils; he was still downwind.

Tag felt a half-mile's worth of trotting in her single pair of legs; she cut to a sharp left and loped at a steady pace, paralleling Mike's trail. If she could catch up to him, the wind would tell her where he was.

On bare patches of ground, she dropped to all fours after all for a few quick lollops to take some weight off her legs, her hands doubled into fists to better enable them to withstand the rough ground and her weight. It was not until then that Tag realized she hadn't brought her AK.

He would stay in the clearer places, where humans could walk with ease. The leaves patted her on the back as she trotted through the thick foliage, doubled over and breathing in noiseless pants, each breath bringing new smells, new information about her surroundings. She slipped through underbrush and dense growth like a knife, happier than she'd been in months. The old familiar acid rush of danger, fear and alertness swam in her blood, sharpening every sense; she thought she could almost feel the veining on the backs of the leaves that brushed her skin. She wouldn't need little birds or canned ravioli to fill her empty belly this night.

Just as the wind brought a silver reek that flared her nostrils, Tag heard shots. Single, sharp reports, from nonrepeaters, coming from where they had bivouacked; the guns used by Nicaraguan snipers. And she had left her company alone, without her nose and ears.

She stopped dead and stood upright, nose high. Humans, not her own company, the scent too far away to get a count. The smell was blended with the smell of her own company.

Fuck Mike!

Tag bolted through the undergrowth, galloping back to camp. Leaves tore off branches as she pelted through on all fours, nose and ears telling her the story before she could change the ending. Everything smeared into shades of black and white.

Sarks were impervious to all but silver when worn, but when peeled off to air-dry they were as vulnerable to rips and abrasions as any soft leather. Like all Lukos members, Tag took pains not to even drag a fingernail across the delicate skin; a punctured sark became a useless wolfskin, its power lost. One-third of each member's salary was deducted for three years to pay for her sark.

One day after a night's work Tag was visited by a new apartment-neighbor who had come over to introduce herself. Susan Bankley was about Tag's own age, friendly and warm. Tag invited her in for coffee, pleased to play hostess in a non-Lukos social situation for a change. Before sitting at the table with Susan, Tag went into her bedroom to latch the window screens and close the door to her bedroom so that air could continue to gently dry the sark, laid fur-side down on the bed.

Susan drank coffee and talked about her cats for an hour. Tag was a little bored but nodded in all the right places. The new neighbor mentioned how clever her Vinnie was about unlatching screens, said, "Oh, it's almost feeding time, he'll come looking for me. He's such a greedy little. . . ." then stared as Tag tore for her room.

I'll know to close the windows now, Tag chanted to herself. She's brand new here, it can't have happened already, I'll know now, so it isn't too. . . . But the jelly side of the bread hits the ground first.

"Vinnie, you naughty wuss!" Susan said as the orange tabby ran out of the bedroom and leaped into her arms, miaowing imperiously. She then looked up at what the cat had done. "Oh, my God, I'm so sorry! I'll pay for that fur myself, please don't worry!"

Rules were rules; no one was issued a new sark if the old one was damaged under the person's care. Tag was made wolfless—and like true wolves, Lukos members stopped seeing or calling her; she had ceased to exist. She was alone, with only naked human skin between herself and the world.

Unsarked Lukos women did not live long. Their instincts were wrong; they did wolfish things wearing only lambskins. They were raped and murdered in droves. Many committed suicide, or disappeared.

When clumsy two-legged stalking didn't work, Tag simply left the screen door open and opened a can of cat food. Vinnie finally came in, begging piteously to be fed. She shut the door, caught the animal up by the scruff of the neck, and pulled it apart. Vinnie's meat was the first thing Tag had eaten in days.

The shooting was louder, closer; there were two—three—four people shooting; one had a silver stink. Tag broke through another clearing. The shaven-headed blur shooting toward the sniper sounds heard the brush crackle, and whirled around to aim the stinking AK at his own commander.

But Mike's aim and timing had been geared to stop a human woman running on two legs, not a four-footed creature at a dead charge. By the time the skinhead thought of lowering the gun's muzzle to aim at a wolf-level head and not a human-level one, Tag's clenched fists, driven by locked forearms, punched through his sternum. The hand holding the gun smacked her shoulder, and silver bullets rattled the clearing as her fists hit a crunchy wet brick wall, plunged in and stuck. She fell with the jerking, kicking wall, and the sweet rich smell of iron drowned out the reek of silver. She reached with her flat round face, teeth groping—but she had hands and fingers now. She unclenched her battered fists, groped through a hot wet sponge with aching fingers; found the throbbing, slippery thing, squeezed here, squeezed there, and yanked hard. The wall bounced once, and was quiet. The thing stopped throbbing in her hands.

All Tag wanted to do was to eat what she had in her hurting hands and then go lie down and sleep, but the snipers' shots screamed at her to get up. Her hands let go of the quiet lump, slid past the splintered sternum, and left dark handprints on Mike's clothes as she pulled herself to her feet.

She raced toward the camp, now hearing three guns, and knowing what she would find—one down, the other one valiantly mowing the jungle for the snipers (two unwashed bodies). Tag hoped Lori was the casualty; Wilbur was the better shot.

The nearer one didn't hear her run up behind him; he did feel her leap onto his back. Her face was bowled out enough, her teeth still long and sharp enough; she bit the back of his neck once, crunching through flesh, bone and soft inner core as if biting a corncob in half. He dropped beneath her. His hair was greasy and filthy, and she spat once as she let go the corpse. Movement to the left, a sour smell. Tag charged toward that movement, yelling, her eyes hot with joy. She saw fire and smoke coming from the gun's mouth head on, felt heat as the barrel thrust into her stomach and kept firing; but she didn't need her ears any more and tuned out the ammo fire. She saw the man's white-rimmed eyes, his narrow crooked nose, his lips forming the word *¡Diablo!* as her open mouth and bared canine teeth landed on the single cord on the left side of his neck and chomped down on the buried artery. Blood rushed into her like a shotgunned beer, a draft of iron and life gushing down her throat and out her nose and spilling down her front as both of them toppled over, locked together.

And then the fury was gone, the pain was going away, and Tag couldn't even free her teeth from the sniper's neck. She lay full length on the quivering warm flesh, gun and all, gave a great sigh, and closed her eyes.

". . . The law protects white males. If a woman and her children are battered for 10 years by the husband, the neighbors and police look the other way because it's the man's personal business. But if the woman kills the abuser, she gets the maximum sentence for first-degree murder. You can't help but wonder how many of those judges and attorneys are terrified that their own wives might try to set fire to THEIR *beds one night. . . . Of course Lukos is hated. We are women attacking the men who have harmed us and ours, armed with centuries of bottled rage as well as teeth and claws, and we cannot be intimidated. . . . Since we are blamed for the crimes committed against us anyway, then by Mother-god let us* EARN *the blame!"*

—Excerpt from an article by Raksha, founder of Lukos, that appeared in The Village Voice

There was crying, dreadful sobbing, the grief of a whole family. A woman's crying, and she had heard it once today already. She knew what it meant. Oh, and the bitter, welcome grief squeezed her chest till she had to yell to let it out. Tag woke, howling and howling, to join the noise Lori was making.

"I thought you were dead, too," she sniffled when she could speak again. "There was so much blood, and you didn't move. . . ."

Tag looked down where the pain was. Black dried blood was caked all down her front—but it was all the sniper's. She had a bloody nose and blood in her mouth—also sniper's blood. Then she pulled up her shirt and found her single wound—a long red mark from the sniper's hot gun barrel raking down her stomach.

How many bullets had gone through her? Not Mike's—she went at Mike under his arm and his stinking bullets never touched her. But the sniper's gun. . . .

Lori had already laid Wilbur out and set up the beacon. There was a small red hole in his forehead and blood all over his punctured clothes; his whole face was puffed up. But his eyes were closed. Tag nodded gently, knowing that that little kindness was Lori's work also. She pulled off her jacket clumsily, her hands stiff with dried blood, and covered Wilbur's face with it.

It was almost day's end, and the chopper would come soon to take them back to base. Tag scouted around the camp and found some of the sniper's bullets: regular lead. His gun had been loaded when he had aimed right at her. From the angle of the bodies and the direction of the bullets Tag deduced that the one who shot at her was responsible for Wilbur's death.

When Tag asked about Wilbur, Lori started to cry again. "He, he covered me till I could get behind the log and start shooting, and then—" She looked down, breathing hard, tears making runnels down her dirty freckled cheeks. Basarnian was smudged with dirt, and there was a thick orange splash on her jacket front that was probably from the tamales, but she had withstood the sniper barrage without getting a scratch.

Tag thought about Wilbur's grin, his acceptance of her former lupine status, his steady gun at her back, the way he'd let Mike's hatred roll off him without sticking. Her eyes burned with grief, her throat tightened, her nose stung. Then—a day of wonders—something *wet* welled up around her blazing eyes and rolled down her cheeks, taking away the fire. She stretched her arms toward the only other survivor of her company.

Lori shrank from Tag at first, terrified by the bulletproof woman; but the young soldier badly needed to hold on to something—and now, so did her corporal. For a long time they sat clinging to each other like shipwreck survivors, tears smudging their cheeks.

Tag sat, weeping for the first time in eight years, and her thoughts ran wild. This was human grief at last, and not lupine; Tag knew this stinging-tender pain of Wilbur's loss would stay with her the way her angry howling for Formaya's death had not.

And yet she was wolf, too. She had changed; but the change had been so gradual she hadn't noticed it before. Her wolfishness had not left her, after all—it had merged with her humanity. Just as her features—her strong arms, long teeth and yellow eyes—had been imprinted by Lukos, so now had her imprinted human skin recovered from the removal of the hermit-crab shell; her exterior had hardened to a wolfsark's immunity from lead bullets.

But why hadn't any of the others—

Lived long enough to notice? That thought held Tag perfectly still, her mind gathering all the wild-flung strands together, just as she had pondered Mike's ammo during the disastrous meal break.

Was it possible that Baynes—and others like her—had gotten fragged just about the time they discovered that their lupine nature had fused with their humanity? Fragged by specially-assigned berserkers sent by nervous generals under orders from a frightened government?

Just suppose the huge murder rate among newly-unsarked civilian women wasn't the result of careless instincts, but was in fact a colossal and deadly cover-up?

Tag clacked her teeth together, and grinned a wolf grin. How much cheaper than dealing with a subspecies of fearless, lethal and invulnerable women!

She heard the chopper coming, and decided that Lori was going to have to be very brave. "Basarnian, you really got baptized today. You're one helluva soldier."

She snuffed. "But Wilbur—he died because I didn't—"

"You did what your superior ordered, Private. Shit happens." Lori's mouth twitched, and Tag let the corners of her own mouth turn up a little. "But you'll have to take Wilbur home by yourself."

Lori sucked in a breath of air fast, not quite a sob, and nodded, her eyes wet and red. She knew the bullets had gone through Tag, and her fear of her superior was now well established. Perhaps there was even a little fear *for* her superior. "They'll look for you. And, and Mike."

"Mike shot me. Tell 'em that for now. True enough."

But after a time, when no Mike came back to base with a new ear on his string to collect his reward, more skins with silver bullets might show up to finish the job. Tag wanted to find the others like her first.

She'd bet anything that a lot of wolfless women did what she'd done immediately after being unsarked—go to ground in a faceless government body to lick their wounds. Their need to use their fighting skills would lead them to join the armed forces, where they'd be shipped out to C.A. as fast as they were trained. Was it when they got too good—when the numbness wore off and they relearned just how much wolf remained in them, when their soft human skin hardened into wolfsarks—that the silver snipers were called in? Socios like Mike could be explained away with ease; could almost be counted on to go berserk on patrol and frag a fellow soldier. And after all, didn't everyone fear Lukos women anyway?

A lot of the women would have died. But surely not all!

The ones who escaped might do what she planned to do, Tag realized. They could live in the jungle, trot through the underbrush, hunt down their own food—and sniff the breeze for lone stalkers that smelled of woman and wolf both, with names like Johnsbane and Momsee.

And what if Tag were the very first ex-Lukos soldier to escape the elimination?

Well, she *could* start roaming the jungle, calling out Lukos pack-signals when she smelled both woman and wolf in a billy-walker. She might persuade enough of the unsarked to MIA themselves and hide out in the jungle while their hides toughened. And from there . . .

Tag considered what they could accomplish when they unified. For starters, there were plenty of stags in the jungle. She thought of them: the lieutenant who only stopped Wilbur's hazing by the skins when a white man got hurt; the skins themselves; the regular soldiers who thought rape was part of the fun of war. Back in the bases lurked frightened officers issuing silver bullets to sociopathic soldiers, and promoting some women soldiers based solely on their willingness to blow their commanders. Beyond even that, back in the states, there was work to be done—right up to the President who had ordered the fighting escalation in Nicaragua just as his connections with druglords were being investigated. There were people responsible for a murderous cover-up to take on.

It would take a lot of work to detect that kind of stag—but a new Lukos formed of ordinary-looking women who smiled with their mouths closed to hide the long teeth, with contact lenses to hide yellow eyes, would be much harder to kill, harder to hide from, than furry four-legged wolves. And the crimes committed by a rapist or slasher paled beside the activities of some respected citizens—after all, Charles Manson hadn't been responsible for My Lai.

We are a new species, then. Homo sapiens lycanthra. *And we are invisible. Once we unify . . .*

Tag wrapped Lori in a big hug, careful not to crush the weary soldier in her arms, and bussed her cheeks the way French officers did. Then she whispered the phone number, several times. Whether Lori remembered, and acted on it, was another matter.

Then Tag was running on all fours through the brush, away from the wind and thunder of the landing chopper, and back into the jungle, following the blood-scent back to where she had left Mike with his heart pulled out of his chest. It had been a long day, and she was very hungry.

A contemporary and correspondent of H.P. Lovecraft and Robert E. Howard, Clark Ashton Smith is better known for his fantasies, usually set in baroque ancient civilizations, than for his occasional works of science fiction. "A Prophecy of Monsters," however, looks ahead to tomorrow for an ingenious mixture of the scientific with the supernatural. It first appeared, appropriately enough, in The Magazine of Fantasy & Science Fiction.

A Prophecy of Monsters

CLARK ASHTON SMITH

The change occurred before he could divest himself of more than his coat and scarf. He had only to step out of the shoes, to shed the socks with two backward kicks, and shuffle off the trousers from his lean hind legs and belly. But he was still deep-chested after the change, and his shirt was harder to loosen. His hackles rose with rage as he slewed his head around and tore it away with hasty fangs in a flurry of falling buttons and rags. Tossing off the last irksome ribbons, he regretted his haste. Always heretofore he had been careful in regard to small details. The shirt was monogrammed. He must remember to collect all the tatters later. He could stuff them in his pockets, and wear the coat buttoned closely on his way home, when he had changed back.

Hunger snarled within him, mounting from belly to throat, from throat to mouth. It seemed that he had not eaten for a month—for a month of months. Raw butcher's meat was never fresh enough; it had known the coldness of death and refrigeration, and had lost all vital essence. Long ago there had been other meals, warm, and sauced with still-spurting blood. But now the thin memory merely served to exasperate his ravening.

Chaos raced within his brain. Inconsequently, for an instant, he recalled the first warning of his malady, preceding even the distaste for cooked meat: the aversion, the allergy, to silver forks and spoons. It had soon extended to other objects of the same metal. He had cringed even from the touch of coinage, had been forced to use paper and refuse change. Steel, too, was a substance unfriendly to beings like him; and the time came when he could abide it little more than silver.

What made him think of such matters now, setting his teeth on edge with repugnance, choking him with something worse than nausea?

The hunger returned, demanding swift appeasement. With clumsy pads he pushed his discarded raiment under the shrubbery, hiding it from the heavy-jowled moon. It was the moon that drew the tides of madness in his blood, and compelled the metamorphosis. But it must not betray to any chance passer the garments he would need later, when he returned to human semblance after the night's hunting.

The night was warm and windless, and the woodland seemed to hold its breath. There were, he knew, other monsters abroad in that year of the twenty-first century. The vampire still survived, subtler and deadlier, protected by man's incredulity. And he himself was not the only lycanthrope: his brothers and sisters ranged unchallenged, preferring the darker urban jungles, while he, being country-bred, still kept the ancient ways. Moreover, there were monsters unknown as yet to myth and superstition. But these too were mostly haunters of cities. He had no wish to meet any of them. And of such meeting, surely, there was small likelihood.

He followed a crooked lane, reconnoitered previously. It was too narrow for cars, and it soon became a mere path. At the path's forking he ensconced himself in the shadow of a broad, mistletoe-blotted oak. The path was used by certain late pedestrians who lived even farther out from town. One of them might come along at any moment.

Whimpering a little, with the hunger of a starved hound, he waited. He was a monster that nature had made, ready to obey nature's first commandment: *thou shalt kill and eat.* He was a thing of terror . . . a fable whispered around prehistoric cavern fires . . . a miscegenation allied by later myth to the powers of hell and sorcery. But in no sense was he akin to those monsters beyond nature, the spawn of a newer and blacker magic, who killed without hunger and without malevolence.

He had only minutes to wait, before his tensing ears caught the far-off vibration of footsteps. The steps came rapidly nearer, seeming to tell him much as they came. They were firm and resilient, tireless and rhythmic, telling of youth or of full maturity untouched by age. They told, surely, of a worthwhile prey; of prime lean meat and vital, abundant blood.

There was a slight froth on the lips of the one who waited. He had ceased to whimper. He crouched closer to the ground for the anticipated leap.

The path ahead was heavily shadowed. Dimly, moving fast, the walker appeared in the shadows. He seemed to be all that the watcher had surmised from the sound of his footsteps. He was tall and well-shouldered, swinging with a lithe sureness, a precision of powerful tendon and muscle. His head was a faceless blur in the gloom. He was hatless, clad in dark coat and trousers such as anyone might wear. His steps rang with the assurance of one who has nothing to fear, and has never dreamt of the crouching creatures of darkness.

Now he was almost abreast of the watcher's covert. The watcher could wait no longer but sprang from his ambush of shadow, towering high upon the stranger as his hind paws left the ground. His rush was irresistible, as always. The stranger toppled backward, sprawling and helpless, as others had done, and the assailant bent to the bare throat that gleamed more enticingly than that of a siren.

It was a strategy that had never failed . . . until now . . .

The shock, the consternation, had hurled him away from that prostrate figure and had forced him back upon teetering haunches. It was the shock, perhaps, that caused him to change again, swiftly, resuming human shape before his hour. As the change began, he spat out several broken lupine fangs; and then he was spitting human teeth.

The stranger rose to his feet, seemingly unshaken and undismayed. He came forward in a rift of revealing moonlight, stooping to a half crouch, and flexing his beryllium-steel fingers enameled with flesh pink.

"Who—what—are you?" quavered the werewolf.

The stranger did not bother to answer as he advanced, every synapse of the computing brain transmitting the conditioned message, translated into simplest binary terms, "Dangerous. Not human. *Kill!*"

Michael Swanwick's first novel, In the Drift *(1984), featured a heroine whose unusual digestive system made her a kind of scientific vampire. Since then Swanwick has proven unusually adept at mixing fantastic concepts with science fictional reasoning, and won the 1992 Nebula Award for his novel,* Stations of the Tide. *"A Midwinter's Tale" is a powerful story of humans, wolves, and transformation on an alien world. Believe it or not, it is also a Christmas story.*

A Midwinter's Tale

MICHAEL SWANWICK

Maybe I shouldn't tell you about that childhood Christmas Eve in the Stone House, so long ago. My memory is no longer reliable, not since I contracted the brain fever. Soon I'll be strong enough to be reposted offplanet, to some obscure star light-years beyond that plangent moon rising over your father's barn, but how much has been burned from my mind! Perhaps none of this actually happened.

Sit on my lap and I'll tell you all. Well then, my knee. No woman was ever ruined by a knee. You laugh, but it's true. Would that it were so easy!

The hell of war as it's now practiced is that its purpose is not so much to gain territory as to deplete the enemy, and thus it's always better to maim than to kill. A corpse can be bagged, burned, and forgotten, but the wounded need special care. Regrowth tanks, false skin, medical personnel, a long convalescent stay on your parents' farm. That's why they will vary their weapons, hit you with obsolete stone axes or toxins or radiation, to force your Command to stock the proper prophylaxes, specialized medicines, obscure skills. Mustard gas is excellent for that purpose, and so was the brain fever.

All those months I lay in the hospital, awash in pain, sometimes hallucinating. Dreaming of ice. When I awoke, weak and not really believing I was alive, parts of my life were gone, randomly burned from my memory. I recall standing at the very top of the iron bridge over the Izveltaya, laughing and throwing my books one by one into the river, while my best friend Fennwolf tried to coax me down. "I'll join the militia! I'll be a soldier!" I shouted hysterically. And so I did. I remember that clearly but just what led up to that preposterous instant is utterly beyond me. Nor can I remember the name of my second-eldest sister, though her face is as plain to me as yours is now. There are odd holes in my memory.

That Christmas Eve is an island of stability in my sea-changing memories, as solid in my mind as the Stone House itself, that Neolithic cavern in which we led such basic lives that I was never quite sure in which era of history we dwelt. Sometimes the men came in from the hunt, a larl or two pacing ahead content and sleepy-eyed, to lean bloody spears against the walls, and it might be that we lived on Old Earth itself then. Other times, as when they brought in projectors to fill the common room with colored lights, scintillae nesting in the branches of the season's tree, and cool, harmless flames dancing atop the presents, we seemed to belong to a much later age, in some mythologized province of the future.

The house was abustle, the five families all together for this one time of the year, and outlying kin and even a few strangers staying over, so that we had to put bedding in places normally kept closed during the winter, moving furniture into attic lumber rooms, and even at that there were cots and thick bolsters set up in the blind ends of hallways. The women scurried through the passages, scattering uncles here and there, now settling one in an armchair and plumping him up like a cushion, now draping one over a table, cocking up a mustachio for effect. A pleasant time.

Coming back from a visit to the kitchen where a huge woman I did not know, with flour powdering her big-freckled arms up to the elbows, had shooed me away, I surprised Suki and Georg kissing in the nook behind the great hearth. They had arms about each other and I stood watching them. Suki was smiling, cheeks red and round. She brushed her hair back with one hand so Georg could nuzzle her ear, turning slightly as she did so, and saw me. She gasped and they broke apart, flushed and startled.

Suki gave me a cookie, dark with molasses and a single stingy, crystalized raisin on top, while Georg sulked. Then she pushed me away, and I heard her laugh as she took Georg's hand to lead him away to some darker forest recess of the house.

Father came in, boots all muddy, to sling a brace of game birds down on the hunt cabinet. He set his unstrung bow and quiver of arrows on their pegs, then hooked an elbow atop the cabinet to accept admiration and a hot drink from Mother. The larl padded by, quiet and heavy and content. I followed it around a corner, ancient ambitions of riding the beast rising up within. I could see myself, triumphant before my cousins, high atop the black carnivore. "Flip!" my father called sternly. "Leave Samson alone! He is a bold and noble creature, and I will not have you pestering him."

He had eyes in the back of his head, had my father.

Before I could grow angry, my cousins hurried by, on their way to hoist the straw men into the trees out front, and swept me up along with them. Uncle Chittagong, who looked like a lizard and had to stay in a glass tank for reasons of health, winked at me as

I skirled past. From the corner of my eye, I saw my second-eldest sister beside him, limned in blue fire.

Forgive me. So little of my childhood remains; vast stretches were lost in the blue ice fields I wandered in my illness. My past is like a sunken continent with only mountaintops remaining unsubmerged, a scattered archipelago of events from which to guess the shape of what was lost. Those remaining fragments I treasure all the more and must pass my hands over them periodically to reassure myself that something remains.

So where was I? Ah, yes: I was in the north bell tower, my hidey-place in those days, huddled behind Old Blind Pew, the bass of our triad of bells, crying because I had been deemed too young to light one of the Yule torches. "Hallo!" cried a voice, and then, "Out here, stupid!" I ran to the window, tears forgotten in my astonishment at the sight of my brother Karl silhouetted against the yellowing sky, arms out, treading the roof gables like a tightrope walker.

"You're going to get in trouble for that!" I cried.

"Not if you don't tell!" Knowing full well how I worshiped him. "Come on down! I've emptied out one of the upper kitchen cupboards. We can crawl in from the pantry. There's a space under the door—we'll see everything!"

Karl turned and his legs tangled under him. He fell. Feet first, he slid down the roof.

I screamed. Karl caught the guttering and swung himself into an open window underneath. His sharp face rematerialized in the gloom, grinning. "Race you to the jade ibis!"

He disappeared, and then I was spinning wildly down the spiral stairs, mad to reach the goal first.

It was not my fault we were caught, for I would never have giggled if Karl hadn't been tickling me to see just how long I could keep silent. I was frightened, but not Karl. He threw his head back and laughed until he cried, even as he was being hauled off by three very angry grandmothers; he was pleased more by his own roguery than by anything he might have seen.

I myself was led away by an indulgent Katrina, who graphically described the caning I was to receive and then contrived to lose me in the crush of bodies in the common room. I hid behind the goat tapestry until I got bored—not long!—and then Chubkin, Kosmonaut, and Pew rang, and the room emptied.

I tagged along, ignored, among the moving legs, like a marsh bird scuttling through waving grasses. Voices clangoring in the east stairway, we climbed to the highest balcony to watch the solstice dance. I hooked hands over the crumbling balustrade and pulled myself up on tiptoe so I could look down on the procession as it left the house. For a long time nothing happened, and I remember being annoyed at how casually the adults were taking all this, standing about with drinks, not one in ten glancing away from themselves. Pheidre and Valerian (the younger children had been put to bed, complaining, an hour ago) began a game of tag, running through the adults, until they were chastened and ordered with angry shakes of their arms to be still.

Then the door below opened. The women who were witches walked solemnly out, clad in hooded terry-cloth robes as if they'd just stepped from the bath. But they were so silent I was struck with fear. It seemed as if something cold had reached into the pink, giggling women I had seen preparing themselves in the kitchen and taken away some warmth or laughter from them. "Katrina!" I cried in panic, and she lifted a moon-cold face toward me. Several of the men exploded in laughter, white steam puffing from bearded mouths, and one rubbed his knuckles in my hair. My second-eldest sister drew me away from the balustrade and hissed at me that I was not to cry out to the witches, that this was important, that when I was older I would understand, and in the meantime if I did not behave myself I would be beaten. To soften her words, she offered me a sugar crystal, but I turned away stern and unappeased.

Single file the women walked out on the rocks to the east of the house, where all was barren slate swept free of snow by the wind from the sea, and at a great distance—you could not make out their faces—doffed their robes. For a moment they stood motionless in a circle, looking at one another. Then they began the dance, each wearing nothing but a red ribbon tied about one upper thigh, the long end blowing free in the breeze.

As they danced their circular dance, the families watched, largely in silence. Sometimes there was a muffled burst of laughter as one of the younger men muttered a racy comment, but mostly they watched with great respect, even a kind of fear. The gusty sky was dark and flocked with small clouds like purple-headed rams. It was chilly on the roof, and I could not imagine how the women withstood it. They danced faster and faster, and the families grew quieter, packing the edges more tightly, until I was forced away from the railing. Cold and bored, I went downstairs, nobody turning to watch me leave, back to the main room, where a fire still smouldered in the hearth.

The room was stuffy when I'd left and cooler now. I lay down on my stomach before the fireplace. The flagstones smelled of ashes and were gritty to the touch, staining my fingertips as I trailed them in idle little circles. The stones were cold at the edges, slowly growing warmer, and then suddenly too hot and I had to snatch my hand away. The back of the fireplace was black with soot, and I watched the fireworms crawl over the stone heart-and-hands carved there, as the carbon caught fire and burned out. The log was all embers and would burn for hours.

Something coughed.

I turned and saw something moving in the shadows, an animal. The larl was blacker than black, a hole in the darkness, and my eyes swam to look at him. Slowly, lazily, he strode out onto the stones, stretched his back, yawned a tongue-curling yawn, and then stared at me with those great green eyes.

He spoke.

I was astonished, of course, but not in the way my father would have been. So much is inexplicable to a child! "Merry Christmas, Flip," the creature said, in a quiet, breathy voice. I could not describe its accent; I have heard nothing quite like it before or since. There was a vast alien amusement in his glance.

"And to you," I said politely.

The larl sat down, curling his body heavily about me. If I had wanted to run, I could not have gotten past him, although that thought did not occur to me then. "There is an ancient legend, Flip, I wonder if you have heard of it, that on Christmas Eve the beasts can speak in human tongue. Have your elders told you that?"

I shook my head.

"They are neglecting you." Such strange humor dwelt in that voice. "There is truth to some of those old legends, if only you knew how to get at it. Though perhaps not all. Some are just stories. Perhaps this is not happening now; perhaps I am not speaking to you at all?"

I shook my head. I did not understand. I said so.

"That is the difference between your kind and mine. My kind understands everything about yours, and yours knows next to nothing about mine. I would like to tell you a story, little one. Would you like that?"

"Yes," I said, for I was young and I liked stories very much.

He began:

"When the great ships landed. . . ."

Oh, God. When—no, no, no, wait. Excuse me. I'm shaken. I just this instant had a vision. It seemed to me that it was night and I was standing at the gates of a cemetery. And suddenly the air was full of light, planes and cones of light that burst from the ground and nested twittering in the trees. Fracturing the sky. I wanted to dance for joy. But the ground crumbled underfoot, and when I looked down the shadow of the gates touched my toes, a cold rectangle of profoundest black, deep as all eternity, and I was dizzy and about to fall and I, and I. . . .

Enough! I have had this vision before, many times. It must have been something that impressed me strongly in my youth, the moist smell of newly opened earth, the chalky whitewash of the picket fence. It must be. I do not believe in hobgoblins, ghosts, or premonitions. No, it does not bear thinking about. Foolishness! Let me get on with my story.

"When the great ships landed, I was feasting on my grandfather's brains. All his descendants gathered respectfully about him, and I, as youngest, had first bite. His wisdom flowed through me, and the wisdom of his ancestors and the intimate knowledge of those animals he had eaten for food, and the spirit of valiant enemies who had been killed and then honored by being eaten, even as if they were family. I don't suppose you understand this, little one."

I shook my head.

"People never die, you see. Only humans die. Sometimes a minor part of a Person is lost, the doings of a few decades, but the bulk of his life is preserved, if not in this body, then in another. Or sometimes a Person will dishonor himself, and his descendants will refuse to eat him. This is a great shame, and the Person will go off to die somewhere alone.

"The ships descended bright as newborn suns. The People had never seen such a thing. We watched in inarticulate wonder, for we had no language then. You have seen the pictures, the baroque swirls of colored metal, the proud humans stepping down onto the land. But I was there, and I can tell you your people were ill. They stumbled down the gangplanks with the stench of radiation sickness about them. We could have destroyed them all then and there.

"Your people built a village at Landfall and planted crops over the bodies of their dead. We left them alone. They did not look like good game. They were too strange and too slow, and we had not yet come to savor your smell. So we went away, in baffled ignorance.

"That was in early spring.

"Half the survivors were dead by midwinter, some of disease but most because they did not have enough food. It was of no concern to us. But then the woman in the wilderness came to change our universe forever.

"When you're older, you'll be taught the woman's tale, and what desperation drove her into the wilderness. It's part of your history. But to myself, out in the mountains and winter-lean, the sight of her striding through the snows in her furs was like a vision of winter's queen herself. A gift of meat for the hungering season, life's blood for the solstice.

"I first saw the woman while I was eating her mate. He had emerged from his cabin that evening as he did every sunset, gun in hand, without looking up. I had observed him over the course of five days, and his behavior never varied. On that sixth nightfall I was crouched on his roof when he came out. I let him go a few steps from the door, then leaped. I felt his neck break on impact, tore open his throat to be sure, and ripped through his parka to taste his innards. There was no sport in it, but in winter we will take game whose brains we would never eat.

"My mouth was full and my muzzle pleasantly, warmly moist with blood when the woman appeared. I looked up, and she was topping the rise, riding one of your incomprehensible machines, what I know now to be a snowstrider. The setting sun broke through the clouds behind her, and for an instant she was embedded in glory. Her shadow stretched narrow before her and touched me, a bridge of darkness between us. We looked in one another's eyes. . . ."

Magda topped the rise with a kind of grim, joyless satisfaction. *I am now a hunter's woman*, she thought to herself. *We will always be welcome at Landfall for the meat we bring, but they will never speak civilly to me again. Good. I would choke on their sweet talk anyway.* The baby stirred and without looking down she stroked him through the furs, murmuring, "Just a little longer, my brave little boo, and we'll be at our new home. Will you like that, eh?"

The sun broke through the clouds to her back, making the snow a red dazzle. Then her eyes adjusted, and she saw the black shape crouched over her lover's body. A very great distance away, her hands throttled down the snowstrider and brought it to a halt. The shallow bowl of land before her was barren, the snow about the corpse black with blood. A last curl of smoke lazily separated from the hut's chimney. The brute lifted its bloody muzzle and looked at her.

Time froze and knotted in black agony.

The larl screamed. It ran straight at her, faster than thought. Clumsily, hampered by the infant strapped to her stomach, Magda clawed the rifle from its boot behind the saddle. She shucked her mittens, fitted hands to metal that stung like hornets, flicked off the safety, and brought the stock to her shoulder. The larl was halfway to her. She aimed and fired.

The larl went down. One shoulder shattered, slamming it to the side. It tumbled and rolled in the snow. "You sonofabitch!" Magda cried in triumph. But almost immediately the beast struggled to its feet, turned and fled.

The baby began to cry, outraged by the rifle's roar. Magda powered up the engine. "Hush, small warrior."

A kind of madness filled her, a blind anesthetizing rage. "This won't take long." She flung her machine downhill, after the larl.

Even wounded, the creature was fast. She could barely keep up. As it entered the spare stand of trees to the far end of the meadow, Magda paused to fire again, burning a bullet by its head. The larl leaped away. From then on, it varied its flight with sudden changes of direction and unexpected jogs to the side. It was a fast learner. But it could not escape Magda. She had always been a hothead, and now her blood was up. She was not about to return to her lover's gutted body with his killer still alive.

The sun set and in the darkening light she lost sight of the larl. But she was able to follow its trail by two-shadowed moonlight, the deep, purple footprints, the darker spatter of blood it left, drop by drop, in the snow.

"It was the solstice, and the moons were full—a holy time. I felt it even as I fled the woman through the wilderness. The moons were bright on the snow. I felt the dread of being hunted descend on me, and in my inarticulate way I felt blessed.

"But I also felt a great fear for my kind. We had dismissed the humans as incomprehensible, not very interesting creatures, slow-moving, bad-smelling, and dull-witted. Now, pursued by this madwoman on her fast machine as she brandished a weapon that killed from afar, I felt all natural order betrayed. She was a goddess of the hunt, and I was her prey.

"The People had to be told.

"I gained distance from her, but I knew the woman would catch up. She was a hunter, and a hunter never abandons wounded prey. One way or another she would have me.

"In the winter all who are injured or too old must offer themselves to the community. The sacrifice rock was not far, by a hill riddled from time beyond memory with our burrows. My knowledge must be shared: The humans were dangerous. They would make good prey.

"I reached my goal when the moons were highest. The flat rock was bare of snow when I ran limping in. Awakened by the scent of my blood, several People emerged from their dens. I lay myself down on the sacrifice rock. A grandmother of the People came forward and licked my wound, tasting, considering. Then she nudged me away with her forehead. The wound would heal, she thought, and winter was young; my flesh was not yet needed.

"But I stayed. Again she nudged me away. I refused to go. She whined in puzzlement. I licked the rock.

"That was understood. Two of the People came forward and placed their weight on me. A third lifted a paw. He shattered my skull, and they ate."

Magda watched through power binoculars from atop a nearby ridge. She saw everything. The rock swarmed with lean black horrors. It would be dangerous to go down among them, so she waited and watched the puzzling tableau below. The larl had wanted to die, she'd swear it, and now the beasts came forward daintily, almost ritualistically, to taste, the young first and then the old. She raised her rifle, thinking to exterminate a few of the brutes from afar.

A curious thing happened then. All the larls that had eaten of her prey's brain leaped away, scattering. Those that had not eaten waited, easy targets, not understanding. Then another dipped to lap up a fragment of brain and looked up with sudden comprehension. Fear touched her.

The hunter had spoken often of the larls and had said that they were so elusive he sometimes thought them intelligent. "Come spring, when I can afford to waste ammunition on carnivores, I look forward to harvesting a few of these beauties," he'd said. He was the colony's xenobiologist, and he loved the animals he killed, treasured them even as he smoked their flesh, tanned their hides, and drew detailed pictures of their internal organs. Magda had always scoffed at his theory that larls gained insight into the habits of their prey by eating their brains, even though he'd spent much time observing the animals minutely from afar and gathering evidence. Now she wondered if he had been right.

Her baby whimpered, and she slid a hand inside her furs to give him a breast. Suddenly the night seemed cold and dangerous, and she thought: *What am I doing here?* Sanity returned to her all at once, her anger collapsing to nothing, like an ice tower shattering in the wind. Below, sleek black shapes sped toward her across the snow. They changed direction every few leaps, running evasive patterns to avoid her fire.

"Hang on, kid," she muttered, and turned her strider around. She opened up the throttle.

Magda kept to the open as much as she could, the creatures following her from a distance. Twice she stopped abruptly and turned her rifle on her pursuers. Instantly they disappeared in puffs of snow, crouching belly-down but not stopping, burrowing toward her under the surface. In the eerie night silence, she could hear the whispering sound of the brutes tunneling. She fled.

Some frantic timeless period later—the sky had still not lightened in the east—Magda was leaping a frozen stream when the strider's left ski struck a rock. The machine was knocked glancingly upward, cybernetics screaming as they fought to regain balance. With a sickening crunch, the strider slammed to earth, one ski twisted and bent. It would take extensive work before the strider could move again.

Magda dismounted. She opened her robe and looked down on her child. He smiled up at her and made a gurgling noise.

Something went dead in her.

A fool. I've been a criminal fool, she thought.

Magda was a proud woman who had always refused to regret, even privately, anything she had done. Now she regretted everything: her anger, the hunter, her entire life, all that had brought her to this point, the cumulative madness that threatened to kill her child.

A larl topped the ridge.

Magda raised her rifle; and it ducked down. She began walking down-slope, parallel to the stream. The snow was knee deep and she had to walk carefully not to slip and fall. Small pellets of snow rolled down ahead of her and were overtaken by other pellets. She strode ahead, pushing up a wake.

The hunter's cabin was not many miles distant; if she could reach it, they would live. But a mile was a long way in winter. She could hear the larls calling to each other, soft coughlike noises, to either side of the ravine. They were following the sound of her passage through the snow. Well, let them. She still had the rifle, and if it had few bullets left, they didn't know that. They were only animals.

This high in the mountains, the trees were sparse. Magda descended a good quarter mile before the ravine choked with scrub and she had to climb up and out or risk being ambushed. *Which way?* she wondered. She heard three coughs to her right and climbed the left slope, alert and wary.

"We herded her. Through the long night we gave her fleeting glimpses of our bodies whenever she started to turn to the side she must not go and let her pass unmolested the other way. We let her see us dig into the distant snow and wait motionless, undetectable. We filled the woods with our shadows. Slowly, slowly, we turned her around. She struggled to return to the cabin, but she could not. In what haze of fear and despair she walked! We could smell it. Sometimes her baby cried, and she hushed the milky-scented creature in a voice gone flat with futility. The night deepened as the moons sank in the sky.

We forced the woman back up into the mountains. Toward the end, her legs failed her several times; she lacked our strength and stamina. But her patience and guile were every bit our match. Once we approached her still form, and she killed two of us before the rest could retreat. How we loved her! We paced her, confident that sooner or later she'd drop.

"It was at night's darkest hour that the woman was forced back to the burrowed hillside, the sacred place of the People where stood the sacrifice rock. She topped the same rise for the second time that night and saw it. For a moment she stood helpless, and then she burst into tears.

"We waited, for this was the holiest moment of the hunt, the point when the prey recognizes and accepts her destiny. After a time, the woman's sobs ceased. She raised her head and straightened her back.

"Slowly, steadily she walked downhill."

She knew what to do.

Larls retreated into their burrows at the sight of her, gleaming eyes dissolving into darkness. Magda ignored them. Numb and aching, weary to death, she walked to the sacrifice rock. It had to be this way.

Magda opened her coat, unstrapped her baby. She wrapped him deep in the furs and laid the bundle down to one side of the rock. Dizzily, she opened the bundle to kiss the top of his sweet head, and he made an angry sound. "Good for you, kid," she said hoarsely. "Keep that attitude." She was so tired.

She took off her sweaters, her vest, her blouse. The raw cold nipped at her flesh with teeth of ice. She stretched slightly, body aching with motion. God it felt good. She laid down the rifle. She knelt.

The rock was black with dried blood. She lay down flat, as she had earlier seen her larl do. The stone was cold, so cold it almost blanked out the pain. Her pursuers waited nearby, curious to see what she was doing; she could hear the soft panting noise of their breathing. One padded noiselessly to her side. She could smell the brute. It whined questioningly.

She licked the rock.

"Once it was understood what the woman wanted, her sacrifice went quickly. I raised a paw, smashed her skull. Again, I was youngest. Innocent, I bent to taste.

"The neighbors were gathering, hammering at the door, climbing over one another to peer through the windows, making the walls bulge and breathe with their eagerness. I grunted and bellowed, and the clash of silver and clink of plates next door grew louder. Like peasant animals, my husband's people tried to drown out the sound of my pain with toasts and drunken jokes.

"Through the window I saw Tevin the Fool's bone-white skin gaunt on his skull, and behind him a slice of face—sharp nose, white cheeks—like a mask. The doors and walls pulsed with the weight of those outside. In the next room children fought and wrestled, and elders pulled at their long white beards, staring anxiously at the closed door.

"The midwife shook her head, red lines running from the corners of her mouth down either side of her stern chin. Her eye sockets were shadowy pools of dust. 'Now push!' she cried. 'Don't be a lazy sow!'

"I groaned and arched my back. I shoved my head back, and it grew smaller, eaten up by the pillows. The bedframe skewed as one leg slowly buckled under it. My husband glanced over his shoulder at me, an angry look, his fingers knotted behind his back.

"All of Landfall shouted and hovered on the walls.

" 'Here it comes!' shrieked the midwife. She reached down and eased out a tiny head, purple and angry, like a goblin.

"And then all the walls glowed red and green and sprouted large flowers. The door turned orange and burst open, and the neighbors and crew flooded in.

The ceiling billowed up, and aerialists tumbled through the rafters. A boy who had been hiding beneath the bed flew up laughing to where the ancient sky and stars shone through the roof.

"They held up the child, bloody on a platter."

Here the larl touched me for the first time, that heavy black paw like velvet on my knee, talons sheathed. "Can you understand?" he asked. "What it meant to me? All that, the first birth of human young on this planet, I experienced in an instant. I felt it with full human comprehension. I understood the personal tragedy and the community triumph, and the meaning of the lives and culture behind it. A second before I lived as an animal, with an animal's simple thoughts and hopes. Then I ate of your ancestor. I was lifted in an instant halfway to godhood.

"As the woman had hoped I would be. She had died with her child's birth foremost in her mind. She gave us that. She gave us more. She gave us language. We were wise animals before we ate her brain, and we were the People afterward. We owed her so much. And we knew what she wanted from us." The larl stroked my cheek with his great, velvety paw, the ivory claws sheathed but quivering slightly, as if about to awake.

I hardly dared breathe.

"That morning I entered Landfall, carrying the baby's sling in my mouth. It slept through most of the journey. At dawn I passed through the empty street as silently as I knew how. I came to the First Captain's house. I heard the murmur of voices within, the entire village assembled for worship. I tapped the door with one paw. There was sudden, astonished silence. Then slowly, fearfully, the door opened."

The larl was silent for a moment. "That was the beginning of the association of the People with humans. We were welcomed into your homes, and we helped with the hunting. It was a fair trade. Our food saved many lives that first winter. No one needed to know how the woman had perished, or how well we understood your kind.

"That child was your ancestor, Flip. Every few generations we take one of your family out hunting and taste his brains to maintain our closeness with your line. If you are a good boy and grow up to be as bold and honest, as intelligent and noble a man as your father, then perhaps it will be you we eat."

The larl presented his blunt muzzle to me in what might have been meant as a friendly smile. Perhaps not; the expression hangs unreadable, ambiguous in my mind even now. Then he stood and padded away into the friendly dark shadows of the Stone House.

I was sitting staring into the coals a few minutes later when my second-eldest sister—her face a featureless blaze of light, like an angel's—came into the room and saw me. She held out a hand, saying, "Come on, Flip, you're missing everything." And I went with her.

Did any of this actually happen? Sometimes I wonder. But it's growing late, and your parents are away. My room is small but snug, my bed warm but empty. We can burrow deep in the blankets and scare away the cavebears by playing the oldest winter games there are.

You're blushing! Don't tug away your hand. I'll be gone soon to some distant world to fight in a war for people who are as unknown to you as they are to me. Soldiers grow old slowly, you know. We're shipped frozen between the stars. When you are old and plump and happily surrounded by grandchildren, I'll still be young and thinking of you. You'll remember me then, and our thoughts will touch in the void. Will you have nothing to regret? Is that really what you want?

Come, don't be shy. Let's put the past aside and

get on with our lives. That's better. Blow the candle out, love, and there's an end to my tale.

All this happened long ago, on a planet whose name has been burned from my memory.

Gene Wolfe is undoubtedly one of the most acclaimed of modern science fiction writers. Perhaps best known for his massive tetralogy The Book of the New Sun, *Wolfe has won the Nebula Award, the World Fantasy Award, and the admiration of numerous critics and readers. In a Gene Wolfe story, things are seldom what you expect—and this "werwolf" transforms into a monster by not changing at all.*

Etymological note: The English word "werewolf" is traced by the Oxford English Dictionary to the year 1000, where it was used in the Laws of Cnut. *Gene Wolfe uses a less common spelling, one used by Thomas Malory. There is no evidence that there has ever been a variant spelled "werewolfe."*

The Hero As Werwolf

GENE WOLFE

Feet in the jungle that leave no mark!
Eyes that can see in the dark—the dark!
Tongue—give tongue to it! Hark! O Hark!
Once, twice and again!

—KIPLING,
"Hunting Song of the Seeonee Pack"

An owl shrieked, and Paul flinched. Fear, pavement, flesh, death, stone, dark, loneliness and blood made up Paul's world; the blood was all much the same, but the fear took several forms, and he had hardly seen another human being in the four years since his mother's death. At a night meeting in the park he was the red-cheeked young man at the end of the last row, with his knees together and his scrupulously clean hands (Paul was particularly careful about his nails) in his lap.

The speaker was fluent and amusing; he was clearly conversant with his subject—whatever it was—and he pleased his audience. Paul, the listener and watcher, knew many of the words he used; yet he had understood nothing in the past hour and a half, and sat wrapped in his stolen cloak and his own thoughts, seeming to listen, watching the crowd and the park—this, at least, was no ghost-house, no trap; the moon was up, nightblooming flowers scented the park air, and the trees lining the paths glowed with self-generated blue light; in the city, beyond the last hedge, the great buildings new and old were mountains lit from within.

Neither human nor master, a policeman strolled about the fringes of the audience, his eyes bright with stupidity. Paul could have killed him in less than a second, and was enjoying a dream of the policeman's death in some remote corner of his mind even while he concentrated on seeming to be one of *them.* A passenger rocket passed just under the stars, trailing luminous banners.

The meeting was over and he wondered if the rocket had in some way been the signal to end it. The masters did not use time, at least not as he did, as he had been taught by the thin woman who had been his mother in the little home she had made for them in the turret of a house that was once (she said) the Gorous'—now only a house too old to be destroyed. Neither did they use money, of which he like other old-style *Homo sapiens* still retained some racial memory, as of a forgotten god—a magic once potent that had lost all force.

The masters were rising, and there were tears and laughter and that third emotional tone that was neither amusement nor sorrow—the silken sound humans did not possess, but that Paul thought might express content, as the purring of a cat does, or community, like the cooing of doves. The policeman bobbed his hairy head, grinning, basking in the recognition, the approval, of those who had raised him from animality. *See* (said the motions of his hands, the writhings of his body) *the clothing you have given me. How nice! I take good care of my things because they are yours. See my weapon. I perform a useful function—if you did not have me, you would have to do it yourselves.*

If the policeman saw Paul, it would be over. He was too stupid, too silly, to be deceived by appearances as his masters were. He would never dare, thinking him a master, to meet Paul's eye, but he would look into his face seeking approval, and would see not what he was supposed to see but what was there. Paul ducked into the crowd, avoiding a beautiful woman with eyes the color of pearls, preferring to walk in the shadow of her fat escort where the policeman would not see him. The fat man took dust from a box shaped like the moon and rubbed it between his hands, releasing the smell of raspberries. It froze, and he sifted the tiny crystals of crimson ice over his shirt-front, grunting with satisfaction; then offered the box to the woman, who refused at first, only (three steps later) to accept when he pressed it on her.

They were past the policeman now. Paul dropped a few paces behind the couple, wondering if they were the ones tonight—if there would be meat tonight at all. For some, vehicles would be waiting. If the pair he had selected were among these, he would have to find others quickly.

They were not. They had entered the canyons between the buildings; he dropped farther behind, then turned aside.

Three minutes later he was in an alley a hundred meters ahead of them, waiting for them to pass the mouth. (The old trick was to cry like an infant, and he could do it well; but he had a new trick—a better trick, because too many had learned not to come down an alley when an infant cried. The new trick was a silver bell he had found in the house, small and very old. He took it from his pocket and removed the rag he had packed around the clapper. His dark cloak concealed him now, its hood pulled up to hide the pale gleam of his skin. He stood in a narrow doorway only a few meters away from the alley's mouth.)

They came. He heard the man's thick laughter, the woman's silken sound. She was a trifle silly from the dust the man had given her, and would be holding his arm as they walked, rubbing his thighs with hers. The man's blackshod foot and big belly thrust past the stonework of the building—there was a muffled moan.

The fat man turned, looking down the alley. Paul could see fear growing in the woman's face, cutting, too slowly, through the odor of raspberries. Another moan, and the man strode forward, fumbling in his pocket for an illuminator. The woman followed hesitantly (her skirt was of flowering vines the color of love, and white skin flashed in the interstices; a serpent of gold supported her breasts).

Someone was behind him. Pressed back against the metal door, he watched the couple as they passed. The fat man had gotten his illuminator out and held it over his head as he walked, looking into corners and doorways.

They came at them from both sides, a girl and an old, grey-bearded man. The fat man, the master, his genetic heritage revised for intellection and peace, had hardly time to turn before his mouth gushed blood. The woman whirled and ran, the vines of her skirt withering at her thought to give her leg-room, the serpent dropping from her breasts to strike with fangless jaws at the flying-haired girl who pursued her, then winding itself about the girl's ankles. The girl fell; but as the pearl-eyed woman passed, Paul broke her neck. For a moment he was too startled at the sight of other human beings to speak. Then he said, "These are mine."

The old man, still bent over the fat man's body, snapped: "Ours. We've been here an hour and more." His voice was the creaking of steel hinges, and Paul thought of ghost-houses again.

"I followed them from the park." The girl, black-haired, grey-eyed when the light from the alley-mouth struck her face, was taking the serpent from around her legs—it was once more a lifeless thing of soft metal mesh. Paul picked up the woman's corpse and wrapped it in his cloak. "You gave me no warning," he said. "You must have seen me when I passed you."

The girl looked toward the old man. Her eyes said she would back him if he fought, and Paul decided he would throw the woman's body at her.

"Somebody'll come soon," the old man said. "And I'll need Janie's help to carry this one. We each take what we got ourselves—that's fair. Or we whip you. My girl's worth a man in a fight, and you'll find I'm still worth a man myself, old as I be."

"Give me the picking of his body. This one has nothing."

The girl's bright lips drew back from strong white teeth. From somewhere under the tattered skirt she wore, she had produced a long knife, and sudden light from a window high above the alley ran along the edge of the stained blade; the girl might be a dangerous opponent, as the old man claimed, but Paul could sense the femaleness, the woman-rut from where he stood. "No," her father said. "You got good clothes. I need these." He looked up at the window fearfully, fumbling with buttons.

"His cloak will hang on you like a blanket."

"We'll fight. Take the woman and go away, or we'll fight."

He could not carry both, and the fat man's meat would be tainted by the testicles. When Paul was young and there had been no one but his mother to do the killing, they had sometimes eaten old males; he never did so now. He slung the pearl-eyed woman across his shoulders and trotted away.

Outside the alley the streets were well lit, and a few passers-by stared at him and the dark burden he carried. Fewer still, he knew, would suspect him of being what he was—he had learned the trick of dressing as the masters did, even of wearing their expressions. He wondered how the black-haired girl and the old man would fare in their ragged clothes. *They must live very near.*

His own place was that in which his mother had borne him, a place high in a house built when humans were the masters. Every door was nailed tight and boarded up; but on one side a small garden lay between two wings, and in a corner of this garden, behind a bush where the shadows were thick even at noon, the bricks had fallen away. The lower floors were full of rotting furniture and the smell of rats and mold, but high in his wooden turret the walls were still dry and the sun came in by day at eight windows. He carried his burden there and dropped her in a corner. It was important that his clothes be kept as clean as the masters kept theirs, though he lacked their facilities. He pulled his cloak from the body and brushed it vigorously.

"What are you going to do with me?" the dead woman said behind him.

"Eat," he told her. "What did you think I was going to do?"

"I didn't know." And then: "I've read of you creatures, but I didn't think you really existed."

"We were the masters once," he said. He was not sure he still believed it, but it was what his mother had taught him. "This house was built in those days—that's why you won't wreck it: you're afraid." He had finished with the cloak; he hung it up and turned to face her, sitting on the bed. "You're afraid of waking the old times," he said. She lay slumped in the corner, and though her mouth moved, her eyes were only half open, looking at nothing.

"We tore a lot of them down," she said.

"If you're going to talk, you might as well sit up straight." He lifted her by the shoulders and propped her in the corner. A nail protruded from the wall there; he twisted a lock of her hair on it so her head would not loll; her hair was the rose shade of a little girl's dress, and soft but slightly sticky.

"I'm dead, you know."

"No, you're not." They always said this (except, sometimes, for the children) and his mother had always denied it. He felt that he was keeping up a family tradition.

"Dead," the pearl-eyed woman said. "Never, never, never. Another year, and everything would have been all right. I want to cry, but I can't breathe to."

"Your kind lives a long time with a broken neck," he told her. "But you'll die eventually."

"I am dead now."

He was not listening. There were other humans in the city; he had always known that, but only now, with the sight of the old man and the girl, had their existence seemed real to him.

"I thought you were all gone," the pearl-eyed dead woman said thinly. "All gone long ago, like a bad dream."

Happy with his new discovery, he said: "Why do you set traps for us, then? Maybe there are more of us than you think."

"There can't be many of you. How many people do you kill in a year?" Her mind was lifting the sheet from his bed, hoping to smother him with it; but he had seen that trick many times.

"Twenty or thirty." (He was boasting.)

"So many."

"When you don't get much besides meat, you need a lot of it. And then I only eat the best parts—why not? I kill twice a month or more except when it's cold, and I could kill enough for two or three if I had to." (*The girl had had a knife.* Knives were bad, except for cutting up afterward. But knives left blood behind. He would kill for her—she could stay here and take care of his clothes, prepare their food. He thought of himself walking home under a new moon, and seeing her face in the window of the turret.) To the dead woman he said: "You saw that girl? With the black hair? She and the old man killed your husband, and I'm going to bring her here to live." He stood and began to walk up and down the small room, soothing himself with the sound of his own footsteps.

"He wasn't my husband." The sheet dropped limply now that he was no longer on the bed. "Why didn't you change? When the rest changed their genes?"

"I wasn't alive then."

"You must have received some tradition."

"We didn't want to. We are the human beings."

"Everyone wanted to. Your old breed had worn out the planet; even with much better technology we're still starved for energy and raw materials because of what you did."

"There hadn't been enough to eat before," he said, "but when so many changed there was a lot. So why should more change?"

It was a long time before she answered, and he knew the body was stiffening. That was bad, because as long as she lived in it the flesh would stay sweet; when the life was gone, he would have to cut it up quickly before the stuff in her lower intestine tainted the rest.

"Strange evolution," she said at last. "Man become food for men."

"I don't understand the second word. Talk so I know what you're saying." He kicked her in the chest to emphasize his point, and knocked her over; he heard a rib snap. . . . She did not reply, and he lay down on the bed. His mother had told him there was a meeting place in the city where men gathered on certain special nights—but he had forgotten (if he had ever known) what those nights were.

"That isn't even metalanguage," the dead woman said, "only children's talk."

"Shut up."

After a moment he said: "I'm going out. If you can make your body stand, and get out of here, and get down to the ground floor, and find the way out, then you may be able to tell someone about me and have the police waiting when I come back." He went out and closed the door, then stood patiently outside for five minutes.

When he opened it again, the corpse stood erect with her hands on his table, her tremors upsetting the painted metal circus-figures he had had since he was a child—the girl acrobat, the clown with his hoop and trained pig. One of her legs would not straighten. "Listen," he said, "you're not going to do it. I told you all that because I knew you'd think of it yourself. They always do, and they never make it. The farthest I've ever had anyone get was out the door and to the top of the steps. She fell down them, and I found her at the bottom when I came back. You're dead. Go to sleep."

The blind eyes had turned toward him when he began to speak, but they no longer watched him now. The face, which had been beautiful, was now entirely the face of a corpse. The cramped leg crept toward the floor as he watched, halted, began to creep downward again. Sighing, he lifted the dead woman off her feet, replaced her in the corner, and went down the creaking stairs to find the black-haired girl.

"There has been quite a few to come after her," her father said, "since we come into town. Quite a few." He sat in the back of the bus, on the rearmost seat that went completely across the back like a sofa.

"But you're the first ever to find us here. The others, they hear about her, and leave a sign at the meetin'."

Paul wanted to ask where it was such signs were left, but held his peace.

"You know there ain't many folks at *all* anymore," her father went on. "And not many of *them* is women. And *damn few* is young girls like my Janie. I had a fella here that wanted her two weeks back—he said he hadn't had no real woman in two years; well, I didn't like the way he said *real*, so I said what did he do, and he said he fooled around with what he killed, sometimes, before they got cold. You never did like that, did you?"

Paul said he had not.

"How'd you find this dump here?"

"Just look around." He had searched the area in ever-widening circles, starting at the alley in which he had seen the girl and her father. They had one of the masters' cold boxes to keep their ripe kills in (as he did himself), but there was the stink of clotted blood about the dump nonetheless. It was behind a high fence, closer to the park than he would have thought possible.

"When we come, there was a fella living here. Nice fella, a German. Name was Curtain—something like that. He went sweet on my Janie right off. Well, I wasn't too taken with having a foreigner in the family, but he took us in and let us settle in the big station wagon. Told me he wanted to wed Janie, but I said no, she's too young. Wait a year, I says, and take her with my blessing. She wasn't but fourteen then. Well, one night the German fella went out and I guess they got him, because he never come back. We moved into this here bus then for the extra room."

His daughter was sitting at his feet, and he reached a crooked-fingered hand down and buried it in her midnight hair. She looked up at him and smiled. "Got a pretty face, ain't she?" he said.

Paul nodded.

"She's a mite thin, you was going to say. Well, that's true. I do my best to provide, but I'm feared, and not shamed to admit to it."

"The ghost-houses," Paul said.

"What's that?"

"That's what I've always called them. I don't get to talk to many other people."

"Where the doors shut on you—lock you in."

"Yes."

"That ain't ghosts—now don't you think I'm one of them fools don't believe in them. I know better. But that ain't ghosts. They're always looking, don't you see, for people they think ain't right. That's us. It's electricity does it. You ever been caught like that?"

Paul nodded. He was watching the delicate swelling Janie's breasts made in the fabric of her filthy shirt, and only half listening to her father; but the memory penetrated the young desire that half embarrassed him, bringing back fear. The windows of the bus had been set to black, and the light inside was dim—still it was possible some glimmer showed outside. *There should be no lights in the dump.* He listened, but heard only katydids singing in the rubbish.

"They thought I was a master—I dress like one," he said. "That's something you should do. They were going to test me. I turned the machine over and broke it, and jumped through a window." He had been on the sixth floor, and had been saved by landing in the branches of a tree whose bruised twigs and torn leaves exuded an acrid incense that to him was the very breath of panic still; but it had not been the masters, or the instrument-filled examination room, or the jump from the window that had terrified him, but waiting in the ghost-room while the walls talked to one another in words he could sometimes, for a few seconds, nearly understand.

"It wouldn't work for me—got too many things wrong with me. Lines in my face; even got a wart—they never do."

"Janie could."

The old man cleared his throat; it was a thick sound, like water in a downspout in a hard rain. "I been meaning to talk to you about her; about why those other fellas I told you about never took her—not that I'd of let some of them: Janie's the only family I got left. But I ain't so particular I don't want to see her married at all—not a bit of it. Why, we wouldn't of come here if it weren't for Janie. When her monthly come, I said to myself, she'll be wantin' a man, and what're you goin' to do way out here? Though the country was gettin' bad anyway, I must say. If they'd of had real dogs, I believe they would have got us several times."

He paused, perhaps thinking of those times, the lights in the woods at night and the running, perhaps only trying to order his thoughts. Paul waited, scratching an ankle, and after a few seconds the old man said: "We didn't want to do this, you know, us Pendeltons. That's mine and Janie's name—Pendelton. Janie's Augusta Jane, and I'm Emmitt J."

"Paul Gorou," Paul said.

"Pleased to meet you, Mr. Gorou. When the time come, they took one whole side of the family. They were the Worthmore Pendeltons; that's what we always called them, because most of them lived thereabouts. Cousins of mine they was, and second cousins. We was the Evershaw Pendeltons, and they didn't take none of us. Bad blood, they said—too much wrong to be worth fixing, or too much that mightn't get fixed right, and then show up again. My ma—she's alive then—she always swore it was her sister Lillian's boy that did it to us. The whole side of his head was pushed in. You know what I mean? They used to say a cow'd kicked him when he was small, but it wasn't so—he's just born like that. He could talk some—there's those that set a high value on that—but the slobber'd run out of his mouth. My ma said if it wasn't for him we'd have got in sure. The only other thing was my sister Clara that was born with a bad eye—blind, you know, and something wrong with the lid of it too. But she was just as sensible as anybody. Smart as a whip. So I would say it's likely Ma was right. Same thing with your family, I suppose?"

"I think so. I don't really know."

"A lot of it was die-beetees. They could fix it, but if there was other things too they just kept them out. Of course when it was over there wasn't no medicine for them no more, and they died off pretty quick. When I was young, I used to think that was what it meant: die-beetees—you died away. It's really sweetening of the blood. You heard of it?"

Paul nodded.

"I'd like to taste some sometime, but I never come to think of that while there was still some of them around."

"If they weren't masters—"

"Didn't mean I'd of killed them," the old man said quickly. "Just got one to gash his arm a trifle so I could taste of it. Back then—that would be twenty aught nine, close to fifty years gone it is now—there was several I knowed that was just my age. . . . What I was meaning to say at the beginning was that us Pendeltons never figured on anythin' like this. We'd farmed, and we meant to keep on, grow our own truck and breed our own stock. Well, that did for a time, but it wouldn't keep."

Paul, who had never considered living off the land, or even realized that it was possible to do so, could only stare at him.

"You take chickens, now. Everybody always said there wasn't nothing easier than chickens, but that was when there was medicine you could put in the water to keep off the sickness. Well, the time come when you couldn't get it no more than you could get a can of beans in those stores of theirs that don't use money or cards or anything a man can understand. My dad had two hundred in the flock when the sickness struck, and it took every hen inside of four days. You wasn't supposed to eat them that had died sick, but we did it. Plucked 'em and canned 'em—by that time our old locker that plugged in the wall wouldn't work. When the chickens was all canned, Dad saddled a horse we had then and rode twenty-five miles to a place where the new folks grew chickens to eat themselves. I guess you know what happened to him, though—they wouldn't sell, and they wouldn't trade. Finally he begged them. He was a Pendelton, and used to cry when he told of it. He said the harder he begged them the scareder they got. Well, finally he reached out and grabbed one by the leg—he was on his knees to them—and he hit him alongside the face with a book he was carryin'."

The old man rocked backward and forward in his seat as he spoke, his eyes half closed. "There wasn't no more seed but what was saved from last year then, and the corn went so bad the ears wasn't no longer than a soft dick. No bullets for Dad's old gun, nowhere to buy new traps when what we had was lost. Then one day just afore Christmas these here machines just started tearing up our fields. They had forgot about us, you see. We threw rocks but it didn't do no good, and about midnight one came right through the house. There wasn't no one living than but Ma and Dad and brother Tom and me and Janie. Janie wasn't but just a little bit of a thing. The machine got Tom in the leg with a piece of two-by-four—rammed the splintery end into him, you see. The rot got to the wound and he died a week after; it was winter then, and we was living in a place me and Dad built up on the hill out of branches and saplings."

"About Janie," Paul said. "I can understand how you might not want to let her go—"

"Are you sayin' you don't want her?" The old man shifted in his seat, and Paul saw that his right hand had moved closed to the crevice where the horizontal surface joined the vertical. The crevice was a trifle too wide, and he thought he knew what was hidden there. He was not afraid of the old man, and it had crossed his mind more than once that if he killed him there would be nothing to prevent his taking Janie.

"I want her," he said. "I'm not going away without her." He stood up without knowing why.

"There's been others said the same thing. I would go, you know, to the meetin' in the regular way; come back next month, and the fella'd be waitin.' "

The old man was drawing himself to his feet, his jaw outthrust belligerently. "They'd see her," he said, "and they'd talk a lot, just like you, about how good they'd take care of her, though there wasn't a one brought a lick to eat when he come to call. Me and Janie, sometimes we ain't et for three, four days— they never take account of that. Now here, you look at her."

Bending swiftly, he took his daughter by the arm; she rose gracefully, and he spun her around. "Her ma was a pretty woman," he said, "but not as pretty as what she is, even if she is so thin. And she's got sense too—I don't keer what they say."

Janie looked at Paul with frightened, animal eyes. He gestured, he hoped gently, for her to come to him, but she only pressed herself against her father.

"You can talk to her. She understands."

Paul started to speak, then had to stop to clear his throat. At last he said: "Come here, Janie. You're going to live with me. We'll come back and see your father sometimes."

Her hand slipped into her shirt; came out holding a knife. She looked at the old man, who caught her wrist and took the knife from her and dropped it on the seat behind him, saying, "You're going to have to be a mite careful around her for a bit, but if you don't hurt her none she'll take to you pretty quick. She wants to take to you now—I can see it in the way she looks."

Paul nodded, accepting the girl from him almost as he might have accepted a package, holding her by her narrow waist.

"And when you get a mess of grub she likes to cut them up, sometimes, while they're still movin' around. Mostly I don't allow it, but if you do—anyway, once in a while—she'll like you better for it."

Paul nodded again. His hand, as if of its own volition, had strayed to the girl's smoothly rounded hip, and he felt such desire as he had never known before.

"Wait," the old man said. His breath was foul in the close air. "You listen to me now. You're just a young fella and I know how you feel, but you don't know how I do. I want you to understand before you go. I love my girl. You take good care of her or I'll see to you. And if you change your mind about wanting her, don't you just turn her out. I'll take her back, you hear?"

Paul said, "All right."

"Even a bad man can love his child. You remember that, because it's true."

Her husband took Janie by the hand and led her out of the wrecked bus. She was looking over her shoulder, and he knew that she expected her father to drive a knife into his back.

They had seen the boy—a brown-haired, slightly freckled boy of nine or ten with an armload of books—on a corner where a small, columniated building concealed the entrance to the monorail, and the streets were wide and empty. The children of the masters were seldom out so late. Paul waved to him, not daring to speak, but attempting to convey by his posture that he wanted to ask directions; he wore the black cloak and scarlet-slashed shirt, the gold sandals and wide-legged black film trousers proper to an evening of pleasure. On his arm Janie was all in red, her face covered by a veil dotted with tiny synthetic bloodstones. Gem-studded veils were a fashion now nearly extinct among the women of the masters, but one that served to conceal the blankness of eye that betrayed Janie, as Paul had discovered, almost instantly. She gave a soft moan of hunger as she saw the boy, and clasped Paul's arm more tightly. Paul waved again.

The boy halted as though waiting for them, but when they were within five meters he turned and dashed away. Janie was after him before Paul could stop her. The boy dodged between two buildings and raced through to the next street; Paul was just in time to see Janie follow him into a doorway in the center of the block.

He found her clear-soled platform shoes in the vestibule, under a four-dimensional picture of Hugo de Vries. De Vries was in the closing years of his life, and in the few seconds it took Paul to pick up the shoes and conceal them behind an aquarium of phosphorescent cephalopods, had died, rotted to dust, and undergone rebirth as a fissioning cell in his mother's womb with all the labyrinth of genetics still before him.

The lower floors, Paul knew, were apartments. He had entered them sometimes when he could find no prey on the streets. There would be a school at the top.

A confused, frightened-looking woman stood in an otherwise empty corridor, a disheveled library book lying open at her feet. As Paul pushed past her, he could imagine Janie knocking her out of the way, and the woman's horror at the savage, exultant face glimpsed beneath her veil.

There were elevators, a liftshaft, and a downshaft, all clustered in an alcove. *The boy would not have waited for an elevator with Janie close behind him. . . .*

The liftshaft floated Paul as spring-water floats a cork. Thickened by conditioning agents, the air remained a gas; enriched with added oxygen, it stimulated his whole being, though it was as viscous as corn syrup when he drew it into his lungs. Far above, suspended (as it seemed) in crystal and surrounded by the books the boy had thrown down at her, he saw Janie with her red gown billowing around her and her white legs flashing. She was going to the top, apparently to the uppermost floor, and he reasoned that the boy, having led her there, would jump into the downshaft to escape her. He got off at the eighty-fifth floor, opened the hatch to the downshaft, and was rewarded by seeing the boy only a hundred meters above him. It was a simple matter then to wait on the landing and pluck him out of the sighing column of thickened air.

The boy's pointed, narrow face, white with fear under a tan, turned up toward him. "Don't," the boy said. "Please, sir, good master—" but Paul clamped him under his left arm, and with a quick wrench of his right broke his neck.

Janie was swimming head down with the downshaft current, her mouth open and full of eagerness, and her black hair like a cloud about her head. She had lost her veil. Paul showed her the boy and stepped into the shaft with her. The hatch slammed behind him, and the motion of the air ceased.

He looked at Janie. She had stopped swimming and was staring hungrily into the dead boy's face. He said, "Something's wrong," and she seemed to understand, though it was possible that she only caught the fear in his voice. The hatch would not open, and slowly the current in the shaft was reversing, lifting them; he tried to swim against it but the effort was hopeless. When they were at the top, the dead boy began to talk; Janie put her hand over his mouth to muffle the sound. The hatch at the landing opened, and they stepped out onto the hundred-and-first floor. A voice from a loudspeaker in the wall said: "*I am sorry to detain you, but there is reason to think you have undergone a recent deviation from the optimal development pattern. In a few minutes I will arrive in person to provide counseling; while you are waiting it may be useful for us to review what is meant by 'optimal development.' Look at the projection.*

"In infancy the child first feels affection for its mother, the provider of warmth and food. . . ." There was a door at the other end of the room, and Paul swung a heavy chair against it, making a din that almost drowned out the droning speaker.

"Later one's peer-group becomes, for a time, all-important—or nearly so. The boys and girls you see are attending a model school in Armstrong. Notice that no tint is used to mask the black of space above their airtent."

The lock burst from the doorframe, but a remotely actuated hydraulic cylinder snapped it shut each time a blow from the chair drove it open. Paul slammed his shoulder against it, and before it could close again put his knee where the shattered bolt-socket had been. A chrome-plated steel rod as thick as a finger had dropped from the chair when his blows had smashed the wood and plastic holding it; after a moment of incomprehension, Janie dropped the dead boy, wedged the rod between the door and the jamb, and slipped through. He was following her when the rod lifted, and the door swung shut on his foot.

He screamed and screamed again, and then, in the echoing silence that followed, heard the loudspeaker mumbling about education, and Janie's sobbing, indrawn breath. Through the crack between the door and the frame, the two-centimeter space held in existence by what remained of his right foot, he could see the livid face and blind, malevolent eyes of the dead boy, whose will still held the steel rod suspended in air. "Die," Paul shouted at him. "Die! You're dead!" The rod came crashing down.

"This young woman," the loudspeaker said, *"has chosen the profession of medicine. She will be a physician, and she says now that she was born for that.*

She will spend the remainder of her life in relieving the agonies of disease."

Several minutes passed before he could make Janie understand what it was she had to do.

"After her five years' training in basic medical techniques, she will specialize in surgery for another three years before—"

It took Janie a long time to bite through his Achilles tendon; when it was over, she began to tear at the ligaments that held the bones of the tarsus to the leg. Over the pain he could feel the hot tears washing the blood from his foot.

One of the classic gems of the scientific vampire genre is Damon Knight's "Eripmav," a cleverly executed short-short that gives the vampire legend a sneaky twist or two. (Spell the title backwards). It seemed a shame that there was no equivalent story in the lycanthropic canon . . . until now.

John J. Ordover is notorious for both his compact prose and bad puns. Recent stories by Ordover have appeared in Splatterpunks II: Over the Edge *and* The Ultimate Silver Surfer.

flowereW

JOHN J. ORDOVER

DNA, it turned out, was much more fragile than anyone had anticipated. On Earth, the double-helix was firm, or at least firm enough that if you started out life as a human being, you pretty much ended it that way. When people left Earth for other planets, they confidently expected that pattern would continue.

People were wrong.

Centrex IV was no bigger than Earth, and very Earthlike in appearance, aspect, and smell—which is probably what made the sudden appearance of ISD—Involuntary Shapeshifter's Disease—so surprising. But it was the reluctance of scientists to learn from folklore and accept the obvious that kept the cause from being identified for so long. Light, reflected from Centrex's single large moon, had a destabilizing effect on human DNA. The human body would re-form, taking on the shapes of various Centrexian animals. Sometimes this was just amusing, as when at some dinner party someone found themselves transformed into a *Bornice*, a kind of Centrexian monkey. Sometimes it was tragic, as when someone changed to fish-like form far from water. And sometimes it was deadly dangerous. That's when they call me.

There'd been reports of formerly human *Kathus Carnivorous Centrexia* preying on the settlers in the woods near New Aspen. The scientists had lots of reasons why *Kathus* wasn't a wolf, but that's what it looked like, and sounded like, and hunted like, except that this one had human intelligence to work with. It was my job to bring him in.

So there I was, squatting in the woods just outside New Aspen, snow everywhere, the Centrexian moon shining brightly overhead, waiting for the *Katha* to show up. See, as long as he was just helping himself to a few deer here and there, nobody minded, but when he starting picking off settlers the city fathers figured that might hurt the immigration drive a bit. So they called my boss, and two days later there I was, freezing my butt off.

I did have one advantage, though. No, it wasn't a gun filled with silver bullets—give the science guys credit, after they figured out the moon thing, that's the first thing they tried. It didn't work. It took them a while, but through trial and error they came up with a gadget that did work. It was a flashlight, basically, but with full UV range and a little extra kicker—a reflector coated with Terran DNA. They were still working on the theory behind it, but it did what it was supposed to do—the lab boys proved that—and I left the whys and wherefores to others.

So all I had to do was track the *Katha* down, zap him with the flash, and instead of a ferocious super-intelligent carnivore I'd be facing a very confused human being. Those I could handle easy.

That was the plan. And the plan might have worked

if the *Katha* hadn't jumped me from the side, his sharp, cold claws cutting right through my flak-jacket and into my ribs. I fell, shouting with pain, and the flashlight flew off into the darkness.

His jaws came for my throat, but I managed to pull my legs up under him, get some leverage, and with a thrust that made my shattered ribs rub together with truly shocking pain, I tossed him up and off of me.

I don't remember how I got to my feet, but somehow I did. Then I was running, running as quickly as I could, the tree branches scraping at my face and eyes. He was after me in seconds. I could hear his body crashing heedlessly through the forest after me, then I could hear him panting, then the soft footfalls of his padded paws right behind me. Thinking quickly, I reached for my belt. I waited until I could feel the *Katha*'s hot breath on the back of my legs, and did the only thing I could.

See, I figured that what triggered the change was light reflected by Terran DNA, any light. That's what the lab boys had shown, that's what was in the flashlight. So that's what I had to come up with. So there, in the brightly lit woods, I did the only thing I could to stop the *Katha*.

I mooned him.

Bertram Chandler was part of John W. Campbell's stable of writers in the Astounding *of the forties and fifties, a professional sailor, and a resident of Australia. None of which would lead one to think that he'd be writing a story with interesting implications about gender roles. But while the narrator of "Frontier of the Dark" is decidedly macho, it doesn't mean that he's the* strongest *character in the story. . . .*

Frontier of the Dark

A. BERTRAM CHANDLER

Falsen had never liked cats, and cats had never liked him. That was one of the reasons why Captain Canning, master of the interstellar ship *Etruria*, had ordered that his second pilot be marooned on Antares VI, an inhospitable planet barely capable of supporting human life and deemed by the Federation not worthy of the time, trouble and expense of any colonization project. At that, Falsen was lucky that the mutual hostility between himself and the feline species brought only marooning as its consequence. Others like himself had been tossed out of air locks without spacesuits, had been carefully shot with specially manufactured bullets, had, in fact, been purged from the body politic by many and divers methods more interesting than pleasant. But Falsen had once saved Canning's life at considerable risk to his own—on the occasion when the bloody-minded Coralians overran and all but annihilated the trading post on their planet—and, as Canning remarked to his senior officers, there *are* limits, you know . . . And, Canning had added, he couldn't be *certain*—

So, at the appointed time, the whine of the Mannschen Drive generators had sagged from the supersonic to the subsonic and *Etruria*, navigating once more in normal spacetime, had made a gingerly approach to the sixth planet of the ruddy sun, had thrown herself into an orbit around this planet. Number Three boat had been readied, and to the boat Falsen, under heavy escort, was taken. He could have broken free even then, he could have slipped out of the manacles around his wrists with ease. But there were too many of the crew to see him off, and Wilbraham, the commander, was carrying a heavy, old-fashioned automatic pistol, an outmoded blunderbuss of a thing that fired, as Falsen well knew, slugs of metal rather than bolts of energy. So he went into the boat, which was to be piloted by Kent, his own junior, and Wilbraham, still carrying his weapon, came too, and Minnie, the ship's cat, spat one last malediction at him before the air lock doors closed.

They set him down on a spongy plain that was more than half swamp, with the last of the daylight almost gone and a thin, persistent rain drifting down from the overcast sky. Falsen shivered as they pushed him towards the air lock door. "You might," he protested, "have let me bring some stores, some heavy weather gear—"

"*You* won't need 'em," Wilbraham told him. "You're lucky," he gestured with his pistol, "that I didn't use this. If I thought that you had the ghost of a chance, I would."

"You could, you know, sir," volunteered Kent. "Shot while attempting to escape—"

"Escape?" asked Wilbraham. "To *what*? He's welcome to all that he finds here. Although I still think that the Old Man was too soft-hearted. *Out*, Falsen. And"—this last in tones of great irony—"good hunting!"

So it was that Falsen stood ankle deep in mud and, with upraised fists, cursed *Etruria*, cursed the boat that had brought him here to this dismal world. The fast fading flare of the lifeboat's jets was reflected from his eyes, made them glow like those of some wild animal. And then there was only the darkness and the falling rain, and the solitary figure clad in low shoes, in shirt and shorts, dressed not for pioneering but for the control room of the interstellar liner from which he was forever barred.

Cursing, Falsen soon realized, would get him nowhere. With one hand he brushed his wet, pale blond hair away from his eyes, then his stocky figure stiffened as he surveyed his surroundings. The rain was not heavy enough to impair visibility, although heavy enough to soak and chill. Enough light still remained, once the castaway's eyes had become accustomed to the darkness following the flare of the lifeboat's departure, for him to make out the horizon—a dim, deeper blackness against the blackness of the overcast sky. Featureless was this line of demarcation, level, unbroken by tree, hill or building, so straight that for one panic-stricken moment Falsen thought that he had been set down upon some tiny islet in the midst of a great, calm sea. Fighting down his fears he tried to remember all that he had ever read, in Pilot Books and Astrogating Directions, of Antares and its worlds. He remembered vaguely that this planet's equatorial zone was encircled by a broad belt of almost level plain and swampland; that it was only in the equatorial zone that temperatures were endurable by Terran standards.

Once again he turned in a slow circle, eyes, ears and nose alert for any indication of life—of life, and warmth, and food. He heard nothing but the steady susurrus of the rain, smelt nothing but dampness and vegetable decay and—and—Surely, he decided, that was smoke, wood smoke, an elusive fragrance that did no more than hint at the presence of some kind of intelligent life. He shook himself then, and purposively started to trudge in the direction from which he judged the faint odor had come. The mud slopped over the tops of his shoes, making his feet even colder, his saturated clothing clung clammily to his body yet, as the exercise warmed him, with a certain moist heat of its own. One hand, as he walked, explored, not for the first time, the pitifully inadequate contents of his pockets—a combination tool that combined pocket-knife with screw driver, tiny adjustable spanner, cork-screw and bottle opener, a pocket lighter, a sodden pack of cigarettes. Whatever he might find at the end of his walk he was armed, after a fashion. He had a cutting tool or weapon, and he had fire. He had, too, his own physical strength and the ability to look after himself in unarmed combat.

Stronger grew the smoke odor, and stronger, and with it another smell, not unpleasant—a smell that in other circumstances would have promised more than the warmth and dryness to which he looked forward now with increasing certainty—yet, paradoxically, a smell that destroyed his hopes of food. He could see something ahead now—a hill that humped its not inconsiderable bulk well above the featureless horizon, halfway up whose denser blackness flickered a ruddy circle of dim light, the entrance, he decided, of a cave—a cave in which dwelt somebody who, in all probability, was a castaway like himself, somebody with the same needs and desires—or, he amended, similar needs and desires. For he was, by this time, reasonably certain that his co-ruler of this barren world was a woman.

He walked cautiously now, treading carefully to avoid snapping the twigs and branches of the low shrubs that covered the relatively dry slopes of the hill. The other, whoever she was, might be armed. And, armed or not, too sudden an awakening from her sleep might make her—vicious. Cautiously he climbed the hill, carefully—yet with a mounting excitement in his veins. It was only now, at this moment, that he fully realized how lonely he had been. Appreciatively he savored the fragrance of the fire, of those other scents that most men would never have noticed, especially at this distance. At last he was at the cave mouth, was peering inside.

The fire burned low, casting a dull, crimson radiance over the clean sand floor, over the pile of twigs and small branches a little to one side of it, over the neatly folded clothing and the huddle of blankets. Walking slowly and softly, scarcely breathing, Falsen entered the cave and, skirting the fire, made his silent way to the little heap of clothes.

Curiously, he picked up the garments one by one. They were a woman's, as he had known, and they bore, as he was now discovering, insignia similar to those on his own uniform. This person had been, as he had been, in the employ of Interstellar Mail Lines. He looked at the epaulettes of the shirt—two silver braid bands on scarlet—and thought: *Nurse*.

Meanwhile, he was cold. He turned to walk to the fire, stepped inadvertently on a dry twig. He turned again, this time with no thought for caution, to see the blankets tossed violently aside and the white figure of a girl leap from them. He caught her in mid-leap, forced her down to the sandy floor. He felt the flesh of her naked shoulders shudder and crawl beneath his hands, flinched from the animal hate that glared from the pale, almost colorless, blue eyes. He bared his teeth in a mirthless grin, said, "Steady, my dear. Dog doesn't eat dog, you know."

Suddenly she ceased to struggle. Falsen got to his feet, gave her his hand to help her up. In the light of the dying fire she looked unreal, somehow, her flesh gleaming with a shimmering insubstantiality. Yet her actions were prosaic enough. She dusted the sand from her body, then walked to her clothing and started to dress. Falsen watched her—the slim, graceful lines of her, the high cheekbones, the pale blond hair and, when she spoke, the strong, white teeth.

She said, her voice low and husky: "Who are you, and where do you come from?"

"Falsen. Nicholas Falsen, late second pilot of *Etruria.* They decided that they didn't like my company. And so—"

"Why didn't they kill you?"

"Some of them wanted to. But I saved the captain's life once." He said sneeringly, "I suppose you were equally obliging."

"Perhaps," she said tonelessly. "I wouldn't be—*now.* I was dumped here, with enough stores to last me about six months. I've been here for three."

"Then you must be from *Calabria.* She was about three months ahead of us."

"Yes. I'm from *Calabria.*" Dressed now, she turned to look at him as he stood in the firelight, stared at his soaked clothing and muddy shoes. She said, "I heard no rockets. You must have come a long way. Wouldn't it have been better to have left your clothes?"

"I didn't know who or what I might find," he told her. "Then there's convention, and training, and all the rest of it. I notice that you've dressed."

"So I have," she admitted. "But as *ex*-officers of Interstellar Mail"— she laughed bitterly—"we must dress the part."

"You haven't told me *your* name."

"Veerhausen. Linda Veerhausen. But you're cold, and I'm no hostess. Get out of your wet things and between those blankets, and I'll bring you something hot—"

"But I wouldn't take your stores."

"Rubbish. I've hardly touched them. There's a sort of crayfish in these pools that's not too bad eating—not the same as red meat, but it serves. But this calls for a can of stew."

She went into a smaller cave opening off the main one, and by the time that Falsen was between the blankets she was back, carrying the can of stew, hot, the smoke still spiraling from the tube of chemicals that had heated it. Falsen took his share gratefully and then, exhausted by the emotional and physical strains of the last few days, slept soundly. The girl built up the fire and sat beside it, alert, unsleeping.

Outside the cave the steady whisper of the rain died, and finally ceased.

Falsen was awake with the dawn, snapping from sound sleep into instant awareness. He threw the blankets to one side, walked on bare, silent feet to the cave entrance. The girl, standing on the little ledge overlooking the downward slope of the hill, sensed his coming, turned to greet him. A smile flickered briefly over her sullen face. "This is it," she said. "Your first morning on Antares VI. At that, it's better than *my* first morning."

Low to the east a sullen, red glow stained the gray clouds. Slowly it spread, spread and lifted, suffusing all the overcast with dull crimson. And then there was a sun in the sky, Antares, with upper and lower limbs vaguely defined, and all the pools and channels of the swamp glimmering like blood among the grayness of vegetation.

"What now?" asked Falsen.

"Breakfast," said the girl. "But we have to catch it first. I've been keeping the stores they left me as an emergency ration. Look!" she pointed, "that pool there, shaped like a horseshoe. That's where I get my crayfish. I'll show you."

"Do we go . . . as we are?"

"You can dress, if you like. But as we are is better for things like crayfish. If it were sheep, now—" She licked her lips with a red tongue.

"Don't!" said Falsen sharply.

The girl ignored him. "On my last leave," she said.

"I *knew* then. One morning, but finer than this, in the Scottish Highlands—" She smiled reminiscently. "I often wonder who, or what, that shepherd blamed."

"And yet, knowing the risk, you kept in the Service?"

"Why not? As a nurse I had access to the drugs—and saw to it that there was a sudden and complete mortality among the cats. If it hadn't been for that passenger, and her pampered Persian— And now"—she spat viciously—*"crayfish!"*

"Let's go and get 'em," said Falsen. "I'm hungry."

Together they made their way down the hillside, down to the pool. The spongy vegetation was soggy underfoot, still saturated with the night's rain. The rising of the sun had brought a steamy, uncomfortable warmth to the air and Falsen was thankful that he had not bothered to dress, thankful in a way that there was only his smooth, hairless skin to get muddy, that the discomfort was no worse. At the pool that Linda had pointed out to him they stopped, and there the girl made a careful search of the vegetation along the bank. She selected, finally, a long tendril having at its end an elongated, yellowish berry. This, with her left hand, she lowered into the water. Watching, Falsen saw that there were tiny fish in the pool, and that somebody, or something, with very weak eyesight might just possibly mistake the berry for one of the fish.

"The thing to do," explained Linda, "is to keep it moving, just so. And you need hands for this. Now we start in earnest."

Carefully, so as not to disturb the water, she assumed a prone position, still angling with her left hand, her right hand poised ready. Falsen watched the pale colored berry, watched the tiny fish—if they were fish—dart up to it, investigate it, then sheer off with a rather elaborate show of disinterest. Then, suddenly, the little water creatures were gone, flashing away to the farthest recesses of the pool, and something big and gray scuttled over the bottom. With scarcely a splash Linda's arm flashed down into the water—and then she had rolled over on to her back, holding with both hands a thing that could have been an oversized, infuriated Earthly spider. Uncertain what to do Falsen stood by, more than a little sickened by the appearance of the thing that the girl had fished from the pool.

"Shall I—" he began doubtfully.

"No. All right. There!"

Something cracked loudly and sharply, and then the crustacean was rolling on the spongy vegetation, a gray, hairy football in size and appearance, dead.

"We cook him," said the girl. "I've tried them raw, but—"

The thing, Falsen admitted, wasn't bad eating. It would have been improved by salt, and vinegar, and bread and butter, but it was much better than nothing. And then, after the meal, there was a cigarette from the pack that Linda had carefully dried when she dried his clothes, a shared cigarette for, as the girl pointed out, she had not yet found any kind of vegetable that would serve as a tobacco substitute. "But you will lose the desire," she said. "After all, it's not natural. I'm just having this one with you to be sociable."

"Then let me finish it."

"No. Funny—with the smell of it the desire came back. After all, we *are* civilized and there's no reason why we shouldn't make the best of two worlds."

"The main problem right now," said Falsen, "is to make the best of one."

He got to his feet, walked to the cave entrance to survey the one world that was left to them after all their years and light-years of interstellar travel. He stiffened suddenly. "Linda!" he called. "Come here!"

"What is it, Nick?"

"Look! Do you see it?"

Away over the swamp, all of seven miles distant, something was moving, something that reflected the crimson rays of the sun. Something brightly metallic it was, moving fast, flying low. As they watched it stopped and hovered, poised over one of the larger pools of water.

"A helicopter," muttered Falsen. "Looks like a survey job."

"But I thought that the Federation didn't want this world."

"There are races outside the Federation." He grinned suddenly. "There are races that don't know anything about the family scandals that the Federation is keeping so quiet about! Quick! Get some damp wood on that fire!"

"But suppose they *are* human?"

"Even then, they won't know why we're here. We can cook up some yarn about shipwreck!"

As he talked he was tearing up armfuls of the brush growing outside the cave, throwing it on to the fire. The white smoke rose, a trickle at first, then great, rolling billows, pouring out of the cave mouth, flowing down the hillside like a heavy liquid. Over the swamp the helicopter rose slowly from the surface of the pool that it was investigating, made directly for the hill and the cave.

"Not one of ours," said Falsen, watching intently. "That's a serrated disk they have rather than rotors. Doralan—? Could be. But we'd better get dressed."

"Why? This is better if we're going to—"

"We're not going to—yet. They're taking us to their ship. Hurry!"

Falsen, coughing and spluttering, came out of the cave again when the humming of the aircraft's approach filled all the humid air. He looked up at the thing, saw the characters on the cylindrical fuselage, decided that his guess had been correct. She was Doralan. But what were the Doralans doing here? Linda came out and stood beside him, watched the helicopter drop to a neat landing a little way down the slope of the hill, watched the door in the fuselage open and three red-cloaked, red-hooded figures clamber out. Falsen, his arm over the girl's shoulders, felt her muscles tense and shift, whispered: "Not *now*! You'll spoil everything."

"But they look," she murmured, "so tempting—"

"And they've got some kind of lethal ironmongery trained on us from inside their ship."

"That shouldn't worry us. Unless—"

In single file, the Doralans marched up the rough path. Their scarlet cloaks were brave splashes of color against the gray of sky and plain, their scarlet hoods shaded faces that were like the grave, piquant faces of little girls. Their bodies, too—what little could be seen of them—were human enough in outline.

"But," Linda whispered, "they're human—"

"No," said Falsen softly. "Just similar conditions, parallel development. Take 'em apart and they're—different. Yet near enough to human for—us."

The leader of the Doralans, she who wore the gold star on the collar of her cloak, addressed them. Her voice was thin and high, clear, and every word was perfectly enunciated.

She said, "You are from Earth."

"Yes," agreed Falsen.

"Why do you make smoke?"

"Because we are cast away upon this world, and we need help."

"That is obvious. But why do you make smoke?"

"That is obvious, too. To attract your attention."

"But in the course of our survey we were bound to have visited this, the only hill within miles. Your call for help that was not urgently required has disturbed our work."

Falsen said, "I'm sorry about that."

"Lady," said the officer to Linda, "I would have no further talk with this so obviously inferior being. It is clear that you are in charge here. Tell the male to follow us to our helicopter. You shall be taken to our Lady Mother."

"Better play ball, Linda," Falsen told her. "They've a sort of matriarchal setup, and the Lady Mother is the captain of their ship."

He followed the three women to the helicopter, was somewhat surprised when the officer gestured to him to get in first. But, he found, he was not to make the ride in comfort. The three who had been left to guard the aircraft grabbed him unceremoniously, pushed him into a compartment at the stern that was already more than half full of specimens—geological as well as others of a softer but even less pleasant nature. From his uncomfortable seat he could see the backs of Linda and the three Doralans—the Earth girl towering head and shoulders above her diminutive companions. He could see a contraption of metal tubing that might, or might not, have been a weapon. He hoped that the proximity, the all too close proximity, of these warm-blooded beings would not lead the girl into doing something foolish. In the confined space the odor of them was almost overpowering.

Silently, smoothly, the helicopter took off. It flew with equal smoothness—but that, Falsen decided, might be due as much to local aerological conditions as any excellence of design. At last a slight forward tilt of the deck told him that they were coming in to a landing; a slight jolt told him that they had made it. Linda turned to look at him before she left the aircraft—her face was white and strained, but she essayed a grin. Falsen grinned back—and much of his grin was relief at being able to lift the fleshy part of his thigh from the rocks upon which he had, perforce, been sitting. He stumbled forward to the door, half fell out on to the spongy, gray vegetation.

He looked around him with interest. Except that the plain here was not level, but gently undulant, the site of the Doralan camp differed very little from the place from which they had been brought. The only high things in sight were a range of hills to the eastward, and the ship. A secondhand job, Falsen decided—Earth-built. One of the old City class that Interstellar Mail got rid of all of ten years ago. But they were good, solid old wagons, he thought, and built to last.

"You," said the officer, breaking into his thoughts, "come with us."

"What are your orders, Lady?" Falsen asked Linda, more than a little sardonically.

"Don't ask me," she said. Then, to the Doralan, "Look, Little Red Riding Hood, in our world we do things differently. Horrid though it may seem, where we come from this male is my superior officer."

"Then come, both of you," said the Doralan. "Here you will both take *my* orders."

They entered the ship by the stern air lock, crowded into an elevator cage and were rapidly lifted through deck after deck, coming to rest, at last, just under—or so Falsen estimated—the control room right forward. They left the cage, walked along a short length of alleyway terminating in a door. On this the officer rapped sharply. Somebody on the other side called out something, and then the door slid open. The furniture in the room beyond the door had been changed, of course, had been modified to suit the dimensions of its present occupant—but otherwise it was still the captain's day room of a City-class liner. Sitting behind the big desk was one of the little women who now owned and operated the ship, dressed, as were her crew, in scarlet—but scarlet well ornamented with gold devices. Her hood was thrown back to show short, iron-gray hair. Her features were lined by experience and authority—yet the mouth was kindly. Sitting on the desk, a little to her right side, was a huge, ginger cat, a Persian if the length of its coat were any guide. This beast, as the Earth people entered, got to its feet and, with arched back, spat viciously.

"Pondor!" said the Lady Mother reproachfully.

The animal replied in a mewling voice—and Falsen could almost have sworn that the reply was in words. *Imagination*, he thought.

The ship's officer made her report to her captain. The Lady Mother heard her story, then spoke a few words of dismissal. To the two castaways she said, "Be seated."

"So you speak our language, Lady Mother?" asked Falsen. He seated himself on the built-in settee, that being the article of furniture best adaptable to his greater weight and bulk. The girl sat by his side.

"Yes," said the captain, "I speak your language. And first I must apologize to you for the conduct of my officer. She is unused to the idea of a world in which the two sexes are equal or, indeed, to one in which your sex is superior."

"That was nothing," said Falsen—then jumped to his feet with a yell, bent and rubbed the calf of his leg.

"Pondor," said the captain sternly. "That is no way to treat guests!"

"They don't like me," the words were slurred, barely distinguishable, "so I don't like them."

"Then leave the room. At once!"

"Why should I? My people were worshiped as gods once."

"*We* never worshiped you, Pondor. Go!"

"Oh, all right." Then as the beast, tail in air, sauntered out, they heard the one word, muttered in tones of great contempt, "*Females!*"

"What a . . . what a charming animal," said Linda. "Do you have any more like him?"

"Yes. I think you'll agree that we've done wonders with your cats—just fifty generations of controlled mutation and we even have a few bilingual specimens like Pondor here. But I am sure that you will like some refreshment."

One of the little women came in with a tray on which were small, spouted cups and plates of tiny cakes, another, an officer, followed her, carrying a pad and a styluslike pen. This latter seated herself and prepared to write.

"Tell me your story," said the captain.

"We are Nicholas Falsen and Linda Veerhausen," said Falsen, "second pilot and nurse respectively of the liner"—he hesitated slightly—"*Etruria*. We were bound from Chylor to Port Gregory, on Mars, in our System, with general and refrigerated cargo and two hundred passengers. It was my watch," he said. "Miss Veerhausen shouldn't have been in the control room with me, but she was. She was there—and it saved her life."

"Why, what happened?"

Falsen sipped from the little, spouted cup that had been handed him, decided that it was like weak tea flavored with aniseed. He sipped again—not because he liked the overly sweet brew, but to gain time. He heard the girl, her voice strained, say, "It was horrible, horrible."

"Yes," he agreed. "It was horrible. The field of the instruments in Control saved us, I guess, but the rest of the ship— Have you ever seen what happens when a Drive Unit runs wild?"

"No," said the Lady Mother. "But I've read about it."

So have I, thought Falsen. He went on, "They were all dead, of course. All of them. Some of them—changed. I'd cut the Drive as soon as the buzzer went, but it was too late. And then, as we were investigating, we heard the thing starting up again. You know, it does sometimes, even with the power cut off. All part of this temporal precession business. So we threw what bits and pieces we could into one of the boats and got out—but fast."

"Where is your boat?"

"I could show you the spot," lied Falsen. "But unless you've got special mud-dredging gear, you'll never find her. We shifted our stores to this cave of ours, and slept there the night—and in the morning she was gone. I should never," he said, trying to make his voice sound bitter, "have left both air lock doors open."

"There will be an inquiry," said the Lady Mother, "when we return you to your own people. Meanwhile, you are our guests. Arrangements are being made for your accommodation." She sipped from her cup, then set it down on the deck for Pondor, who had just returned. The animal, using his fore paws to tilt the vessel, drank noisily and appreciatively. "You will be wondering," she went on, "what we are doing here. It is not a secret. In return for certain trading privileges your Federation has ceded us this planet, and this is the first prospecting and surveying expedition. We expect to remain here for two hundred days. I trust that you will not mind being separated for so long from your own kind."

"*I* mind," mewed Pondor unexpectedly. "Find their boat for them, mistress, tell them to go. They are not our people. They—smell. They smell wrong."

"Rubbish, cat. If you'd spent all your life aboard an Earth ship, you'd say that I smelled all wrong."

"No, mistress. You wouldn't. Make them go."

"Lend us a boat," said Falsen, "and we shall go. When an *animal* tells me I . . . stink it's time that I went."

"Don't pay any attention to Pondor," said the Lady Mother, smiling. "He's jealous. He's used to being the center of attention and now he's having to . . . how do you put it? . . . take a back seat. Just ignore him, and he'll stalk out, all outraged dignity, and cuff his two wives to restore his self-esteem."

"A charming animal," said Linda.

"If I thought you meant that," Pondor told her, "I *might* like you."

"How intelligent are these . . . things?" asked Falsen. "Or are they no more than sort of glorified parrots?"

"I don't know. Of course they couldn't solve an equation or build a ship—"

"Our people were gods once," said Pondor, "and gods don't build ships."

"Could you make a world, then?" asked Falsen.

"I don't know. I've never tried."

"Prenta, here, will show you to your cabins," said the Lady Mother. "You will mess with my officers. I shall see you again."

"I hope that I shan't," muttered the cat.

The cabins to which they were shown were comfortable enough by Terran standards, although the furniture was on far too small a scale for comfort. Each cabin, however, boasted a little shower cubicle—and this, thought Falsen, would be useful. Having explored his tiny, temporary home he sat on the edge of his bunk, waited until the murmur of female voices, heard indistinctly through the thin bulkhead, should cease. At last it stopped, and shortly after came a soft rap on his door. It was only the captain's cabin that was fitted with a voice-controlled door opening device, so Falsen had to get to his feet and open his himself. Linda Veerhausen came in.

"That purser, whatever she is," she began, "was in a talkative mood. I think that she was trying to convert me to these people's way of thinking. She kept harping on this big ship of theirs, with a crew of a hundred, and not a single male among them. Not counting, of course, Pondor, or whatever the beast's name is—"

"A hundred—" said Falsen thoughtfully.

"Yes," she said. "A hundred. And we are only two. But there's the value of surprise—"

"We have to do it," muttered Falsen. "How we do it—that has to be worked out." He paced up and down in the narrow confines of the little cabin, like some caged wild beast. "They won't have changed the controls of this ship much, if at all. I'm a good pilot, and I can navigate. There are worlds out towards the Rim, out past the Rim, that'll not be colonized for generations, if at all."

"What sort of worlds?" she asked. "Like this? Or arid deserts? Or with atmospheres of chlorine or something equally toxic?"

"Some of them. But there are good worlds, too. Planets with rivers and forests, and timid, fleet-footed animals not unlike the Earthly deer."

"You're not lying?"

"Why should I lie? And get this straight—if we stay here the balloon is bound to go up sooner or later. We have to get somewhere where there's no explaining to do. And that fast."

The girl was not listening. She stood tense, alert. Suddenly she strode silently to the door, opened it, pounced with the same speed that she had shown in her capture of the crayfish. Swiftly and silently she backed into the room, the thing between her hands struggling viciously, trying to cry out, succeeding, in spite of the pressure on its throat, in giving a strangled squeal.

"What—?" began Falsen. Then he saw what it was. It was a cat—not Pondor, but, presumably, one of his two mates. Like him, it was of Persian descent, but it was black. And the Lady Mother had said that all the cats could talk.

"This *thing*," said Linda, "was spying."

"Can it understand English?"

"I don't know. But it may have learned it from that other brute. You may have spied," she went on, addressing the animal, "but you won't talk!"

Claws drew angry furrows down her face as she lifted the cat to her mouth. There was one, semi-articulate cry—then a silence broken only by a steady, rather horrid dripping sound. Suddenly the woman choked: "This fur gets between your teeth."

"The fur will have to go the same way as the rest of it," said Falsen in a matter-of-fact voice. "We can't leave the body around."

"Help me, then."

"All right."

A little while later Falsen carefully inspected the cabin. "It's a good thing," he remarked, "that this soap of theirs is so strong smelling. I doubt if even Pondor could tell that his girl friend has been here."

"It must be almost dinner time," said Linda, "but now I haven't much of an appetite."

"Neither have I,' admitted Falsen, "but we shall have to go through the motions. Anyhow, if that horrid aniseed tea we had was a fair sample of their food, a small appetite will be understandable."

A little later the survey ship's chief officer, at whose table they had been placed, remarked, "Earth people never seem to appreciate our food. Is yours, then, so very different?"

"Very," said Falsen.

Falsen awoke, that next morning, much refreshed. He did not need to be called—for him the first light, even when he was in a metal box with no outward looking ports or windows, was alarm clock enough. He threw back the light blankets of his bunk, jumped out. Silently the door opened and Linda came in.

Falsen turned to face her. He saw that she had made concessions to the ship's conventions, was wearing a gaudy wrapper loaned her by one of the officers. She was fully dressed by the standards of the burlesque stage, but by no others, even though the kindly owner of the wrapper had explained that the garment was too big for her.

"Careful, there's somebody coming," whispered Falsen.

He was dressing when the door flew open without ceremony. One of the officers looked in and, ignoring Falsen somewhat pointedly, addressed Linda Veerhausen.

"Lady! The Lady Mother desires the presence of both of you, at once."

"What's wrong?" asked Falsen.

"Something dreadful. Last night, when the ship slept, huge, savage beasts attacked the night watch. Clenni is dead, and four of her people. Not only dead, but—parts of them eaten. Hurry!"

In a minute or so—Falsen having finished his dressing with more regard for haste than for appearances, Linda still in her wrapper—they were in the captain's day room. The Lady Mother faced them across her big desk, and her face was grave. On the desk sat Pondor, who did not forget to spit a curse at them as they entered. The captain cuffed him absent-mindedly, then spoke.

"Sit down," she said. "You will have heard something of what has happened. Perhaps you can help."

"In what way?"

"You, Mr. Falsen, were an executive officer on your last ship. You must have read astrogating directions. You might, just possibly, have read those astrogating directions applying to this planet. Can you remember any mention of any large, dangerous animals among the fauna?"

"I can't remember," said Falsen.

"Well, then—you were living here for some time before we came. Did you see anything, hear anything?"

"Yes, Lady," said Linda, while Falsen was still considering his answer. "Some nights we heard something howling. And early one morning we saw something big and gray slinking away from our cave. After that we kept our fire going."

"You should have told me."

"But we thought you knew."

"I have explored all around the ship," said Pondor suddenly, "and I have neither seen, heard nor smelt anything—until this morning. The smell hangs strong, even in here."

"I examined the—bodies," said the Lady Mother. "What was left of them."

"Then you might be able to reconstruct—"

"Only this far. Whatever it was—it used teeth as its main weapon. Perhaps its only weapon. Whatever it was, was immune to the fire of my crew's blasters—and some of them must have been fired at close range. Was this thing you saw—armored?"

"It seemed to have a scaly hide," said the girl.

"I ask your advice," said the Lady Mother. "On your world, or so I have read, there are still large tracts of wild forest, of savage jungle, where men and women still go to hunt, and kill, large dangerous beasts. We have nothing of that kind, we never had, even in our barbarous past. We have no experience. You have. You must help us."

"What steps have you taken so far, Gracious Lady?" asked Falsen.

"I have sent both my helicopters out, and they are searching all the area of which the ship is the center. Should they see anything they will signal in at once."

"Useless," said Falsen, an idea germinating in his mind. "The only way to track any kind of game is on foot. You'll never do it with aircraft."

"How big a party will you require?"

Falsen hesitated. Then—"Six," he said, "not counting

ourselves. Somebody in charge who can speak English. And, of course, weapons."

"You had better break your fast before you go."

"No. This is too urgent. Give us a few moments to get dressed and we shall be ready."

"As you please. The party will be waiting for you in the after air lock."

Falsen, dressed himself, went into Linda's room while she was hastily donning her uniform.

He said: "We'll try that range of hills. There's bound to be caves there. And where there are caves you might find—anything."

"Yes," she agreed. "But shall we?"

"Why not?" He went to the door, opened it, looked up and down the alleyway. It was deserted. He returned to the cabin, shut the door. While the girl finished dressing he talked rapidly, pausing at intervals to give her time to object or to elaborate. Then, together, the two of them made their way to the after air lock where they found the ship's people waiting for them.

The Lady Mother was there, and she handed weapons to the man and the girl. Falsen examined his curiously. It was a pistol, its grip a little small for his relatively large hand. It had a bell-mouthed muzzle, and a firing stud instead of a trigger. It could be set either to paralyze or to kill, and its maximum effective range—here the captain paused while she did a conversion sum in her head—was fifty yards.

Prenta, the officer who had brought them in from the cave, was in charge of the party—and she showed little enthusiasm when she learned that, to all intents and purposes, she was to be under Falsen's orders. She snapped a command, however, and her five women shouldered their packs. She herself carried nothing but her weapons, and neither did Falsen nor Linda Veerhausen.

She said, hesitating over the title, "What first, Mr. Falsen?"

"We shall examine the scene of the—killings," said Falsen.

One by one they clambered down the ladder to the spongy vegetation. The Lady Mother halted them at the foot of the gangway. "They came," she said, "as far as this. They must have wanted to get into the ship, but could not negotiate the ladder."

"Why do you say 'they'?" asked Falsen.

"There were at least two. Some of the bodies bear teeth marks—and one of the things had smaller jaws than its mate—or mates. But look, there's blood around here—smeared blood, not freshly shed blood. They must have prowled, and jumped, and rolled on this mossy growth."

"Could be."

"And here," said the captain, leading them farther from the ship, "is where we found the bodies. They have been taken into the ship, of course, but, as you see—there was a struggle."

"Hm-m-m. They must have attacked," said Falsen, "from that clump of shrubs. Have you looked there?"

"But of course."

A mewling voice broke into the conversation. Falsen looked down, saw that it was Pondor, who was addressing the Lady Mother in her own language. She replied to the animal briefly, then said to the man: "He wants to know if anybody has seen Kristit—that's one of his two mates." She smiled briefly. "I'm afraid that I was rather short with him."

"I'm rather sorry for him," said Linda. "After all—he will feel a loss as deeply as any of us."

"I suppose so. But he might make himself useful—he *should* be able to follow a trail. Why not take him with you?"

"Why not?" said Falsen.

"Are you *walking*?" asked the cat. "No. I do not wish to go. I shall stay here and look for Kristit."

He stalked off, tail in air.

▼▼▼

Linda, who had been carefully examining the low shrubs, suddenly straightened and pointed, crying, "They went that way!" Falsen, following the direction of her outstretched arm, saw that it led towards the low range of distant hills. The Lady Mother hurried to where the girl was standing, asked, "How do you know?"

"See," said Linda, "how the tendrils of this mossy stuff have been disturbed—"

Falsen looked, expecting to see nothing—and was not disappointed. The Lady Mother looked, and said that she thought she saw the trail found by the girl. Prenta looked—and remarked superciliously that, of course, Earth people were much closer to the animal than the Doralans. Falsen, lying, said that the trail was as easy to read as a tri-di chart.

They followed this doubtful trail, then. The Lady Mother standing by her ship watched them go, and, thought Falsen, she still would be standing there when they returned, anxious to learn that vengeance had overtaken the thing or things that had murdered her people.

Overhead one of the two helicopters dipped and hovered, its buzzing distracting. At last: "Tell them to go away," said Falsen to Prenta. "If the things are lurking anywhere around, it'll scare 'em off."

At the word of command one of the Doralans pulled out a fishing rod aerial from her pack, put on a headset and spoke into it. The flying machine bumbled off in the direction of the gleaming tower of metal that was the ship. Meanwhile Linda, on hands and knees, was examining the vegetation. "They traveled in a straight line," she announced. "And fast."

"I don't know how you can tell all that," said Prenta. "But I suppose that it is as you say."

The sun, a vague, ruddy ball of light in the overcast sky, rose higher, drawing a steamy moisture, a stench of decay, from the numerous stagnant pools. A diversion was caused by something that splashed loudly over to the left of the party. Three of the Doralans ran to investigate, and loosed their fire on it. But it was only one of the crustaceans—a huge beast, its body at least two feet in diameter. The energy bolts from the Doralan pistols had cooked it—and so Falsen called a halt for lunch; he and Linda satisfying their appetites with the stringy, but far from flavorless, flesh. Prenta and her women, although offered a share, preferred their little, oversweet cakes.

After they had eaten, and after Falsen and Linda had shared one of the precious cigarettes—which neither of them enjoyed—the party pressed on. The ground rose gradually, became drier, and the air, although still hot, was drier, too. Here and there bare rock showed through the gray, spongy, mosslike growth. And once something small and lizardlike, too fast for Prenta's skill as a markswoman, scurried from one stunted bush to another.

They pressed on—and had now and again to climb from ledge to ledge. Then—"There!" cried Linda. "They went in there!"

"There" was a narrow opening between two boulders, an opening that, by its very darkness, gave promise of depths beyond and below. *Promising*, thought Falsen. *Promising*— He said: "You brought lights, I suppose."

"Of course," replied Prenta. "We may not have the skill of your so marvelous people as trackers of wild beasts, but we are not devoid of intelligence." She started snapping orders to her women. Three of them produced large, powerful hand torches from their packs. The one with the walkie-talkie started a conversation with somebody—presumably with the ship. She repeated whatever it was she had been told to Prenta, who turned to Falsen and said, "The Lady Mother says that we are still under your orders."

"And why not? That was the understanding. And we have yet to find the beasts for you."

"Give me one of those lights," said Linda. "I shall go in first."

"No," said Falsen. "I shall. There might be something in there."

"I thought that that was why we had come here," remarked Prenta in acid tones.

"He is prone to understatement," replied Linda.

Falsen took the light, switched it on, then squeezed his body between the two boulders. There was a little more room inside the cave—but, even so, his body blocked the tunnel from the view of those behind him. He called: "You were right, Linda. They came this way."

"Let me see," cried Prenta. Then—"These clumsy males! Your big feet are obliterating the tracks."

"Do *you* want to go first, then?" asked Linda.

"Yes."

You would, thought Falsen, but said, "I'm sorry, Prenta, but your Lady Mother put me in charge. I must go first."

The cave, to Falsen's nostrils, smelt dry and sterile—not the sterility of death, but a sterility that had never known life. He said nothing, however. After all—Linda had led the party here, and her senses were at least as good as his own, perhaps better. And some extra sense that he possessed told him of the girl's mounting excitement, of the eager anticipation of the hunter with the kill almost within sight. *An extra sense?* On reflection he was not quite sure. Perhaps it was only that his other senses were keen enough to appreciate her quickened breathing, the subtle change of the very smell of her, just as the same senses brought him evidence of the fear—a fear that was kept well down, well under control, but still *fear*—of the Doralans.

The beam of his torch suddenly touched something smooth and gleaming, something that shone like a huge, black mirror. Falsen hurried forward, ran to the water's edge, his feet stirring up fast falling clouds of the powdery sand. He saw that they had come into a huge cavern, a vast, subterranean hall that was almost filled by the glassy waters of the lake. Only here, where they had come from the tunnel, and directly opposite, was there any beach. And behind the farther beach, black in the grayish rock wall, was the mouth of another tunnel.

"They must have crossed the water," said Falsen.

"If you say so," replied Prenta. "You've destroyed what tracks there were."

"We shall have to cross," said Linda. "It looks deep."

"There's another tunnel mouth," said the Doralan officer. "And another. Which one?"

"The one over there, with the beach, I think— Yes. I can see tracks," murmured Linda.

"*I* can't," said Prenta rudely. "I'm beginning to wonder just what special senses you people have got."

"You'd be surprised," said Linda. "Nick—I'm going across. Tell her ladyship that I want four of her people with me. You, with Prenta and the other one, had better stay here to guard our rear."

"Are you sure that you'll be all right?"

"Of course. Prenta, will you tell these women of yours to get ready for a swim? I suppose that these weapons and torches of yours are waterproof?"

"They are." The Doralan officer snapped orders in a bad-tempered voice.

Four women unbuckled and dropped their packs, swiftly divesting themselves of their scarlet uniforms. Their almost human bodies glimmered pallidly in the reflected glow of the torches, the beams of which were trained on the entrance to the nearest tunnel. Each of the women, Falsen noticed, buckled her belt, with its holster and pistol, back about her waist after she had stripped. Linda did not. Falsen supposed that she knew best, said nothing.

The girl picked up one of the torches and, holding

it high, waded into the lake. She said, "It's *cold—*" But she kept on and dropped suddenly, with barely a splash, into a swimming posture, struck out for the farther beach. The beam of her torch, which she had not extinguished, made fantastic, shifting patterns on walls and cave roof. Prenta snapped something in her own language, and the four Doralans followed the Earth girl. One of them also carried a torch.

Falsen and the two women watched the swimmers reach the other side of the lake, watched them clamber up to the tunnel mouth. Linda dropped to her hands and knees, seemed to be examining the sandy floor. She straightened then and, hands cupped to her mouth, shouted across the water: "They went this way!"

"Be careful!" replied Falsen.

"Don't worry! I shall be all right!" came the reply.

Prenta called something incomprehensible to her people, then sat on the sand, her back to the rock wall. Her pistol, though, was in her hand, ready for instant use. The other Doralan sat beside her officer, pulled the radio antenna from her pack, put on the headset and started to talk. Falsen, pacing up and down, watched the mouth of the tunnel into which the others had vanished. He watched the glow of the torches fade and, as those using them turned a corner, die. And the faint whisper of bare feet over dry sand died with it.

He said, to make conversation, "I wonder what they'll find."

"Nothing!" snapped Prenta. She turned on him a face in which worry and responsibility struggled with indignation. "What are the words in your crude language? A wild goose chase? That is what you have led us on."

"That is what you say," countered Falsen, resuming his moody pacing.

"For Korsola's sake stop that!" almost screamed the Doralan. "It's bad enough being stuck on this world, in this cave, without having to watch a half-witted male walking miles to get nowhere!"

Falsen grinned. "I give the orders here. Your own Lady Mother said that it was to be that way."

Prenta started to make a vicious reply, then stiffened. Across the lake, in the dark tunnel, somebody was screaming. And with the screaming came a crackling sound—the same crackling sound that Falsen had heard when the Doralans had used their energy guns on the crustacean. Abruptly the crackling of released energy ceased, and the screaming— Something howled, a dismal ululation that was not human, that echoed from the rocky walls, that seemed to be amplified rather than diminished with each reverberation.

The silence fell like a blow.

Falsen stripped hastily, flinging his garments from him. He entered the water in a shallow dive, gasped as the icy chill of it shocked his skin. Something passed him, going like a torpedo. It was Prenta. Behind them the walkie-talkie operator gabbled a few hasty words into her microphone, flung aside her garments and followed them. Although the two women had belted on their pistols nobody had thought to bring the torch, the beam of which still shone across the lake on to the mouth of the tunnel.

Prenta had entered the dark opening when Falsen, the other Doralan close behind him, scrambled up the shelving sand. He heard Prenta scream, heard the crackle of her pistol and saw the blue flare of it, heard, too, a loud and frenzied snarling. Prenta screamed again and staggered backwards out of the tunnel to the beach, knocking over both Falsen and the other woman. All three fell into the water—and with them there fell something huge and gray and furry, something whose eyes gleamed green and evil in the light from across the lake. Its eyes gleamed, and its teeth gleamed, and those teeth were at the throat of the radio operator—and the white body sank into the bloodstained water.

Falsen and Prenta fought the thing—hands against teeth and claws, human intelligence against a more than animal cunning. The full fury of the attack seemed directed against the woman, however, and the man was fighting for her life rather than for his own. He got his fingers into the shaggy mane, his legs around the beast's body, pulled it somehow from the Doralan officer. It broke away then, and it was gone—and Falsen was alone, paddling with an exhausted stroke, barely keeping himself afloat. Something glimmered pallidly below the surface, and the man dived. It was Prenta. He got his hands into her hair, towed her to the beach, dragged her up the shelving sand.

She was alive still, although unconscious. There were deep scratches on her shoulders and neck. He shook her brutally until her eyes opened, said, "I'm going to find Linda." She made a sound that could have been assent, that could have been merely a moan. He left her there.

It was dark in the tunnel, but Falsen found his way sure-footedly, only occasionally putting out a hand to steady himself against the rock wall. The odor of freshly spilled blood was heavy in the air, and his nostrils tingled as he smelled the ozone that told of the recent discharge of electrical weapons. His foot caught upon something metallic. He picked it up. It was one of the torches that had been carried by Linda's party.

All of them were there, sprawled ungracefully on the blood-soaked sand. The three Doralans were dead. No close examination was necessary. They were too close to humankind, Falsen knew, to live with their throats torn out. Linda was there. There was blood on her face and on her white body. She blinked in the beam of Falsen's torch. She said, in a matter of fact voice: "It's you."

"Yes," said Falsen. "I left Prenta by the water. She'll live."

"Hadn't you better—?"

"It would be as well," agreed Falsen.

"In case *she* comes, put the light out."

There was a little cry of pain from the girl. Then: "Couldn't you have been gentler?"

"I could," said Falsen, his voice curiously muffled, distorted, "but this has to carry conviction."

The light flashed on again.

"She's coming now," said Linda.

Together they listened to the whisper of unsteady feet on the sandy floor, together they watched the Doralan stagger round the bend of the tunnel. In her right hand she carried a pistol. She stared at the bodies of her women, whispered something, her bloodless lips scarcely moving, in her own language. Then, turning her pallid face to the two Earth people, she said, "Dead. All dead."

"Yes," said Falsen.

"But," said Prenta to Linda, "you are wounded."

"It is only a scratch," said the girl.

"Which way did it go? I could have sworn that I hit it, with my first shot. Which way did it go?"

"I think," said Falsen, "that it swam across to one of the other tunnels. I can't be sure which one. I was too . . . busy to notice."

"Yes," Prenta said slowly, "you saved my life. I had forgotten. I must thank you."

"Skip it," Falsen told her. "Have you got any first-aid kit in those packs we left? You're in a mess, and Linda, here, is badly torn around the shoulders."

"Yes. Of course."

Together they made their way back to the lake, Prenta first of all collecting the weapons of her dead shipmates. Slowly, with Falsen and Linda taking it in turns to assist the Doralan, they swam across the dark expanse of icy water. Then, while Falsen broke out antiseptic and dressings, Prenta got in touch with the

Lady Mother on the portable radio set, announced that a helicopter was being sent at once.

As soon as the plastic "skin" that Falsen had sprayed on to the wounds of the women had set they dressed, then made their way to the tunnel entrance. The sun was not far from setting and a damp chill was in the air. In the distance they could see the glaring lights of the ship and, soaring and dipping, fast approaching, the dark, low flying shadow that was the helicopter. Prenta led the party from the aircraft into the cave, supervised the removal of the mangled bodies. A second helicopter came, bringing the Lady Mother herself. At her orders a large, metal cylinder was carried into the tunnel. At her orders the two helicopters took off hurriedly, put as much distance as possible in as short a time as was practicable between themselves and the range of hills.

Sitting with the Lady Mother Falsen and Linda watched, as she watched—but all her attention was not on the landscape astern of them, some of it was on the timepiece at her wrist. At last she sighed and said—"*Now.*" With the word the hills lifted—a huge mushroom of smoke and dust and rubble that climbed slowly towards, and through, the overcast. From the riven earth rose a dull, baleful glow, and a dreadful, sullen thunder caught and drove their flimsy flying machines like leaves before a gale.

And as her pilot tried to hold a steady course for the ship—"I should have liked specimens," said the Lady Mother. "But I refuse to risk the lives of my crew or"—and she smiled briefly—"my guests."

That night six more of the Doralans were killed and partly eaten.

Falsen and Linda Veerhausen were asked to the conference held by the Lady Mother in her cabin. Out of courtesy to the two castaways English was spoken, the words of any officers not conversant with the language being at once translated. Prenta's story was told and retold, discussed from all angles. Even Pondor—after all, he was animal and therefore presumably conversant with the habits of other animals—was called in, but he could do nothing but whine about his lost mate, Kristit, a cat who, it would seem, served as a repository for all the feline virtues. The Lady Mother, her nerves frayed with strain and worry, cuffed his head and sent him squalling away.

More and more did Falsen and Linda sense the hostility of the ship's people. After all, they were from Earth, and Earth had ceded this planet to the Doralans. And it was a well-known fact that Earth was not in the habit of making free gifts. There must, said one of the officers, evidently proud of her grasp of idiom, be a catch in it somewhere. There must be a nigger in the woodpile, a fly in the ointment. Furthermore, she said, the presence of the two Earthlings had never been explained to her satisfaction. How long was it they said that they had been away from their ship? And yet, when found by the survey party, the man was clean shaven, had only begun to produce a facial growth after he had become a guest of the Doralans, whose hospitality he was no doubt abusing.

"Carlin," said the Lady Mother. "You are being insulting. Mr. Falsen and Miss Veerhausen have risked their lives in our service. I, myself, have seen Miss Veerhausen's wounds. All the same—it seems odd. But I am sure that Mr. Falsen has an explanation."

"I have, Lady Mother. I do not use a razor, I use a depilatory cream. And my last tube was finished the day before you found us."

"Thank you. I am sure that my pharmacist will be able to make something up for you. Have you any more . . . theories, Carlin?"

"No, Gracious Lady. But—"

"But *what*?"

"I would suggest, Gracious Lady, that the disappearance of Kristit be investigated more closely."

"Rubbish, Carlin. It is obvious that whatever it was that killed our people, that attacked Mr. Falsen and Miss Veerhausen in the cave, could have swallowed a *cat* in one gulp. Anything else?"

All were silent. The Lady Mother absent-mindedly scratched Pondor's ears, looking from face to face. At last she spoke, directly to her chief officer.

"Mardee," she said, "there are one or two questions I have to ask *you*." She looked at a slip of paper in her hand. "Last night Canda and Weltin were killed. According to the watch list you gave me they should have been on duty *inside* the ship."

"That is correct, Gracious Lady."

"Then why were their bodies found *outside*?"

"The only thing I can suggest, Gracious Lady, is that they heard, as they should have heard, the noise outside and rushed down to help their comrades."

"Without sounding the alarm?"

The officer's manner was defensive. "As you know, Gracious Lady, all the watchkeepers had written instructions, signed by yourself, to the effect that all hands must be roused at once at the first signs of anything suspicious. Canda and Weltin must have disregarded those instructions. Unfortunately we cannot deal with them as they deserve."

"They have been punished," said the Lady Mother slowly, "with even greater severity than their offense deserved." There was silence again, broken only by the purring of the big cat. Then—"As and from tonight, there will be no watches kept outside. The air lock door will be kept shut. You, Letta, will see to it that searchlights are rigged to cover all the surrounding terrain, so that an efficient lookout can be kept from Control. You, Mardee, will arrange watches, and see to it that a reliable junior officer is in charge of each. And you and I will split the night between us. And you, Pondor"—the cat stretched and yawned—"will prowl through the ship all night, in company with your mate, Tilsin. It is possible that your keen, animal senses might detect something outside the range of ours."

"Can I get some sleep now?" mewed the cat. "And will Mardee see that some saucers are left out for me?"

"All right. Don't forget to tell Tilsin, will you?"

"Can we help?" asked Falsen.

"Why not? You are guests here—but this . . . *thing* menaces you as much as it does us." She said thoughtfully, "I'm still not happy about Canda and Weltin. I'm still not sure—"

"People do silly things," said Falsen.

"Yes. I suppose so. And it's the last silly thing that they'll do. Thank you, ladies, and you, Mr. Falsen and Miss Veerhausen. Stay with me, Mardee, and we will draw up our watch lists."

As they filed out of the room the woman Carlin fell in beside them. She said, rudely, "What do you know about the Mannschen Drive?"

"Not much," said Falsen shortly. "I didn't invent the thing."

"But you were a navigator."

"No. Second pilot. Another five years' service, and study, and school, and I'd be qualified to sit for master astronaut. And not everybody who sits passes. Come to that—even our best navigators know only how to use and to service the Drive. The actual workings of it are a mystery."

"Come to my room," said Carlin.

She led the way to her cabin. Waited until her two guests were seated on the settee, then curled up in a large, overstuffed chair. She looked, thought Falsen, like a huge, sleek, slightly overfed cat. He disliked her, and knew that she disliked him. He was rather surprised when Carlin got up, went to a locker and produced a bottle and three of the little, spouted drinking vessels. The wine was heavy, and too sweet, and had a strong, spicy flavor that at once repelled and attracted. The second cup was much better than the first.

"When you had the accident to your Drive," said Carlin, "you said that people were—changed. In what way?"

"What way would you expect?" countered Falsen. "All sorts of odd things had happened to space-time, and there was a certain . . . reversal? No, that's not the right word. Turning inside out is near enough."

"So the Temporal Precession had no effect?"

How much does she know? thought Falsen. *Is she the navigator of this packet?* He said, hoping that his memory of what he had read of disasters on the interstellar tracks was accurate, "The only thing I noticed was that some of the clocks seemed to be running backwards. And the perspective of things was—wrong. And the colors. Why do you ask?"

"I have my—curiosity. After all, such a thing might happen to this ship at some time. Especially with our Earthbuilt Mark XVII unit."

"If you're so clever," said Falsen, "why don't you build your own ships instead of buying our worn-out tonnage?"

Carlin smiled cattily. "We regard our survey ships as being expendable. So when we can get cheap old crocks for the job—we do so."

"She's a better ship than any of the spacefaring boudoirs that are turned out by *your* yards!" flared Falsen.

"At least," said Carlin, "they don't—*stink*."

Falsen bit back the reply that he could have made so easily. He had been conscious for some time of the odor of the little cabin—a smell that made him want to bare his teeth and snarl, that roused the urge to—kill. He glanced sidewise at Linda. She was conscious of it, too—he could tell by the tenseness of the line of her jaw, by the taut skin over her cheekbones, by the subtle shifting of skin and muscle that he could feel when he laid his hand lightly on her shoulder.

He said: "Let's go, Linda. We appreciated your hospitality, Lady Carlin—until you started to become insulting."

Carlin got to her feet. She said—and Falsen could not doubt her sincerity—"I'm sorry. But there's a certain—incompatibility. After all, in spite of our outward resemblance, we are members of different races—"

You don't know how different— thought Falsen.

He said, "Thank you, anyhow. Come, Linda."

Outside, in the alleyway, the door shut behind them, Linda said, "*Phew!* I couldn't have stood it any longer in there. That horrid wine—and that horrid woman! Better tell that chief officer of theirs to invest in about twenty tons of deodorant!"

"She's not the only one," said Falsen. "There're one or two of the officers and about six of the crew— But what was she driving at?"

"As she said," suggested Linda, "just curious. After all—the disasters befalling others are almost as interesting as those befalling oneself—and far less dangerous."

"She'd have found the truth even more interesting."

"If she'd believed it. These people haven't any frontiers of the dark in their Cosmos."

"I suppose not. I wonder why we should be the only ones?"

"Some accident of radiation and mutation. Perhaps even an experiment by some race before history—or a race whose history went up in flames in some catastrophe that blasted them back to first beginnings."

"I suppose you know where we are?"

"Frankly, no. I thought that you knew which way we were going. And if we didn't want any Doralans they'd be treading all over our toes—and now we do want one they've all vanished."

"If we keep going down ladders, we're bound to hit the right deck. Ah! Here's a hatch!"

"Storerooms," said the girl, halfway down the ladder. "And"—wrinkling her nose—*"cats!"*

"Or *cat*," amended Falsen. "One tom has a nuisance value out of all proportion to his size. Pondor!" he called. "Pondor!"

"He'll never come to you."

"He's wise. If he did—I'd wring his neck."

"That was strong wine she gave us," said Linda thoughtfully. "Watch your step, my dear, and I'll watch mine. If we aren't careful we'll be doing something silly."

"Something moved!" snapped Falsen suddenly. "Look!"

"The storekeeper," suggested Linda, but Falsen did not hear her words. He was attacking a pile of bales and cases like a terrier at a rat hole. As the girl watched he put all his strength into pushing a huge bale to one side, then squirmed into the aperture thus made. There was a brief scuffle, a cry of pain—and then Falsen backed out from the opening, dragging with him a limp figure. It was dressed as were the other Doralans and to outward appearances was one of them.

"Have you killed her?" asked Linda.

"Her?" demanded Falsen. "Use your senses, woman. This isn't a female."

"No . . . you're right. A stowaway?"

"Stowed away," said Falsen. "But—by whom?" He laughed. "These people with their marvelous, matriarchal society! And yet one of them—perhaps even the Lady Mother herself—has brought along some company for her idle moments!"

"Are you reporting it?"

"Why should I? I might make enemies—open enemies. No, let 'em enjoy themselves while they can. It's no skin off our nose."

The little Doralan moaned and stirred, opened his

eyes. He stared at the two Earthlings, muttered something in his own language. He seemed to be making an appeal. Falsen said nothing in reply, made a gesture of dismissal. The stowaway scrambled to his feet, ran silently to a corner of the storeroom. He seemed to melt into a stack of crates.

"Somebody should be grateful to us," said Linda. "But come on! We've still to find our way back to our own quarters."

It was light in the big ship's control room—light with the reflected glare from the big searchlights. All shutters around the greenhouse were down, and through them Falsen could see the featureless plain surrounding the ship, looking, in the harsh brilliance of the lamps, as though it were covered with fresh snow. Another glow, not of reflection, hung in the sky over where the Lady Mother's bomb had destroyed the cave system. Falsen wondered what would have happened to himself and Linda if they had been there when the bomb exploded. It was an interesting problem.

"It is very quiet," said the Lady Mother.

Falsen agreed with her. His keen ears could hear the subdued whine of the generators that supplied the current for the searchlights, could hear—but faintly—the soft breathing of the sleepers throughout the ship. He made a mental calculation—one hundred minus sixteen makes eighty-four; plus one stowaway—eighty-five. Six on deck watch, two in the engine room, and the captain, leaves seventy-six sleepers. And Linda. *I hope*, he thought, *she's sleeping.* Something padded almost silently along the alleyway outside the control room. Instinct made Falsen stiffen, reason told him to relax. Pondor crept in through the half open door, spat at Falsen in passing, rubbed against the Lady Mother's legs.

"Well, cat," she asked, "is all well?"

"I have a name," said the animal. "I wish you'd use

it." He condescended to allow the Lady Mother to tickle his ears. Then—"All is quiet," he said. "I left Tilsin making her rounds of the lower decks."

Falsen, the very presence of the cat making him nervous, started to pace up and down. Prenta came in, flashed him a smile and made a report to the captain in her own language. She fell in beside Falsen, tried to match her stride to his, tried to make conversation. Falsen answered in monosyllables, thought: *Was it your boy friend we found, my dear? Is this why you're being so nice to me? But I forgot, I saved your life.*

"It's too quiet—" said the Lady Mother suddenly.

Falsen stopped his nervous pacing, stood still with every sense alert. He did not join the Doralans at the windows, in their scanning of every inch of the terrain with their high-powered binoculars. But—*There is something wrong*, he thought. *Linda . . . I should have had her on watch with me. It would not have looked suspicious.* Out of the corner of his eye he saw a little light flash on among the dark instruments, dismissed it from his mind as something of no importance. But, in spite of the dismissal, its very presence was an irritation, a warning. Falsen tried to remember the layout of the controls of the City-class liners, in one of which he had once served—then suddenly realized what the little light was. He thought, *The silly little fool! She shouldn't.*

The sudden clangor of the alarms struck like a blow. The Doralans fell back from their windows, dropping their glasses with a clatter. The Lady Mother gripped Falsen's arm, cried: "Look! The air lock door is open!" The man tore his attention away from the little, betraying light, followed the Doralans as they ran from the control room.

Already the ship was in an uproar. Lights flashed on in very alleyway, through open doors poured the crew—in night attire, half dressed, but every woman among them armed. Somebody, somewhere, was already firing at something—the vicious, sharp crackle of the energy guns was distinctly audible above the tumult of near panic.

I must be first, thought the man. *I must be first on the scene. Perhaps, even now, I shall not be too late.* Knocking down the little Doralans as he ran he buffeted his way through alleyways, down companionways. The air was thick with the smell of fear, of anger and, as he approached the deck where his own living quarters were situated, of blood.

Carlin was beside him, running, her cat-face almost smiling, her cat's eyes alight with excitement. Oddly, illogically, at this moment, Falsen felt a feeling of kinship with the Doralan, thought:

She's better than the others. She's not frightened. Then he cursed her as, accidently or by intent, she tripped him. When he scrambled to his feet the chase had surged past and over him and the alleyway was deserted. He drew his pistol then and, walking cautiously, made his way to the head of the companionway leading to the next deck—the deck on which he and Linda were living. As he walked he heard the babble of excited voices stilled by the clear, authoritative commands of the Lady Mother. He walked slowly, alert, ready to fight or fly, descended the companionway step by wary step.

It was Prenta who met him when he was halfway down. She said, "Come quickly. But she will live, I think. She is asking for you."

"I was knocked down," said Falsen. He quickened his pace, but feigned a limp.

The crowd of Doralans parted to let Falsen through. There were bodies on the deck, which was slippery with blood. Each one had been torn and gashed and—disemboweled. Falsen shuddered. He forced himself to ignore them, walked slowly to where the girl was sprawled against the door to her own cabin with the Lady Mother and the ship's surgeon bending over her. He tripped over something, half stumbled, looked down and saw that it was Tilsin, Pondor's mate—or what was left of Tilsin. Something had torn the animal's head from its body.

"Nick," said Linda.

Her face was pale beneath the blood, and there was blood on her shoulders and down the front of her body. Falsen looked at the deep gashes and wondered how they could have been inflicted. He said, his voice unemotional, "Well?"

"She did it!" screamed Pondor. "She killed Tilsin!"

Squalling, he launched himself upon the wounded girl, his claws reaching for her eyes. The Lady Mother caught him in mid-leap, held him at arm's length while his scrabbling hind feet tried to rend her wrists. Violently, she threw him from her. There was a dull thud as he hit the bulkhead, and then his voice was upraised again in mewling protest. "She did it. I know she did it. Kill her."

"Take him," said the Lady Mother, "and lock him up until he comes to his senses." Her voice became gentle. "How is she, Magadja?"

"She has lost some blood," said the surgeon. "But her injuries are little more than superficial." Deftly she cleaned the wounds, sprayed them over with the quick-drying plastic skin. "Can you get her moved to her cabin?" she asked.

Falsen followed the surgeon and the Lady Mother into Linda's room. He walked to her bedside, caught her limp hand in his. He felt her fear, a blind fear that almost induced a like panic in himself. He said, "Don't worry."

"Miss Veerhausen," said the Lady Mother, "I am sorry to have to question you. But this has been—dreadful. Fifteen of my people murdered in their cabins, including my chief officer, another five in the alleyways. Can you tell me what happened?"

"A . . . little," said the girl. Falsen felt her hand tense in his. "I did not sleep well. And I woke up, feeling that something was wrong. There was a strange odor in the air. I got up and went out—and something attacked me."

"What was it like?"

"I don't know. It had teeth, and claws. It was like an Earthly tiger, but not the same. It seemed to run on its hind legs only—"

"Was there more than one?"

"Yes. I'm almost sure that I saw others while I was fighting it off."

"Miss Veerhausen?" The words cracked like a whip lash. "Did you open the air lock doors?"

The girl's eyes opened wide in an amazement that, thought Falsen, must convince almost anybody. "Of course not," she said.

Prenta slipped silently into the room. "Lady Mother," she said, "there's blood on the moss under the air lock door. I followed the trail as far as I could, then it faded out. What shall we do?"

"Order out the helicopters. Go in one yourself. Fly in the direction indicated by the trail." She turned to Falsen, who felt an acute stab of pity at the sight of the pale, careworn face. "What else can we do?"

"You were a fool," said Falsen. "You tried to do too much by yourself. You could have ruined everything."

"But, Nick, I *didn't*. Oh, I did kill Tilsin—the sound of her padding up and down outside was driving me frantic. Then, while I was dealing with her, this other . . . *thing* jumped me. Luckily I was . . . prepared, so I could fight it off."

"A cross between a kangaroo and a tiger!" scoffed the man. "That's even better than your big, gray beast with the armor-plated hide! Save these tales for the Doralans."

"No," she said. "Why should I lie to—you? This planet has got dangerous beasts, after all." She started to laugh. "Funny, isn't it?"

"It's not so funny. But—it suits us. Anything,

everything will be blamed now on these . . . these . . . Antareans? As good a name as any. But we shall have to be careful still."

"There's somebody at the door," the girl said suddenly. "Come in!"

It was the Lady Mother. She said abruptly, "I have called the roll. I have taken account of all those killed. But, even so, there are three of my women missing."

"Could they," suggested Falsen, "have been eaten entirely?"

"I thought that myself at first. But Carlin tells me that she saw them being dragged away from the ship by the beasts that attacked. Carlin thinks that they were still living."

"But why should they take prisoners?"

"That puzzled me, too. But I have a fairly clear idea now as to what the things are really like. Funnily enough, they're remarkably similar to one of our own animals—a beast that is now extinct save for a few specimens in zoos. The *simbor*, we call it, and in its wild state it was carnivorous. And in its wild state it used to carry living victims back to its lair for its young. It would cripple them so that they could not escape, and sometimes it would be days before they were eaten."

"There couldn't possibly be any . . . what was the name? . . . *simbors* here," said Falsen.

"Oh, I know, I know. But there is parallel evolution. You and I are examples of that. And, you must admit, similar habits often go with a similar external appearance."

"Could be."

"Prenta's helicopter has returned. She reports that she has seen the beasts, two of them, in a crater to the southwestward. She opened fire on them, but they bolted for cover in time. She thinks that she saw, too, one of our people—but the creatures dragged her down into a narrow opening between the rocks." She paused. "I want my three subjects back alive. And I want these bloodthirsty beasts exterminated. I'm stripping the ship, Mr. Falsen, of all hands but the merest skeleton of a watch. Both helicopters will go, and the bulk of the party will proceed on foot. You have shown your skill in the past. I should like you to lead the ground forces."

"I want to go, too," said Linda.

"But you are wounded," said the Lady Mother.

"I was," said the girl. "But you don't know just how tough we are."

The Lady Mother bent to examine Linda's wounds, the scars of which were visible under the transparent, plastic skin. She said, "That is remarkable. If you feel fit enough—"

"But I do. And I want my revenge."

"As you wish, then. Please report to my cabin with Mr. Falsen for instructions."

The instructions were brief and to the point. The helicopters were to guide the ground party and also to act as air cover. The ground forces were to press into every tunnel, opening immediate fire on anything and everything that moved. The ship's armorers had been working on the Doralan energy guns, had tuned them so that they were just short of being as great a danger to the marksman as to the target, so that, in fact, one sustained action would inevitably burn them out. Meanwhile, one of the helicopters would carry a bomb similar to that employed before. After the three Doralans had been rescued—or after proof positive of their deaths had been found—the bomb would be used.

The sun was already up when the two helicopters took the air, when the ground party clambered down the ladder from the after air lock to the spongy soil of the hostile planet. Carlin was in charge of the bomb-carrying aircraft, another officer, who had flown with Prenta when she discovered the lair of the Antareans, commanded the other. Prenta herself marched with Falsen and Linda Veerhausen.

"Tell me, Prenta," said Falsen, "how did you find the things? This crater of theirs must be out of range of our lights."

"It is. But one of the prisoners was using a pocket torch, and, as luck would have it, we saw the feeble glimmer of it. And Merru, who flew with me, had suggested that the crater—we found it on our first survey flight—might be where the things were living."

For a while they marched in silence, then Prenta said, "I saw them only by the light of our flares. But I could have sworn that they were *simbors*."

"Impossible," said Falsen. "Unless you brought them with you."

"Impossible!" snapped Prenta. Then she started to laugh. "You were joking."

"Of course. You people couldn't bring half such queer things with you as ours do."

Conversation flagged then, a fragile plant wilting in the steamy heat. The party marched on and on, possessed by a sense of urgency. Ahead of them the helicopters soared and dipped, the steady humming of their rotors hypnotic so, at the finish, the ground party marched as in a dream. Falsen was hardly interested when, at last, the flat horizon ahead was broken by a low, serrated ridge. He had literally to force himself into a state of alertness, discovered that the mere act of drawing his pistol taxed all his reserves of will power. By his side trudged Prenta and Linda, both of them, to outward appearance at least, more than half asleep. He had to shout at them to arouse them—and they, in turn, had to bully those following into complete wakefulness.

"Tell the helicopters," Falsen ordered Prenta, "that we're having a breather before we attack. Tell them to let us know if they see any signs of life."

Prenta called her radio operator to her side, passed the orders on to her in her own language. Ahead of them the two helicopters dipped and hovered. The operator said a few words and then listened. Again, briefly, she spoke, then turned to Prenta and passed on to her what had been said by those in the aircraft.

"No signs of life or movement," reported Prenta.

"I rather think," said Falsen, "that they sleep by day."

"Never mind when *they* sleep," said Prenta. "Haven't *we* rested long enough?"

"All right, we have. Pass the word for the crater to be encircled. Tell the helicopters what we're doing."

Falsen stood and watched the little, red-cloaked women, obedient to his command, straggling out into a line that would surround the crater and all that it might contain. *I'm getting fond of the little beasts*, he thought, *and that won't do at all.* He looked down from his superior height at Prenta, watched her face as she snapped orders, noticed the capable way in which she held the weapon that she had already drawn. He felt a sudden, strange pride, and a regret, and his active mind was already considering schemes in which marooning was an alternative to death.

"This is fun," said Linda, a bright spot of color on either cheek relieving the pallor of her face. "But I wish we could hunt them *our* way."

"What is your way?" asked Prenta. "We are under your orders, you know."

"On elephants," said Falsen quickly. "But I don't suppose that anybody has brought *them* along."

Prenta's radio operator was in touch with her similarly equipped sisters. She made a report to Prenta, who said, "The encirclement is complete."

"All right. Give the word that all weapons are to be ready. Give the word to advance."

Slowly they climbed the gentle slope, pausing to examine every boulder. There was a sudden, sharp crackle of fire to the right; and a large rock shattered and a small lizard-thing killed. A considerable area of the mosslike growth was set on fire. Falsen ordered greater caution—wondering, as he did so, if he were making a wise command. This was war, he told himself, and the old principle of firing first and asking questions afterwards still held good. He thought, *I'm a fool. I should be in one of those helicopters, running the show from up top. But it wouldn't be the same.*

Falsen's sector of the line topped the crater rim—paused for a minute until the others had done so. Falsen surveyed the shallow depression, the saucer shaped hollow, his eye noting the boulders that would serve as cover, the rocks that might mask the entrances of caves. He saw a splash of scarlet on the gray ground, decided that it must be the cloak of one of those taken by the beasts. Opposite him, from the other side of the crater, somebody fired. The beam of the weapon was barely visible—but the flare of the disintegrating boulder was blinding. The sharp crackle of the bolt was followed by sudden thunder—and by an almost human scream. From where the boulder had been something ran, something that progressed in almost kangaroolike hops. Yet, Falsen decided as he saw it over the sights of his gun, it had a leonine head and body.

"You missed," said Linda. "We all missed."

Falsen blinked his smarting eyes. "Which way did it go?"

"Between those rocks."

"Must be a cave. Anything from the helicopters, Prenta?"

"Yes. They reported the thing after we'd all shot at it."

"What now?" asked Linda.

"We continue to advance. Tell them, Prenta, to post a strong guard over every cave mouth, every possible hole. After we've got them all located we call for volunteers."

The going was hard—harder still when one hand was needed to grip a weapon, when undivided attention could not be given to the secure placing of feet. At the finish about two thirds of Falsen's force met in the center of the crater—the rest having been left at various points to watch the mouths of caves and tunnels. And here, almost equidistant from all points of the crater rim, was the most promising cave of all, a tunnel sloping down into the blackness at not too steep an angle, an almost horizontal shaft floored with a damp pumice dust, on the surface of which were the almost human footprints of the Doralans and other marks, larger, like those of an Earthly lion.

Already Prenta held a torch in her left hand, her pistol ready in her right. Already the Doralans were quarreling among themselves as to whom should descend to the rescue of their shipmates. But Falsen was not happy about it—neither, he saw and sensed, was Linda. It was all too easy, somehow. There was a trap—he was sure of that. A trap baited with footprints, with a rag of scarlet cloak. And there were marks just inside the tunnel entrance that, to his acute senses, begged for investigation.

He said to Prenta: "Get that boulder shifted. I think it will roll. I know it will."

Four of the Doralans laid hands on the rock, contrived to get their fingers into inequalities of its surface. It was stubborn at first, and then it came easily. Behind it was a smaller cave—a mere niche, rather—and in it were three huddled bodies, the three missing Doralans. Two of them were fully clad, the third was naked. They were alive.

Willing hands lifted them, carried them out to the open air. They seemed too dazed to speak. Prenta stilled the excited babble of the rescue party with one sharp order, then turned to Falsen. She said, "We've done what we set out to do. The bomb?"

"Those were the Lady Mother's orders."

The bomb-carrying helicopter was already dropping, the roar of its rotors making further conversation impossible. Looking up, Falsen saw the woman Carlin peering from the cabin of the thing, decided, when he saw the expression of triumph on her face, that the three rescued Doralans must be especial friends of hers. With a creaking of landing gear the helicopter grounded. The cabin door opened. Moving swiftly and efficiently the aircraft's crew passed the three ex-captives into their ship. The rotors started to spin again, the ship to lift.

"What about the bomb, Carlin?" shouted Falsen.

"You shall have it!" she screamed in reply.

From the open cabin door toppled the shining metal cylinder, striking the rocky ground with a dull *clang*, rolling a few feet before it fetched up against a boulder.

As the helicopter drifted overhead Falsen turned to Linda and bellowed, "Jump!" At the very peak of his own leap his outstretched fingers caught the horizontal struts of the undercarriage, caught and held. For long seconds he hung there, his body buffeted by the slipstream; dimly he realized that Linda was beside him. Working slowly, carefully, he succeeded in transferring the grip of one of his hands to a vertical member of the undercarriage; first one hand, and then the other, and then he was able to pull himself up until he was sitting, insecurely, on the cross strut. Using his right hand only he got a firm hold of Linda, pulled her up until she was seated beside him.

They looked down. Below them, in the crater, the scarlet clad Doralans were getting out, and fast. Only one of them had not joined the general panic, and that one was Prenta. Grimly, intently, she was working at the gleaming cylinder left by Carlin, worrying at it like some small, conscientious terrier at a rat hole. Whether to defuse, whether to procure a premature burst and thus involve the helicopter and its crew in the explosion, Falsen never found out.

There was the other helicopter still to be reckoned with. It came dropping down on Carlin's ship like a noisy falcon, all its guns spitting bolts of energy. There was the smell of ozone, the acrid stink of hot metal. But Carlin did not falter in her flight, held the nose of her craft steady on that point of the horizon beyond which lay the ship. And then, suddenly, one of her guns began to speak—not a mere projector of electrical forces, all but ineffective against a metal hull, but an old-fashioned weapon firing solid slugs of metal. Abruptly the other aircraft fell within Falsen's field of view, and he saw that the shining aluminum of its hull was perforated, and as he watched a great piece broke off its whirling vanes and gyrated Earthward. And with the shattering of its rotor the helicopter faltered, faltered and fell, following its own wreckage in unsteady, wavering descent, accelerating wildly and suddenly towards the end so that where it fell there was a sudden geyser of water and mud—followed, after a moment, by a second, high climbing geyser of flame and steam.

Linda Veerhausen clutched Falsen's arm, her nails digging painfully into his flesh. She screamed, trying to make herself heard above the slipstream, the roaring rotors, "What . . . what are they doing?"

"I . . . I don't . . . know. Mutiny—"

He looked astern, to where the low crater had already dipped beneath the horizon. He saw the flash, the beginnings of the flash, and shut his eyes. When he opened them there was the climbing column of flame-shot smoke, reaching up to and through the overcast. Then the wind came—the hot, searing wind that lifted the helicopter like a toy, that drove the aircraft before it like a dead leaf before an autumnal gale. He clung to his strut with one hand, kept his other arm tightly around the girl's waist. With the wind came the thunder, peal after dreadful peal, beating at them like blows from a giant's hammer, threatening to tear their desperate grasp from the frail construction of light metal that still, miraculously, kept its course and even keel.

Prenta must be dead, thought Falsen numbly. Prenta, and all her people. He was sorry, in his way—although, he told himself, this woman Carlin had, by her mutiny, made things so much easier for himself and Linda. He did not fear the energy guns of the Doralans, although their possession and use of old-fashioned machine guns caused him a certain degree of apprehension. But, he told himself, they would never have the right ammunition for them. The need for ammunition of that kind could never exist, possibly, in more than one world of the galaxy.

Astern the column of smoke still stood high and dreadful in the sky but, save for a certain hot, gusty turbulence the air was almost calm again, and the sullen thunders of the bomb were now no more than a distant, forbidding rumbling. And ahead the ship lifted above the horizon line—a tower of dull-gleaming metal, the wandering home of a new race, the great, sky-faring argosy that would bear them to the last frontier of the dark. A fortress it was, too—a fortress of the snug, secure interstellar civilization, a fortress that had fallen, or was soon to fall, by the treachery of its own people.

The helicopter was flying lower now, losing altitude steadily, barely skimming, it seemed, the mossy surface of the Antarean planet, the scum covered surface of the stagnant pools. Falsen noticed this, shouted to Linda, "We shall have to drop!"

"Why?"

"Carlin's bound to find us when she lands! We'll approach the ship on foot!"

Swiftly they approached one of the pools—almost a lake it was, hundreds of feet across. Falsen waited until the helicopter was almost above its nearer shore, then wriggled down from his sitting posture until he was hanging, once more, by his hands. He waited until the girl had followed his example, then shouted, *"Now!"*

Together they let go, together they fell, hitting the water with barely a splash, sliding deep, deep down below its surface. Falsen felt his feet touch soft mud, kicked out and, long seconds later, broke through to the light and air. He was afraid that Carlin or one of her women would have seen him, would have brought the aircraft back to deal with the two survivors of the massacre in the crater but, he was relieved to see, the helicopter still flew onward heedlessly and straight for the ship.

There was a splash beside him, a splash and a splutter as Linda broke surface. She shook her head to throw the wet hair away from her eyes, gasped, "What now?"

Falsen treaded water. He said, speaking jerkily, "We'll swim for the shore—this way. If they *do* come back for us, we can dive."

Side by side they struck out, swimming in a silence broken only by the splashing of their passage and their sharp breathing. Side by side they reached the lake edge, the shore that was no more than the gradual, unpleasant merging of land and water. Side by side they scrambled out and stood, muddy and dripping, regarding each other.

"There will only be a few of them," said Linda at last.

"Yes. We must be ready to fight—any way."

In silence they stripped. Linda Veerhausen made as though to resume her holstered belt, then thought better of it. She took the pistol from the holster instead, held it ready in her right hand. Falsen did likewise. Naked and muddy, weapons ready, they trudged slowly and warily over the spongy, mossy terrain, through the gathering night to the bright lamps that marked the ship.

Carlin had no guards out, although there was one member of the survey ship's complement who sat, miserable and terrified in the mud, staring towards the bright lights that marked what had been, what never again would be, his home. Linda pounced upon him before he was aware of their coming, held him high, squeezing him with deliberate cruelty.

Pondor spat and scratched, cursed the girl in the Doralan tongue, then lapsed into English. He said, his mewing voice little more than a whimper, "They are killing, killing—They have killed the Lady Mother."

Falsen felt rage surge up within him. He had known that he himself must, at the end, slay the foreign woman, the kindly, tolerant captain of the Doralan ship—but he hated Carlin for having done what he himself could not have escaped doing. *Besides*, he told himself, *I'm different. Carlin is not.* He said, his voice cold, "We shall kill them."

"Be careful!" squealed Pondor, "they are—"

His voice died in a choking gurgle as Linda's teeth found his throat. The girl threw the little, lifeless body to one side.

"You shouldn't have done that," said Falsen sharply. "He was trying to warn us of something."

"I hated the beast, anyhow. As well kill him now as later."

It was dark now, but the glaring lights from the ship threw every prominent object into sharp relief. Falsen realized that he was a prominent object, that both he and the girl were prominent objects, that their pale, naked skins must stand out against the surrounding grayness as though luminous. He said, "We're too conspicuous. We shall have to change."

"What about our pistols?"

"Carry them in our mouths."

He watched her, watched the white flesh creep and shift, darken and change. He felt the pain that was not a pain, the sense of freedom that was, at the same time, a sense of bondage. He dropped his pistol when he could hold it no longer, then picked it up between his teeth. Crouching low, moving swiftly and silently, a gray shadow among the gray shadows, he led the way to the square of yellow light that was the air lock door. The smell of warm machinery, of lifeless, inanimate metal, was strong and repugnant in his nostrils, and the smell of warm flesh and blood was strong—but not repugnant. The last few yards of the journey he made on his belly and then, only a foot or so from the ladder into the ship, he crouched motionless, listening and—feeling.

Carlin, he thought, must be lax. There was nobody on guard in the air lock. She must be certain that he and Linda had perished in the explosion. But what of the cat-things, the carnivorous beasts indigenous to this planet whose bloody ravages had given Carlin the opportunity for her treachery? Perhaps, he thought, with hope and disappointment, they've all killed each other.

Once again the sense of loss and gain, the queer, painful ecstasy—and Falsen stood erect, picked up the pistol that had fallen from his mouth. He looked around, saw that the girl had followed his example. Swiftly, silently, he climbed the ladder to the air lock door, clambered into the ship. The air lock itself was, as he had known it would be, deserted—and so was the alleyway beyond it—and the companionway leading from it to the next deck above. And yet the ship was not—dead. It pulsed with unseen life, with unseen, inimical life, spoke vaguely yet threateningly of the menace that lay just beyond that bend of the alleyway, that lurked just at the top of this companionway. Linda was beginning to whimper softly, but Falsen said, "We must go on. We *must* go on. After all—*they* can't hurt us."

And so they climbed, deck after deck, alleyway after alleyway, smelling now and again, the death that had come to those loyal to the Lady Mother—yet finding nowhere any other evidence of death, no bloodstains, no charred and contorted bodies, nothing but the dead, yet alive, ominous emptiness.

And so they climbed, deck after deck, until at last they stood in the alleyway outside what had been the captain's quarters. From behind the closed door they heard voices—low, indistinct, speaking in the Doralan language. Pistols ready, the two Earthlings approached the door, their bare feet silent on the soft, plastic deck covering, hoping that the automatic control of the door was still working, that Carlin, hearing them knock, would absent-mindedly utter the words that would cause it to open.

Falsen knocked—and a voice inside, Carlin's, said the words. The door opened.

"I could kill you now," said Falsen, his pistol covering the group behind and around the big desk. "I could kill you now—and I shall kill you later. But I want you to know who is killing you, and why. It should help to make your last moments uneasier."

He looked at the group behind and around the big desk—at Carlin lolling at ease, smoothly insolent even now, at the other five women, at the six men, one of whom was the stowaway found by himself and Linda. And he hated them, the fat, satisfied sleekness of them, and the treachery that had brought them to where they now sat and stood, masters and mistresses of a huge, sky-cleaving ship in which they could escape, in which they would have escaped had it not been for the intervention of the man and woman from Earth, the justice of their kind.

"You," said Carlin," are as bad as we."

"No," snarled Falsen. "We should never have killed the Lady Mother. We should never have murdered our shipmates with a bomb."

"*You* might not have done so. But could you answer for your . . . companion?"

"So you know?"

"So we know—what? All right, then. We aren't all fools, Mr. Falsen. We aren't all like our late, sorely lamented Lady Mother. We know your language, we read your books. We learn of your rather intriguing legends. And we know, as you know, that the Drive does queer things to Time as well as to Space, and that if there is a tendency towards atavism— It was Pondor who put me on the right track. He told the Lady Mother of his suspicions at first—but she, poor fool, would not believe him. So he came squealing to me. I didn't believe him either—officially."

"Believe *what*?" demanded Falsen, his grip tightening on his pistol. He felt that things were going wrong, that this little group of Doralans, regarding him steadily with their big, almost luminous eyes, was playing with him. His gaze flickered to Linda, standing close beside him. He noticed the white tautness of the knuckles of her pistol hand, sensed the unease of her. *Shoot!* screamed a voice in his brain. *Shoot, and get it over with.*

"You were marooned, of course," went on Carlin, "from your ship, or ships. It doesn't matter. They should have killed you. But perhaps they couldn't. I'm rather intrigued to see that you survived the bomb. But we didn't expect you here so soon."

"We came back with you," Falsen told her. "Riding the undercarriage of your helicopter."

"Indeed? I had assumed that you had lost your clothing in the blast."

"We took off our clothing," snarled Falsen, "so that we could—fight! Just as we did the first time, in the caves."

"Oh? So it *was* you. An almost masterly piece of planning that—especially making sure that there was one survivor of our people to tell the tale. You know, Falsen, we could almost respect you."

Shoot! screamed the voice in his brain. *Shoot!*

The hand holding the pistol had dropped slightly. He raised it, pointing the muzzle squarely at Carlin. He was about to fire when, "Don't," said Linda. "*I* want her, the other way."

Carlin smiled. "Yours is the dominant sex," she said. "Why don't you smack her down? You know," she went on, "we've found the pair of you most useful. Your activities served to lay a most confusing smoke screen. And now the ship is ours."

"*Was* yours," corrected Falsen. "Anyhow, just what did you intend doing with her?"

"There are worlds," said Carlin, "out towards the Rim. Wild worlds that will not be colonized for generations yet. Worlds where we"—and her voice caressed all those standing around her—"can lead the kind of life that we were meant to lead."

"And that," said Falsen, "is the very reason why *we* are taking your ship."

He stared at the hateful face before him—the grave, unsmiling cat's face, the big, unwinking eyes. His thumb pressed the firing stud of the pistol. The crackling bolt leaped out, played briefly over Carlin, then passed on to the Doralan at her left hand, paused and passed on, paused and passed on. At his side Linda was firing—first at Carlin, then at the people on her right. With a thud the big desk burst into flames, flared briefly, smoldered redly and smokily. The air stank of ozone, of charred wood and fabric, scorched paint—

Through the acrid fumes he stared at the hateful face before him—the grave, unsmiling cat's face, the big, unwinking eyes.

"You never bothered to learn our language, did you?" asked Carlin. "And if you had, you'd never have bothered to read our books, to study our history and mythology." She smiled briefly, showing very white teeth. "I must admit that, luckily for us, our people haven't been quite so quick on the uptake as yours. A certain effect of the Interstellar Drive, of its temporal precession, has, so far, escaped their notice. They do not know, as your authorities know, as *we* know, how short a way we have come from the frontier of the dark—"

Falsen kept a tight grip on his useless weapon. "I don't understand," he said, understanding only too well, the last pieces of the jigsaw puzzle falling into place, with inexorable logic, in his mind. "I don't understand."

"But you do," said Carlin. "You must." Her little, pointed red tongue flickered out between her red lips, flickered briefly over her lips. She said, "I am glad you came. We are—enjoying this."

She gave a brief order to her people, two of whom, a man and a woman, cast aside the scorched and still smoldering remnants of their clothing. With fascinated, horrified eyes Falsen and Linda Veerhausen watched them, watched the firm, golden flesh creep and shift and change, watched the terrifying metamorphosis of humanoid into *simbor*. Standing erect, the tiger-like animals snarled at them wordlessly, extended the long, razor-sharp claws of their fore paws. Snarling, Falsen hurled his pistol at one of them. The beast evaded the missile easily, then fell into a crouch preparatory for the killing spring.

Falsen snarled back at the *simbor*, and by his side the girl snarled, too. He fell to all fours as he changed, as he sloughed off the remaining shreds of his humanity. *At least*, he thought, *it will be a good fight. And we might even—who knows?—win after all. They're only*—cats. He was aware of Linda beside him, changed too, the fur of her body erect and bristling, the lips drawn back from the sharp teeth as she growled deeply and ominously in her throat.

Carlin chuckled. "Yes," she said, "it would have been a good fight, and I should have liked to have watched it, even to have taken part in it. But I have so few, Falsen, with whom to start my colony."

Her hand came up from beneath the smoking ruins of the desk holding a pistol—not one of the energy guns, but a huge, old-fashioned weapon that could well have come from some museum. She said, "Luckily the cartridges didn't explode—" Then, as she fired, "Silver bullets, of course."

The larger of the two werewolves died scrabbling vainly at the door. The other, his mate, was struck down in mid-leap.

So there we were, finished with Tomorrow Sucks, *our first science fiction vampire anthology, and playing around with an idea for a similar collection devoted to futuristic lycanthropes, when what do we see on the cover of the December 1994 issue of* Asimov's Science Fiction *magazine but a fanged and furry werewolf in an astronaut's suit, complete with bubble helmet, and the title "Werewolves of Luna." It was an omen! Suddenly, we knew we* had *to do this book, if only to include this rip-roaring tale of aliens, virtual reality, and at least two different kinds of science fiction werewolves.*

Werewolves of Luna

R. GARCIA y ROBERTSON

"It was a unique, almost mystical environment up there."

—Edwin E. "Buzz" Aldrin, Jr.

Down and Out in Orbit

Ian was lost, listening to the last of his air hiss away, when he saw the moon faerie—a silvery form flitting on gossamer wings among the slumped peaks and scree slopes. He snapped his head about, trying to hold the glimmering light in focus. Lunascape reeled and tilted, but his battered tourist helmet couldn't turn quick enough. Horizontal reference is haphazard on Luna—limited field of vision and the short horizon made local features lean alarmingly. Before Ian could compensate, the faerie had slipped from sight.

Hallucination, was his first thought. Oxygen starvation. Hypoxia. Rapture of the Void. He had been stretching that last of his air (Heaven knows *why*), cranking the intake valve down to a whisper, letting blood oxygen dip into the danger zone, ignoring seductive warnings from his suit. "Do not lower your air flow," advised a husky, come-hither voice, whispering into his left ear. Even idiot suit computers knew that young males paid more attention to *sexy* voices. This throaty whisper had swaying hips, pert nipples, and a neck like Nefertiti. Ian could *hear* the willing smile. "Time to renew your air supply—*please* return to your vehicle."

"Fine advice, but I *cannot find* my goddamned vehicle!"

Unless the faerie returned, Ian was going nowhere. The surrounding bit of moonscape seemed familiar—a low saddle between two slumped peaks, littered with pebble, talus, and house-sized boulders. But so much of Luna looked the same.

And all the while, his air kept hissing away.

No natural complainer, Ian still resented this slow measured extinction. He was near to thirty, with three advanced degrees, a solid career in mass conversion maintenance, a dry Scots humor, and even decent judgment—when he deigned to use it. Cosmetic medicine gave him trendy unblemished features, and he owned a thatch-and-stone bothy in the Hebrides. Damn it, he played the *bagpipes*, too—"Practically a lost *art* for Christ's sake! What a waste!"

On the Moon less than forty hours, his death had to set a record for non-impact fatalities—fastest tourist kill since a load of Zen sightseers aboard the *Dharma Bum* completed their current incarnations by carving a fresh crater inside Tycho. Barely two hours before, Ian had been atop a peak, able to *see* the goddamned rover, sitting on the *mare*—a shining silverfish on a basalt plate. That's when he thought he'd take a new route back. "No sense seeing the same Moon twice."

The suit's mapping program was supposed to project an optimum route onto his visor, using broken yellow lines. But the dotted lines had not taken him back to his rover. Instead, the lying yellow brick road only led him deeper into the *Montes Carpatus*, the Lunar Carpathians, part of a highland arc forming the southern shoreline of the Sea of Showers. (The *montes* were named for a range in Poland or Hungary—Ian was not sure which, and never likely to know now.) He was lost amid the protruding bones of the ancient moon, blunt peaks and scree slopes older than the surrounding *mare*. Older than life on Earth. A bouldered moonscape, saturated with impact craters, filled with stark shadows so solid he couldn't see into them.

Halo comsats and lagrange navigation stations were supposed to instantly locate anyone, anywhere on Luna. But the same suit-flu that infected the mapping program had locked his comlink on Radio Ganymede. Upsun rockabilly jammed the wavelength. Right now he was listening to a folksy refrain by "Jolly King Jove and the Red Spots," accompanied by mouth harps, guitar, ceramic jugs, and an electronic washboard:

Us gud ol boys ahn Ganymede,
Got us ah gee-tar an a band . . .

Amateur night in the Jovian moons was drowning Ian out. He could *see* Jupiter, eight-hundred-million kilometers away, a yellowish disk among the hard sharp stars. He shouted for Jolly King Jove to "Shut the hell up!" A futile gesture. At light speed, the signal would take forty-five minutes to reach the Jovians—Ian would be dead long before Ganymede could reply. He reached up and gave the suit antenna a vicious jerk, snapping it at the base with an armored gauntlet. That did not solve his communications glitch, but at least he could hear himself think. Suddenly, everything was as quiet and cryptlike as only the Lunar Highlands could be. Silent and spooky beyond belief.

Softer sounds filled out the silence. His suit and helmet formed a compact little coffin, whirring with life, holding back burning daylight and freezing night. Air hissed in at the nape of his neck. He had water in his helmet tank. By turning his head to the right or left, he could pop pills onto his tongue—glucose and vitamins on one side, hard drugs on the other—synthetic opiates to block out pain and fear, powerful amphetamines to pump him up. Readouts on his visor told him his pulse and respiration rate, blood oxygen, air supply, radiation exposure, interior-exterior temperature, even the time of day in Greenwich, England. When the hiss of air gave out, his treacherous, friendly-faulty suit would continue to hum for months—maybe years. Micrometeorite erosion takes eons, a millimeter every ten million years. His body would be there for a good, grotesque little warning for future tourists.

The faerie came back, a silver form leaping between bright sunlight and black shadow, its gossamer wings shot with rainbow colors. Why wings on an airless world? "Ian, old son—you are not just dying, but flipping your set switches as well." (Suit tapes of hypoxia victims were full of fanciful imaginings, mirages of home, mother, and rescue ships that weren't there.) The first faerie was joined by a second.

Just as quickly, they were both gone, disappearing into dense shadow. Ian had the impression that they were playing with him.

He gobbled several white stim pills, washing them down with tepid water from his helmet tube—long term addiction was not an immediate worry. Drugs snaked through his veins, snapping the moonscape into sharp, crisp focus, like a 3V negative of some brilliant desert scene, where sand and sky are black and shadows glaring white.

Ian pushed off, full of drugs and anger, dizzily determined to find the dancing lights and force them to take him to the rover.

"Warning, you are now on 120 second reserve—kindly return to your vehicle."

Reaching around, Ian clamped his helmet intake valve down tight, cutting off the hiss of air, saving his last breaths for when he really needed them. He still had the stale air in his suit and helmet, sweaty as a jock strap, but breathable. He shuffled forward. Short steps. Shallow breaths. With no rush of air to cool his sunlit helmet, perspiration collected in the suit's itchy plastic collar. Suffocating closeness dulled his sense of self-preservation. Even before he'd started seeing moon faeries and talking back to his suit, Ian had noted an insane desire to tear off the confining helmet, breathe the pure, cool vacuum. Catastrophic decompression might rip his lungs out, but it would save him from dying in a slobbering brainless stupor. Ian did not look forward to lying facedown in the *regolith*, drowning in his own sweat and CO_2, while sultry recordings told him he was in trouble.

With his air shut off, he actually felt better. No annoying little hiss to remind him of his troubles. Best of all, the faeries came back. Ian admired their low gliding leaps, touching down every ten or twenty meters—barely making contact—skimming prima donnas with a million years' practice. They had no faces, just gentle hollows where the mouth and eyes should be.

Ian's blood oxygen blinked red. He ignored it. The sensuous voice in his suit pleaded, "Please open your helmet intake valve." The brute mechanical valve could not be overridden by his suit computer. He told the sexy, synthesized voice to, "Put a sock in it." Ian was not ready to take his next-to-last breath. The faeries did not seem to bother with breathing.

He started to step off again, meaning to meet the hallucinations halfway—but his legs were locked. Looking down, Ian found that he was kneeling. He had fallen without knowing it. Fine cohesive sand, produced by eons of micrometer impacts, had softened the impact, sliding and caking, spreading the force outward.

Blood oxygen blinked angrily. Time to obey that sweet persistent recording—"Please, open your intake valve." Reaching back, Ian fumbled about, finding the intake tap—but he could not make it turn. He struggled to close his gloved hand. Numb fingers no longer had the strength to work the tap, to get at those last breaths. He pitched headfirst into the lunar dust.

Dust falls gently in one-sixth g, like a slow-mode damask curtain. Through the falling motes, Ian could see the highlands tilted sideways, butted against stark cosmic night. *What a stupid way to die!* Ian loved life, loved it so much that being on the moon had made him want to climb mountains. Cold emptiness crept through the sweaty heat of his suit, descending his spine, balling in his gut. He had gone too far. Fucked up once too often.

As Luna faded, Ian felt himself rising, cradled in silver arms, borne up by gossamer wings. The faerie's silver-clad face did not look the least bit human—it was shaped more like a wolf's snout. Not that it made an angstrom's difference to Ian. The dead don't care who gets them.

Nothing beats going to bed dead and waking up alive. Ian lay on his back, eyes closed, feeling the moon's feeble pull. Air moved in and out of his lungs. Somewhere, water was dripping. In a burst of panic, he realized that his helmet was off, his suit unsealed, exposing face and chest to vacuum. Groping wildly, he tried to close his suit.

"Human, quit batting the air and *breathe* it."

Ian lowered his arms. Shadows flickered against

stone high overhead. He lay in a huge cave lit by hundreds of stubby wax candles. Dark air tasted cool and musty. A caninelike humanoid crouched next to him. Ian's first impression was "wolf," then "hyena," but the beast was not nearly so close akin to him. It was a xeno—an Eridani Hound, human-sized, vaguely baboon-shaped, with dark beady eyes and tufted audio antenna set on either side of a short snout. Twin rows of white fangs showed through parted lips. The Hound's body was hidden by silver fabric; a hooded mask hung to one side; rainbow wings covered with solar cells sprouted from the beast's shoulders. A standard speakbox rested on the Hound's silver chest.

Lounging beside the Hound was a human, a man with the face of a blond, blue-eyed faerie king—handsome, devil-may-care features that screamed biosculpt. His silver body suit showed off nearly sixteen stone of muscle and bone to stunning effect. Neither of them were Loonies. Loonies looked like the "before" holos advertising a cheap health spa—the man was too well-built, and the dog came from the far side of Human Space.

"Clive Barrow," the muscular faerie said, giving Ian a relaxed two-finger salute. He jerked a thumb at the wolf. "A Hound. He doesn't figure he needs a human name."

The xeno's six-digit hand keyed his speakbox. "Howdy, human," drawled the box, "welcome to the Wolf Pack."

Ian looked around. The gravity felt right, but everything else was wrong. He was lying in a vast limestone cavern—Tom and Becky's cave, transported from Hannibal, Missouri, to the moon. Stalactites hung down from the cave vault, and massive stalagmites rose up from the floor, some meeting halfway to form tremendous flowing columns, like pillars of half-frozen ice cream. From far off came the drip, drip of falling water, and the high, faint squeak of bats. The leather-winged rodents flitted back and forth in the candle light. Little blackish-brown vampire bats—Ian could picture their evil beady eyes and bright fangs.

"Where the hell am I?"

"Luna." The Hound hit a dictionary key: "Earth's largest natural satellite, thirty-five hundred kilometers in diameter, surface grav . . ."

Clive cut in, "And your name is Ian MacNeil. From the Outer Hebrides—Earth. Today is Tuesday, Greenwich time. Does that help?"

Aside from the short personal bio, none of this made the least sense. There were no vampire bats on the moon. There was no air for them to fly in. No mammalian blood to feed on. Nor did lunar caves have stalactites or stalagmites, which are caused by water seeping through limestone—the moon being bone-dry. *Mare Imbrium* was a sea in name only. Luna does not even have *limestone*, which is formed from the remains of ancient marine creatures pressed to stone.

Ian's senses were plainly on a drug-induced holiday, but that did not stop him from feeling better, overwhelmingly better—on top of the world. Or at least, on top of the moon. Instead of worrying over where the bats came from, Ian marveled at how really superb life was, picturing summer afternoons off the Hebrides. White sails on the water. Sea turning sunset colors, copper-red and deep lilac. He remembered the devilishly beautiful stewardess who had served him dinner aboard the shuttle. Ian felt as happy as if she had whispered, "When we land, let's rent a futon and fuck," instead of merely saying, "Have a nice stay."

Insanely thankful for his second shot at life, Ian babbled on about how glad and grateful he was. . . .

"How grateful?" asked the Hound.

"Could you put it in money terms?" Clive suggested.

"Well, really, really grateful. I feel like an absolute fool. . . ."

"Humans often are," observed the xeno. "Did you know that your intake valve was clamped *down*?"

Ian gave a guilty nod. "I was saving air."

The Hound's speakbox chuckled. Clive wagged an admonishing finger, "Boy, ya gotta breathe *now*, not next week!"

Ian laughed with them, looking off into the deep recesses of the cave—the gallery above seemed to go on forever. "Where *do* these bats come from?"

Clive looked at the Hound. "Bats? What bats?"

"Human's hallucinating," concluded the Hound.

Okay, I'm cracking up, thought Ian. Can you blame me? The last few hours had been enlightening. Ian now knew that humans were never meant to leave Earth; since his first ancestors wiggled free of the anaerobic slime, they had been adapting to live in the open air—and nowhere else. The ease with which Luna could kill you was eerie. You could suffocate in vacuum, drown in CO_2, be bent by nitrogen, OD on oxygen, freeze in the shade, or fry in the sun. Slow falls could puncture your suit. Flash fires could turn you to toast. Or a tiny lapse in shielding could let in a particle of hard radiation, carrying the seed of inoperable cancer that would cream you twenty years down the line, when *la Luna* was merely a memory.

Outrageous. Unfair. Such casual deadliness made staying alive cheerless drudgery; checking and double-checking, looking before each step, always having healthy margins of everything. *Being good all the time.* With no slack for daydreaming, or just enjoying the moonscape.

Nothing had properly prepped Ian for this, not 3V, not the shuttle ride, not the stewardess' "Have a nice stay." Instinctively, he reached into his open suit for the return ticket, wanting to touch the plastic promise that there was a shuttle berth set to take him home.

The ticket was gone. Ian sat bolt upright. His sweat-soaked pocket was empty. No ticket. No ID. No credit key. He glanced about. Neither of his rescuers were looking his way. "Where's my stuff?"

"Stuff?" Clive lifted an eyebrow. "What stuff?" The Hound's evil grin broadened a millimeter or two. Xenos have a beast's ability to observe without making eye contact.

"The stuff in my pocket. My ID. Credit key. Shuttle ticket?"

"We took 'em." Clive patted a small packet adhering to his silver ribs. It was no great admission. Who else could have emptied his pocket? Ian calculated furiously. Weird as these two were, they had saved his life, and he hated to tangle with them. Clive had height and weight on him, and the Hound looked inhumanly strong. The ID was replaceable, he could spare the credit, but he had to have that prepaid ticket.

"You're sort of like salvage," Clive explained. "Unwritten law says we get half—and unwritten law's got to be strictly obeyed, since there's no one to enforce it."

The fare home was more than Ian made in a year. If anyone cashed the ticket, or used it to disappear dirtside, he might as well never come back. "Hey, I don't mind splitting with you—you deserve some *reasonable* reward—but I have to have that ticket home."

The xeno set his speakbox to extra harsh, "Human, a minute or two more, and we wouldn't be dickering. We'd have had that ticket, along with a slew of body parts and valuable bio-implants, while the rest of you did dust to dust in an organics dump."

Clive grinned amiably, "Absolutely—you can't thank us *enough*. Without air, you don't have a ticket *nowhere*. Not even out the door. If you think you can do better, then get up and go. Just reseal the lock when you leave."

What lock? Ian saw no sign of a cave entrance.

"Look," Clive reflected, "what real use is half a

ticket? Shuttle's not going to take you *halfway* to Earth. The only way for a fair and even split was to make you a full, 100 percent, voting member of the Wolf Pack."

"What's the Wolf Pack?"

His ignorance provoked pitying looks. Clive turned to the Hound. "Claims he never heard of the Wolf Pack."

The Hound gave his shoulders an exaggerated shake, as if to say, "Your stupid species."

"*We* are the Wolf Pack," Clive explained. "What's left of her."

The Hound stared up between the hanging stalactites, looking past the limestone roof. "Would say the jumpbug is just about *due*."

Clive produced Ian's helmet from behind him. "There's a motion on the floor that we suit up and meet the jumpbug. All in favor?"

"Opposed," objected Ian. "I vote you give me my stuff and show me the way back to my rover."

Clive shrugged. "Sorry, I got to go with the xeno. That's a two-thirds majority—motion passed and veto-proof. Want a recount?"

"No. This isn't fair."

"Hell, *no*! It's *democracy*." Clive pulled his silver hood over his head, handing the helmet to Ian. "You're gonna love being a Loonie."

The Hound thumbed a switch sitting incongruously on a stalagmite, and the cave vanished, bats and all. Ian found himself sitting in a transparent half bubble, pitched under an overhang at the edge of an extensive *mare*.

Clive pointed a silver finger, "Gotcha!"

The whole cavern had been a 3V holoprojection. The air holding the bubble taut no longer tasted cool and musty, turning flat and metallic. The 3V had been good. Feelie quality.

The Hound pulled on his own hood and unplugged a seal. Air spilled into the void. As the bubble collapsed, Ian set an amateur indoor record for donning a helmet and sealing a suit. Untangling himself from the deflating shelter, he stepped out onto the Sea of Showers, the vast lava plain connecting the *Oceanus Procellarum* to the Sea of Serenity—carved out four billion years ago by the Rhode Island-sized rock that gave the Man-in-the-Moon his right eye.

Earth hung overhead, nearly full, bigger by far than the fullest moon. White cloud torrents streamed across blue seas. So much air, so much life! You never knew what a blue-white jewel Earth was until you saw her from the surface of her dead sister.

Ian had a full million complaints, questions, and accusations—none of which could be voiced. His comlink was still out, and there was no point shouting into vacuum. Clive and the xeno were a few meters off, wings full extended, pulling in afternoon sunlight, the collapsed shelter tucked casually under Clive's arm. Neither of them looked his way. Ian could hardly run off. He had to stand anxiously checking his oxygen—with his helmet valve wide open, pouring final seconds of air into the suit.

A point of fire appeared overhead, growing larger, outshining Jupiter, then Earth. Waiting on an open *mare* for an incoming lander can be uncanny. The jumpbug appeared to be coming down right on top of them, aiming to grind them into the regolith.

At the last instant, the angle of descent steepened and the jumpbug came down a short ways off, raising a fiery red cloud of dust and exhaust gases. The lander looked old and boxy, a three-legged spider with porthole eyes. "Little Deuce Coup" was stenciled in white across the lock door.

Ian hustled for the lock. Hustle did not mean run, but sort of a fast shuffle, leaning far forward—in Luna's light gravity, it was always a long way to the ground. The others beat him easily. Clive let the xeno cycle through, then made an "after you" motion. Ian took the rungs two at a time, diving into the lock. The outer door closed behind him.

As the little chamber filled with air, Ian tore off his suffocating helmet, happy to breathe whatever the jumpbug offered. Through the tiny square window on the hatch cover, he caught sight of Clive backing off—Ian's first hint that he and the Hound were making this jump alone.

He felt the soft shudder of paired oxy-hydrogen engines, muffled by insulation and lunar vacuum. Acceleration replaced gravity. Too much had happened too quickly. Too much was *still* happening. Ian watched Luna drop away—taking his ID, his credit key, his ticket home, and the rented rover he had no hope of returning. Meanwhile, he was sealed in a hurtling metal box, headed fast for who-knows-where. Music rattled out of a pair of scratchy speakers—Radio Ganymede again. Jolly King Jove had given way to the *Callisto Tabernacle Choir*, coming in a cappella, with "Higher than the Angels" and other hits of the last century:

Flying higher than the Angels,
In the heavens so free,
I hear the sinners a sighin',
"Why me Lord? Why me?"

HOUSTON: Watch for a lovely girl with a big rabbit.

APOLLO 11: (Static) Say what?

HOUSTON: Legend says a beautiful Chinese girl named Chango is living on the moon. Been there four thousand years. Should be easy to spot. (Static) Companion is a large Chinese rabbit standing on his hind legs in the shade of a cinnamon tree. (Static). Name of the rabbit not recorded.

APOLLO 11: Check. Keep a lookout for the bunny girl.

Little Deuce Coup

Prying open the inner pressure door, Ian wormed his way between blue propellant tanks into the jump-bug's command cabin, a cramped metal closet, old and awkward. Modern shuttles and mass conversion ships hid their guts behind hardwood paneling and plush carpets, but here tubing snaked around vents, electronics bays, and indicator boards. Two huge trapezoidal view ports dominated the clutter, showing bright slices of Luna's sunside. Glare and interior lights blanked even the brightest stars, and the sole feeling of flight came from the double throb of oxy-hydrogen engines.

The Hound was in the far couch, half-hidden by the combustion chamber cowling. The near acceleration couch was empty. The command couch sat atop the cowling, with the primary axis of thrust running straight through the seat of the pilot's pants—if the pilot were wearing pants. From where Ian stood, the pilot seemed to be wearing nothing. A smooth, bare leg sprawled alongside the high definition screen, relaxed and professional, heel nestled comfortably in a crook of the optical alignment mount. Nearest to Ian was a nude shoulder, and a head of short-cropped hair, dark as the starless night outside. The pilot was saying something to the xeno, so Ian could not see her face. He stood there feeling hugely overdressed, swathed in layers of nylon fabric and spun silicone.

She turned abruptly. "Welcome aboard, stranger. Where ya headed?"

Ian was too struck to answer. The pilot's face had deep natural lines, untouched by biosculpting. It was not an ugly face—merely the face of a woman who had lived long and worked hard without the benefit of chemo-surgical cosmetics—something you seldom saw on the Dirtside dating circuit. But what hit him was her tattoo. A diamondback rattler covered the right half of her face, rattles touching the corner of her mouth, body coiling up her cheek and arching over her eyebrow—the gaping mouth and thin curved fangs filling her right forehead, ready to strike. Not another pretty face.

"Name's Angel O'Ferrall." Her upsun accent was smooth as cream and honey. Looking down at her bare body, she laughed, "Well, pardon my tits. I didn't know I had to put on panties to pick up a pecker-headed Hound." She nodded toward the far seat. "Xenos don't give a damn what you wear—or look like. Ain't got human feelings."

The Hound's speakbox made noises of grateful agreement.

Angel bent forward, snagging a black top draped over the doppler hood. While she struggled into the synthetic fabric, Ian managed to introduce himself, finding it easier to talk to her bare back and shoulder blades than to that rattlesnake tattoo. Angel straightened up, pulling the black top down to her waist. "Hound and I are headed for Lagrange Farside," she explained. "Sure hope you were, too."

Lagrange Farside was an empty point in space teetering at the edge of the Earth-Moon system—farther than ever from where Ian needed to be. "Good God, no! Why the Hell would . . ."

She silenced him with a snakey look. "We got business, there. Private business. If you're not headed for Lagrange Farside, why are you tagging after the Hound?"

Private business? Ian could easily believe it. He did not want to know more, hoping to stay as clean and innocent as possible. Angel would hardly be burning reactant mass merely to give some canine ET a get-acquainted look at the Earth-Moon system. Clive and the Hound had larceny punched all over them—having offhandedly robbed Ian of everything worth taking. Angel looked only an angstrom more honest. It was hardly in Ian's best interest to know the details of whatever criminal alien-smuggling enterprise he had tumbled onto.

He felt nervously compelled to assure Angel that he was exactly what he seemed—a hapless law-abiding tourist gone astray. He hastily told his whole story. How he had come up from Terra to do an onsite inspection of a new-style mass conversion furnace—then set out on some private lunar exploration. He had rented a suit and rover from a tourist shop in Copernik North—in retrospect, a ghastly mistake—but "My God, I was on the moon!"

Ian had wanted to do a Neil Armstrong, heading off into the unknown. Or at least the unvisited. The Lunar Carpathians had scores of unclimbed peaks. He merely meant to stand on a virgin summit, mentally naming the mountain for himself. Where else in the Earth-Moon system could you put your footprint where no fool had ever tread? Luna made Antarctica look grossly overpopulated—a bubbled tourist trap with polluted ice and hordes of tiny panhandlers in tuxedos. But the vendor had been your typical Loonie, a spindly little weasel—sending him off in a terminally defective suit with a smile, and a hearty clap on the back. (That got a chuckle of sympathy from Angel.) He had gotten lost (outright laughter). And rescued (applause from the Hound's speakbox). And *robbed* (mixed laughter and applause).

"Sounds like Luna." Angel shook her head. "Always pays to see Lady Selene at a distance. I purely do want to hear the finish of this *really funny* story, but I got to do a bit of piloting." Angel cut her throttle, reaching down for the attitude controller between her legs, playing with her thrusters. Roll. Yaw. Then counter thrusts. Farside swung into view, filling the jumpbug's ports. She cut her thrusts. They were in freefall. Farside was in half phase, and they were falling past the sunlit half, seeing the pockmarked plain in maximum contrast. Craters lay on top of craters. No dark *maria* here. The broad ancient lava seas were all on Nearside, facing earth's pull, created by tidal action. Farside was a tortured moonscape of secondary and tertiary impacts, dominated by the big bull's eye of Orientale Basin.

"Gorgeous, isn't she?" sighed Angel. The Hound's speakbox pounded out a rolling crescendo, the intro riff from "Great Wall of Galaxies" by *Gas and Dust*.

He saw Angel's features soften, the snake relaxing—charmed by music and moon magic—no longer about to strike, becoming merely a bizarre and intricate design inked into a woman's face. She gave her shoulders a wistful shake, "*La Luna* and Big Blue are the best reasons to come downsun."

Ian shrugged, "I'd trade my next ten-dozen looks for a ticket to Earth." With each passing second he slid farther from his home in the Hebrides.

"Can't take you to Earth," she told him. "Not if Big Blue still has that steep gravity well and soupy atmosphere. My bug would fuckin' fly apart before we hit bottom."

Angel considered for a moment, "I *could* drop you off in low orbit, at a factory or research station—wouldn't be hard to hitch a ride Dirtside from there."

Ian calculated. The jumpbug might make it down to low orbit, stripped and carrying only two people. Definitely not the way he wanted to return—Ian far preferred the shuttle's air cushion couches, elixir bar, and inflight entertainments (feelies, 3V gaming, and maneuvering nimble flight attendants into semi-private berths). But . . .

"It'll cost," Angel added. "Have to burn like hell to get there, then refuel in low orbit. Give you a straight freight deal—fuel plus 10 percent trouble and overhead. Course, it'd be cheaper to drop you on Farside, or even to take you around to Tycho or Armstrong Station."

Cheaper *maybe*, but any return to Luna was a step backward. Ian hadn't half a chance of finding Clive, and without his ticket, he'd be at the mercy of the

Loonies. The scrawny bastards would be thrilled to send him home, charitably billing his agency double or triple for room, board, travel, damages to the suit and rover, use of the lavatory, and for every deep breath he took. Loonies were adept at wringing a living out of visiting Dirtsiders. Going back down to the moon dead broke, with no ticket home, would be like slitting his wrist in a shark tank and ringing the dinner bell. Much as he might enjoy a chance at force-feeding his virus-ridden suit to that Copernik shopkeeper—Ian needed to get home. On Earth, he could file a claim for the lost ticket and credit, suing the tourist shop in a Dirtside court, charging fraud, punitive damages, and outrageous pain and suffering.

Angel looked him over, "I'd have to know how you planned to pay."

Ian hedged. "I can pay. But I would need to contact my agency, arranging some reasonable compensation . . ."

She cut him short, "This bug does not run on promises, reasonable or otherwise." Angel patted a panel with affectionate intimacy. "Only solid reactant mass is gonna change your vector."

Ian glared at the Hound lounging in the far couch. The xeno knew he was good for the nut, but was saying nothing. Not taking sides.

Angel bent forward, "Got more flying to do." Main thrusters burped. The jumpbug pitched and yawed. Ian had to grab a handhold to keep from rattling about like a bean in a box. Farside slid back behind them. Their destination swung into view. Lagrange Farside is the farthest libration point in the Earth-Moon system, a spot where a ship's fall around the Earth exactly balances its fall around Luna, leaving the ship at rest relative to those two bodies. (Nothing ever stops relative to everything.) Even this limited stability is an illusion—the least displacement gives the Earth or moon an advantage, causing the ship to fall away from the libration point. It was an inherently unstable location that Ian had never dreamed of visiting.

There was a lone ship orbiting the Lagrange point, looking like a three-bladed exhaust fan, slowly rotating in space. Judging size is difficult against a dimensionless black backdrop, where even the stars seem small, but Ian figured the ship had to be fairly big, and quite old, powered by solar collectors married to a fusion reactor. The one or two rpm rotation was a rube goldberg gravity simulator, using circular motion to create internal acceleration.

Angel did a neat job of docking, sliding the jumpbug's stubby lock into a port on the ship's main axis. Ian felt a slight bump. Locks opened automatically and they were joined. Freefall returned. Through the cabin ports, Ian could see kilometers of slowly rotating solar collectors, their flat surfaces pitted by micrometeors.

Angel kicked off the control console, flipping with knees tucked into a tight back somersault, ending up in *demi-plié* at the lock entrance—a neat bit of zero-g gymnastics, proving she knew every millimeter of the cabin. The tight black top came only to her waist, dividing her neatly in half, adding to her mystery—half of her was dark and remote, topped by her menacing tattoo, the other half of her was unclad, open, even enticing. Unembarrassed by semi-nudity, she slid past Ian, entering the big ship through the open lock, vanishing into the revolving hatch of a de-spin system—not bothering to look back.

Ian dived after her disappearing rump, unwilling to be left aboard the jumpbug with only a big ugly xeno for company. As soon as he had joined her in the de-spin system, Angel reached up and banged the inner hatch shut, saying, "Room for two. The Hound can take the next drop."

They began to fall toward the tip of the solar panels. Weight built up. Angel looked him over, head cocked, deliberately showing the profile not disfigured by her tattoo. By now, Ian was used to this trick. She would flick the snake back toward him whenever she wanted to shock. "You're really damned cute," she decided. "Do you have a body to match that face? Earth men usually do." This was all challenge and bravado. She *knew* there was no chance of Ian taking advantage of her at close quarters, not when he was suited up tighter than Sir Galahad.

The capsule thumped to a stop at somewhere near two-thirds standard gravity. Angel kicked open the deck hatch with her heel. Humid misty air steamed into the capsule. She swung her bare legs over the lip and dropped through the hatch. Ian followed, struggling to compensate for coriolis effect, and his bulky suit.

He landed in a photosynthetic greenhouse. Vines clung to the bulkheads. Wavering illumination and light gravity made Ian feel like he was standing on the bottom of a weed-choked pool. A brown pigmy goat stared curiously up at him from amid the undergrowth.

"Mind the goat shit." Angel pushed aside some creepers, exposing another pressure hatch. "And take off that suit. You'll be so much more comfortable." She slipped through the hatch again without a backward glance.

Ian unsealed as quickly as he could, opening the pressure suit down to one knee like a pair of kid's pajamas. Stepping free of the suit, he stuffed it into the open hatch above him, to keep the elevator lock from closing. With the hatch held open, tons of air pressure kept the elevator capsule from returning for the Hound. The xeno might as well be back in the Eridani.

Proud of his ingenuity, Ian swaggered after Angel. Now it was him and her. No clumsy suit. No freefall antics. No superhuman Hound. Earth-trained muscles in two-thirds *g* made him feel strong and agile, and very much in control. For the first time since getting lost, things would go his way. Angel had her bold talk and brash habits—but he had the law behind him (or what passed for law on Luna). She had to cooperate—and at least punch through a call to Earth—or be an accessory to robbery and kidnapping. He opened the pressure hatch, prepared to be firm but reasonable.

The inner cabin was free of vines and creepers. Instead, a great stone eye stared sideways at him. As Ian stepped through the hatch, the bulkhead behind him turned into sand dunes, rising and falling beneath a cloudless sky. He saw that the eye belonged to a colossal face, half-buried in desert sand. Ian recognized the face at once. It was Ramses II. Beside it stood two tall trunkless legs of stone.

It was, of course, a projection, hiding the real decks and bulkheads behind a 3V image of the broken monument of Ramses II. Not a true image either. (Ian had seen the real thing, flanked by a ruined temple complex, rent-a-camel stands, and tourist shops.) It was a projection of Ramses' fallen statue *as Shelley pictured it* in his poem "Ozymandias":

Nothing beside remains. Round the decay
Of that colossal wreck, boundless and bare
The lone and level sands stretch far away.

But it was every bit as good as the bat cave. He could taste hot barren air, and hear the *sirocco* moaning off the dunes. Flecks of illusionary sand struck his face.

Beneath Ian's feet was a brightly colored Persian carpet, stretched flat. Angel sat crosslegged on the big embroidered rug, filling china cups with tea from a brass samovar. Ian guessed that only the rug and tea set were real, everything else was sensory illusion. Determined not to be impressed, he sat down, taking an offered cup.

"So, you cannot pay for a trip home, or even the drop to Farside?" As Angel spoke, the rug began to rise. Ramses' face and legs sank out of sight. Dunes dwindled. The carpet took off, winging over sunlit waste.

"I cannot pay for anything," Ian admitted, trying to ignore the desertscape unrolling below.

"A lot of us up here are in that income bracket."

"Come on, how much could it cost to punch a signal through to Terra for me?"

Angel considered. "If I did put a signal through, would they come to get you? And arrest the Hound?"

"I hope so." Ian heard caravan bells tinkling on the wind. A line of camels plodded nose to tail beneath them, casting dramatic shadows over the plain.

She shook her head. "No good. I need that xeno. Right now there is a Gypsy Mother Ship in a decaying orbit around Neptune, in terminal need of repairs. Everyone aboard is in desperate trouble—and that xeno is my link to credit that can save them."

Jesus, a Gyp. It made a sick sort of sense. The antique equipment. Angel's brash talk. And the Arabian Nights 3V show. Gyps lived their whole lives between cramped decks. Illusions like this kept them just this side of being psychotically claustrophobic. They were as witless as Loonies, and twice as wild, with a fine disregard for the rights and opinions of Dirtsiders. Ian was going to have to work hard to get her sympathy. "Look," he protested, "I can't think flying about like Ali Baba. Land this rug."

The carpet picked up speed. A double line of palms poked over the horizon, marking a pair of rivers. Harun-al-Rashid's Baghdad hove into sight. The carpet descended, just clearing the huge circular walls. Banking between tall minarets, they flashed over sweating porters at dockside and crowds haggling in the bazaars, making straight for Harun's domed and turreted palace at the heart of the city. Swooping into the palace precincts, the carpet slid under an ornate portico, coming to rest in a sunlit harem court.

Women and girls lounging under citron trees beside a rosewater fountain played with dwarf deer and an ape with a gold collar. Tough-looking eunuchs guarded the pointed doorways. Angel's fantasies had casts of thousands and vivid detail. Ian could hear the deer's tiny silver horse shoes clicking on the tiles. She set down her tea cup. "You're a Dirtsider. Check?"

"I thought I said that?"

"Got a job?"

"Yes, I told you . . ."

"Pension, paid vacations, health plan . . ."

"Well, sure."

". . . and dental plan?"

"I don't see . . ."

"Clearly not a charity case. I got *none* of those. My problems are all cash and carry—yours don't impress me much. People *depend* on me. Oldsters and babies who don't have agency grants or pension funds. If their ship isn't fixed, they will all die when the orbit decays."

"That sounds harsh, surely . . ." Ian groped about for a solution, but no easy one came to mind.

"Harsh? Hell, it's just *gravity*. And gravity's the *law*—it keeps the system together. Can't bitch about that. But with that Hound's help, we can afford to fix the ship."

"Why is this Hound so precious? They are more obnoxious than rare."

"We mean to enter him in the Great Games at Tycho."

Gamers. My God! Why couldn't Angel and the Hound have been into something sane and sensible, like credit fraud, or hijacking interstellar liners? "No one wins at gaming," he protested.

"The Wolf Pack does!" Angel's rattlesnake seemed to leap out, reminding Ian how often gaming addiction went with disfigurement—a deepseated distaste for mere flesh, even your own.

Despite being a hundred percent voting member of the Wolf Pack, Ian hadn't the least faith in this phantom organization. "From what I've seen, I wouldn't stake a microcredit on them, much less my sanity." Gaming was the most insidious, dangerous addiction ever invented. Ian liked his brain undegraded.

"They've won before." Angel's eyes glittered with the gambler's fallacy—because something had happened once, it had to happen again. "Turning that Hound over to the law is a null program. No payout. He's a xeno. No clothes. No pockets in his moonsuit. The only way he could have your ID and ticket is if he ate them."

She leaned forward, putting her whole body into her plea. "Forget your crummy little job. We're going to hit a *sweepstakes* jackpot! Getting rich by doing good. Saving you, and saving my ship. I'll see you fly back to Earth in style. A private shuttle. Your own orbital yacht!"

"And if we *lose*?" Addicts never considered that—they were hooked on the game itself. Earth had millions of feelie addicts, but there the disease was more or less under control, with clinics to help you kick, cut back, or live with the addiction. On Tycho, things were wide open. Addicts were soaked until their credit went sour, and the gaming casinos owned them—body and soul. "God, why can't you guys earn an *honest* living!"

Angel laughed, "This is absolutely the most legal thing Clive has ever done. And win or lose, I'll *personally* make it worth your while."

No need to ask how. The fountain was pouring out some hellish pheromone, jacking his hormones into overdrive—reminding Ian *why* the Caliphs built these perfumed harem courts. In case he somehow missed the message, the houris began to strip and bathe, splashing rosewater over each other's breasts and thighs, engaging in erotic play, while caged birds broke into a chorus of "Sheherazade."

Ian fought to shake off the spell. "This is mad. And illegal. And I am not going *near* Tycho."

"Look, I'm giving you a hundred percent free choice." Angel leaned back, letting him look her over. "You can come *with me* to Tycho. Or I'll have Tiny sit on you until the Hound and I come back rich and happy."

"Tiny?"

She pointed her chin, flashing the snake, indicating the gold-collared ape in the garden, the only male member in the lesbian garden party. This was the problem with gamers, they found it impossible to tell illusion from reality. It would take more than a 3V gorilla to terrorize Ian into obeying. "I'm going to insist on you bouncing a call to Terra off one of the Lagrange stations."

Angel smiled and snapped her fingers. The ape shambled away from his playmates, stepping onto the carpet. A moment later, Tiny was towering over Ian, looking like the colossus of Ramses come to life. Clearly this was a real three-hundred-kilo SuperChimp, able to stuff Ian into his tea cup. "Tiny or me, take your pick." Angel looked him straight in the face, half woman, half snake. "Either way, I promise not to be insulted."

The lady or the behemoth? Ian had little choice. Tycho might be a first class brain-fuck, but it beat hanging about Lagrange Farside with Tiny for his keeper. There was no way he would stay here, not even if Harun's harem were real and ready to indulge him.

He threw up both hands. "Okay, let's take Tycho apart!"

Angel's congratulations were interrupted by an insistent rapping on one of the harem gates. A bored eunuch drew his scimitar and opened the cedarwood door, revealing a plasti-metal airlock, full of EVA gear and deflated pressure suits. The Hound stepped out in full silver suit, having obviously just climbed several kilometers of solar paneling to reach the living quarters. "The capsule did not come back," his speakbox complained. "Some witless human jammed the elevator lock."

Hail Caesar, we who are not *about to die salute you.*
—Motto of the *Circuit Maximus*

The Great Games

Smack, crack, crank, speed, booze, acid, hash, bhang, poppies, and belladonna; none of the above (or all of them taken at once) had even half the addictive power of gaming. As proof of that, all these drugs (and a hundred others) were offered free or *at cost* to customers by the gaming palaces in Tycho. Not to *compete* with gaming—which could never be done—but to provide a relaxing come-down between sets, taking the edge off tattered neurons.

Angel set the jumpbug down just inside Tycho's massive ringwall, amid long afternoon shadows. Like a lot of inhabited Luna, the landing-field looked really low-rent, tramped-over, scarred by blast craters and crawler tracks. Posh automated pressure vehicles scuttled out to greet them, like great scavenger beetles competing for a fresh cadaver. Each sported the logo of a different gaming palace. Angel picked the one marked *Circuit Maximus*, and they were piped aboard by a corny, full-orchestra version of *"Also Spracht Zarathustra."* Ian pointed out that this was pure hype, to impress the marks, setting them up for plucking.

Angel waved off his sour attitude. "Of *course* it's a shuck—so lie back and *enjoy it.*"

He gave in, settling back on a plush sofa facing the forward viewport. Angel snuggled next to him. The Hound sat hunched on the deck, visibly bored by human luxury. Tiny wedged himself into a plastic seat, like King Kong trying not to fill a small living room. Through crystal vacuum, Ian could count the notches on the crater's central peak. Tycho was only a couple of billion years old, blasted out by a flying mountain somewhat smaller than the one that had carved Copernicus. The gaming palaces were perched on the central massif. The surrounding crater floor was graded like a giant Japanese rock garden, covering-over centuries of crawler tracks. A massive pillar and lintel shrine stood over a small black depression, dedicated to the *Dharma Bum* and her passengers.

The crawler rolled right up to a private lock, to keep *Circuit Maximus* from losing customers to another casino. They disembarked directly into the autobar and gaming area, done up to resemble a Roman forum. Holos made the place look huge, throbbing to the beat of "Nero's Treat," by *Smug and Insincere*.

A tasteless triumphal arch opened onto a 3V arcade blazing with simulated life. "Come this way!" it shouted. "Choose from HUNDREDS OF ALIEN WORLDS—fight WILD BEASTS in the sun-scorched ARENA, win the SLAVE MAIDEN caged overhead—TAKE HER on the burning sand!" Ian could tell by the frantic appeal that the arcade booths must be nearly empty. Such synthetic vice was amusing enough in its own robust way—especially if you lacked the energy and imagination to jerk-off on your own—but it could never compare to the Great Games. The real action did not begin until you plugged in.

Demi-gods in tights and togas and women with impossible tinsel-wrapped figures were having such a raucous good time that they had to be shills or holos. As soon as Ian passed up the penny-ante arcade, a suave majordomo stepped forward with a wave and a bow. He was a Loonie, with spindly limbs and the distant unflappable smile of a feelie addict. Minor employees were almost always Virtual Reality junkies, endlessly working off their debts to the casino.

Ian ordered up a room, only to find Clive had already rented them a suite. Angel's bold tattoo, Tiny the SuperChimp, and the outlandish xeno did not get so much as a blink. Clearly nothing happening in the here-and-now could possibly compare to this Loonie's off-hours. Ian suspected that he could have spit in the majordomo's face, and the smile would not have wavered. It was impossible to annoy someone who was merely going through the motions of life—in his spare time he could easily be Caligula or Kublai Khan, lord of some synthetic Xanadu, with a seraglio of nubile young houris and painted boys waiting for him to plug in. Greeting the public was so many hours of hum-drum, endurable so long as it paid for his pleasure. It would have taken a plasma torch between the man's toes to get more than a polite, "Right this way."

Angel took Tiny to their suite. Ian went with the Hound to inspect the gaming arena, a steep high-tech pit smelling of blood and sand, surrounded by pillowed couches and low tables. Two towering holos rose out of the center of the pit, ten meters tall, and sweating under an indoor sun. A huge *retiarius*, armed with fish net and trident, stalked an amazon *samnite* in half armor, who was defending herself with an oblong shield and Spanish short sword. The female holo limped from a leg wound, and a ribbon of blood cut across the *retiarius'* muscular chest.

The phantom combat got scant attention from prospective gamers crowded around the pit, huddled in groups and pairs, striking deals, debating tactics, or going over map displays of nineteenth century Africa and medieval Transylvania. Tables were spread with a typical Loonie tourist buffet: curried bulgar and garbanzos, a three-fungus salad, peppered leeks, *champignons farcis*, and edible pond algae. Every so often, someone would look past the giant gladiators, glancing at the hexagonal display floating overhead, getting a readout on games in progress.

Ian noted that most of the games were now closed competitions, of interest only to touts and gamblers. A Renaissance Italy team elimination was down to a dozen pairs, stalking each other with stilettos and poison cups through the back alleys and banquets of fair Verona. In the Arthurian tourney, Lancelot looked to be mopping up. Gawain and Galahad trailed in the standings, Tristram and Mordred had been eliminated by a bad fall and a broken lance. Bedivere remained a long shot at 20 to 1. Of the open heats, the Cape to Cairo rally had yet to begin, and attention focused on the Grand Luna Sweepstakes, still accepting latecomers at bargain rates. A timer showed that the moon over Dracula's castle was waxing, nearly full.

The base of the hexagonal display bore a cheery warning—ALL OUTCOMES ARE FINAL.

Clive came strolling through the crowd, dressed as a blond Alcibiades in a gold toga, its purple border trailing behind him. He paused several times to listen in on strategy sessions, exchanging comments, sometimes aloud, sometimes in a stage whisper. When he got to Ian, he clapped him on the shoulder. "Perfect timing—I've entered us in the Sweepstakes. We go in at 0700."

A gawky sharp-faced Loonie with slick black hair and a spade beard slid up, looking furtively from side to side. Clive introduced the Loonie, saying "This is Philaemos, but you can call him Phil—he's on our side, I think."

Phil nodded eagerly. "Until the Castle."

"Until the Castle," Clive said, and laughed.

Ian knew that alliances and conspiracies were an integral part of team competitions. But once you plugged in, anything was fair; surprise, duplicity, and betrayal were standard tactics. The sweepstakes competition had a single prize, "The Vampire's Heart," a blood-red ruby hidden away in the heavily defended tower of Dracula's Castle. Each team could increase its chances by cooperating with the others—until the Castle was breached, or an advantageous double-cross presented itself. But whoever seized the ruby was sole winner of the accumulated credit—minus the casino's cut.

Phil looked warily about. "The White Company has put out a call for allies."

Clive looked up at the display. "Of course, they got waxed in the opening rounds. Well, tell 'em the Wolf Pack's back."

Phil scuttled off, happy to have a confidence to betray. Clive lowered his voice. "Philaemos hangs around the pit, talking up games he hasn't the credit to enter. People call him Phil the Shill, but he's pretty harmless, unless you happen to trust him."

The White Company did not look much like Conan Doyle's band of chivalric adventurers; clumped together at one end of the arena, their casino togas haphazardly arranged, they looked more like a load of soiled laundry. The only thing *Roman* about them was the hollow-eyed Romulus and Remus look—abandoned at birth and suckled by wolves. One of them growled at the Hound, "This table's for humans."

Clive flashed a smile. "He's not fussy."

According to the readout above, the White Company had already been overrun by Tartars in the early innings. Ian recognized the nervous brooding of gamers at the closing end of a bad run. Several sat hunched on couches, staring past their eyebrows at the timer ticking overhead.

"Brilliant, absolutely brilliant," muttered a big blonde amazon in a man's toga. "You sure gave 'em hell, Gertrude. Screaming for mama until they slit your throat."

"No shit, Sheila. You weren't so fuckin' slick yourself." Her companion, small and dark, was dressed more like a woman in an ill-fitting Ionian chiton.

"What was I *supposed* to do? Those Tartars just creamed us, coming out of nowhere. It was hardly fair." Sheila's appeal for fairness got a grim laugh. "I mean, how can they bring in a fuckin' Kipchak killing machine from out of Central Asia just to roll over us?" There was no answer, except for the obvious one: so long as the casino stayed within the game parameters, *Circuit Maximus* could tilt the play any way it pleased. It was up to the gamers to beat the system or go away broke.

Ian looked over toward the readout, to get a fix on the time. Almost 2200. He should be resting. Or better yet, in bed with Angel.

The Hound got into a spirited argument with the *Circuit Maximus* management, absolutely refusing to go into the game in human guise, citing several treaties and insisting that his rights as an extraterrestrial were being violated—threatening to *sue*. If the casino had no provisions for ET players, he could at least go in as a dog. Any sort of human would be too degrading.

Sheila took a sharp bite out of a peppered leek. "Well next time out, I hope to see all you fuckers dying *hard*."

A man protested. "You think it was *fun* getting feathered with iron-headed arrows? Feeling yourself bleed to death?"

"Right," Sheila snorted. "Want to hear what the Kipchaks were doing to *us* while you were lying on your backs restfully bleeding to death?" She nudged the smaller woman. "Gertrude, *tell* 'em about it." Gertrude merely grunted.

Phil the Shill took the chance to cut in. "Hell, one time I was tortured by Hurons, for *days*."

"Hurons? This was the bloody Balkans."

White Company members blinked at him, staring as if he had lost his wits. "It was another game," Phil admitted. "But it was real bad—they had red-hot tomahawks."

"Shit, that's *nothing*."

"God, I hope they hacked you in the crotch!"

The White Company tried to go back to their argument, but they had lost the thread. Soon everyone was comparing their most gruesome, horrendous deaths—burning, impaling, crucifixion, flaying, and dismemberment. It seemed that every form of violent, bizarre extinction had been suffered by *someone* at the table. Hollow eyes lit up. A false bravado seized hold. Whatever else had happened, they were still the goddamn White Company, and they could sure as hell take it!

Ian got up and looked around. Sicker than the stories themselves was the *way* they were told, full of verve and energy—*as if it actually mattered.* He hated to hear gamers spilling their guts, trying to sound *bad.* All it showed was how totally delusional they were. The most elemental rule of gaming was that if you die, you lose—your original stake is gone. You have to give up, or buy your way back in. This tough talk amounted to a bunch of chronic losers bucking themselves up by boasting about how badly they had lost. Somehow he had to *win.*

Disgusted by the whole show, he went to look for Angel, to get what he could out of the game—*up front.* The Wolf Pack's suite was immense—three bedrooms, two baths, a full galley, a salon and an autobar. Tiny had his own room. One of the salon walls was 3V, tuned to show an indepth surface projection of Kikku, Chi Draconis III, with its planetary ocean rolling under china-blue skies. Twin moons hung low on the watery horizon. All charged to Ian's line of credit.

Angel was wearing a green silk casino chiton and snacking on dishes brought up from the buffet downstairs. "Try the curried bulgar," she suggested. "Come tomorrow we're likely to be living on it—along with this edible pond scum."

Ever since he'd agreed to go to Tycho, she had shown him nothing but her good side. Now was the time to take advantage of that. He sat down next to her, resting his hand on her thigh. She did not flinch or draw back. Her leg felt strong and warm through the thin fabric. His fingers slid inward. Hardly suave, but he was in a hurry.

"Save it for the games," she told him. "At seven A.M. sharp, we've got to cut our way to Dracula's Castle, storm the sucker, then steal a ruby out from under some mean opposition."

Ian assured her that he'd be better able to wrestle Bulgars in the morning, if she would loosen up a bit now.

Angel turned slightly, showing only the fangs and tail of the snake. "Come morning, we are going to be in a megacredit sweepstakes competition. Bulgars will be the least of our worries. We have to beat the House. Beat the White Company. Beat *everybody*—you know what the odds on that are like?"

"Not good."

"Bad enough that *Circuit Maximus* is willing to bet a thousand-to-one on us fucking up—and feel sure of winning. Look around you; none of this was paid for by backing bad bets."

She held up her hand edge-on in front of her face, defining an invisible plane dividing her face down the middle, an eye on either side. By moving her hand forward, she indicated that the plane extended outward, as far as the mind could take it. "We have to walk it tight if we aim to win. No missteps, no mistakes. Our energy has to be on line. We better damn well *hum*, or my people orbiting Neptune will die. And we'll all end up losers, like those sad fuckers downstairs."

"Sure, sure, but . . ."

"No buts. Did you see that duded-up corpse that greeted us at the door? Talk about your undead, *that* was a goddamn zombie! Give the casino a week or two, you could be *him*. Totally glazed-over in some electronic Neverland. In a gaming casino, you check your sanity at the door. So don't blow it. You've got to promise me that you will *never* think it's not real."

"I promise." Ian would have promised her the

whole godforsaken moon at this point. What did he have to lose?

She gave him a swift kiss on the lips. "Good. Now get some sleep. In a day or two, we'll be dodging vampires in the dark—if we're real lucky."

At 0600, the crowd in the gaming pit was gearing up for the start of the Cape-to-Cairo Rally. Tarzan wanna-bees were poring over projections of German Tanganyika, swearing in Swahili. Clive was there to prep Ian on plugging in. "Remember—go light. The Board is going to offer you all kinds of weapons, armor, and paraphernalia—tempting you to turn yourself into a walking arsenal."

"What's so bad about that?" Ian was having second and third thoughts about the whole business.

"First, you have to lug it about, and edged weapons weigh a lot. Have you ever hefted a halberd or a broad ax?"

"Not lately."

"Would you know how to use one when the time came?"

"Maybe . . ."

"Most likely, you'd never get the chance. The casino *wants* you to load up on weapons and spells, figuring you'll be blindsided before you can ever use 'em. Going in overarmed is worse than being bare-assed—if you're naked, you at least feel *exposed*. You'd know to take cover and keep alert. All an arsenal does is lull you into making mistakes—it can even give you away. Have you ever *heard* someone walking in plate armor? It sounds like a convention of drunk tinkers. Are you ready to take on every Turk and Tartar who hears you coming?"

"Probably not. So what's best?"

"Dress like a peasant," Clive advised, "with a dirk or dagger—and one distance weapon. How are you with a bow?"

"I don't know." Except for the bagpipes, Ian had never handled anything that could be called a "distance weapon."

"Try a light crossbow. They're easy to aim, and can be fired from hiding—always the preferred position."

"What about magic?"

"Way too expensive. That line of credit you came here with wasn't endless. It took your ticket and most of that credit to get this far."

"Next time, I'll do better." *Next* time, he would stay on *Terra*. "So if we lose, *Circuit Maximus* will be expecting me to pay up?"

Clive grinned, "Sounds too perfect to be true."

"Could only happen on Luna," added the Hound. He had won his tussle with the casino—happily going in as an ugly black mastiff.

Ian grinned back, secretly wishing he could flatten them both—but they easily outmassed him. Besides, he was trapped. Back out now, and *Circuit Maximus* would present him with an absolutely unpayable bill. Somehow, the Wolf Pack had to win.

Clive patted him on the back. "Just remember the Pack motto."

"What's mine is yours?"

"No," Clive laughed, "though that's a good'un. It's 'All for One and One for All.' Punch *French Crusader* so that we can go in together—and never think it's not real."

Circuit Maximus had a whole phoney ritual connected with plugging in—part of the casino hype, delivered at *no extra charge*. Servants stripped off Ian's toga, leading him down marble steps to a subterranean Roman bath. Light streamed down from stone vents onto pale steaming water. Here he was washed, toweled, rubbed, and scented, then escorted to his gaming compartment, as though he was a gladiator going into single-combat, the casino's champion, instead of its chump.

Gold letters decorated the Roman arch above the entry vault—DACIA, the name of Trajan's Romanian province.

Inside, lying on slabs, were rows of high-tech coffins, plasti-metal cocoons covered with tubes, circuitry and instrumentation. Inside his was a tiny human-shaped space, adjusted to Ian's size and physique. Casino flunkies helped him in, tightening the seals until the chamber fit like a surgical glove, with dermal transceivers touching every centimeter of skin. Then the chamber was screwed shut, light-tight.

He was in total darkness, silent and disorienting. Then the Board appeared. The display floated about half a meter in front of his face, listing identities, physiques, languages, arms and armor, spells and counter magic, mounts, pack animals and special equipment, each item paired with a price in credits. All had tiny red dots beside them. He could make selections by reaching up and touching the dots, turning red settings to green. His hand would not really be moving, any more than he was actually "seeing" the board. Movement and sensation were already wired in. The Board was a projection onto his retina. Blinking made it go away. Opening his eyes brought it back. The decision to lift his arm and touch a setting triggered complex feedback loops that registered his choices, while stimulating his kinesthetic and pressure receptors, making him feel touch and movement.

All contestants came into the game from outside Transylvania. Identities ranged from the Khan of the Golden Horde or Osman Sultana (both hideously expensive) down through Prince Philip of Artois (merely overpriced) all the way to Crippled Beggar (the casino was willing to *give* credits to anyone who thought they could win with one leg and spastic shakes). Under *French Crusader* a double column of entries included:

Jean the Fearless	Chevalier
Marshal Boucicaut	Esquier
Admiral de Vienne	Hospitaler
Comte Jacques de la Marche	Courtesan
Enguerrand de Coucy	Monk
Henri de Bar	Gross Valet
Gendarme	Crossbowman

And so on, down to Common Whore and Scullery Knave.

The titled nobles all came with armed retinues (handy no doubt, but way out of his price range). Ian skipped over the various forms of men-at-arms, concentrating on the lowly and affordable personas at the bottom of the list. He doubted his abilities to perform as a Monk or Courtesan, but Crossbowman seemed to fit, and supplied him with the distance weapon Clive had suggested.

There was a whole list of physical features—height, weight, hair and eye color, etc. A make-over cost nothing. He could go in as handsome as Clive and hung like a god *at no extra charge*. Or as a woman, if he wanted that thrill. Something told him he would do better as he was.

The first couple of languages came cheap. French was free with the character. Magyar, German, Romany, Turkic, Yiddish, and so on could all be had at reduced prices. But the ability to plead for mercy in Mongol did not seem all that much of an edge. He selected the local Romanian dialect, which would at least let him know what the poor folks were saying.

The list of edged weapons read like a grotesque military museum catalog:

Broadsword	Halberd
Brown Bill	Mace
Claymore	Pole Ax
Double Axe	Rapier
Falchion	Sabre
Flamberge	Scimitar
Gisarme	and so forth . . .

A dirk came with the costume. The only other piece of cutlery that tempted him was a silver stiletto, for dispatching *loups-garous* and vampires, but it cost more than all the rest combined.

He lingered over the lists of spells and magics—not because he could afford or use them, but to get an idea of what he was up against. In general, any sort of central Balkan ghoul or beastie seemed to be allowed, everything from werebitches to bottled *djinn*. God, what a disaster this was going to be.

He punched ENTRY. Let the games begin!

The Undead

Ian stood on a gallows hill. A narrow rutted cartpath at his feet wound down the knoll toward an almost treeless plain, dotted with villages, each with its domed church. In the near distance, a gaily colored pavilion stood by a silver stream. Farther off was a walled town with leaden roofs, and an outlying Byzantine tower. A crossbow and quiver dug into his back.

The gaming compartment, tons of rock, Tycho, and all of Luna had vanished at the press of a button. His sole companion on this place of punishment was a mummified body, impaled from pelvis to collar bone. The half-rotted head lolled to one side, wearing a wide toothy grin. Whatever software ran the scenery had a perfectly macabre sense of humor.

None of this is real, he reminded himself. He was *really* back on Luna, in a plasti-metal womb, being force-fed sensations. But it damn well *felt* real. Open skies and Earth-normal gravity seemed totally natural, a relief from the tunnels of Luna. Rough homespun itched against his skin. The clink of chains on the gibbet and the moan of the wind through the spokes of the tall breaking wheel raised hairs at the nape of his non-existent neck. Ian smelled horse-leather, and heard the clank of armor.

Spinning about, he saw a knight on horseback, framed by the flogging post and burning stake. Fear and amazement shot through him. He had been caught flat-footed, mooning over the reality of the set-up, his crossbow uncocked and untested, leaving him nothing but a dirk to save him from this armed apparition on a warhorse.

"Yo, villain," the knight called down, couching his lance. "Give my regards to Beelzebub!"

Ian ducked behind the gibbet, to keep from being ridden down in the first rush—all the time thinking, this is impossible. Unreal. Grossly unfair. The knight bearing down on him was armed with a lance, mace, broadsword, and even one of those thin silver vampire-killing stilettos. Right out of the chute, he was supposed to somehow gut and kill this heavily armored horse and rider, with nothing but bare hands and a sliver of sharp steel *that did not even exist*. There was no way this could happen. Not even in a feelie.

Sir Asshole rattled right up to the gibbet, taking a couple of lively stabs with the lance, laughing as Ian jumped from one side to the other. Then he lifted his visor. "Gotcha!"

It was Clive. Ian cursed, calling his teammate every rude anatomic name he could come up with on short notice, ending the string with, "You bugger-headed bastard, you lied! 'Go light,' you told me, 'Dirk and crossbow.' Then *you* terrorize the shit out of me, dressed like a steel scarecrow!"

Clive shrugged, letting his shoulder armor rattle. "Your line of credit was nowhere *near* long enough to arm us both. Besides, just moving in a suit like this requires training." Clive did a swift mounted pirouette, showing off his costume, which was that of a *gendarme de la Garde*, a Scots Archer armored *cap-à-pie*, à la Quentin Durward—gorget, greaves, and back-and-breast over chain-link hose and hauberk. Ian recognized the Robertson coat-of-arms in Clive's shield, three wolf's heads on a red field.

"Look, I'm the one who's disappointed"—Clive brought his lance down, resting the point against Ian's chest, pressing gently—"finding my teammate thumb-up-the-butt, gawking at the landscape. That ain't the Wolf Pack way. This is an elimination sweepstakes, not a goddamn *sightseeing* contest! You're a French bowman far from home, on an incredibly suicidal quest." Clive pushed harder with his lance. "Start fuckin' *acting* the part. Or you are going to be *dead*. Gone. Out of the game. Explaining to *Circuit Maximus* why you can't pay up."

Ian wanted to groan, or mayhap scream. Instead, he grimly unslung his crossbow and took a few practice pulls at cocking it. The bow came with a stirrup, goat's foot, and spanning belt, so that he could use his thigh and back muscles to bend the steel bow. Slip the goat's foot over the bow cord, put his foot in the stirrup, then straighten up. The bow was cocked. Stick in a wicked looking quarrel, and he was set to do damage. The immediate impulse was to test the bow's effectiveness by sticking it under the skirt of Clive's hauberk and squeezing the trigger. Only the threat of being left alone stayed his hand.

He unstrung the bow, and they set off, leaving the gallows hill behind. The gray mud and the dour medieval landscapes were supposed to match Transylvania, the Land Beyond the Trees—not as it was, but as it might have been in the days of Dracula. The white peaks of the Southern Carpathians poked through blue haze. How long was it since he had been lost among the Lunar Carpathians? Hours? Days? It seemed like centuries.

Fields and vineyards butted up against the blue mountains. The undead live more or less forever, so game time was telescoped. Anything from thirteenth century Kumans to Ottoman Timariot cavalry could come out of the Carpathian passes—Transylvania had been threatened or overrun by nearly everyone. In actual fact, the doomed crusade of Jean the Fearless had gotten no closer than Nicopolis, seventy or so leagues to the south, but considering how totally botched that crusade had been, ending up on the wrong side of the Transylvanian Alps was no more unimaginable than the actual disaster that had engulfed the cream of French chivalry on the Danube.

The cow path dipped down to ford a stream. On the far bank, a knight's pavilion stood planted in a field of stubble. A slim raven-haired damsel lounged in the shelter of the tent fly, black eyes shaded with kohl, bare feet peeping out from under a blue flounced skirt. Diamonds sparkled in her dark hair. She gave Clive a languid smile. Foot-slogging cross-bowmen did not even rate a glance.

The knight himself came trotting round from behind the tent, a gruff bearded giant on a black charger, face flushed and beaded with sweat. He challenged Clive for "the right to cross the stream, and the hand of yon fair maiden."

Clive tipped his lance. "You may keep your fair maiden—hand, tits, toenails, and tiara. As for the stream, we will gladly back up and go around."

But the knave in black armor made it plain that his challenge was mere formality; Clive would not get away without a fight. Ian hurriedly cocked his cross-bow, doubting the light bow would even dent the big man's armor, but in a crude set-up like this anything could happen. The "knight and lady" had to be part of the program—real villains with posh pavilions, and pretty maids at their mercy, had better things to do than camp by a brook, hoping to break lances with some stalwart stranger.

Clive grinned, then lowered his visor. He and the behemoth cantered to opposite ends of the stubble field. The black knight lifted his bridle; his lance came down. Clive did the same. Ian swallowed hard, no longer grudging Clive the horse and armor. Let Mr.

Handsome go in and take the whacks. Ian would not have traded places for all the maidens in Transylvania.

The lady let fall her kerchief, and the two cavaliers in sheet metal launched themselves at each other. Hoof beats shook the stubble as chargers chewed up the turf. The galloping pair came together like a combination anvil chorus and ground-car collision. Ian flinched.

An instant before contact, Clive leaned in, angling his shield, throwing his whole body into the impact, a move that called for incredible concentration and timing. The black lance struck Clive's tilted shield, and was tossed outward. Clive's point caught the inner edge of the black shield, and skidded off, slamming into the man's breastplate at belly-button level. The lance bowed on impact, but Clive was braced for the shock, his body angled into the blow.

His opponent rose up out of the saddle, stirrups flying. He hung for a moment in midair, arms splayed, as his warhorse ran out from under him—then he came crashing down, bounced, and lay prone. Clive reined in directly in front of the pavilion.

The dark-eyed beauty in the blue dress raised her diamond crowned head a notch higher, giving Clive a haughty so-you-think-you've-won-me look. Clive answered with a jaunty salute, turned and trotted over to poke at the prone man with his lance. The fellow refused to respond. Clive lifted his visor, calling to Ian, "Get his purse and broadsword. I'll go after the horse."

The black charger had come to a halt by the brook, saddle empty, drinking nervously. Before Clive got there, Phil the Shill emerged from the weeds by the bank and seized the bridle, bringing the horse over to Clive. Phil was dressed in a jester's outfit, with three thin juggling knives thrust through his belt—acting as helpfully inoffensive as ever.

Ian frisked the Black Knight, finding the man's

purse full of aspers, and his broadsword a bit heavy. Clive called to him, "Finish the fucker."

"What?" Ian looked up.

Clive tapped the silver stiletto with his gauntlet, then made a swift stabbing motion. "Use your dirk. Through the eye-slit." Ian stood rooted. Clive sighed, and waved to the jester. "Phil, show him how."

The tall scrawny jester ran up, bells jingling on his cap. Drawing a juggling knife, he tilted the man's helmet and slid the thin blade between the bars of the visor. Leaning forward, Phil put all of his weight behind the knife. The prone man shook till his armor rattled, then lay still.

"Good job," Clive called down. Ian felt like having a virtual vomit. Phil beamed, saying he knew where the White Company was rallying. Clive lifted an eyebrow. "Can you get us there?"

The jester nodded eagerly, "A few leagues farther on, this path crosses an irrigation ditch at a proper bridge—ignore the bridge, but follow the ditch until you come to a cherry orchard. Through the trees you can see a farmstead with a walled court. That's where the White Company will be."

Clive leaned down, took the black purse from Ian, counting out five silver aspers, giving them to the jester. Grinning his appreciation, Phil cocked his head toward the pavilion. "And what about her?"

Clive laughed, "Feel free. But give her half a chance, and you'll be joining him." He tapped the dead man with his lance.

Phil tucked the aspers in his purse, looking longingly at the pavilion.

"Some kept women will thank you for killing their lord and master, others might take it amiss." Clive handed Ian the reins to the black charger. "Between here and Dracula's Castle, we're going to be offered enough virtual tail to kill you out of sheer exhaustion." The French crusade's riotous progress through the Balkans was infamous for murder and debauchery.

Beautiful concubines. Spearmen drowned in butts of wine. Monks scandalized. "It doesn't cost the casino a thing to jerk you off. Feelie-fucks are part of the programmed obstacles. Hell, a half-dozen gamers are coming in as eunuchs, just to avoid temptation."

The dark-haired damsel laughed at Clive, a high musical laugh, light and inviting. Her hand rested on a silver table set with wine and sweetmeats. Ian mounted up, not tempted in the least. The early morning entry meant they had been sent off before breakfast; Ian's stomach was already inquiring about lunch—soon the sweetmeats on the silver table would be more seductive than the perfumed bed within.

They passed more pavilions, and more women. Also some lumpy-looking peasants, who did not look happy to have bogus French knights tramping about. Crusaders had earned an evil reputation, even in Transylvania.

Clive hardly gave them a glance until well into the afternoon, when he stopped before a golden tent with a well-upholstered blonde seated by the entrance. Here Clive dismounted. A towering *djinn* in Turkish armor with boar's tusks and a wicked scimitar stood guard over the woman. Ian expected him to square off with Clive, but the damsel merely told the muscular demon to see to the horses. Then she gestured toward a low table decked with wine and fruit.

Clive rested his armored seat on the table, reaching for a wine goblet. The woman poured. She had big blue innocent eyes, lips soft as a child's and a friendly open smile.

"Is the food safe?" Phil asked.

"The wine is," Clive told him. "The fruit might give you diarrhea."

The blonde woman laughed and washed an apple in wine, offering it to Ian. "It's not poison," she promised solemnly, sounding like a girl determined to do good, whatever her natural impulse might be.

"But how do you *know*," Phil whined nervously.

"I know." Clive and the blonde exchanged mischievous looks. He would not say more—but they ate and survived.

As they rode on, Clive kept joking with Phil, going over old games, refusing to say how he knew the food was safe. Finally they found the bridge and irrigation ditch, and after that, the cherry orchard. Phil leaped the ditch and disappeared beneath the trees. Clive paused to pluck and eat some cherries. He handed a few down to Ian, saying sotto voce, "Cock your crossbow."

Ian did as he was told, wondering what had made Clive suddenly wary. Phil called out to them from under the trees. Clive spit out a seed, saying, "Phil is going to come running back—when he does, shoot him."

"Say *what*?" Ian stood holding a squareheaded armor-piercing quarrel and a handful of cherries.

"When Phil comes back, shoot him. Through the heart if you can. Point your bow at his chest and pull the trigger."

"My God, *why*?"

"A head shot's too hard. And a gut-shot would be cruel."

"Why shoot him at all?"

"Why do you think you brought that bow? You're going to shoot people. Might as well start with Phil. We don't *need* him anymore, and this is an *elimination* sweepstakes, remember?"

The jester leaped the ditch again, and came jogging back. "What's taking you guys?"

Clive shook his head, and started fumbling for something on the far side of his saddle. Ian stood mesmerized, clutching the cocked bow, telling himself it was all a hideous game and no one was *really* going to die. But he still could not just put a quarrel into Phil's chest.

"What's wrong?" Phil demanded.

Clive nodded toward Ian.

The jester turned to him. "Well, what is it?" Clive rose up in his stirrups. The arm on the far side of his high saddle was holding his heavy flange-headed mace. Swinging it through a tremendous arc, he brought it down on with a wet smack on the back of Phil's jester cap. Ian saw Phil's eyes go wide and his jaw drop. The jester crumpled face forward, the back of his head a bloody mess.

Clive tried to flick the blood off the mace, with not much success. Hair and skin clung to the steel flanges. "See what you made me do? The crossbow would have been so much neater." He tossed the mace to Ian. "Clean it off."

Feeling numb, Ian knelt, trying to clean the mace in the orchard runoff, while Clive rolled Phil into the ditch with his lance. The cool green shade of the ditch smelled heavily of cherries. He handed back the mace and they set out again.

Halfway through the orchard, Clive reined in, saying, "At least the little shit wasn't lying."

Sheila and Gertrude came riding up, looking like Britomart and Amoret fresh out of the *Faerie Queene*. Sheila wore full armor and rode a big chestnut warhorse, carrying her lance half-couched to fit under the cherry branches. Her surcoat and shield bore the red lion of the White Company. Gertrude wore a ball gown and rode a dapple gray palfrey. Both looked wary.

"Where's Phil?" Sheila leaned forward to see under the lanes of trees.

Clive answered with an armored shrug. "He went his own way." Flecks of gore still clung to the mace.

Sheila and Gertrude were not totally taken in, but seemed willing to let Phil fend for himself, asking, "We still have a truce, don't we?"

Clive smiled cheerfully. "Until the Castle."

Ian marveled at the man's ability to lie. Some truce. Sure, it was a *game*—and he had never much liked Phil. But the pain was as real as the smell of ripe cherries. Ian could hardly stomach what he had seen so far. And worse was sure to come. At any moment Clive could start hacking at these two women—shouting happily for Ian to lend a hand.

As they rode on, Sheila and Gertrude started ribbing each other to keep up their spirits. They had gone through grisly deaths already, and bought their way back into the game. But at least these two hopeless addicts had a lively good humor. Already, Ian liked them more than he cared for Clive.

Trees thinned. Through the branches, Ian saw another ditch, and the white walls of a farmstead. "Load your bow," Clive whispered.

The bow was still cocked. Ian looked about, seeing no sign of trouble. No one but Sheila and Gertrude, riding just ahead.

"Load your bow, damn it!" Clive demanded.

Ian hesitated, hating to reach for the quarrel.

Gertrude turned to see what the commotion was. Her curly dark hair framed a round, pleasant face. Not plain. Not pretty. Just pleasant. She had not bothered to make herself beautiful—but Ian still felt moved. He was damn well *not* going to shoot her, even if it cost him the game. He smiled, trying to set her at ease.

Clive cursed and couched his lance.

Ian saw a flash of color over Gertrude's shoulder. A line of men rose out of the ditch. The nearest man wore a sleeve-shaped turban and a short flashy green jacket, over baggy maroon pants. Ian smelled burning sulfur, and realized the men were pointing big crude matchlocks at them. Janissaries, elite Turkish infantry.

With a hideous crash, the whole line exploded in flame and smoke. The black horse beneath him screamed and jerked. Instinctively, Ian turned his mount about—neither he nor the horse wanted to face that hail of lead.

The beast stumbled on for a dozen yards, before going down in a thrashing heap. Ian struggled free of his dying mount. For a moment, he lay amid fallen cherries, mouth open, his jerkin smeared with horse blood. Janissaries swarmed out of the smoke, howling with glee, waving scimitars and short curved daggers. Sheila was down. She and her horse both looked dead. Clive was down, too. A janissary tore off the knight's helmet, and Ian caught a glimpse of Clive's cosmetic features grimacing in agony. A neck wound pumped blood onto his blond hair. Gertrude's horse was down, but she was up and running, trying not to trip on her gown.

Ian bolted, knowing he had no chance against a platoon of Turkish musketeers. None of this was *real*, but he aimed to be gone before they reloaded. Ducking branches and stumbling over furrows, he risked a panic-stricken glance back. Gertrude was pinned against a cherry tree, holding three colorful attackers at bay with a dagger. A dozen more stood around her, laughing and loosening their harem pants. Another pair was busy sawing off Clive's head. Janissaries were slave soldiers, raised from boyhood under rigid barracks disciplines, trained to take out their urges for sex and aggression "in the field." Murder, mayhem, and rape were as fundamental to them as the manual of arms.

He did not stop until he was huddled in the irrigation ditch. Ian could clearly see how insanely idiotic the whole business had been—thinking that they could beat *Circuit Maximus* at the casino's own game. He and Clive had gone up against a perfectly integrated program that suckered players in, then ground them up. The Wolf Pack, the White Company, Phil the Shill, and god knows how many others were all being dealt with swiftly and efficiently. It was only a matter of hours before the program hunted him down and finished him off in some painful dramatic fashion.

With no future worth worrying over, Ian decided to attend to the present. He was cold and miserable, lying in a clammy ditch. Virtual hunger gnawed at him. The need to eat was hardwired into the program, to keep him from just lying low and waiting for an opening. Well, he might as well die comfortably. Getting up, he followed the ditch back the way they had come. He knew he was nearing the cartpath when he came on Phil's body, head down in the ditch. Corpse beetles crawled over the back of his broken skull.

Dusk was descending on the virtual world by the time he came upon the line of pavilions. He sought out a cloth-of-gold tent lit by tall burning cressets and guarded by a huge *djinn* in Turkish armor. If the demon wanted to do him in, the monster had the strength to do a quick, neat job of it. Otherwise, Ian was determined to eat.

The silent colossus with the gleaming scimitar looked him over and let him in. As the silk tent-fly closed behind him, he saw the blonde was waiting, wearing the same good-girl, bad-girl smile that she had seen him off with. Her table was set with couscous and stewed chicken, sprinkled with saffron. Ian set at once to eating, too hungry to care what the meat might contain. Love potions. Sleeping draughts. Slow poison. Whatever kept him from getting into Dracula's Castle was fair game.

She watched, blue eyes alight with amusement. "Where are your friends?"

"Couldn't make dinner," Ian replied. He gave a brief brutal description of Phil's murder and the Turkish ambush. She looked sad and offered more couscous.

Maybe there *was* a love potion in the saffron chicken, because the more he ate, the better the blonde looked, with her upturned nose and infectious good humor. There just had to be a computer-perfect body under her golden robe.

She stood up, taking him by the hand, heading toward her curtained bed. What the hell. She was clearly programmed to please. If she was also programmed to slip a stiletto into him, he only hoped she'd let him come first; anything else would be cruel.

The bed was lit by a single candle suspended in a slotted brass ball, a sort of orb-shaped censer giving off shafts of light. A golden haze filled the curtained chamber. Somewhere in the gaming software, there was a real artist at work. She knelt beside the perfumed coverlet, hands clasped in her lap. "Would it please M'Lord if I undressed?"

Ian grunted and sat down on the bed, kicking off his boots. He'd never thought much of virtual sex. Programmed partners always seemed so slick, so perfect, so ready to please. Real women did not eagerly submit to every semi-sordid act the male mind could imagine, and then come at a touch—just when you wanted them to. Not all the time, anyway.

She let her robe fall and leaned forward, helping him with his pants. As he pulled his homespun shirt off over his head, he felt her go to work, first with her hand, then with lips and tongue. Letting out a little gasp, he lay back on the bed. This was more like it.

Without warning, she bit him. He yelped, struggled up onto an elbow, and looked down at her. The virtual bitch had *bit* him, hard, in the soft hollow of his thigh. He could see the red teeth marks.

"Why the hell did you do that?"

She looked impishly up from between his legs, all smiles and innocence. "To show my Master that this is real."

Then she rose up and kissed him, covering his face in a cascade of golden hair. "This is Transylvania," she told him, "land of the love bite." To prove it, she nibbled on his neck.

It seemed to work. What followed did not feel like virtual sex. To Ian's intense surprise, he found himself really fucking, in a perfumed bed with an utterly real woman that he had met that afternoon over lunch. She was wild, winsome, and headstrong, with her own ideas about pleasure, playfully unpredictable. By the time they were done, he was exhausted, and utterly pleased.

"Was it worth waiting for?"

"Waiting?" Ian stared at her. How do you properly thank a program, especially one with soft curves and an impish grin?

"Doesn't this beat a *Circuit Maximus* guest suite?"

He sat up in bed. "Angel?"

She rolled her blue eyes. "Who else?"

"But how?" He gestured at the tent and bed.

"Protective coloration." She started to redo her hair. "Mobile hazards are programmed to avoid the line of pavilions. Can't have Mongols messing up the casino's honey trap."

Seeing her lift her arms up to redo her hair was too much. He reached over to slide her closer. "It was worth waiting for. You feel ungodly wonderful."

She laughed, not resisting, letting him run hands over her. "That's just programmed hormones. The casino jacks up your testosterone, to keep you virile and distracted. And we have serious work to do. With Clive out of the game—you, me, Tiny, and the Hound are the only ones left to tackle the Castle."

Ian did not like the odds. "Shit—I think I'll take my testosterone to the tent next door."

She gave him a peaches-and-cream pout. "Please don't be such a mark. So Clive is out. He served his purpose."

"The only purpose Clive served was to get his head planted on a virtual pike."

"He got us here. He's the one who infected your suit."

"My suit?" He stopped, thinking back to the *Lunar* Carpathians and the convenient virus in his suit programming.

"I mean, what were the chances of Clive just *finding* a ticketed tourist lost in the highlands? A zillion to one—right? He helped out the odds."

"Fuck." Ian shook his head. "I've been screwed from the beginning."

"And you'll keep on being screwed until you learn to get going and take *control*." She stamped her foot, blue eyes blazing, beginning to look like the old Angel—minus the rattlesnake tattoo. "I for one can't wait forever. I've got my people around Neptune to worry about—and a sweepstakes to win. This is *real*. No one's going to rescue you. Not Clive. Not your agency. No one but you and me can do it."

He had been made into a total mark. First by Clive. Then by the casino. "Okay, okay, I'm in. Just one thing."

"What?" Angel went back to fixing her hair.

"How much is this virtual virility good for?"

She grinned. "Near infinite."

A bright, full summer moon turned the Transylvania plateau into a velvety landscape, half blue moonlight, half dense shadow. It was near to midnight, but Ian kept feeling it was neither night nor day, but some weird in-between world, cloud-wracked and peopled with ghouls and blood-sucking phantoms. The Hound led, loping ahead, sniffing out snares and sentries. Tiny's dark bulk loomed behind Ian. Angel was at his side, warm and comforting.

Since the Hound retained his nominal intelligence, the Wolf Pack got a werewolf without having to pay the steep prices attached to any sort of magic. The xeno lost his speakbox, but he'd never been much of a talker. He continued to radiate his usual superhuman confidence, slipping past one dark obstacle after another, until Dracula's tower loomed ahead, huge and lonely, rising straight out of the plain, casting a deep immense shadow. It was a twelfth-century keep, copied on Byzantine works, seven stories tall, pierced by nothing but loopholes. The inner floors had to be as black as the devil's basement, even at noonday. At night, Ian found it utterly uninviting.

The remnants of the White Company were laying dilatory siege to the place, having beaten back the janissaries. Too weak to storm the tower, they were merely patrolling the approaches, killing or turning back any gamers who refused to join them. They hadn't enough players to picket the entire tower, and posting sentries in the Transylvanian darkness was semi-suicidal, so they relied on strong roving patrols, which the Hound artfully avoided.

Crawling from one moonlit hummock to the next, Ian edged after the Hound. The xeno led them right up to the base of the tower—a massive battered plinth, topped by blocks of dark stone rising toward black battlements blotting out the stars. Here the Hound faded and Tiny took over. The *djinn* disguise was all tusks and muscle, no magic came with it, but he still had the innate talents of a SuperChimp—including balance and climbing ability. Taking out a pair of pointed hooks tied together by a couple of fathoms of rope, he went straight up the wall.

Standing in the dark shadow of the tower, Ian could hardly tell how Tiny did it. Using the hooks as both grapples and pitons, the SuperChimp swarmed up the side as easily as if he were walking on all fours. In a matter of minutes, a line snaked down.

The were-hound yipped a warning.

Angel whispered, "Let's go," seizing the line and starting to walk up the wall, almost as freely as Tiny had. Living in spin ships had stripped away any inborn fear of heights. Ian grabbed the dangling line, planting his feet against the wall, doing his best to imitate her. Bats brushed past, squeaking in the blackness. He could feel the rope jerk as Angel went hand over hand above him. Strangely enough, he was not scared. Everything was tinged with a virtual invincibility. Probably part of the trap, like his heightened testosterone—a hormone rush that would carry him up the wall into who-knows-what.

The outer battlements were bathed in moonlight.

Ian pulled himself through a narrow embrasure, sliding softly onto a stone guard walk between the parapet and inner wall. Angel crouched in the shadows, her hand over his mouth. Her thin fingers felt warm and fresh, absurdly sexy. She pointed silently down the walkway.

Ian saw empty, curving stonework. He nodded. Angel took her hand away and they set out together. Less than a quarter of the way around they came on a pair of bodies in plate and mail armor, their necks bent at odd angles. Tiny's work.

Farther on, they found Tiny himself, looming over a third body at the head of a dark stairwell, his *djinn* fangs shining hideously in the moonlight. They had breached the tower. No other team had gotten this far. Win or lose, the Wolf Pack was living up to its dubious reputation. What came next did not look so inviting. Aside from the scant light filtering down the spiral stairway, and the odd moonlit loophole, there looked to be absolutely no interior illumination. Dracula did not need light.

Angel tied the rope around her waist, signing that she would go first. Ian took the rope end, passed it around his middle, tied it tight, then handed it to Tiny—glad that Angel had volunteered to lead. Nothing could have convinced him to go first into that darkness, where the undead had every advantage.

Flint scraped on steel, and a thin sliver of light appeared, shining down the back stairwell. Angel had the brass candleball in her hand, the light that had hung above her curtained bed; by holding the ball in her gloved hand, she let only a thin shaft fall on the stairs. They descended.

Ian held tight to the rope, feeling each step with his toes. Moonlight ended at the first turn in the spiral stairs. There was nothing beyond but the dark castle odor of cold wet stone. The stair wound counterclockwise, anti-sunwise, so the defenders retreating up the stairs had their left hands free. Vampires were notoriously left-handed.

At the bottom, Angel paused, motioning for him to stop, then stepping over something in the blackness. She spoke for the first time since coming into the tower, "Watch that last step, it's a baddie."

By the thin light of her candle, Ian could just make out the shining jaws of a mantrap, lying on the last step, set to snap shut on his leg. The jagged teeth would tear through muscle and break bone, leaving him to writhe in very real agony until the game ended or some softhearted ghoul came along.

As he stepped over, Angel caught him, keeping him from coming down where he naturally would have. As she set him down, he saw the outlines of a second mantrap, right at the foot of the stairs—blackened and sprinkled with straw, making it nearly invisible. You were *supposed* to see the first one, sitting on the last step—then step over it onto the second.

Angel whispered softly, "A good sign."

Ian nodded. Not your normal stairwell. The passageway led where no one was supposed to go. You could not have sentries losing legs as they went on and off duty. Angel called to Tiny, and the apish *djinn* leaped over both traps, landing next to his mistress.

They set out. Bats squeaked overhead. Clumps of the little beasts hung from cobwebbed stonework. Ian had his crossbow out, expecting to see guards or worse. The passage curved, following the contour of the tower. Ian silently counted steps. He calculated that they were about halfway around, when suddenly Angel's light vanished.

The rope at his waist snapped taut, jerking him forward. He let out a muffled squeal. His boots slid on straw, then the stone flags beneath his feet disappeared. He fell into blackness.

For a horrible moment Ian pictured himself splattering on a stone floor, or crashing down on top of Angel in some spiked pit. Then the line about his waist jerked tight. He caught the rope above him, pulling himself up, taking the strain off his waist, which had to support Angel's weight as well, keeping himself from being cut in half. Swinging in the dark, he realized that they had fallen into an oubliette, a wide mural chamber several stories deep, with no exit except the hole at the top.

Once you stumbled in, you were lucky if the fall killed you, since the alternative was to lie broken on the floor below, waiting in utter blackness for thirst or internal injuries to put you out of the game. A fine way to go mad.

Between labored breaths, Ian felt himself moving. Bit by bit, the rope was rising. He bumped against the domed ceiling of the oubliette. Tiny was pulling them out. Ian let go of the rope. When his waist was flush with the stone lip, he scrambled back into the passage, feeling absurdly "safe." Another nanosecond to catch his breath, then he and Tiny drew Angel up out of the dark pit.

The only way to get past the oubliette was to brace feet and back against the stonework—like climbers in a rock chimney—and inch across. On the far side was another mantrap, waiting for anyone incautious enough to try to leap over the opening. Ian hoped these hellish entanglements showed that they were headed in the right direction.

Beyond the oubliette, he saw moonlight at the end of the tunnel. Ahead was a wide recess, with a tall window niche opening onto an inner court topped by bare battlements. Ian could see windows running around the inner wall, turning the enclosed court into a vast airshaft that brought air and light into the tower. Bats fluttered by the window. Next to the niche was a heavy wooden door, reinforced with iron bands. From the placement of the windows, Ian guessed that the door led into a series of mural chambers spaced around the upper floor of the tower. Tiny tried the door. He might as well have tried to move the tower.

The window niche was too cramped for a battering ram, but there *had* to be a way in. Game rules required that obstacles be prodigious, but not absolutely impossible. Angel stuck her head out the window. Blonde hair shone in the moonlight. She grabbed Ian by the shoulder. "Look, we can go around."

Ian gauged distances between windows, and silently shook his head. The windows were well spaced, and the inner shaft was faced with small flush stones. It could not be climbed the way they had gone up the outer wall. "Tiny can do it," Angel assured him. She told Tiny to stop grunting over the door and take a look out the window.

The SuperChimp in *djinn* disguise stuck his head out, nodding eagerly. Angel played out more rope, then she and Ian braced themselves against the stonework. Tiny swung out the window, cutting an astonishing arc, just catching the stone sill of the next window. Tiny did not seem perturbed by height or distance, reminding Ian of Poe's pitiless killer ape in *Murders in the Rue Morgue*—monstrous and unstoppable.

Tiny pulled them after him. The neighboring window opened on a mural chamber, and another ironbound door. So they tried the next window, and the next, swinging silently over the stone court six stories below. Bats flew back and forth, excited by their passage.

Finally they came to a window sealed with leaded glass. Angel peered through one of the dim little panes. "Bingo," she breathed softly, signaling to Tiny. The *djinn* took off his Turkish helmet, using it to shield his hand, giving the window a ferocious tap. Panes splintered. The sash buckled. Shards of glass tinkled against the stone, falling like snow crystals into the court below. They were in.

The trophy room was a cross between some *ancienne noblesse* dining hall and Kublai Khan's rumpus room. Curved and pronged weapons lined the walls, along with Gothic armor and silk tapestries. Turkish battleflags and the heads of weird steppe antelope hung over a huge hand-carved table surrounded by Roman-style cushioned stools. A silver table service glittered in the light from the broken window.

The only door was a brass monstrosity, bolted on the inside, that looked as if it could not be cracked with a tactical nuke. But what they wanted sat right at the far end of the banquet table. A tall barred cage contained an emir's ransom—gold chains, jade rings, big bevel-cut emerald necklaces, silver orthodox crosses, a diamond coronet or two. Perched atop the heap was a ridiculously large blood-red ruby. The Vampire's Heart.

Angel bounded down the length of the banquet table and went to work, picking at the lock. Tiny shambled after her to lend a hand. Ian stood by the window, thinking that it all had been too easy.

He was right.

A bat flitted by, looping between the candlesticks, side-slipping into a neat split-s, and coming down behind Angel. As the beast descended, it started to grow, extending its legs, lengthening head and torso, assuming human form. Wings became a great billowing cloak. Ian stood rooted. Too late he realized why the tower had so few human defenders.

As the face formed, the vampire's features took on a familiar cast, showing a sharp spade beard, thin smiling lips, and slick black hair. It was Phil the Shill. There was no sign of the mess Clive's mace had made. The undead could not be daunted by normal means.

Tiny leaped at him. It looked to be no contest. Vampire or not, Phil was still a Loonie, with long spindly arms and legs, looking barely able to stand in a one-g field, much less put up a fight. The *djinn*-cum-SuperChimp outmassed him handily.

And it *was* no contest. Tiny lunged. Phil batted aside one outstretched hand and grabbed the other one, grinning. He twisted the hand sideways. Through Tiny's wounded bellowing, Ian could hear the bone crack. Phil twisted more, all the way around, until the hand came free, separating from the wrist with a bloody snap. Tiny howled and staggered back, swinging with his sound arm. Phil seized it with both hands, planting a foot in Tiny's chest and yanking. The arm came off at the root.

Tiny dropped to his knees, screeching in pain. Phil leaped at his prey with fangs and nails; when he was finished, Tiny lay dismembered and half-decapitated. White cervical vertebrae poked through bloody flesh.

Ian was horrified and sickened. Not just by what he had seen, but by the gruesome unfairness of the game. All this time, Phil had been tracking them, letting them think they were winning, while *Circuit Maximus* laughed up its collective sleeve.

Phil wiped gore from his lips. "Don't look so shocked. Any decent Greek scholar would have known that Philaemos meant 'blood-lover.'" Ian could see Angel working furiously at the lock. He raised his crossbow. Fighting was hopeless, but if he could hold the vampire's attention, Angel had a chance to open the cage, grab the Vampire's Heart, and end the game.

Laughing at the antique weapon, Phil advanced. Ian took a step back, keeping the corner of the table between him and the vampire. The window was open beside him—but that was no escape. Without Tiny, Ian would splatter on the black stones.

Phil glided around the table. "Give my regards to Clive."

Angel gave the lock a last twist. It snapped open with a hideous click you could have heard in Constantinople. She threw open the barred door.

Spinning about, the vampire sprang the length of the table, slamming the cage shut, holding it closed with superhuman strength. With his free arm, he backhanded Angel, sending her flying across the table.

She landed in a heap against the wall, taking a velvet stool and sterling place setting with her.

Ian could only think how horribly, monstrously unfair it all was. There *had* to be a way to win—it said so in the goddamn casino contract. But he had no hope, nothing to fight with, not even Clive's silver stiletto. In a second, the vampire would be on him, tearing at his neck, twisting his head until it came off. He wanted to cry.

Phil looked down at Angel, huddled behind the stool. He blew her a kiss. "Don't bother to get up, girl. I'm saving you for last."

Then he turned back to Ian, trapped against the window. Ian saw Angel scoop something long and thin off the floor, tossing it to him. It turned and flashed in the moonlight. "Shoot him!" she shouted.

Instinctively, Ian caught the object; it was an oak-handled silver-bladed knife. He knocked the iron bolt from his crossbow, slipped the knife in its place and took aim.

Phil screamed in baffled rage, leaping forward. Ian shot him straight through the heart.

They brought him out of the vaults and hoisted him onto a chariot. Touts dressed as nymphs and satyrs dragged him onto the casino floor. Holos thundered overhead.

And not just Ian either. The whole Wolf Pack was on chariots, even Tiny, who was not much of a burden in one-sixth g. Clive flashed him a grin of triumph. It was weird to see them alive and ecstatic after being decapitated and/or dismembered. Sheila and Gertrude were in the throng, as deliriously happy as if they had won. Half the White Company was there to cheer someone else's triumph. Addicts to the last.

Casino shills crowded around as *Circuit Maximus* broke out the cheap champagne; gaming palaces loved to record mob scenes around a big winner. It was their best advertisement. A life-size animated holo, done up like a slave in Roman leather, held a laurel wreath over his head, whispering in a sexy synthesized voice, *sic transit gloria mundi*—passing are the glories of the world.

So enjoy them now. He looked over at Angel. She was no longer blonde and bouncy, but, by God, she had guts, and purpose—and enough credit to save her people orbiting Neptune.

A crisp smartly dressed Dirtsider, with an outdoor tan and earthbound muscles shoved his way through the crowd, easily parting the Loonies, asking if Ian was really who he claimed to be. Short of a chromosome match, Ian no longer had any proof of identity—but what the hell. "Ian MacNeil at *yer* service."

The fellow demanded to know why he had cashed his ticket in. Didn't he *know* that gambling with agency credits was a termination offense, possibly a felony? This *had* to be a casino touch. No one could be so obtuse—but Ian was ready to play along. He yelled down from the chariot, "I quit."

Loonies cheered, laughing at the ridiculous groundhog, trying to bully someone who had just won several lifetimes worth of credit. Casino beauties in body paint and moonstone g-strings climbed aboard the chariot, happy to start helping him spend it. A newsie from some Tycho-based casino network thrust a recorder at him. "Ian MacNeil, you have just won a *Circuit Maximus* grand sweepstakes! What are you going to do next?"

Angel smiled over at him—showing only the good side of her face. Ian grinned back. "I'm going to Neptune."

The Cultured Werewolf

T.K.F. WEISSKOPF

If vampires are the gentlemen of the monster kingdom, werewolves are distinctly lower class. We picture Dracula in evening dress, complete with black tie and cloak. Even though he wears blue jeans, TV's "Forever Knight" is a gentleman; his motives are noble. It's much easier to be a vampire than a werewolf. For to be a werewolf is to eschew civilization, to become a beast. No werewolf ever wore a cummerbund.

Most people in our enlightened technological age have a pretty good idea of what it means to be a werewolf. We know that lycanthropism involves a physical change, preferably to a mammalian predator form, usually brought about by the light of the full moon. The changed human then proceeds to lose his sense of humanity and rampage like a wolf—uncontrollable, irresponsible, unaccountable—often acquiring in the process a taste for human flesh. An unnatural creature of incredible strength and viciousness, the werewolf can be killed only by a silver bullet. This assortment of defining traits feels like folklore passed down through the ages. And, in truth, werewolves and their ilk are a worldwide, ancient phenomena.

On the island of Java in Indonesia, the *anjing ajak* are men of impure spirit who change at night into werewolves in order to eat people. The Javanese *macan gadungan* is a tiger's body inhabited by the spirit of a man. In Sumatra and in Malay, too, there are tales of tiger men, indeed whole villages of tiger men, who wreak revenge for injustices. And in Bali, there is a sort of combination vampire/werewolf in the *leyak*, a person who is outwardly normal except that at night he wanders cemeteries to obtain the entrails of humans—with which gory ingredients he transforms himself into a tiger. Also on Java, a magician can transform himself into a man-killing tiger by wearing a piece of a special sarong. In fact, legends of transformation of shamans into animals are found on all continents, from Australia to America.

In Europe the primordial predator was the wolf. Tales of lycanthropia go back to the Greeks. In his *Metamorphoses* Ovid gives a Roman version of the Greek myth of Lycaon, who was turned into a wolf after feeding Jupiter human flesh. Pliny tells of the family of Antaeus, one of them chosen by lot to fulfill a curse by spending nine years in lupine form. The idea of children being raised by wolves, as were Romulus and Remus, the mythical founders of Rome, has been associated with the idea of humans turning into wolves as well. (In China, the legends speak of humans raised by tigers.) One of the legends surrounding Saint Patrick has it that he turned the King of Wales into a wolf. In England and Scotland witches are associated with shapeshifting, most commonly into cats, but also mares, hares and other animals. And it was believed that if wounded with silver shot, the transformed witch would be forced to reassume human shape. The werewolf appears in historical records dating from the time of the Plague, when the real wolf enjoyed a renaissance in Europe. In France particularly, arose stories of the *loup garou*, leading to actual trials—and burnings—of accused werewolves. In almost all cases of medieval historical or literary werewolves, those transformed were peasants, not nobles. The method of transformation, however, varied wildly, from the use of an ointment, to the wearing of a wolf pelt, to a pact with the devil.

But despite all this shapeshifting precedent, the current "folk" picture of the werewolf, as Greg Cox has pointed out, comes from twentieth century horror movies. The werewolf is a modern monster. So too the vampire, who has been transmogrified over the ages from his legendary material into his current semi-literary construction. But the vampire is conceived of as a supernatural phenomena—which is another way of saying that it doesn't exist in nature, but is a human invention. The werewolf on the other hand is a product of strict metaphor. Wolves do exist, and to be a werewolf simply means being a man and a wolf at the same time—with all the implied give and take and double reality that such a metaphoric existence bestows. But why is the werewolf metaphor so powerful today?

And what does being a wolf really mean to the twentieth century? It's not just about being hairy and howling at the moon; the transformation goes deeper than that. Robert A. Heinlein said in "The Notebooks of Lazarus Long" in *Time Enough for Love*, "Beware of altruism. It is based on self-deception, the root of all evil." Even if that's true, it still doesn't preclude humans acting nobly because it makes them feel good to make others feel good. In contrast to that impulse to do good is the wolf's nature: that thing which we strive *against* when we create something glorious or act nobly; it's the impulse to bestial behavior, the cannibalistic fascination with suffering that drives the tabloids; it's all that is low and cruel about humanity—

the seeds of civilization's downfall.* The power of the werewolf icon as currently configured is the suspicion that the wolf's nature, fighting (or perhaps balancing) the desire to do good, is present within us all and can rise to the surface with just a flick of fate's figner. We see it happen every day.

So the werewolf metaphor points up a real science fictional problem: what should a civil society do with those who would be wolves? Michael Flynn's story gives one purely science fictional solution: we leave those who choose to be wolves behind when the rest of us have gotten to the stars *per aspera*. But Flynn doesn't leave us feeling terribly superior about this solution: he tells the story from the viewpoint of the werewolf.

And what happens if we bring the werewolves with us? A. Bertram Chandler addresses that in his story "Frontier of the Dark." He tells of a space travel technology that inadvertently brings back werewolves. While his gloss of scientific explanation isn't especially integral to the theme, he nevertheless tells a particularly science fictional *sort* of story. Falsen, the narrator, (I won't call him the hero), approaches with an admirable attitude being marooned on what his captors fondly think is a deserted planet. After taking an inventory of the contents of his pockets, Falsen sets out to explore his new world: "Whatever he might find at the end of his walk he was armed, after a fashion. He had a cutting tool or weapon, and he had fire. He had, too, his own physical strength and the ability to look after himself in unarmed combat." As it turns out, though, mere physical strength—the power of the wolf—is not enough. Falsen has neglected the lesson that culture is stronger than

---

*Speaking of tabloids, note the cover story and headline for the March 14, 1995 issue of *The Sun*: "Devil's Curse Turns Girl Into Werewolf." The reader is directed to note the "amazing pictures" her husband has taken "as she slowly changes."

nature, and he doesn't bother to study his neighbor's history. Thus, the werewolf's doom is sealed for all time. The werecat, on the other hand, might just go on to conquer the galaxy—so long as she doesn't get too arrogant. . . .

But that's what good old rational science fiction stories about monsters from the id are for: to prepare us for the fight in a future of cultured werewolves. For inevitably, even as humanity changes and evolves and yearns toward perfection, so too will the wolf within us. . . .

Bibliographic note: *The Beast Within: A History of the Werewolf* by British writer Adam Douglas, (copyright 1992 and published in paperback by Avon in 1994) will tell you all that you could ever possibly have wanted to know about werewolves in Western society, in exhaustively researched detail, from psychiatric cases to medieval lays. (But he is wrong about the lack of legendary precedent for using silver bullets: Stith Thompson's *Motif-Index of Folk Literature* includes "Silver bullet protects against giants, ghosts and witches.")

ANNOUNCING:

THE ARCANA

A GROUNDBREAKING NEW SERIES FROM THE BESTSELLING AUTHOR OF *LION OF IRELAND!*

They are **The Arcana.** Collectively, they are the ultimate symbols of cosmic power. Millennia ago they were the treasures of the gods of creation, honored and cherished in four great cities since swept away by the rivers of time. The Spear of Light came from Gorias. The city of Falias contained The Stone of Destiny. From Murias came The Cup of Blood. The Sword of Flame was enshrined within Findias.

Properly used by an adept, these four together have the power to create worlds—or to destroy them. The three volumes of The Arcana by Morgan Llywelyn and Michael Scott tell of the desperate quest to rediscover the ancient tools of creation and restore a world that lives only in memory. A world everyone longs to return to, in their most secret dreams. The lost world at the outermost limit of human desire.

Book One tells the story of Silverhand, he who was foretold, he who is destined to save the world from Chaos and begin the long climb back to the world that lives within us all.

Silverhand is the first novel in an extraordinary ground-breaking fantasy world created by a multiple New York Times bestselling author. ***Silverhand*, Book I of *The Arcana***, represents her first foray into pure fantasy, and in it Llywelyn makes it obvious that she needed a larger framework than that provided by the Celtic fantasy genre, even though her contributions to that genre have made her one of the two or three most successful fantasy authors that we have ever seen.

"One of my all-time favorite authors."

—Jude Devereaux

"[*Red Branch*:] One of the most powerful stories I have ever read....The result is a total captivation of the reader into a landscape that is vivid, vital and victorious even in tragedy...."

—Anne McCaffrey

WATCH FOR VOLUME ONE OF

THE ARCANA:

SILVERHAND

COMING IN HARDCOVER

APRIL 1995

FROM BAEN BOOKS

0-671-87652-X ✦ 480 pages ✦ $22.00